"Is that a Burberry?" I heard in a breathy whisper behind me.

I clutched the strap of the handbag in a death grip and whirled around, ready to take on the enemy.

"Yeah," I said, centering my weight.

A flat-faced woman with a hungry expression and wide nose narrowed her heavily made-up eyes.

Women in this store were vicious, and it was extremely rare for a Burberry to escape the first onslaught of interest on delivery day. These patrons were hellbent on getting first-tier fashion at reduced prices.

"Cute, isn't it?" I said in a blasé tone. Summoning all my confidence, I settled the strap just a little more firmly onto my shoulder before walking around her. "I might just take it for a stroll. See if I like it."

I started off at a speedy clip, using the sassy movement of my upper body to hopefully distract her from the tattered shoes painfully squeezing my feet. I wasn't worried about my white top and slightly wrinkled khakis. They were clean and stain-free, and I doubted she'd know they were actually a uniform. In her eyes, I might just take home this fantastic handbag.

I could feel her stare digging into my back as I rounded a rack of clothing. A woman down the row had her hair done up in a ponytail tied with a familiar green bow that I knew read *Proud to Be a Chester*, a somewhat derogatory term for non-magical people. She glanced

S0-BIA-424

up before giving me the once-over, looking for signs that I might be *different* (a.k.a. magical). Wings, fangs, the ability to sprout fur and teeth…

I didn't have any of those, sadly.

Those would give me status in the magical community. And status was one thing I'd never experienced. But I did have this fabulous handbag, for now, and a real bad attitude. We had to work with what we were given.

I matched her narrowed eyes with my own, silently letting her know I wasn't to be trifled with. Fear was a strong deterrent to treating someone badly, even though she had nothing to fear when it came to me specifically.

A bad attitude and a bullshitter. There could be worse things.

My forceful gaze worked—her body stiffened and her head jerked away. But before she could completely go back to her perusal, she caught sight of the unicorn slung over my arm.

Hunger sparked in her muddy-brown peepers, and she swiveled her tanklike body to face me.

Fear did deter bad treatment, usually, but it wouldn't keep the patrons in this store—a place cheaper than anywhere else because of the dual-society location—away from a Burberry.

Her gaze coated my body, taking in every inch. She

paused on my shoes, then flicked to my tiny canvas sacklike...*thing* I used for a purse, draped across my cheap cotton shirt. Suddenly, I knew stainlessness wasn't enough.

Excitement lit her eyes. "You can't afford that bag," she said in an accusatory whisper.

My knuckles turned white on the handbag strap. The effort to keep my chin up made sweat pop out on my forehead. Even though we were in the dual-society zone, something like the Wild West of San Francisco, this store only employed non-magical people. If this woman raised a big enough fuss, the non-magical management would check my ID, which would reveal that I had absolutely no clout whatsoever in the magical community. Management had the right to refuse service, and throwing me out to appease their customer base would be a no-brainer. I knew this from experience.

Not that I let that stop me.

"Yes, I can," I lied, strutting past her. "It would take all my inheritance, but I could. I'm wondering if I *should*."

"I saw it first," the flat-faced woman from before called, now rounding the clothes rack, following me. Three other women looked up from around the store. A man in the back wisely minded his own business. "I already called dibs on it," she continued.

Ms. Proud to Be a Chester frowned and clenched her jaw. "I didn't hear you call dibs."

"Dibs," the flat-faced woman said.

I tried to block out their shrill voices as they argued about the use of dibs when it pertained to Burberry handbags, and headed toward the mostly deserted men's section. The smell of newness flirted with my senses and the weight of my latest dream bag sat comfortably on my shoulder. I glanced at a button-up shirt that might look great on Mordecai's thin frame, then a pair of slacks, something he'd never owned.

My heart sank.

Mordecai. His illness was the whole reason for this outing. The only thing I should dream about was the ability to afford his medicine. Or, pie in the sky, the procedure to cure him.

I slipped the purse from my shoulder and unceremoniously dropped it to the ground. The women were on it in seconds, battering each other to grab hold of it first. Without stopping, and ignoring the startled looks from the silent man, I made my way out of the store.

Mooning over luxury items wasn't worth it. Not at this stage of my life, anyway. And honestly, probably never. Maybe once Mordecai and Daisy, my wards, were on their own two feet and happy, I could figure out a way to rake in money. But honestly, just like my mother, I had a habit of taking in strays. That wasn't conducive to making money, but this world was the pits for anyone who didn't belong. If I could keep one kid from dying on the streets, I would, even if it meant hustling for the rest of my days.

Dreaming small. That was the ticket.

For example, I'd always wanted a sleek little cell phone like all the powerful people had, with its app-ridden screen and impractical fragility. So, what did I do? I made friends with a dickface at my latest place of poorly paid employment who was horribly clumsy. This guy dropped his phone all the time, often while talking shit to someone or inappropriately flirting. I waited until the newest model phone came out, then for him to crack his screen again, and threw out a few comments about how the new phones were *super* durable, not to mention the height of cool.

In a week, he had a new phone. A week after that, when his sexual innuendos were really beginning to scrape my last nerve, he tossed me his not-that-old phone with three cracks in the screen and said, "Here. You can have the run-down piece of shit. It matches your whole...*look*."

He'd been making fun of me, as usual, which had made the transaction so much easier. I'd mock-refused to take it, I'd kissed his ass for the rest of the day, and then I'd gone home with that sleek little number.

The week after I'd gotten what I wanted, I chastised

him every time he was a dickhead, and often stormed off afterward. As desired, the pseudo-friendship fizzled quickly, and I was back to zero headaches and one stylish, newish phone.

It was a small dream turned reality. And my conscience was clear, too, because he was universally acknowledged to be an asshole, and everyone knew those types had it coming. They deserved a little manipulation once in a while.

I dug in my purse for the phone as I made my way down the sidewalk within the shopping complex, headed for the store I'd originally intended to solely visit. The phone's large, bright face read twelve thirty-four. Irresponsible fashion bargain hunting had bled away half of my lunch hour.

Seeing a message alert from my home number, I tapped into my voicemail and watched the transcription slowly load. I stepped off the sidewalk and into a rarely used service driveway cutting through the stores.

The scream of tires on concrete stopped my heart. The flash of light on a red hood dotted with a black stallion in a plate of yellow caught my eye. Some rich somebody in a sweet ride was bearing down, ready to cut the legs out from under me! He or she wouldn't think to stop for a poor girl—I was about to be a new hood ornament.

Chapter 2

KIERAN

T HE ECHO OF his father's grating voice telling him to have a little pride played through Kieran's mind as he eased his new Ferrari through a dilapidated shopping complex in a disgusting part of town.

Of the magical community, only derelicts with no self-respect or outlaws hiding from the magical governing body spent time in dual-society zones. Kieran was neither of those things, but he needed the cover of this shadow zone to meet privately with his crew. Only here, amongst the dredges of both societies, mostly unwatched by either government, could he be sure none of his father's spies were watching. If Valens got one whiff of Kieran's plans, he would rip his world out from under him. He had the power to do so.

Kieran sped down a row of cars, aiming for the service driveway that would take him to the back of the complex where his Six waited. The handpicked group of dedicated acolytes, who'd given a blood oath to protect him to their dying breath, were the only people on this

9

planet he trusted implicitly.

Before he turned, he caught sight of a woman striding purposefully along the sidewalk, her long legs eating pavement while her focus remained fixed on the phone in her hand. She reached the driveway first and stepped off the curb without so much as bothering to glance up. Apparently, she expected others to navigate around her.

She needed a lesson on how the world worked.

He let the car roll until the last possible moment before slamming on the brakes. The supercar screeched to a noisy stop, his bumper sliding to within a couple feet of her thighs.

She jolted in surprise, jerking her arms. Her phone broke free from her grasp, tilting in the air before gravity got hold of it.

Kieran grinned. A cracked screen wasn't much of a lesson, but hopefully the scare would make her pay a little more attention next time.

He waited for the fearful glance in his direction, followed by a look of surprised realization when she saw just whom she'd inconvenienced, but instead she braced herself and bent forward, her hands sinking low. The phone bounced off her waiting palms, but she adjusted gracefully and trapped it, cradling it like a little baby bird.

A strange fascination momentarily wiped away his annoyance. She was athletic, this woman, with good and quick reflexes. But she'd ignored an obvious threat on her life...for a phone. That wasn't usual in a mundane part of the world.

He pushed the button to lower his window. Half of him wanted to sarcastically congratulate her on having saved a replaceable commodity instead of worrying about the continued functionality of her legs. The other half wanted to deliver a warning that would do what his screeching tires had failed to.

But before he could decide, the salty oceanic breeze wafted into the car and flirted with his senses. The feel and smell of it reminded him of home. Of the good times, hunting and fishing and roaming the green fields of Ireland on horseback. Almost immediately, though, the sorrow that had been plaguing him for years took over. Followed by the sharp, consuming bite of loss, remembering his mother's death six months ago.

Images crowded his mind, unbidden—of his mother's withered face, of her pained eyes, of her paper-thin body, wasting away to nothing.

She'd sacrificed herself for him. She'd let him feel free, and live wild, while she endured a hellish cage. One that had eventually killed her.

A wave of guilt tore through him, hot and sharp. He gritted his teeth.

No. That wasn't true.

Kieran had to remember who was truly at fault: his

father. He had essentially kidnapped her and forced her to live a half-life. Stolen her vitality and, slowly but surely, her desire to keep living. Valens had killed her. Slowly. Painfully.

Kieran's hands tightened on the wheel as rage burned through him.

His foot lightened on the brake. Giving this woman a hard metal tap right now would surely teach her a lesson, and maybe alleviate some of his burning anger at the same time. There wasn't a damn thing anyone would do about it if he were to hit her. It was illegal, sure, but charges didn't stick to a Demigod. His father would wave the incident away. And, because of the location, the non-magical government would be all too happy to cooperate. His foot lowered on the brake again. Did he really feel like dealing with the repercussions of his father finding out where he was?

It was at that moment that the woman, her phone clutched in her hand, finally looked up.

Without warning, her fierce, deep brown eyes burrowed into him. A burning sensation sliced down his middle. His small hairs stood on end as his skin, tissue, and bone were peeled away like tissue paper, revealing what lay inside of him. Revealing his very soul for her analysis.

He'd never felt anything like it. The strength of her magic…

He marveled at it for a solid beat. He felt vulnerable, of all things. Like, at any moment, she could rip the life force out of him and toss it away.

His heart sped up and adrenaline pumped through his blood. He barely kept himself from looking down to make sure the effect was from her intense, thick magic, not some sorcery that had actually cut through him physically.

Before he could swell his magic to defend himself, the feeling washed away. In its place, a new sensation crawled across his skin before buzzing through his entire body. Delicate, sensual, spirited, and exciting, it was like nothing he'd ever experienced. It was so strong and carefree, yet as solid as the earth, and as old as time itself. The feeling...was better than sex. More fulfilling than intimacy. And even though he'd only had a small taste, he knew it had to be desperately addictive.

His eyes narrowed as he looked over her ill-fitting clothes and holey shoes. Even an oversized shirt, sports bra, and rat's nest of hair couldn't disguise her sexy form and beautiful face. She was trying, though, that was clear. Trying to look poor and mundane, like all the other dwellers of this dilapidated place.

But with magic that strong and unique, she had to have gotten training when she was little. It was her unlucky day that she'd almost been run down by someone who could assess magic without electronic instruments. Her disguise had just been ripped away.

Now, to find out what she was doing here, and whom she was working for…

Chapter 3

ALEXIS

A CHERRY-RED FERRARI idled in the mouth of the service driveway, the yellow equine emblem two feet from my legs. A shockingly handsome man in his late twenties with high, arching eyebrows and sharp cheekbones glared at me from the driver's seat.

Oh good, a rich and probably important guy whose parents likely owned one of the stores in this complex. He was probably skirting around to the back to fire a delivery guy or something. He'd be pissed I got in the way of his oh-so-important business. These snooty bastards thought the sun shone out of their asses, and people like me were of little use. He wouldn't accept an apology for accidentally stepping in front of him. My death, however, he'd accept just fine.

Thankfully, a store could kick me out, but the complex as a whole could not. I was legally allowed to be here, and he was not legally allowed to kill me.

Which meant I needed to own my space and up my confidence. When you didn't know if you were dealing with the magical or non-magical, but were sure the arrogance level would be high, it was best to bluff about your self-worth. It often threw the snobs off their high horses long enough for you to get out of Dodge.

I turned on Beast Mode.

"Are you serious right now?" I yelled at him, waving my hand to indicate the nonexistent crosswalk. "Pedestrians have the right of way. Watch where you're going. You could've killed me."

I braced a fist on my hip and waited for a moment, like I expected an apology.

He didn't so much as twitch, continuing to stare at me through the shiny glass of his elegant and extremely classy car. His wife or girlfriend would definitely have a Burberry, and not one she'd had to wrestle out of a discount store in Bumfuck Nowhere.

I lifted my eyebrows and leaned in a bit, as though exasperated he wasn't replying. "I nearly dropped my phone," I accused, before loudly huffing and shaking my head.

That oughta do it.

Projecting all the self-importance I could muster, I started forward.

"You're lucky I don't sue," I faux-muttered loud enough for him to hear me through his slightly cracked-open window.

His unwavering stare, and complete lack of a reaction, sent a cold trickle down my spine. I picked up the pace, sincerely hoping he wasn't an unhinged, extremely powerful magical type. He might then hunt me down, drag me to magical soil, and kill me for sport.

"Watch where you're going next time," I said over my shoulder. "A nice car won't keep you out of jail."

There. A subtle hint that I was non-magical.

Only the non-magical believed in throwing criminals into rent-free cells with free food, exercise breaks, and warm beds, where they did little but wait an arbitrary amount of time to get free again. Magical people were a lot more barbaric. They handed out judgments harshly and quickly, then meted out punishment in whatever manner they deemed fit. Cross a shifter, get your head beat in. You had it coming. Cross Valens, the Demigod of San Francisco, and hope for a quick death.

I shivered.

I *sincerely* hoped he wasn't magical. This altercation reaffirmed why I stuck to dual-society zones. Chesters, the worst of the non-magical bunch, could be crazy, but at least they followed stricter laws with less insane punishments. Also, they ignored me instead of picking on me. Win-win.

The stagnant smell of recycled air greeted me as I stepped into the bright store at the far end of the complex. Another non-magical-owned establishment, this one sold homewares and various other domestic items. This was where I should have gone straight away instead of getting swept up by unrealistic fantasies.

The small clock by the door said I needed to get in and get out so I could make it back to work in time. But the call of all that sparkled and shone dragged my feet off course. Immediately, I spied something I desperately needed: a lovely scented candle that would mask some of the mildew smell of the bathroom.

Or over there, by the strange painting of a dog face—a garbage can whose lid rose and fell by sensor. I wouldn't get sticky when I threw away the kids' messes in the kitchen.

Or there! A sponge holder that suctioned to the side of the sink so I wouldn't have to leave the sponge on the side of the dirty basin that Mordecai and Daisy were supposed to have cleaned, said they'd cleaned, and definitely hadn't.

I drank in the sight of all the stuff I definitely needed or could at least use while calling up in my mind's eye my embarrassingly low cash balance. A balance so low, I only had wiggle room in the budget for the single item I'd come for.

"Dream small, Alexis," I muttered, staring at the shelves of kitchen gadgets. "Dream small."

I was a sighing machine today.

I headed back toward the other side of the store,

making my way to the blanket section.

When asked what color he would prefer, Mordecai had needed to be convinced that yes, he needed a decent blanket. Central heating wasn't a luxury we could afford, and his other blankets were all threadbare. Finally, he'd admitted a cheery color would really suit him. Apparently, the drab color scheme of our house wasn't to his taste.

My hand hovered over a bright yellow blanket with little tassels on the ends. He wanted cheery, and yellow was certainly cheerful, but I also knew he absolutely detested the color. I loved playing jokes, but this one seemed too harsh, even for me.

I thought about pink, which was soft and happy. He was into those sorts of things, but I wasn't, so I moved on. Turquoise…might work. It seemed a little kiddish, but who was I to judge?

I checked the price, nodded, and pulled it from the shelf. Good enough.

As I turned toward the checkout, a puffy gray blanket caught my eye. Affixed with a ridiculous price tag of nearly three hundred dollars, it boasted gridded stitching and a classy red ribbon around its folded girth.

The packaging suggested a quality item. A luxury item.

I loved luxury. I would've done great as a rich person. It was a role I'd been born for. Maybe someday I would marry a prince and find creative ways to shrug off running his country while I ran up his credit card. I smiled at the possibilities.

"This blanket isn't dreaming small, idiot," I said, fighting with myself to keep from reaching out and touching the fabric. It would be soft, I knew it. It would make love to my hand and beg to be bought.

But I didn't have that kind of money. If I did, we'd have heat, and I wouldn't need the dang thing in the first place.

But doesn't Mordecai deserve the best?

"He'll get the best. He'll get the turquoise best..."

He has a hard time sleeping, which only makes his condition worse. He loves a crapload of blankets. This would help.

"So would the heat being turned on."

The sign mentioned that it was a weighted blanket, which I'd never heard of before. Reading up on its other attributes—premium and therapeutic, both things Mordecai needed and deserved—I hefted it, for research's sake.

"Oooh," I said, running my face across its finely woven surface. It kissed my cheek, then pushed itself into my arms, begging me to take it home.

Whoa, down, girl.

My months-long dry spell was starting to mess with my head and materialize in inanimate, premium-grade objects. Maybe Mordecai wasn't the only one who needed therapeutic devices, though mine didn't usually take the form of a blanket…

I bit my lip, staring at that price. It was just so much money.

How hard would it be to steal this beast…?

Before I could talk myself out of a terrible idea, a strange feeling washed over me. Like eyes digging into the back of my head. Only this time I could tell it wasn't another customer coveting the luxury item wrapped in my arms.

My hardwired danger sensors roared to life.

No way would that guy have followed me. No way. Guys like him, rich and entitled, had business to do. Important things dragging at their attention. An idiot like me shouldn't even register past the initial annoyance.

Unless he was that crazy magical type, looking for sport. Maybe he was bored, and the cat had found a canary.

"Bugger," I said between clenched teeth. Of all the rotten luck.

Moving ever so slowly, I put the thick and wonderful blanket back onto the shelf and slightly turned to look over my shoulder.

Cold washed through my middle. Fear crawled up my spine and sent tingles of apprehension racing down my legs.

Stormy blue eyes under high, arching brows surveyed me from over a shelf of unnecessary doodads. His lush and shapely lips, which softened his rugged face to something distractingly handsome, twitched downward, the budding of a grimace.

Grimaces on crazy people weren't good. His following me wasn't good.

None of this was good.

Time to go.

Chapter 4

ALEXIS

I TURNED TO stuff the turquoise blanket back onto its shelf, but stopped myself.

"Mother-trucker biscuit fucker," I said, a saying my mother had always used when I was in the room and she was trying not to swear. By the last word, she'd apparently given up.

Mordecai needed that blanket. He was trying to fight off a serious cough, and given his chronic illness, another cold night could easily propel him toward bronchitis or worse. Since my place of employment was run by stingy non-magical people, they only offered non-magical health insurance. Being that the world largely kept the two worlds separate, even if certain zones did not, magical people like me and Mordecai could only get medical treatment through magical establishments, and only then with magical health insurance, or the money to pay. I had neither. If Mordecai got worse, not even the local emergency room would take him. I'd have no way to help him.

I needed this blanket.

Blanket tucked under my arm, I pretended I wasn't shaking with adrenaline as I headed to the checkout. The man's body came into full view, and then I couldn't even pretend anymore.

He was built like a god. Large, thick shoulders tapered down to trim hips. His formfitting white T-shirt showed off muscular biceps, the bumps of his pecs, and the plane of his stomach. To complete the picture of mighty strength and power, his muscular thighs strained his snug jeans.

The man would be jaw-dropping if not for the raw intensity rolling from him in heady waves. His eyes held a haunted viciousness that spoke of imbalance. Live in the cracks of society for long enough, and you become an expert on spotting danger. This guy would kill, or had killed, without batting an eye. He wasn't here to chat. If he'd had something to say, he would've said it by now. If he'd wanted a groveling apology, he wouldn't be tracking me silently, like a predator does his prey.

Everything in me said to run like my hair was on fire. I was the little brown mouse in this scenario, and he the snake, coiled and ready to strike.

But I was a caretaker if not a pseudo-mother, and I would not let Mordecai down because of an outrageously scary though equally attractive stalker. I just had to hope this man was not so unhinged as to accost me in plain sight.

Which meant I'd better damn well stay in plain sight.

"Gotta buy this," I mumbled to myself for encouragement while quickening my pace. "He's too sick not to. Just gonna…move faster."

This guy was big, but was he fast? Because I was fast. I was super fast, especially when a huge man with lots of working muscle was chasing me.

At the cashier, I praised all things holy that there was no line and I had cash in my pocket. There would be no awkward pauses as the curly-haired checker verified my ID against a debit card, realized I wasn't "like her," and tried to figure out if she could wait on me or not. Sometimes the answer was no, true, but a teller should really know the rules of the establishment in which she worked.

I flicked my hair to hide some of my anxious tremors as she reached for the blanket. Her wide smile was reassuring, and I let a smile linger on my face in response. Peers, that was what we were. Just two normal gals going about their lives.

An intimidating presence filled in behind me, and I swallowed past the sudden lump in my throat.

"Sir, I can help you over here," the cashier beside us called in a sweet voice.

My cashier, Darlene, going by the nametag, looked

up. Her eyes widened and she paused before putting the blanket into a bag.

"Sir?" the cashier next to us called again.

"I'll stay here." His voice was barrel-deep and raspy. The confidence in it vibrated through my body and burned across my skin.

I sucked in a deep breath, feeling a pull in my core, the kind of warm tug that made a girl stand up and take notice. Both female checkers, older but no less immune, mirrored my reaction. I nearly didn't notice the lilt to his words, a slight accent pleasantly riding his speech. I absolutely noticed, however, the force of his presence, beating into me in a way I'd never felt before. It was lovely and disconcerting and horrible all at the same time.

I leaned forward, my legs shaking harder and my feet tingling. "Hurry there, if you wouldn't mind," I said softly, cash held out in front of me.

Her smile was less sure, and her eyes kept darting to the man in line behind me. "Of course."

A moment later, I took the bag and forcefully told myself not to glance back. Not to make eye contact and possibly excite the little gremlins cranking the wheel in his head.

I could knife myself for how infrequently I listened.

His stormy gaze found mine immediately, his eyes the blue-gray of the ocean right before a squall. I guessed his height at six two, topping mine by only five or so inches. Usually that wouldn't feel imposing, but with his size and stature, it felt like he towered over me, impossibly large and powerful.

His hands were empty. He wasn't buying anything.

"Did you want your receipt?" the cashier asked, but I was already striding away.

Outside the door, I walked as fast as I could, ready to break into a sprint if he came running after me. I made it down the walkway and out of sight from the store, however, and no one followed me.

That didn't slow my pace.

My dilapidated Honda with rust patches and various shades of blue paint waited where I'd left it, blessedly alone. Heart hammering, I stuck the key into the lock as fast as possible before ripping open the door. I threw in the blanket and pulled my purse up over my head.

A large motor revved, capturing my attention. Cherry red and ultra-sporty, a Ferrari turned the corner into my parking aisle.

"Oh crap," I said in a hasty release of breath, clutching the handles of my purse.

The sports car stopped right behind my Honda. My heart tasted acidic in my throat. The predator had me cornered.

The door swung open, and the stranger crawled free

of its depths. Movements lithe and athletic, he walked around the car with a purposeful gait, his shoulders back and air confident.

I did what any sensible woman would do. I dove into my purse and fished out a small can of mace.

I straightened up with the mace at my side, holding it near my leg so as not to be obvious. He stopped in front of me and stared down for an intense, silent moment. Tremors ran through my body and shook my knees. I licked my parched lips. Was he waiting for me to speak first? Because I'd play ball if it would help me figure out what kind of trouble I was in.

Right after I unstuck my tongue from the roof of my mouth.

"Can I help you?" I asked as calmly as I could.

"You should watch where you're walking." His voice was oh-so-pleasant. The harsh stare with a vicious glimmer was not. Sweat trickled down my back.

"I should. That's true. But that service driveway is for authorized personnel only. Your car doesn't fit the bill. I didn't realize it would roll through." The excuse was a poor one, but it was all I had.

The intensity of his gaze increased. Silence stretched between us. My tongue re-stuck to the roof of my mouth.

"You're lucky," he finally said, and the raw danger in his voice cut right through me. "If this were the magical zone, I could have killed you outright. But clearly you know that…"

Ah, crap. He was magical.

My brain churned furiously, and I cursed myself for not knowing more about the magical hierarchy. There were a ton of rich guys driving nice cars in either society, but only the people toward the top of said hierarchy could dole out punishments to civilians.

"Exactly," I rushed to say, pushing the advantage. In the back of my mind, I was scratching this complex off the list of areas I would visit…ever again. "I'm out of your jurisdiction. I don't even live in the magical zone. Your rules don't apply to me. When here."

His eyes dipped to my lips then back up, the flicker so quick that I half wondered if I was seeing things. "I can feel the magic in you," he said accusingly. "Unless you are here for other reasons…it is beneath you to reside in this place." His words dripped with disdain, and though he didn't turn to survey the shopping complex, his tone gave the effect that he had. His gaze delved into me, searching. For what, I had absolutely no idea. "But you are correct. It is mutual soil. I can't do to you what I would like."

Shivers washed down my body, and I flicked off the safety on the mace. If he could sense magical power, it meant he was either a Sensor, and I was moderately in the clear, or he had a *shitload* of power himself. Those who were close to the pinnacle of power could quite literally get away with murder. The only things I had going for me were a bottle of mace, a good sprint, and witnesses.

"But you can rest assured—" He stepped forward, the movement so fast that I instantly panicked.

I yanked up the mace, aimed, and pressed the button in one quick movement.

He dodged to the side, his reactions superhumanly fast and his movements so smooth they looked oiled. His hand sailed up out of nowhere to slap the bottle away, but he stopped before he made contact.

Because nothing had sprayed out.

Cold liquid bubbled out of the spout and dribbled over my fingers.

"Freaking Daisy and her crappy hookups," I muttered, before doing the only thing I could think of: I threw the bottle at his face and looked around for help. But despite the half-full parking lot, no one else was around.

Of all the rotten luck!

He batted the bottle away lazily, and a tiny smile ghosted across his lush lips. He straightened up slowly, eyeing my hand.

"You've got a bit of problem there," he said, and I could detect the faint accent again, though from where it came, I couldn't say.

I braced myself to run, but what was the point? At the speed he could move, I wouldn't even get one foot off the ground before his fingers were wrapped around my neck. Fighting was pointless, too. I had a couple years of martial arts training, plus a couple months of boxing, but I was rusty, and this guy was way beyond what I could handle on my best day. He'd bat me down like that bottle of mace.

Please don't drag me into the magical zone and make an example of me...

"Sorry about the attempted macing," I blurted, trying to keep it light and respectful. Maybe smoothing the ol' ego would help. "You scared me. And also, sorry about stepping out in front of you earlier. That was my bad. You have places to be. I'm nobody. I shouldn't keep you..."

His stormy, vicious gaze beat into me, and a small crease formed between his brows. My words trailed away into a thick, suffocating silence. The desire to run was so strong that I could barely breathe.

Without warning, he pivoted.

I jumped and lashed out. My fist sailed through empty air.

With my heart trying to punch through my chest, I panted and stared after him, incredulous.

He was walking away! He didn't even glance back. After stalking me through the complex and basically threatening me because I'd stepped out in front of his car, he was choosing to ignore my obvious attempt at violence.

Was he off-kilter, or was I? Because my brain was having a hard time with the logic on this one.

He paused by his door. "You said you were buying that blanket for a sick kid?"

I lifted my eyebrows and tried to work my brain around to the change in topic. "Yes?"

"Was that true? The blue blanket?"

"It's turquoise," I corrected him without thinking.

"Why that one and not the other?"

I couldn't stop blinking in confusion, which made me uncontrollably blunt. "Just so we're clear, spying on people as they make life decisions is not appropriate whether we're in a dual-society zone or not."

"Choosing a blanket is a life decision?"

The fear for myself bled away instantly. All I could think about was Mordecai's situation. "For the kid, yeah. It is."

He rested a large arm on the edge of the door and his other hand on the roof. "Then why not go for the fluffier one?"

I shifted uncomfortably.

Usually, I didn't mind admitting I was dirt poor. I couldn't even get handouts. The non-magical government said I didn't qualify because I was technically magical, and the magical governing body didn't give a shit about me or my situation because I wasn't useful or powerful. I'd set up camp in the crack of the two uninterested societies, my meager earnings just enough to keep me and my two wards off the street. I was doing what I could, and it was for a good cause. Why would anyone be embarrassed about that?

But...for some reason...I didn't want to share my nitty-gritty with this guy. I didn't want him shining a light on my life and commenting on what he saw. For once, I didn't want to admit that I was essentially the dog poop ruining important people's shoes.

I lifted my chin defiantly. "Because he likes cheery colors, and turquoise will fit the bill."

His penetrating stare made me squirm, even from that distance. Finally, he nodded with a flat expression, then sat into his car and closed the door behind him. Without another glance, he revved the engine, and the car lurched forward.

Body shaking, I watched the Ferrari head back to that service driveway as the fake or too-old mace dried on my fingers.

He had stopped his business earlier to follow me. He'd admitted he couldn't kill me outright here, which meant he'd thought about killing me in the first place. And now he had my license plate and could easily find out where I lived.

The question was, would he? And if he did, what was it about me that had triggered such a hardcore reaction? I was a nobody, and this was the Wild West of San Francisco—if he was really that important, he could've just run me over and kept going. Stopping and tracking me like prey, then letting me go, spoke of a big cat playing with its food.

I had no illusions of my place on the food chain in this duo. And now he knew how to find me.

Chapter 5

ALEXIS

"HOW WAS YOUR day?" Frank asked as I fitted the key into my front door lock later that evening. His thinning gray hair streaked across his balding head in a bad comb-over. His thin lips pressed into a slightly downturned line and his watery blue eyes were draped in loose skin.

I slumped against the door, really not in the mood for Frank's idle chitchat.

"Kind of crappy, actually," I said, wiping moisture off my forehead. Fog rolled and boiled around us, August one of the worst months for it in San Francisco. While Valens, the Demigod at the pinnacle of our magical governing body, could affect the weather, he didn't bother in the dual or non-magical zones.

"At lunch, some rich, handsome guy stalked me around a shopping complex—"

"That doesn't sound crappy," Frank interrupted. "A pretty girl like yourself? Rich and handsome is what you deserve."

Frank had lost touch with how the world worked.

"You must've missed the word *stalked*, but sure—"

"We don't call it stalked, honey, we call it *interested*. You need to alter your perceptions a little, is all."

Or maybe Frank was just creepy.

"What have I said about calling me 'honey,' Frank?"

"See, now, that's just it." He waggled a gnarled finger at me. "You're too prickly. You need to loosen up if you ever hope to land a husband."

I laughed, and a woman with short hair gave me a wary look as she passed by on the sidewalk.

I quieted and analyzed my keys. It was best to keep my head down. The non-magical government couldn't kick me out of the neighborhood because it was a dual-society zone and I was closer to the magical line than not, but if all the Chesters banded together, they could make my life hell until I had no choice but to leave. I couldn't afford that option.

Best to keep my weird on the down-low.

"The last thing I want is a husband, Frank," I whispered, turning the lock. "I already have two people to look after; I don't need one more."

"Ah." Frank nodded like it all suddenly made sense. "One of those bra-burning feminist types, huh? You don't need a man. You want to roar. I get it."

"But do you?" I leaned against the door as a smile crawled onto my face. For reasons unknown, it tickled me how out of touch Frank was.

"Sure, sure. Women's lib. Flag burning. Damn shame."

"Nope. Those are different things."

He waved the thought away. "Someday, when you realize that it's a tough world out there, you'll come to your senses and want a man to take care of you."

"Well, if you know any rich ones who want to actually take care of me, or even know how to use their words as opposed to creeping me out with penetrating stares, send them my way, would ya?"

"You may have missed your chance. Earlier, at the shopping mall."

"That guy didn't want to take care of me, Frank. He wanted to scare me. Or...actually, I'm not really sure what his end game was, now that I think of it. But it certainly wasn't to propose and take me away from this charmed life."

"Ah now, it ain't all that bad." Frank reached out to chuck my chin.

"Stop that. No touching, remember?"

"Right, right." Confusion stole over Frank's expression. "No touching, right."

"Anyway." I put my hand on the doorknob. "I was late getting back to work and my boss gave me a warning. One more and I'm done."

Frank stared down at his shoes for a moment. "No

touching, no… Where am I?"

I grimaced and turned the knob. Frank was about to slip into one of his episodes. He would head home for some alone time, where, much to his cohabitants' dismay, he'd likely move everything around and open all the cabinet doors.

"See ya around, Frank." I nodded at him and slipped into the house.

Mordecai sat wrapped up in his inadequate blankets on the worn couch. He looked up from a book at my entrance, and his smile revealed straight white teeth that I was forever proud of. I'd been hounding him to keep those pearly whites in tiptop shape ever since I took over this outfit. His light hazel eyes sparkled with happiness in his dark face, the contrast exceptionally striking. He'd be a real looker when the treacherous journey through puberty finally ended.

He fitted a bookmark into the roughed-up paper before closing the volume.

"What's today's lesson?" I asked as I dropped my purse onto the small stand by the door.

"I'm reading a really neat book about trees. Did you know that they can communicate with each other?"

"Really?" My keys clinked as they fell into the bowl next to my purse. "Do they use sign language with their branches?"

"They communicate through fungi in the soil."

I added my shoes to the others neatly placed by the door and crossed the trampled brown carpet to the tiny kitchen with its cracked flowered countertop and scuffed linoleum. "That right? What do they say to each other?"

I heard him grunt before his skeletal form drifted into the kitchen after me. A knit cap covered his tightly curled hair, still falling out in patches. If I could just keep us fully stocked with the anti-morphing serum, his body wouldn't have to constantly fight the shifter magic snaking through his genes.

Mordecai was a rare case among shifters. He had plenty of magic to shapeshift, but the human part of him treated that magic like a virus. The surge of magic it would require him to shift would send his body into defense mode, putting him in shock. He'd never shifted because of this.

Thankfully, he had enough power to keep from shifting, even at the full moon, but a war constantly raged inside of him, depleting his energy and inviting in other sicknesses. Shifters could heal at amazing rates in animal form, and somewhat in human form, but that mostly just kept him alive. It did nothing for the pain.

That was where the anti-morphing serum came in.

Lesser-powered shifters used it to control the urges to change at inopportune times, especially at the full moon. For Mordecai, it dulled his body's reaction to the magic. It calmed the internal fight, and relieved much of the pain. Not all, but a lot of it.

Unfortunately, it was incredibly expensive, and without magical medical insurance, we often ran out for a good week before I could get more.

I'd appealed to the shifter pack he'd come from, begging for their help. That had been about as useful as asking a starving man to share his steak. The current pack alpha wouldn't hear it. He'd taken over after Mordecai's father and mother had died, and didn't want to risk their kid rising up to steal his mantle.

I'd explained that I wasn't asking for the somewhat risky medical procedure that would cure Mordecai's health issue (huge dream), just asking for a steady supply of the anti-morphing serum to keep him healthy (small dream). No go. It turned out that killing a kid outright was frowned upon, but letting nature take its course was considered acceptable.

Fucking shifters.

I'd then appealed to the local Demigod's office, asking for help.

I'd been told it was a shifter problem, and to take my concern to them. When I explained I had, they returned with "It seems his fate has been decided."

Fucking Demigods.

So here we were. Nestled in the crack of both societies, just trying to stay alive.

I plastered on a smile to hide the fear and sorrow filling my middle. "Through fungi, huh? Neato-mosquito."

He sat at the round table straddling the line between living room and kitchen. "You sound like your mom."

I frowned at him. "Not cool, man."

His carefree laughter warmed my soul. "How was your day?" he asked.

"Normal." No need to worry him. He wouldn't have the same regressive view as Frank about being stalked, and he'd blame himself for my being late at work as soon as I showed him the blanket, which would ruin the surprise. "You?"

"Good. I straightened up a little in between lessons."

"Yes." I glanced at the crumbs littering the yellow countertop and the pile of dirty plates and utensils in the sink. "I saw the shoes."

"That's as far as I got."

I nodded, pain stabbing my heart. Maybe I should've just given him my blanket. San Francisco didn't get that cold, after all. It wouldn't have killed me, and then I could've put that thirty bucks toward more of his medicine.

Thirty bucks toward the four hundred and fifty total I needed for the serum.

"How's this online school? Any better than the last one?" I asked, keeping my voice light.

"A bit. It's still a little slow."

"Or you're just a little smart."

He grinned and shrugged.

"So trees are your new object of study?" I looked through the fridge, picking out the items closest to going bad. I wasn't a great chef, but I was a creative one. Give me a few ingredients, however odd, and I'd make a dinner out of it. I'd learned from the best and had a crapload of practice.

"Yes. Trees first, then on to the ocean."

"Are you still doing history?"

He leaned his elbows onto the table and his smile dwindled. "I'm keeping pace, but…"

"You have to keep that up."

"Why? It's mostly about Chesters."

"You shouldn't use that term. It's not polite."

"Fine, whatever, but all the stuff in the books is about them. Magical people have only been in the open for the last hundred years, but we've existed since humans have. Why can't I read up on our history?"

"You can. You should. But you need to do both, remember?"

"They don't teach human history in magical schools…"

"Yes, they do."

"Only in high school, and then only the essentials."

"That's because they are elitist assholes. You need a

thorough understanding of your world, Mordecai. And that includes human history."

He let out a frustrated sigh. "Fiiiine."

He might've been the sweetest kid on the planet, but he was still a teenager. I personally couldn't remember how long puberty lasted, but apparently fifteen wasn't out of the woods yet. More's the pity.

"What's for dinner?" he asked, crossing his arms and leaning back.

"No idea. I'm just looking over all these super-tasty ingredients."

"Your grimace says you're lying."

Didn't I know it. I wasn't a huge veggie fan in general, but I absolutely hated half of the ones laid out in front of me. Whoever had cultivated Brussels sprouts should be shot.

But beggars couldn't be choosers. Una down at the Natural Earth Shop, a non-magical crack-dweller who had made a nice little life for herself, was kind enough to give me some produce and other essentials. It was much better than starving.

"Need me to chop something?" Mordecai asked, wrestling his hands out of the blanket wrapped around his shoulders.

"Yeah." I pulled a few potatoes out of the bottom cupboard. "Handle those, will ya?"

The front door slammed, rattling the glasses. "Bitch

better have my money!"

"Daisy's home," Mordecai murmured, sticking a hand out for a peeler.

"Jesus. What's up with her?" I delivered a cutting board, peeler, and knife as Daisy's petite frame stalked by with balled fists.

"Bitch clearly owes her money, and she wants it," Mordecai answered.

I gave Mordecai a chastising look. "No swearing."

"You swear all the time."

"That's because I'm a surly adult and the owner of the roof over your head. Do as I say, don't do as I do." I stepped out so I could see down the short hallway that led to the two bedrooms in the back. "Daisy?"

Daisy reappeared in the doorway of her and Mordecai's shared room. She stalked toward me with a clipboard in hand, red blotching her porcelain, doll-like face. She was the sweetest *looking* kid ever, but with a very colorful personality.

"I need your phone, Lexi. The cordless is out of battery." She stopped in front of me and put out a hand.

I let my stare beat into her for a moment, not moving.

She gave me a dramatic sigh. "What?"

"What do you mean, *what*?" I left it at that. Like Mordecai, she was in hormone hell. Right in the thick of it, too. Fourteen going on fifty going on nine, she was at war with her body and womanhood. She was non-magical and had been sucked into the system as a toddler when her mother died of a heroin overdose. Bouncing from one foster home after another, she'd been battered and beaten, ignored and forgotten, until she'd run away at ten.

I'd found her offering herself to a homeless guy in a box in exchange for food and a place to sleep. At ten. Hunger would drive a person to extreme things.

Because of me, she was still a virgin. Also because of me, she had been declared lost and presumed dead in the non-magical zone. She lived in the crack of the societies with us because she had nowhere else to go. Not if she didn't want to be returned to the system until she was eighteen.

Over my dead body.

So here we were. Irresponsible me and two teens, one magical, one not, both with troubled pasts. It could be worse.

"Okay, here's how it is." Daisy jutted out a hip. "I sold this guy weed, right? And—"

"I'm going to stop you right there." I held out my hand. "Selling drugs is a *nope*."

She rolled her eyes. "It wasn't *real* weed. *Hello?* How dumb do you think I am?"

"Do you really want me to answer that?"

Her glare could've peeled paint. "It's just a bunch of

herbs all mixed up," she said. "And before you ask, the coke is actually flour."

"Nope." I grabbed her by the arm and dragged her into the kitchen.

"Ew, stop!"

She tried to pull her arm back, but I held on tight until I deposited her in front of the judge and jury.

"Tell Mordecai what you are doing," I demanded.

"I heard. The house isn't very big." Mordecai slid the peeler over the potato in purposeful motions.

"I'm going to go ahead and say that selling fake drugs is worse than selling real drugs." I braced my hands on my hips.

Mordecai nodded slowly, and Daisy aggressively crossed her arms over her chest.

"I second that," he said, not losing stride with the peeling.

"Collecting money for fake drugs is going to result in a bad situation, like a broken bone or a crushed head," I continued.

"And it is morally wrong," Mordecai said.

"Right, yes." I pointed at him. "Morally wrong. That's the real reason not to do it. And *also* because of the busted-head situation."

I already mentioned I was irresponsible. In fairness, my mother hadn't been any better, and I'd turned out okay, all things considered.

"Either way, though, you need to stop." I faced Daisy. "You can't do anything illegal. You know that. You have to stay out of trouble."

Her mouth dropped open and her eyes widened, as though I was the most irrational person alive. "Denny owes me two hundred bucks. With what you have already, we'd be able to get Gollum's serum."

Mordecai rolled his eyes, an action he rarely did. "I should've never let her watch *Lord of the Rings*."

"Really? Because you're somehow in charge of the movies I watch, Sauron?" Daisy tilted her head at Mordecai in what I could only describe as a snarky way. A teenager's body language spoke volumes.

"Wait...what?" I asked, easily distracted.

"*Mord*-ecai has the same start as *Mord*-or," Mordecai said dryly, pushing the peels aside on the table and pulling the cutting board closer.

"Ew, *really*? Look at the mess you've made." Daisy stomped over to the counter. She slapped down her clipboard and snatched up a rag. She scraped the peels off the table and into her palm before depositing them in the trash.

"I can't very well stand over the sink right now, can I?" Mordecai retorted, stooping to her maturity level, as he so often did. It was hard to rise above it, I had to admit. "You saw me earlier. And you should put the peels in the compost bin."

"It all ends up in the ground—"

"What happened earlier?" I asked, rounding on Mordecai.

"He tripped over his own feet and fell on his face." Daisy grabbed her clipboard again. "Seriously, Lexi, I have this covered. Denny is a complete moron. He'll smoke it and think it is legit. I said I'd smoke it with him just to help his buzz along. I figure I'll do—Stop shaking your head. I figure I'll do some weird stuff, laugh a lot, and he'll have a good experience. I'll even kiss him. That'll take his mind—Lexi, seriously, stop shaking your head. This is a good plan. Ol' One-Eye needs that serum. His coughing is driving me crazy."

"Touching speech," Mordecai said, but his soft eyes didn't match his dry voice. You couldn't show too much compassion around Daisy for entirely different reasons than you couldn't show it around me. Where I would burst into tears and be hard-pressed to stop the water-works because of my worry and anxiety over the kids, she just didn't know how to handle emotion. She'd had no experience with it in her life. Pity she'd seen a lot of, anger she was an old pro at thwarting, but honest-to-god compassion stopped her up and made her blink stupidly.

We were a messed-up lot.

"All of that is a no." I shook my head at Daisy. "Hard no. You are not going to sell fake drugs—or real drugs, for that matter, to anyone—and you most certainly are not going to offer PG-rated sexual favors. I'll get the money. I have a plan."

"You always say you have a plan. Working and saving is not a plan." Daisy looked over her clipboard. "And fine. I'll draw the line at selling him the fake coke. I don't know how that would go down anyway. But the fake weed is harmless. And it's not sexual favors, give me a break. He's cute. I'd totally hit that."

"You're not hitting anything. You are way too young. Do we need to have another sex talk?"

Her face soured. "I meant I would kiss him. Not have sex with him."

"You don't have a firm grasp on your sexual slang," Mordecai mumbled.

"Shut up. Like you know."

"Okay, okay," I said, putting out my hands. "Enough. Daisy, no fake anything, and no extorting money for kissing. Have a little respect for yourself."

"I have a ton of respect for myself. I'm a damn good kisser. People should be paying for that shit."

"No. Stop." I looked at her in exasperation. "No swearing, no getting money for kissing—just no to everything. No across the board. Like I said, I'll get the money."

A sound very close to a growl rose out of Daisy's throat before she stomped to the junk drawer and extracted a pen. She wildly scratched items off the list on her clipboard.

"Stop stomping around; it's giving me a headache," Mordecai grumbled.

"Also..." I put my finger in the air. "I'm pretty sure you guys shouldn't be talking about sexual stuff. Right? You're too young."

"Oh my God, you are the worst at parenting," Daisy said.

"Yeah. I know. That's why you two need to help me. Because, spoiler alert, I'm not actually your parent."

"We're not children, and we've seen far too much to be sheltered now," Mordecai said, ever the voice of reason. "And don't worry, your mother, God rest her soul, wasn't any better."

My mother was the one who'd taken in Mordecai when he was five. She'd gone to a local market to steal food, and had ended up saving a starving boy instead. He'd lived in my crammed room until she'd died of an undiagnosed internal infection six years ago.

"Thanks for trying," I said, heading back to the vegetables, "but she somehow managed to support three strays and her daughter on a meager salary. I can barely feed you two ingrates."

"I think you're forgetting that you've been working since you were Daisy's age. She had two meager salaries." Mordecai smiled sadly. "I miss Jane and Eddie, though. I wonder what they are up to. We haven't heard from them in a while."

Jane and Eddie, both of them my age and old enough to go out on their own, had taken off after my mother passed. They'd worked, too, but my mother had insisted they save all their money so they could get a good start when they flew the coop.

"They both have families now in the Midwest. They're busy." I washed off the cursed Brussels sprouts.

"When are you going to settle down and have a family?" Mordecai asked.

I huffed as Daisy said, "Don't worry, Samwise. Master will never leave us. No one would have her."

"Well…I *might* leave," I grumbled.

"Okay, so fine." I heard scribbling on the clipboard. "Fine. No selling fake drugs. So I'll just take his offer to work for the family vet business under the table. I'd rather not clean up dog poop, but I will do it."

I stilled as guilty excitement ran through me. "You shouldn't have to work at your age."

"Kids my age don't work because they are usually in normal school. Since I can't go to normal school because my society thinks I'm a missing person and likely dead, and my online classes can be done at any time, I can just move my studying to the evening or night, when I'm not working. My social life is limited. I have time for all this stuff. Like you guys."

She had a point there. Mordecai was forced to be a recluse because of his condition, Daisy was forced to be a recluse because of her situation, and I didn't have any money to go out and meet anyone. The extent of my social life was the local pub filled with derelicts where the owner, an ex-boyfriend who knew I was dirt poor and enjoyed lording it over me, paid for my drinks. His pity tasted like stale beer and stress relief. Dumping him was the smartest thing I had ever done.

Daisy dropped her clipboard onto the table and grabbed a bell pepper from in front of me. "That's settled. Pretty soon we won't be forced to be vegetarians."

"I don't think it's a bomb," I heard yelled through the front door. "But you may want to be careful, just in case."

I exhaled and slumped against the counter. Freaking Frank. I sure wished he'd find somewhere else to be on a permanent basis.

"Looks pretty benign..." Frank's words were muffled, but I still heard them over Mordecai and Daisy's chopping. "There's hope for you, after all. He'll do just fine. Strong and sure. He'll make a good match if *you'd let someone take care of you.*"

"What is he on about now?" I muttered, debating going to the door to check.

"What?" Daisy asked.

"Is it Frank?" Mordecai dropped the knife next to the chopped potatoes.

"You'll want to come out and grab it before someone steals it off your porch. I've got my eye on things, but you never know," Frank said.

"Yes, it's Frank," I said.

"Oh, gross." Daisy shook her head.

"No note that I see, though," Frank hollered, clearly desperate to be heard. "He's trying to be a secret admirer. Well, I won't spoil it for him. I don't want to quit his game, as the kids say."

"They don't say that," I muttered, losing my battle to curiosity and heading to the door.

"Say what?" Mordecai asked.

"Don't encourage the situation," Daisy told him.

I took the few steps out of the kitchen and to the front door. Frank stood on the stoop, his back to the house and his head moving from side to side, standing guard.

"What's the—" The words died on my lips. Shock bled through every fiber of my being.

Just off to the side, behind the browning bush, sat an opened brown bag with *Bed, Bath & More* written on the side. Inside lay the gravity blanket I'd been fawning over. The one that had been way too expensive for me to seriously contemplate buying.

The super-handsome psychotic stalker had bought a

blanket for a sick kid.

Tears clouded my vision and gratitude melted my heart.

Chapter 6

ALEXIS

"I PROBABLY SHOULDN'T accept it, right?" I asked Frank quietly, a tear running down my face. "I mean, when he first followed me, he didn't even know about Mordecai. Maybe he just intended to bully me. I mean, later on, even after hearing about the blanket being for a sick kid, he talked about punishing me. That suggests dangerous intent. Not to mention, rich and powerful people only perform acts of goodwill to get something in return or as a tax write-off." I wiped the tear away with the back of my hand. "The situation is suspicious, at best. I mean, he looked up my house! He just took his stalkerdom to a whole other level. Despite the blanket situation, that's not good."

"It's a gift to a woman," Frank said, lifting his eyebrows as though I were dense.

"Yeah? And?"

"Of course he wants something. Gifts are down payments for sex."

I ran my hand down my face. "Great. Good input," I

said dryly. "Except I don't think that applies here."

"Of course it does. Why wouldn't it? You're a pretty girl." He scratched his permanent white five o'clock shadow. "Granted, you could put in a little more effort. Some makeup and a hairbrush, for starters. Maybe clothes that actually fit—"

"Yes, Frank. Thank you. I know what I look like." And I did. My stringy blond hair was in a ponytail with a messy halo of flyaways. My sports bra flattened what a padded bra could turn into a C-cup, minimizing my already scant curves, and my pants ended at my ankles because the cheap-o store didn't have my size in *long*. Except for good skin that hadn't seen much of the sun (living in eternal fog will do that to a person), I was a wreck when it came to most beauty standards. But I worked in a place that merely tolerated me, with people who rarely spoke to me, and had the resources of a pauper. I wasn't trying to impress anyone, and no one wanted to be impressed by me. There was no point in getting gussied up, even if I had the energy. Or makeup from this decade.

I smoothed my somewhat wrinkled shirt down my stomach, thinking of the stranger's chiseled face, his stylish jeans, and the way his plain T-shirt fit his perfect body in all the right ways. Somehow, the arrogance he wore like a cape didn't detract from all that unreal beauty, or that power and athletic grace.

His stormy, vicious blue eyes invaded the mouth-watering image. A tingle of fear worked up my spine at the haunted depths to his intense, unwavering gaze.

He'd looked at me like I was prey. I had *felt* like prey, and not of the sexual variety. He was dangerous, and if he was playing a game of cat and mouse, the blanket was bait. He probably hoped I'd let my guard down.

"Everything okay?"

I jumped at the sound of Mordecai's voice and spun around, smoothing over my expression. "Yup," I answered automatically.

He slowly walked from the kitchen, clutching his threadbare blanket around his bony shoulders. Each step jolted his body in ways that a healthy shifter would never experience, even on his deathbed.

He was hurting, and I bet the cold had already settled deeply in his bones.

Desperation tugged at me. Maybe the blanket was a trap, but it was one I'd happily walk into if it would help Mordecai. "Get this! I won the most awesome blanket. Check it out."

Without another thought, I turned back and snagged the handles of the bag. It was probably a bad idea, but if it gave him a warm night in an otherwise shitty existence riddled with pain, I'd handle whatever came of it.

"It's the Rolls-Royce of blankets," I said. "It was going to be a surprise, but...well, you ruined it. Here." I pushed the bag toward him.

"What?" he said slowly, clearly confused. I had that effect on people.

"You shouldn't lie—"

I shut the door on Frank to shut him up. Also because I hoped he'd eventually get the message and buzz off.

"What's going on?" Daisy peeked around the corner, saw that the front door was closed, and fully emerged. "Did you say something about a Rolls-Royce?"

Mordecai extracted the folded blanket with more effort than it should've taken, even for him. His eyebrows knitted together as he hefted the bundle.

"What?" Daisy pushed in close. "What's the matter? Wow, this looks—Oh my God, this is so soft." With rounded eyes, she looked my way. "Did you steal this?"

"No! I said I *won* it," I replied.

She gave me a flat look. "We all know you are the unluckiest person on the planet. Even if you'd cheated, you still wouldn't have won it. How'd you get it?"

I sighed and headed back to the kitchen. "Fine. Don't believe me. It's awesome, though. It's a weighted blanket to...like... It's therapeutic. And super soft. You'll love it."

"Where did you really get this?" Mordecai asked,

carefully putting the blanket back into the bag and stepping away.

"Honestly, Mordecai, I did not steal that. Or buy it. You can relax, since I didn't spend money on you." I gestured with the knife. "Use the thing."

"I'm with Viggo, here—"

"Viggo is the actor," Mordecai said in a pained tone. "The character was Aragorn."

"Fine, whatever. I'm with noble Aragorn here. You clearly found that bag on the front porch, you're acting shady, and this isn't adding up. Where'd you get it? Because you know you can't get caught stealing. Three strikes means you stay in jail. I ain't running this bitch on my own, I will tell you that much. Although then I could sell those fake drugs to that hot moron…"

Was nothing in my life easy?

"Fine!"

I gave in. I always did. As I made dinner, I went through what had happened at the shopping center, including finding that Burberry bag, because I knew these two would be just as excited on my behalf. By the time we set the table and sat down to eat, I'd told them everything.

"Give it back," Mordecai said without hesitation. "I love turquoise. I'd rather have that blanket, anyway. And you know I hate surprises, so this works out better."

"I know you do. That's why I like giving them to you." I blew out a breath. "So that's one vote for giving it back." I spooned some vegetable glop into my mouth. It wasn't much to look at, but it actually tasted all right. "I'm for keeping it. I mean, he did ask about the sick kid. Clearly he was making sure his goodwill would go to a worthy cause."

"What'll happen when he finds out I'm not actually a kid?" Mordecai asked.

I paused in chewing. I hadn't thought about that.

"Teen, kid, whatever." I waved the thought away. "And he won't find out. I'm never going to see the guy again." I shrugged, almost completely hoping it was true. Only a very tiny part of me lingered on the image of the stranger's robust body, his gorgeous face, and intense, turbulent gaze. He spoke to the part of me that liked to chase assholes and fall for bad boys. The part I knifed whenever it reared its ugly head. "Daisy? What's your vote? We should obviously keep the blanket, right? Mordecai needs it while we wrestle up a few more bucks."

"Okay, but…" She stabbed her fork into her mashed potatoes. "Mordecai also needs a guardian, and this guy *stalked* you, Lexi."

"He *followed* me," I countered. "And to him, it was for good reason."

"Telling someone to watch where they're going, after nearly being run over, is a good reason to drop everything and stalk the person?" Mordecai asked incredulously.

My case was collapsing.

Daisy shook her head. "Stalking is *not* sexy, Alexis, no matter how hot you think the stalker is. It denotes an unbalanced, possessive personality, the kind of person who will manipulate the object of desire into isolation so that they'll fall into dependency and subservience. The object loses themselves and becomes property, basically."

There was the fifty-year-old side of Daisy. She could sound extremely clinical when she needed to. She'd also seen that particular scenario firsthand in one of her many foster families.

"I think we all know that I will *never* fall into dependency and subservience," I said, eyeing the two of them. They both nodded, however grudgingly. "And besides, this is a different situation. I have nothing he could possibly want. He didn't even leave a note with which to manipulate me. I can claim ignorance. Seriously, he's just giving a sick kid a blanket, you guys. There is bound to be one gem among a sea of rich turds."

"Rich guys look down on people like us," Mordecai said, concern in his eyes.

"She knows that." Daisy moved the food around her

plate. "She's clearly bullshitting right now. You can see it in her shifty eyes."

"No swearing until you're eighteen. Or…while…" I grasped for what my mother always used to tell me. "Not while you're under my roof."

I earned another eye roll.

"You have to see that the whole story is very strange, Lexi," Mordecai said. "I've never heard of any magical person acting like this. Are you sure he was? Magical, I mean?"

"Definitely. No human could've moved that fast."

"And you think he was definitely important and not some stuffed shirt with an overinflated ego?"

I paused, running through the facts. "I'm not sure, no. He spoke like a guy with power, and he clearly had a lot of money because he was driving a Ferrari, but I don't actually know his position in the magical government. Or even if he has one."

"He could've stolen the car," Daisy said.

"Car boosters don't drive their extremely obvious stolen cars around shopping malls," Mordecai responded.

"Are you dense? It was a shopping *complex*, idiot," she retorted.

"Daisy, don't call your brother an idiot," I said automatically.

"He's not my brother."

"Then don't call your roommate an idiot." I rubbed my temples. "Regardless of whether he has magical authority or not, what could he possibly want with me?"

"Well… You had a point earlier with Frank," Daisy said, eyeing me. "You look like you just rolled out of bed, so it might not be a desire thing. Still, plenty of people have questionable taste. He could be softening you up so you'll let him get close, then he'll show you his sadistic side. A side he can't show to his peers or they'll think less of him…"

"He already showed her his sadistic side. By *stalking* her." Mordecai gave me a poignant look. "I really don't think we should take gifts from sadists."

"I agree." Daisy nodded decisively. "I vote no. You need to give the blanket back. Normally I would say you should chuck it at his face and call him a stalking sonuvabitch, but in this case…maybe just place it at his feet and run."

"Right. Sure. Except I don't know who he is, where he lives, or where he hangs out." I put my hands up and flashed them a winning smile. "So, you see? We have to take it."

"Keep it in that bag until you see him again." Daisy shoveled dairy-free mashed potatoes into her mouth (people didn't usually give away dairy products), then talked around them. "And you will see him again, because he's a stalker."

"When you see him," Mordecai added, "tell him I said thank you—"

"I certainly will not," I cut in, iron in my voice.

"Ha!" Daisy pointed her fork at me. "See? You won't mention Mordecai because you're trying to protect him. Which means you know this isn't legit, but you're prepared to accept the terms anyway." She shook her head. "Now it's a definite no. Tell that stalking bastard to shove his luring-type gift where the sun don't shine. Mama didn't raise no fool."

"I decree that this house is no longer a democracy. It is now a dictatorship." I scooped up more glop. "I get the only say."

"Tell him thank you," Mordecai amended, "but that you can't accept such a generous gift. Then ask him how to get it back to him. Or better yet, just get his license plate and we'll find him the same way he found you."

"Not good that he has our address," Daisy mumbled.

"Agreed," Mordecai said.

I agreed with them but didn't say so. Nor did I tell them I was a little relieved I wouldn't be accepting the blanket. I didn't know what that stranger's game was, but guys like him didn't give handouts without an ulterior motive.

I just wondered what that ulterior motive had to do with me.

Chapter 7

KIERAN

"WHAT HAVE YOU got for me?" Kieran asked as he stepped out of his car. His shoe splashed down into a small stream of murky brown water running from the side of the alleyway behind several prospering businesses. Large metal trash containers dotted the other side, most with trash nearing the top. Cars sped past on the busy street at the far end, their colors muted in the late evening light.

He eyed his car, only a few months old. He hated leaving it in such dimly lit, unmonitored areas, like this back alleyway within the busy magical San Francisco downtown, but he didn't need to attract attention to his whereabouts.

His Six waited off to the side, standing in a staggered line. Tough warriors all, and each with something powerful and unique to bring to the table, these guys had laid down their lives to enter the service of a Demigod—him. Through the blood oath with which they'd pledged their loyalty, they'd inherited a boost of power and certain additions to their skill sets. They were his eyes and ears when he couldn't be present.

Zorn stepped forward; he was a medium-statured man, the most vicious fighter Kieran had ever seen, and as close to a friend as he'd ever been allowed. Zorn had been the first of the Six, and would've been by Kieran's side even without the inherent perks.

"She's a nobody, sir," Zorn said, handing forth a file. "Very little power, next to no talent, and as poor as they come. What you pulled earlier is the extent of it."

Kieran frowned and flipped open the file folder before running a finger down the report within. Sure enough, it was the same information he'd seen in the database, easily pulled up and viewed when he'd searched for her license plate. Not one detail was out of place.

He checked the picture again, then the name and address, before shaking his head. "Can't be right."

He flipped the file closed and walked the few steps to the nearest trash container. He chucked the report inside. What he was looking for wasn't contained in that report.

"She had a lot of power," he said, comparing his own details to what he'd read. "A high class five."

"You've never been wrong on the power scale before, sir," said Jack, a tall, robust man who was happiest navigating deep waters.

"Even so, the report says she's a weak class two." Donovan crossed his arms, his short, dirty blond hair spiked in all directions. "A weak class two is quite a bit different from a strong class five. The assessment for magical people has been known to be wrong from time to time, but never *that* wrong."

"You said she did fit the part she was playing, sir," Zorn said, clearly remembering their earlier conversation. After leaving her, Kieran had parked behind the row of subpar stores in that tattered shopping complex and just sat there for ten minutes, reflecting. Trying to make sense of all he'd just encountered. Of the feel of the woman's magic curling through his bloodstream and exciting his senses. It had been the most unique feeling he could remember. The most invigorating. Finally, he'd summoned the will to meet with his men— but he'd asked them to find out more information about *her.*

He shook his head to clear it, poring over what he'd observed, and trying to make sense of the report.

"She's definitely poor," he said, remembering the look of her clothes. "A spy or assassin might don ill-fitting, cheap clothes, but the woman's shoes had been worn to the point of distress. They were molded to her feet. That look couldn't be duplicated by anything but time."

"Something a highly skilled and trained assassin,

packing enough power to raise eyebrows, wouldn't need," Zorn said. He would know. He was such an assassin, when Kieran needed one.

"Her house has been registered to her since her mother died, and to her mother nearly since Alexis was born," Kieran said. "She's lived there all her life. Or so the records have it."

"A person with that much power would never be left to their own devices," Thane said, scratching his chin through his thick brown beard. "At least not that dual-society zone. Your father would want you to keep tabs on her."

"But on paper, she doesn't have that much power," Jack said.

"And there's the rub," Kieran said softly.

"You said she didn't realize you were following her around the home goods store." Zorn's brow furrowed. "Anyone half trained would've sensed it."

"Easily," Kieran said, remembering the potent trail of magic she'd left behind, like fairy dust, almost as if she were daring him to follow. He'd sensed a trap, but, knowing he had the resources to combat such an attack, had seen it through to see what she would do. The answer, much to his increased confusion, was absolutely nothing. She'd only noticed him once he stepped out in plain view. "That sort of ignorance can't be faked. Not from me."

"Which means...she hasn't been trained," Zorn said with finality.

"Not a chance," Kieran replied. "Everything about her checks out, except for her power level...and her magic."

"What did you say the magic did again?" Donovan asked.

Kieran used a finger and drew a line down the center of his chest. Then, with fisted hands, he mimed spreading open each side of the line.

"It felt like she reached into my middle and grabbed hold of my vitals. I knew one moment of utter, primal vulnerability. But before I could answer in kind, she pulled it away." He shifted his weight, remembering when she'd done it—then remembering when she'd brought out the mace and done it again. "She didn't seem to know she was doing it. When she realized the mace didn't work, she acted like a sitting duck. She was afraid of me; I could sense it." He shook his head. "A person with that kind of magic should never feel afraid. I don't know what kind of magic it was, but it was arresting."

"Her file says she's a Ghost Whisperer," Zorn said.

Kieran huffed out a laugh and led the way down the middle of the alley. "She's no Ghost Whisperer. I've seen enough of them to know." And was about to see another one. Anything to help his mother. Loss pierced his gut, driving away his breath. "Even still, I'll compare her to the woman I'm about to see. This Ghost Whisperer is supposed to be the best in the city. I doubt she'll give me anything more than anyone else has been able to." He blew out a breath, trying to regain his composure. "Have we made any headway in my father's office?"

A tremor of violence ran through his Six. Kieran could vaguely feel their emotional turbulence and anger through the blood bond. The woman was a sideshow curiosity, but their plan to overturn his father required their utmost focus. Focus...and courage.

Henry spoke up. "I've made contact with Valens's secondary assistant, and his bed warmer. Both are more than happy to give up his secrets—"

"As long as they get something in return," Jack said with a smirk.

"Naturally," Henry replied with a smile. He hadn't met a woman he couldn't make scream, or so he claimed. No doubt he'd charmed the bed warmer. "Valens is pretty tight-lipped, but I can get a good idea of his movements and plans through them."

"I've been working through the security staff," Zorn said. "Most of them are disgruntled. They can be paid off, but we'll need to go through a third party to use them."

"I've got third parties all day long." Donovan chuckled. "All day long. I've got a list of organizations Valens consistently uses. Everyone else is fair game. They're not picky. I've also been working my way through the government building, chatting and making friends."

Kieran rounded the corner and emerged onto the busy sidewalk. Street lights rained down a yellow glow, barely lighter than the pink- and orange-streaked sky. Magical people strolled along in the heart of the magical half of San Francisco, most hardly discernable from their non-magical cousins, but a few drawing notice with pale green skin or the flutter of their heavily feathered wings. Delicious smells drifted out from ritzy restaurants, and street vendors beckoned tourists over to see their wares.

"How big is our window?" Kieran asked quietly, his stomach fluttering in anticipation of what was to come.

"Valens will have people monitoring you in about an hour," Zorn said, not needing to check a schedule. He made it his job to track Valens's attempts to keep tabs on his son. Dear old Dad had trust issues. "We'll need to cut the meeting short if necessary."

"And we're positive *this* Ghost Whisperer doesn't have ties to my father in any way?" Kieran saw the sign he was looking for. Clare's Clairvoyance. In small letters below the name, it said, *We see clearly in the beyond.*

"Without question," Donovan said. "She's never spoken to the man, or any of the people who directly report to him."

Kieran nodded, knowing his father frowned upon many of the traits Hades had passed on to the world, clairvoyance being one of them. As a descendent of Poseidon, his father took the old rivalry of the Olympian brothers to heart.

Kieran took in the shop face, with its extravagant gilded scrollwork and fresh paint. This corner location on one of magical San Francisco's busiest tourist streets had to be pricy. This woman obviously charged a lot, and still had the clientele to keep her operational. That alone meant she must be good.

But he'd been fooled by such things before. Many times.

Zorn stopped by the door before pulling it wide. Donovan and Jack entered first, and the rest of the Six waited for Kieran to follow.

He took a deep breath, feeling the familiar press of loss and pain from his mother's passing. He knew something of what he was about to hear, and he dreaded it.

"Let's get this over with," he murmured, crossing the threshold into the dimly lit lobby. Soft music drifted through the space and the faint aroma of incense tickled his nose. Silk-draped dark gray walls surrounded a low glass table and surrounding chairs. A plush Oriental rug stretched out across the concrete floor to the cherry wood front desk.

When the woman behind the front desk saw him, her eyes lit up and an excited smile crossed her face.

"She didn't recognize me," Kieran said, half turning to Zorn. It hadn't dawned on him at the time. "Alexis. She didn't show one glimmer of recognition."

"Hello, Demigod Kieran," the woman at the desk said, flicking her hair. Red infused her cheeks. "So great to see you. Clare will be seeing you personally, of course, and she's ready for you in room three."

"She acted and spoke to me like she would anyone else." Kieran turned away from the woman without a word. Usually he gave everyone a passing moment of politeness, something his mother had expressly requested of him and something his father tolerated, but his brain was churning furiously, fitting this next piece into the puzzle of his new favorite enigma. "Most people have at least heard of me, even if they don't recognize me."

"Did you give her your name?" Donovan asked quietly as they passed through the curtain of hanging glass beads.

"No..." Kieran spied the door of the room they'd be walking into. Three was a relevant number to the mystics, but it didn't get his hopes up. Such things never seemed to help them do their job.

"If she's as she seems, she doesn't sound like the

kind of person who'd be up on current events," Donovan said, his voice also hushed. He glanced around with tight eyes. He didn't much like the thought of spirits lingering in the world of the living. None of the guys did.

"But to not know the son of San Francisco's ruling Demigod is in town?" Kieran asked, stopping outside the closed door of room three.

"Even if she did know, without seeing a picture, why would she assume it was you?" Jack asked.

"I think it proves she's thoroughly entrenched in the dual-society zone, like the report states," Donovan said. "People live there for a reason, and unless they are criminals hiding from the government, they have no reason to know what goes on in either society. Politics rarely affect them."

Kieran nodded, because that was absolutely true. That piece fit, and it connected with her living arrangements.

Her magic and her power level were the odd ones out. Someone like her shouldn't have slipped through the cracks, which typically meant someone like her hadn't.

The whole thing was dangerously mysterious.

Chapter 8

KIERAN

"TIME IS WASTING," Zorn reminded him.

In other words, quit stalling.

Kieran turned the handle and pushed into the room, fighting the gloom that descended on him whenever he allowed himself to think about his mother's long convalescence.

This time, the thought reminded him of Alexis debating, aloud, over the price of that blanket.

If there was one thing that drove Kieran to his knees, it was the memory of the large, sorrowful eyes of the children in the hospital in Galway. The sight of their suffering, and their tiny, frail bodies, had stayed with him.

He clenched his jaw with the memory.

He hadn't been able to do much for them or their parents, for fear of stepping on the local governing body's toes. Not nearly enough. He believed in karma, and his bucket had to be next to empty.

The least he could do was buy a good, warm blanket

for a sick kid, even if that "kid" was actually a teen. Or so the file had said. He'd be fifteen now, infected with a terminal ailment affecting one percent of magical people. Apparently, a non-magical teen girl lived with Alexis as well. He hadn't been able to verify this, but then, he didn't need to. He'd seen the fear and sorrow on Alexis's face when she mentioned the kid. It was the same look he'd seen in the mirror for years as his mother deteriorated before his eyes.

It was a look he'd do nearly anything to banish.

"Demigod Kieran, how nice of you to visit…"

The low, thick voice jogged Kieran out of his reverie. He didn't even have time to point out the inconsistency to Zorn—the magical government knew about Alexis's wards, but not about that potent, dangerous magic. Something still wasn't lining up…

"Demigod Kieran." Kieran found himself facing a middle-aged woman sitting on the other side of a rectangular table. Her elbows rested on the table's surface and a smile sat on her slightly wrinkled face.

"Yes," he said, taking two steps toward the empty leather chair facing her.

"Hello." Her smile widened and her eyes glimmered. "I'm Clare. Please, sit down."

His guys filed out of the room, though Zorn gave Kieran an assessing look before shutting the door.

He was alone with a clairvoyant…and possibly his

mother.

His gulp was loud in the quiet room.

"Now, let me get up to speed," Clare said, moving her hand to touch a deck of tarot cards resting just off to her right. Various bells waited to her left, each with characters inscribed on its surface. Candles of various colors, heights, and smelliness glowed on either side of the table. "You learned of your mother remaining in this world from an Oracle?"

"From a Ghost Whisperer, like yourself. Her services were a gift. A passing amusement."

"But she heard the voice of your mother."

A familiar heaviness pressed on his chest. Though he'd asked Zorn to explain the situation to her before setting up the meeting, hearing a stranger talk about something so personal sent shock waves of unease racing through him. He maintained focus so as not to accidentally lash out.

"Yes," he said.

Clare took her hand back from the tarot deck and reached with her other hand before lightly resting her two fingers on the second bell. "You believe she is trapped in this world?"

"That is what I have been told, yes." Told by a handful of Ghost Whisperers, plus one Necromancer who'd felt her, but hadn't been able to summon her spirit.

Clare's brow lowered and she touched the third bell.

"Hmm," she said, her eyes losing focus. "And you want to help her cross over?"

"Yes." A wave of sadness threatened to drag him under. He struggled to the surface, and a strange tingling sensation crawled into his shoulder and through his middle. "I want her to finally be at peace."

"Yes, I see." Clare picked up the last bell of four before jerking it. The toll pealed through the room, crawling up his spine. She set the bell down before picking up the first bell. This time, she held it daintily before gently moving it side to side, the toll higher and slow.

Kieran tried to ease his stiffness. Tried to stop the flutter of hope in his belly that this woman, unlike all the others, would have answers. That she'd be able to help his mother find peace, once and for all.

"Let's see…" Clare picked up the tarot, movements slow. Dramatized. She shuffled them, a highly practiced movement, before laying them out in a cross-like pattern. "Now…"

One by one she read the cards, mostly mumbling. She asked him a few questions along the way, and stopped often, tilting her head and listening. Halfway through, she stopped what she was doing altogether.

"She's here," Clare finally said, putting her finger up. "She is…speaking…" Her voice dipped lower, and each word took on a different lilt. "Live…happy…"

Kieran's heart stopped. Only one other Ghost Whisperer had been able to replicate his mother's tone and way of speaking—the first one he'd sat with. The way she'd mimicked his mother's speech had convinced him. And now, those two simple words were enough to confirm his mother was trapped in the world of the living, and moreover, she was in the room with him right then.

"Go…life…the place…" Clare moved from side to side, lightly shaking her head. "She wants you to live your life in peace. She's happy here. She wants you to be happy, too."

He sat forward and braced his elbows on his knees. "Are you sure? Because the first Ghost Whisperer—"

Clare held up a hand. "Find…the place—there's *the place* again—life…peace." She kept swaying from side to side. "Hmmm. I feel… I feel…" She shook the third bell three times, filling the room with sound. "Find the place. It must be the place where her skin is kept. And life… That could be 'live.' Live in peace."

She was guessing, Kieran could tell. She was one of the better Ghost Whisperers he'd sat with, but she wasn't as good as the first one he'd met. And she hadn't been able to tell him all he needed to know.

Clare's eyes fluttered open. "She is coming through very strongly," she said, before slightly bending to her right side. She came back with a small silver tape recorder. "Let's try the EVP recorder and see what we find."

Kieran's heart sank as quickly as his hope. This was exactly the same road he'd been down all those other times, and like those other times, he foresaw nothing useful would come of it. If his mother was indeed trapped here, he had no way to break her free. His failure meant her continued suffering.

Just like when she'd been alive.

Chapter 9

ALEXIS

S OMETHING I COULDN'T identify dragged me out of a deep sleep. I looked around my small room. The closed curtains hung placidly, lit from behind by a streetlight that barely cast its glow over the backyard fence. No shadows interrupted the plane, indicating there were no trespassers outside my window.

Frigid air caressed my face, but there was no draft to hint at an open door. The shadows lay as they normally did, a murky soup collecting in the corners and draping my furniture.

I took a deep breath. I'd probably been awakened by some nightmare I couldn't remember. My mind had been playing tricks on me all evening. Every little noise jarred me; every shadow falling across the windows had me looking more closely.

But everything was as it should be in my room. All of it. If the stranger had come back tonight, he wasn't peeping in the windows.

A wet, barking cough shattered the silence. As it was

ending, another vibrated through the walls.

My heart lurched, and I jumped out of bed. My door burst open a moment later.

Huge, fearful eyes adorned Daisy's thin face.

"Something's wrong," she said, emotion choking her voice. "He won't wake up. He just keeps coughing."

Chest tight, I wrapped a robe around myself to keep out the chill and rushed to the next room. A small nightlight projected a forest scene in a circle on the ceiling. Daisy still needed a nightlight to keep the memories of life's beasties away. Mordecai always chose the theme, which coincided with what he was learning.

Soft green light fell on the blanket atop his body. A wet cough shook the pile, as though Mordecai's lungs were filled with mucus. As though he might soon drown in it.

"Steam," I said in a harried breath, rushing forward. "Get the steamer."

"It's on! It's right there." Daisy flung a finger at the old air purifier in the corner, which I'd found on the street in a pile of items set out for donation.

"The *steamer*," I repeated, gently laying my palm on Mordecai's forehead. Clammy. No fever. Thank God.

"Right, right. The steamer." She rushed out of the room.

I checked his pulse. Slow and steady. At least that was okay.

Another cough racked his body. His eyes fluttered but didn't open.

Usually these coughing spells would have the whole house awake, starting with him. The fact that he wasn't waking up...

"Oh God," I choked out, putting my hands on his cheeks as hot tears crowded my eyes. "Please be okay. Please."

"Here." Daisy held out the steamer as she entered the room. Not paying attention, she kicked the post of his bed in her haste. "Motherfucker shit-eating cake fucker!"

I closed the distance and grabbed the steamer, ignoring her swearing. A toe would heal. Whatever was going on with Mordecai might not.

"Come on, Mordie," I said, barely able to speak through my panic. "Wake up, Mordecai. Wake up."

"Shit fuck damn. Motherfucker, that hurt." Daisy limped out of the room.

"Mordecai...wake up." I shook him softly. Then harder. "Limp back in here and fill this steamer up," I yelled at Daisy. "I'm going to get him to sit up."

"I got the cough syrup." She limped back in, grimacing with each step.

"Turn the light on."

"Right, right."

Harsh yellow light saturated the room, making us

both squint. Mordecai's eyes fluttered again, and this time, slightly opened. He squinted, too.

"Good. That's good." I handed back the steamer and took the cough syrup. After placing that on his side table, I pulled his ratty old blanket away, unable to help a smile and another wash of tears as I discovered the new turquoise blanket wrapped tightly around his person. He was using it for comfort, keeping his family close.

That meant he was worse off than I'd thought. He only got sentimental when the pain was at the breaking point.

A sob ripped from me. "We have to get more anti-morphing serum, Daisy," I said, burrowing my arm between his back and the mattress. "He's...he's..." I couldn't say it. I didn't even want to think it. The D-word.

"How much do we need?" She limped back in with a bleach-white face and fear-soaked eyes. I rarely cried in their presence, so when I did, she rightly thought the world was ending. "How close are we?"

"I've got three hundred and two. I get paid on Friday."

She waited until I had muscled Mordecai to a sitting position before putting the steamer on the edge of the bed. "What about rent?"

"It's mortgage, not rent, and...the bank will give us

a couple months before kicking us out. They always gave my mother a grace period when things were tight. And I'll try to get some overtime at work."

"Your boss hates you. He won't give you an extra dime if he doesn't have to."

"Then I'll sell fake drugs to your friend. We'll figure it out."

Mordecai slumped forward. A cough tore through his chest and he hacked on the liquid building up in his esophagus. Air stopped. His chest worked, but nothing was happening.

"Oh God, Lexi, he's not breathing!"

"Help me straighten him," I yelled, getting behind him and pulling on his shoulders. "Never mind. I got it. Plug in that steamer. Set it to full blast."

She knocked over the air purifier in her haste, extremely clumsy from panic. The prongs of the steamer's plug hit off the wall, then the plastic panel of the outlet, before finally finding the holes and slipping into place.

Wrapping my arms around Mordecai to keep him upright, I sobbed again, this time in relief, when he sucked in a wheezing breath. Daisy fiddled with the settings of the steamer, nearly knocked the thing off the bed, and then straightened it and angled it toward his face. Tears dripped down her cheeks.

Minutes trickled by. I held Mordecai. She held the steamer. Together we cried softly as he labored for breath through the violent coughing episodes. But finally, *finally*, the wetness of the coughs eased. His breathing evened out.

He wiggled in my arms and coughed some more.

"Oh, thank God." Daisy flung her arms around him, *thwapping* me in the face as she did so.

"What happened?" I asked, afraid to let go, lest he slump over and fall off the bed.

"He opened his eyes. His eyes are open!"

"What's going on?" Mordecai said quietly, his voice scratchy from all the coughing.

"Get him the syrup." I pushed my captured hand against Daisy's chest. "Get him the syrup."

"Why can't we just take him to the emergency room and pretend we have money until after they treat him?" Daisy asked, unscrewing the cap. "No one can pay upfront. They bill people."

"They run credit, and I don't have any," I said, guilt tearing at me. "I've tried."

"Then fine. I've got a new plan." She wiped her face with the back of her hand, smearing tears across her cheek. "I'm going to find someone with magical medical and marry them. Then I'll claim Mordie as a dependent, and we can take him to the hospital."

"Your plan needs work," Mordecai said weakly, and I struggled to hold my sobs back. He didn't need to know how much we worried about him. He'd feel guilty for causing us grief. He didn't need to expend energy on anything other than staying alive.

"We got this. Just hang tight for a few more days, Mordecai, and we'll have medicine for you." I chanced easing up the hold. He tipped forward, but caught himself.

"I don't know why it's getting worse. It's only been a week since my last dose," he said softly.

"Puberty." I rubbed his back. "Your body is probably going through some big changes right now, bud. A growth spurt, maybe. I've heard that your dad was a big guy. And shifters feel puberty harder than humans."

"We don't have the money to support my habit—"

He barely got to finish the word.

A slap rang out and he fell back into me. Daisy kneeled in front of him with new tears streaking her face, her expression screwed up in anger. "Don't you talk like that. We *do* have the money. It's just a matter of finding it. You two are my family. I need you. Both of you. So, don't you dare give up. We'll get you that medicine. And fuck you for scaring me."

Silence fell over us, gooey and thick with emotion. I should've berated her for slapping him. I should've yelled at her for swearing.

But as the chuckles bubbled up through my middle, all I could do was laugh and hold on to Mordecai for dear life.

"Fuck you, too," he said, reaching out for her.

She was right—it was only the three of us. Our family was all we had in this world, and it was unthinkable for us to lose him. We couldn't.

Somehow, I had to get that medicine.

Chapter 10

ALEXIS

EYES PUFFY AND fatigue dragging at me, I lugged my tired butt into work the next morning. Mordecai hadn't made any kind of recovery, but the syrup had eased his coughing enough to let him sleep soundly.

Neither Daisy nor I had gotten a wink. We'd sat on her bed, hugging each other, watching over him to make sure he was okay.

Stale air greeted me as the glass doors slid open. The cream floors shone in the bright fluorescent lights attached to the ceiling overhead. Racks of clothes spread out in front of me, and shelves of undergarments rose up behind them. Toiletries were to the right, and way in the back was my section—the bed and bath section.

In a national chain that had everything, why had I gone to that other store for a blanket? Because this particular store was owned by a bunch of magic-hating jerks, run by another jerk, and its products were designed by jerks to break or fall apart within a few months so customers would have to come back for more. Still, it was a job I sorely needed, so I dealt with it.

You get what you get, and you don't get upset.

I sighed. I hated when my mother's sayings randomly crowded into my head to sour my already bad mood.

After dipping my timecard into the time-stamp machine, I made my way to my section and stared for a moment at the utter destruction only a few hours had wrought. Bathroom mats lay trampled on the ground, towels were wadded up, the colors mixed, and a toothbrush holder littered the floor in pieces—people were slobs when it came to perusing the wares of a cheap store with no personality.

Or maybe they treated every place with this level of disrespect. I had no idea, but if Daisy and Mordecai treated our house like this, they'd get a thumping.

Thinking of Mordecai dashed my righteous annoyance. With a heavy heart, I went about my managerial duties in a "department" of one, working from one end of my area to the other, cleaning up after patrons. When that was finished, I started over, cleaning up the same amount of destruction I'd just set to rights. It was an endless loop.

A few hours into the mindless daze, my phone vibrated in my pocket. Hoping it was my alarm signaling lunch, I dug it out of my too-tight pocket and looked at the screen.

Fear blasted through my chest. It was home calling, and since Daisy and Mordecai knew I wasn't allowed to look at my phone or take calls on the floor, it meant this was an emergency.

"Hello?" I said, hurrying toward the stockroom.

"It's me." Daisy's voice was filled with fear and determination. "He's at it again and I can't get him to wake up. Alexis, he's going to die if we don't do something. He can't last two more days. You know it as well as I do."

Bands of steel squeezed my chest, but I swallowed my fear. It wouldn't help this situation. "Get him sitting upright and use the steamer. Give him the cough medicine. I can ask for a cash advance. That'll buy us time."

"The fees for doing that are enormous." I had no idea how she knew that, but it was true, so I didn't say anything. "Besides, you've tried that before and they wouldn't let you. You're magical, remember? They don't trust you. But that bitch Denny does owe me two hundred bucks. That's our play. Grab a sword or something from the store. If I call again, it means everything went to shit, and we need to fight back."

"No! No." I lowered my voice when a guy on a forklift looked up. I scurried toward a large stack of unopened boxes. A woman in a different uniform stood idly in the far corner, picking her nail while watching me with solemn eyes. I had no idea what she was doing there. "I'll apply for the cash advance. You take that job with Denny's dad. And please don't call that boy a bitch to his face. People don't take kindly to that. He is a *boy*, right, not a man? He's your age?"

"If he doesn't pay up, I'll call him a bitch! And yeah, he's fourteen. Why do you think he bought fake weed? He doesn't know any better."

"Good point. But... Just take the job at his family's vet clinic."

"Lexi, I love you, but you are shit at making decisions—"

"You've *got* to stop swearing."

"—and money doesn't grow on trees..." Her voice trailed away as a hoarse, hacking cough sounded in the background. "Shit. Oh shit. That's blood."

"*What?*" I clutched the phone so tightly it dug into my palm and fingers. The woman down the way took a step in my direction, confusion on her face.

"He just coughed up blood. He just coughed up blood! What do I do?"

Adrenaline flooded my body. "Fuck it. Get that money from Denny. I've got a bat at home. If he gives you trouble, tell him I'll personally bash his face in. Please don't hold this horrible parenting against me."

"What about Mordie?"

"I'll be right home. I'll watch him." I was running

through the store before I knew it, headed straight for the office. Once there, I burst in, out of breath.

Jason Bertram's shiny bald head jerked toward me. His annoyance at having to momentarily lift his eyes off a clearly riveting game of solitaire was evident. As the store team lead, he sure was busy. Of course, it wouldn't help my case to point that out. I needed him on my side.

"Sorry to barge in, Mr. Bertram." I put my hand on the doorframe to show I wasn't technically invading his space. It was the little things. "But I have a family emergency. I need to take lunch early."

A cloud settled over his round face, something fairly common when he was talking to me. He'd only hired me because the labor force willing to work in the dual-society zone was small. "Your lunch isn't for"—he checked his watch—"another three hours."

"Two hours. I came in at nine. But I don't really have a choice. My ward is sick. He needs someone to watch him while my other ward goes and gets his medicine."

His brown eyes were cold and flat. "Your lunch is in two hours. I suggest you have your *ward* wait until then—"

"He might not have two hours. Please, Mr. Bertram—"

"As a woman who is out of sick and vacation leave because of these types of situations—"

"I don't get sick or vacation leave. I don't qualify because I'm mag—"

"—I think you should really take a hard look at your life. A place of business cannot juggle its schedule around a flighty employee."

"But Mr. Bertram, it's only two hours—"

"End of story. You leave early, and you can hand in your resignation." His lips pressed into a thin, colorless line.

I stared at him in shock for a moment with my mouth hanging open. All the odds-and-ends jobs I could conceivably do until I found another job rolled through my head. Followed by Mordecai's sick, exhausted face.

I let a humorless smile contort my lips. "You miserable bastard." I took off the nametag pinned to my shirt and thought about stabbing it into his leg. But then he could call the cops, and I didn't need that. "You can keep your joke of a job. And for the record, I know *for a fact* that I have the cleanest, best managed section in this entire store. I have been nominated for employee of the month every month since I started. Guests find me attentive and courteous. In just six months, I've already earned a star for excellent service. A star I've never seen, of course." His eyes widened and his cheeks turned red. "Yeah, I've been peeking at the files. I like to know when I'm doing a good job, or when I need to improve, and because no one here has ever done me the favor of filling me in, I had to self-educate. Us magics can be resourceful, which you should know, you filthy, black-hearted bastard. I hope a bird shits on your head at lunch! In fact, maybe I'll use my 'superpowers' to ensure that it happens."

He sucked in a breath, and I could barely hear the word "witch" escape his colorless lips. I was sure that if we lived in the days of witch trials, he would be one of the shortsighted, puritanical hypocrites spearheading my stoning.

I wasn't a witch. I'd give my left arm for that kind of magic. But ignorant guys like Jason Bertram—the quintessential Chester—assumed anyone with magic was a witch, didn't want to hear differently, and would tell anyone who'd listen that fire was the best way to rid the world of us.

Try telling that to a fire elemental. They'd laugh and laugh.

My last paycheck would be ready in twenty-four hours. That was the law in this zone, regardless of what happened here today.

When I pushed through the door of my house, I ran to my wards' bedroom. A limp Mordecai was lying on his bed with red-tinged drool leaking out of his mouth. I knew Daisy was right. He was dying.

"Frank, how long has Daisy been gone?" I asked as I

jogged back to the door, belatedly seeing a note left on the kitchen table. I wasn't sure if she'd left immediately after talking with me, or if she'd tried to bring Mordecai around first.

"That foul-mouthed, doll-faced girl took off about fifteen minutes ago," he answered. "She ran down the street. You know, it's against the law to keep minors out of school. They are delinquent—"

"I got it. Now get off my lawn." I slammed the door and hurried to the kitchen table to read the note scribbled in Daisy's careless hand.

Out of time. I took your stash. I'll be back with meds and change.

My stash—she meant every cent I had to my name. I kept it in a hiding place the kids knew about for just such a situation.

Back with Mordecai, I propped him up in my lap, made sure his airways were open and the steam was reaching him, and did the only thing I could.

I waited.

Chapter 11

ALEXIS

AFTER WHAT FELT like forever, I heard my front door crash open. A glance at the alarm clock on the bedside table said I'd only been home a half-hour. That wasn't nearly enough time for Daisy to have done all she needed to.

Footsteps stalled in the entryway before heading right, to the kitchen. Rustling, followed by a small thunk, coincided with the crashing of my heart against my ribcage. Who the hell had just entered my house?

The footsteps pounded the floor toward the bedroom, and the door flew open, swinging so hard it slammed off the wall and left an imprint.

Daisy stood in the frame, her sheet of dark hair falling around her set expression. An object I couldn't see was wrapped in her bloodied fingers. "I lost that job opportunity."

"What?" I croaked out.

"Turns out the bastard knew the drugs were fake. He just wanted to spend time with me. He doesn't even have any money. So I punched him in the face, then searched his whole room." She stopped at the bedside table and gently set down the item in her hand.

My heart surged. It was the anti-morphing serum!

"How'd you get that?" I breathed out, relief and dread taking turns running through my body.

She dug into her pocket and pulled out a wad of money. "How is he?"

"His pulse feels weak, but he's hanging on. How did you get that?" I repeated.

"I stole it, that's how."

"But... Your hand..." I was having a hard time piecing this one together, and was a little concerned that whatever she'd brought home would turn out like that faulty can of mace.

With quick economy, she left the room and stepped into the bathroom down the hall. I heard a drawer roll open.

"During the shake-down, I found a stash of nude magazines in that lying bastard's room," she called. The drawer rolled again, and she stepped back into the hall. "In that stash was a gay one. The shock on his face when I found it said it likely wasn't his, and whatever friend he got the stash from, some guy named Martin, has a secret. But anyway, his dad is super uptight. He would *not* like to find out his son has a gay porn magazine, because then he'd think his son is gay. See where I'm going with this?"

"So you blackmailed him? But you said he didn't have any money."

She set a syringe next to the serum. "He didn't. But it gave me an idea. Here, we need to switch places. I hate needles."

I carefully slid out from behind Mordecai. "Gay porn gave you an idea?"

"No. Well, yeah. His reaction to the gay porn gave me an idea. I told him that I wouldn't rat him out if he distracted his dad long enough that I could get in and steal something from the vet office."

"But...why would a vet have anti-morphing serum?"

"A dual-society vet." Her smile declared her brilliance. "He keeps this stuff to sell on the side. Like a black market for magical people who don't want to be in the system. They can pay a premium and get their drugs, no questions asked. He had all sorts of stuff—the serum for vampires to walk in the sun, the lotion to keep fairies from shedding pixie dust everywhere, and..."

My smile came up from my toes. "The serum to block the moon's call."

Her eyes glittered. "Exactly. That stuff is legit. And yes, I took out the surveillance camera, used a cloth so I didn't leave prints, and stole a bunch of stuff to make it seem like I wasn't just after the one thing. I did leave behind a little blood—I put too much weight behind breaking the window and fell forward—but it should be fine. I'm not magical and this was a small job. It's not worth a detective's time, and *certainly* not worth the expense to do blood work. If I keep this a one-time situation, I'm good."

I paused in picking up the syringe. I wouldn't have thought of any of that.

How the hell was someone eleven years my junior so much better at this stuff?

My thoughts must've come through on my face, because she rolled her eyes while delicately situating Mordecai so that his arm was easy to access. "I grew up in the foster system, in case you'd forgotten. What I did back there would've been deemed saint-like compared to the antics of some of the other kids. One was trying to start up a prostitution ring, just to give you an idea. Thankfully, I left before that panned out, because you've seen these goods and they would have been a hot commodity. I'm sure he ended up getting his ass beaten anyway."

"I had to quit my job," I blurted as I tore the syringe out of the plastic, trying to slow down so I didn't mess up. "That miserable bastard wouldn't let me take an early lunch, so I took a long, permanent walk instead."

I heard her release of breath. "Shit."

"We're going to be all right." My hands were shaking. I took a couple of deep breaths. Mordecai would be fine, just as long as I got this serum into his arm. "Look at what you did this morning. You saved the day!"

"Well, I got three other bottles of that stuff. So we're good on his medicine for a while." She rubbed his hand, also taking deep breaths. "And I got that other crap. Once we figure out what it is, we can sell it off to keep us going until you find another job."

I put the normal dose into the syringe, afraid to do more in case it would give him a bad reaction. Despite having done this for years, I wasn't a doctor. Or a vet. The bottle wobbling in my hands proved it.

I closed my eyes, stilling. I *had* to calm down. He was going to be okay. Now that we had the serum, he'd bounce back. He'd done it before.

He had to bounce back.

"Maybe you earn money with your magic?" Daisy said, her eyes tight as she watched my movements. She shivered. "Gross."

I huffed, not able to laugh just yet. My ability to see spirits creeped her out. She hated the thought that the dead walked amongst us. So did most people. It was why I was seen as a weirdo, even in the magical community.

I held up the syringe to check the level of the serum, my shaking a little more under control. Adrenaline still coursed through me, but it was manageable. "It pays shit, you know that. Unless you are the absolute best, and have a good track record, there aren't any jobs for people like me. But I'll put in as many nights at the freak show as I can until I find something else. Okay?"

One more deep breath, and I gingerly sat on the bed next to them. *Nice and easy.* Taking Mordecai's arm, I prepared to give him the dose.

"You should've gone to college," Daisy whispered, holding as still as she was probably able. The bed still trembled under them.

He'd bounce back. He would.

"I did. In a way." I took a deep breath, held it, and jabbed the needle into the muscle on Mordecai's upper arm. With my thumb, I pushed the dispenser, forcing the serum into his arm.

"Reading a bunch of books from the library is not college," Daisy said.

"You'd be surprised. My mother went to college. She guided me on what to learn."

"A college certificate would make it easier for you to get a better job."

The clear liquid emptied into Mordecai's arm. I pulled the needle out and rose, allowing myself a small bit of laughter at what she'd said. "No, it wouldn't. I'd need magical blood...or some actual power to go with my magical blood. Or a type of magic people actually want to use—"

"I get it, I get it." Daisy rubbed Mordecai's hand again, looking down at him.

After ten minutes of silence, waiting with bated breath, I checked Mordecai's pulse.

I forced down a sob. "He'll be okay," I said, back to shaking. Tears filled my eyes. "His pulse is already stronger. He'll bounce back."

A hard exhale deflated Daisy's chest. "Thank God."

It never ceased to amaze me. The serum worked almost immediately. Already his pulse had resumed beating, strong and sure. In a moment, I knew his breathing would even out as well. A shifter had to change for the fastest healing, but that didn't mean a shifter's body wasn't resilient in human form. Now that his human side wasn't warring with his magic, his shifter side would fight for health.

"Do you ever wish for a better life?" Daisy asked quietly.

"Sometimes. You?"

She rested her cheek against Mordecai's head. "I used to. All the time. And then you found me. Now I *have* a better life. My prayers have been answered. And soon, yours will be, too. I can feel it; we're on the brink of change."

Chapter 12

ALEXIS

I TOOK A deep breath with my hand resting against the worn wooden door of the local Irish pub. The green paint was peeling away, revealing the faded brown beneath. Night cloaked the damp streets, and thick fog blocked out any hint of the moon or the stars. My mind still spun from all that had happened earlier that day, and my body ached with fatigue and the press of worry.

Even without shifting, Mordecai was healing at an impressive speed. Faster than he ever had before. It was a testimony to how much magical power he truly had. What an absolute shame his pack leader wanted him dead, and I didn't have magical medical, because if he could get healthy, he'd be unstoppable.

Curing him was too big of a dream. At least for right now.

Dream small.

He had medicine for three months. Or, worst case, two, if he kept needing it like he had this month.

Small miracle number one.

Daisy was *positive* Denny wouldn't buckle and tell his dad on her. In fact, when she'd called him with the intent to deliver a few post-theft threats, he'd fallen over himself to apologize for how he'd treated her. He'd begged to still be friends.

He'd apparently told his father that he'd heard of some out-of-town thugs blowing through San Francisco to get magical supplies to take back to Los Angeles and sell at a premium. Since Los Angeles was trying to eradicate all its magical people, and many of the poorer magical people didn't have the funds to get out, they were desperate for the medicine to which they'd grown accustomed.

Maybe Denny wasn't so dumb after all.

Daisy was in the clear.

Small miracle number two.

I now had extra money, since I didn't have to buy Mordecai's medicine.

Of course, I was minus a job.

That miracle was a wash.

Last miracle: the kids had ganged up on me and forced me out of the house. They were basically sending me out to get roaring drunk so I could forget all my woes for a few hours.

In times like this, they were more like roommates than wards, and I loved them dearly for it, because I could definitely use a reprieve from the constant anxiety of thinking about the future. Of the job I had to get. Of what would happen when that medicine ran out again. Of how I might offload the stolen goods from that vet without getting in trouble with the authorities, or winding up in a drug ring with a bunch of power players who had deadlier weapons than an aluminum bat and a non-working bottle of mace.

Yeah. I needed to forget for a few hours.

Daisy had even forced some of my money on me in case the bar had suddenly decided to stop giving me freebies.

I snorted as I willed myself to pull open the door.

There was no way in cold hell Miles, the bar owner and my ex, would stop giving me free beer. He, a non-Irishman who owned a filthy "Irish" pub, thought only someone sliding along rock bottom would accept such blatant pity. He was fascinated and smug that I clearly had not one ounce of pride left. Boy what a loss, dumping him, he surely thought. And now look at me, needing his condescension to keep on going.

I chuckled.

I had plenty of pride. And plenty of street smarts. My mother's racket had earned me more than a free phone.

Feel bad for my scrawny arms and skinny frame and want to sneak me in the back of a gym?

Yes, please.

Want to build karma points by letting a street urchin like me hang around for free martial arts lessons?

Cool.

Need to fill a quota of underprivileged kids in your dance studio?

I'm game.

I'd learned more things than a rich kid, all because I looked a mess and didn't say no when someone offered a freebie. If people wanted to help me out, I would absolutely let them.

I glanced at the cracked sidewalk and scraggly bushes lining the walkway up to the bar. A few cars sat in the parking lot off to the side, and various beat-up automobiles lined the street. A heavyset man slouched as he made his way past on the sidewalk.

This wasn't a good part of town, even though it was backed up against the wall of the magical zone. Maybe *because* it was backed up against the wall, though still in the neglected dual-society portion of the city. We could see the lovely weather on the other side of the six-foot-high wall, reminding us that Valens cared about his territory, and blessed them with his magical weather-changing abilities. The clear skies, which sometimes pushed away some of our fog, rubbing our faces in how pristine and well-tended the houses were over there. Those who lived there had money (mostly) and quality food (probably). They had good jobs (I assumed) and access to all the finest things (the bastards).

All we had were surly dispositions and not much of anything.

Then again, we also had loose rules with over-worked and underperforming law enforcement. We had the cover of anonymity. We weren't watched, or forced to keep our stuff in excellent condition. We could live our lives in peace, even if it was with cracked concrete and crappy weather.

Yeah, they could keep their nice houses. Loose rules worked just fine for me, thank you very much.

"Quit stalling, Alexis, and get your drink on," I muttered to myself.

For a medium-sized miracle, this outing sure seemed like a chore. I was starting to think the kids had forced me out so they could have the house to them-selves without my tight-jawed fretting, the little bastards.

I grabbed the handle and yanked the door open be-fore propelling myself into the dimly lit interior. Wood beams lined the ceiling overhead, closing down the space. Picture frames covered the walls, crowded together and often crooked. Empty tables with chairs tucked beneath them were backed up to the far wall, leaving ample space for me to walk through to the back room. On one side, a few guys loitered around a threadbare pool table, and a dance floor pushed up against the electronic jukebox with outrageous prices; on the other, the bar curved in a slight semicircle lined with high-backed chairs, mostly filled.

At six in the evening, these were likely all regulars, watching the TV or staring at nothing, content to keep their own company. It was still too early for the party crowd that would eventually wander in, consisting of magical and non-magical kinds alike, all looking for a last drink in their neighborhood bar before heading home.

A broken-down, leaning wooden chair sat in place of my usual sturdy, magically protected seat. I paused, glancing next to it at Mick, the biggest asshole in the bar, who sat next to the wall so as to cut down on the number of people who tried to talk to him. He was partly the reason why my seat was always vacant, and the vacancy was why it had become my seat in the first place.

"What happened here?" I asked in a collection of grunts. It was the language Mick responded to best.

He glanced at the chair with absolutely gorgeous pale blue eyes. It was his best and only noteworthy feature. His ruddy, sun-damaged face stayed perfectly flat. "Some fat coont took yer chair," he said in a thick Irish brogue.

"Aww. You called it mine. You must be used to me

now."

I laughed and glanced down the bar. I'd gotten awfully used to the C-word from hanging around him. I also knew that he never used that word to describe women unless he was falling-down drunk and spoiling for a fight. A fight that the women at this bar would happily give him. Typically, though, he reserved the term for men and non-living objects. Which meant a large, heavyset, or stocky man had my chair.

Familiar faces lined the bar—some of the regulars seemingly never left this place. It wasn't until my gaze neared the other end that fireworks blasted through my middle and my stomach flipped over and threatened to come up through my mouth.

Stormy blue eyes surveyed me quietly from within a shockingly handsome face that seemed much too familiar, given that I'd only seen it briefly the day before. The man's muscular arms rested on the edge of the bar, stretching his button-up shirt across the expanse of his broad shoulders. A large hand curved around a half-finished pint of Guinness, the perfect rings of creamy foam lining the sides of the glass.

"Crap," I said softly, my feet rooted to the floor and my whole body tightening up to flee. Daisy had been right. He'd found me again.

The two chairs flanking the stranger were pushed away to give him ample space. Though they were filled, he was clearly there by himself.

"Is that the guy you were talking about?" I asked Mick softly, unable to tear my eyes away from that steady gaze.

Mick grunted, which meant yes.

"That guy is anything but fat, Mick. You'd make a terrible eyewitness. Has he been here for a while?"

"Fer feck's sake. What am I, his fecking nursemaid?" Mick growled. "I don't feckin' know."

"It's been a pleasure speaking with you, Mick, as always."

Mick grunted and took a swig of his beer.

I let out a slow, trembling breath as Liam, the ancient, non-magical bartender who had been there forever, slowly made his way down the bar.

"Guinness?" he asked when he reached me.

I shook my head quickly, but then stopped myself. Why would I pretend not to drink Guinness just because the stranger liked it?

And why would I run? This wasn't a normal day for me to be here, and he couldn't have possibly known I'd show up. I hadn't even known until a couple of hours ago. I usually popped into the bar on Friday or Saturday evenings when it was busy and I knew Miles would make an appearance. I liked to give him the opportunity to not-so-subtly congratulate himself on doing better than me. It was the least I could do in exchange for the freebies.

Anyway, running would only make me seem guilty of something, and this time I didn't even have anything to apologize for. This guy was on my turf, in my chosen place of degradation, and I had every right to dig in my heels and stand my ground. If anything, this was my territory.

Besides, I had a blanket to return.

"I should act normally, shouldn't I?" I asked Mick, still working up the courage to approach the guy. I had every right to be here, but that commanding, authoritative gaze gave a girl pause. "I've been coming here long enough to have earned a spot. He can't do anything to me."

"What da feck?" Mick leaned away as though I'd slapped him. "What are you on about? I'm here to enjoy a few quiet fecking pints."

Usually I liked that Mick kept to himself and didn't want to chat idly. Small talk was draining. But now, when I needed a sounding board, it was damn unfortunate.

"Alexis?" Liam said, waiting for my order.

"Yes. Please. A Guinness. Hey, Liam, how long has that guy been here?" The stranger's eyes were burning into mine, sending tingles through my body. If he was shocked or delighted that I'd happened into the bar, he didn't show it.

Liam glanced behind him and back again. "That's his second pint." Without another word, he moved off toward the glasses.

It was an entire bar of unsociable people. Which, again, was usually a good thing.

But I didn't usually need answers!

If he was on his second pint, he'd shown up here before I'd even left the house. Whatever had happened yesterday, he definitely wasn't stalking me today.

The muscles in my shoulders minutely relaxed. That was good news.

"Well, this chair will never do." I patted the misshapen back of it. "And I need to talk to him so I can return a blanket."

Mick ignored me. The tanned guy on the other side of the broken chair glanced over, but his gaze didn't stick.

"Right." I nodded in determination and forced my feet to move. I needed to nip this situation in the bud.

Ignoring the butterflies in my belly, I moved behind the row of patrons at the bar. The stranger's eyes tracked me, the intensity of his focus acting like a solid weight coating my body. I breathed through the strange reaction, not sure if it was the effect of his magical power or his stellar looks.

The stranger leaned back, dropping a hand down to his thigh as I made my approach.

"Hey," I said, coming to a stop behind a grizzled old man with a hunched back and the rosy cheeks of a habitual drinker.

The stranger stared at me without comment or a glimmer of recognition.

Suddenly unsure, I lightly touched my fingertips to my chest. "Remember me? From yesterday? I'm the chick that you tried to mow down with your fancy Ferrari?"

The smile accompanying my jest wasn't returned.

"Yes," he said, and that rough, gravelly, though strangely entrancing voice washed over me.

I blew out a breath, then tensed as a thread of heat wormed through my middle.

This wasn't normal. He might've been hot enough to scorch the eyes, but I was a girl who liked to look. I usually didn't have a desire to sample the goods.

But as I stood there, the kindling heat inside me turned into fire, setting my core to aching. That aching turned into pounding, and something yanked at my gut, urging me to step forward and touch the origin of this delicious feeling.

It had to be his magic. Within this guy's bag of tricks, he must possess the ability to force desire or lust. I could usually withstand that little scam (which had annoyed Miles to no end), but I'd never felt someone put this much power behind it. It threatened to sweep me away.

"Great, I can see you're not going to make this easy." I blew out a breath and forcefully ignored the dull pounding sensation. "So, listen, that blanket that you dropped off…" A glimmer of recognition finally lit his eyes. It had definitely been him. "Thanks for that. It was really nice of you. But I'm afraid I—*we*—can't accept it. It's just too much. If you're going to be here for a while, I can run and get it. Or…do you live around here? I can drop it off…"

"You keep the blanket," he said. Heat sparked in his eyes. "I'd rather get you into mine."

His voice dripped with sex. Images of glistening muscles and twisted sheets invaded my thoughts and stole my breath. Furious shivers warred with the blazing fire inside me, and the butterflies from earlier turned into a swarm. His delving stare tickled areas deep and wet, which suddenly demanded satisfaction.

God, I hoped I didn't give in to the craving for satisfaction.

Chapter 13

ALEXIS

A LOOK OF confusion flashed across the guy's expression—almost like he couldn't believe he'd just said something so forward. But I couldn't summon the focus to interpret that look, not through the delicious desire swimming through me.

Oh yes, this man had the ability to inspire lust, all right. Lust, passion, intense yearning... I loved the feeling of it, pushing and pulling and pounding and aching. It was like sex without the contact.

But there was a serious downside to this type of magic. The men who possessed it relied on their magic rather than prowess. A lot of flashy bells and whistles without anything solid and real to back them up. The end result was always a letdown. It was one of life's real cruelties, I was certain. At twenty-five, I'd learned my lesson.

Dream small.

I opened my eyes, smiling. "Thanks for the offer, but I'll pass. Anyway, as I was saying, I need to know where to drop off that blanket. I'd offer to mail it back, but shipping prices would be outrageous. Also, I don't want to."

His eyebrows pinched together, and this time, I had no trouble reading his expression. Surprised. Confused. "Women don't say no to me, Alexis," he said, his tone smooth and decadent, like rich chocolate. "They say *please*."

My breath hitched, and not from hearing my name in that luscious voice. From him knowing my name at all.

But of course he knew my name. He'd looked up my address, hadn't he? It wasn't like my car was registered to Jane Doe.

"Are you sure they aren't really trying to say, 'Please pass the pepper spray'?" I asked with a flare of annoyance.

The glorious shivers and sparks of passion I'd felt moments before had morphed into warning tremors and unease. The blanket gesture had been a kind one (possibly), but all of his intrusiveness and arrogance set me on edge. He'd ruined my high, and with it, my mood.

I sighed, entirely put out. "You're in my seat. Get out."

"Sit." He gestured at the chair holding the grizzled old man.

"It's taken." I pointed at the chair. Surely bluntness would work to get that fine ass off my seat. "Look, the chair you're sitting on has special value for me. It's important that you return it to the spot you took it from, next to that extremely grumpy paddy." His face could give a stone a run for its money in the expressiveness department. "No compute?"

"It has your magic," he said without inflection.

"Good guess. It does. Which is why I'm partial to it."

"It wasn't a guess. I felt it as soon as I walked into the bar. Why do you think I grabbed this chair in particular?"

Goosebumps covered my skin, and I stilled for a moment.

Only supremely powerful magical beings could feel magic left on an item like a barstool. And of those supremely powerful beings, none of them were usually the sexy-times magical type.

What was I dealing with here, and why wasn't I walking away from this potential car wreck?

"I don't know why you grabbed it," I said. "Here's what else I don't know. Why are you here? Why'd you follow me around yesterday? Why'd you go to the trouble of looking me up just to give me a blanket, and then not even sign your name? And why did you give me that blanket in the first place?" I put up a hand.

"Take your time. That was a lot of questions."

A small smile played across his full lips. "I grabbed it because I like the feel of your magic. I want to feel that magic pulse through you as you wrap your lips around the head of my cock."

I sucked in a breath. The pounding grew more persistent. His eyes danced with desire.

He was so fucking sexy.

I struggled for control as my grip on reality wobbled.

It's the magic, Alexis. Your desire is because of the magic.

Or is it?

I clenched my jaw at that last traitorous thought. I was turning on me. I hated when I did that almost as much as when I didn't listen to myself.

"You win the blunt award," I struggled out, trying to play it cool. Predators liked a chase. I couldn't let him know he was getting to me.

Or how hard he was getting to me.

Or how badly I wanted to feel how hard he was.

"Still a firm 'no,'" I managed, unable to believe I was reacting like this. He'd stalked and threatened me, for criminy's sake. And now he wanted to get me into bed? Was he Dr. Jekyll and Mr. Hard-On? Because I wasn't buying it.

Except I clearly was, because my core was throbbing

and fire raged through my body.

I opened my mouth to...retaliate, or call him a fooking coont like Mick might've, or...something I hadn't thought of, because my brain was buzzing strangely, when he went on.

"I'm here because I wanted to see the place a creature like you frequents. Before you ask, I stayed because the Guinness is good."

"Wait...how'd you know I frequent this place—"

"I bought the blanket because you weren't lying about the sick boy, though he's less of a boy than I'd originally expected." He paused, and cold replaced the heat from a moment before. Warning signals pulsed through my body again, but they didn't eradicate the hot pounding. "I followed you yesterday because your inner fire and the strength of your magic, mixed with your apparent lack of status, intrigued me. I wondered what you were up to. Who you were working for." He paused again, his eyes narrowing slightly. "But you're not working for anyone, are you? Not anyone magical, at any rate. You are exactly as you appear on paper...except for everything to do with your magic. Your situation is incredibly perplexing, Alexis." He shifted, studying me. "You live below the poverty level, doing odd jobs that require little skill. Your decrepit little house was passed down to you by your mother, who bought it shortly after you were born. She could've survived if she'd had access to treatment. You happily hole up in the worst part of town. It is as though you want to constantly struggle. You're a hard and thorough worker—even the Chesters acknowledge that—but you never strive for more. Why is that?"

My mouth worked, but nothing came out. He *was* here because he was stalking me, and he'd done a lot of homework in a very short period.

His steady gaze never shifted from my eyes, as though we were the only two people in the room, and nothing short of the world ending could tear his focus away. I wished he were a little more easily distracted.

"How do you know all that?" I finally uttered.

His eyebrows lowered marginally. "We keep records on magical people. You must know that. For those with a larger-than-average power level, we usually keep extensive records, and the subject is strongly encouraged to live within the magical zones, at least part-time. But in your case…it seems there are varying reports in regards to your ability and the magnitude of your power. None of the reports are accurate. Not even remotely. What they have on file for your magical talent is ridiculous. Laughable, even. The bad reporting is another…perplexing aspect of you."

It wasn't perplexing at all. I just didn't like people sticking their noses in my business, so whenever the low-level magical governing body employees brought me in for routine testing, I fluctuated my magic to mess with their equipment.

My magic wasn't useful to society at large, but it was plenty useful to me.

I palmed my chest and took a step away. "I don't have an above-average magnitude of power—this non-magical place has clearly bamboozled you. I don't strive for more because all the jobs I could do are already being done by those with a lot more experience. Find someone else to stalk. I'm good right where I am." I took a deep breath and straightened my shoulders. Throwing my weight around worked a lot better when I could keep up the facade of confidence. "Now, if you wouldn't mind, get out of my chair."

Our eyes met, and locked, the distance between us reducing until it was just him and me, his power and intensity washing over my body like a physical presence. Silence descended on the bar, and out of the corner of my eye, I could see more than a few people looking our way.

My legs shook, but I held my ground and his stare. Finally, slowly, a tiny smile tickled his lips. His eyes sparked fire.

"Sure, if that's what you want." He took his time lifting the Guinness to his mouth before draining it. The glass thunked softly as it hit the wood of the bar. He stood, still in no hurry, unfolding to his full height, which, as predicted, topped mine by at least five inches.

He stepped closer. His body came within inches of mine. Heat and electricity sizzled across my skin and fire pounded in my core. His sweet breath fell across my face, and it took everything in me not to back away. It took even more willpower not to close the distance and run my hands up his chest, exploring those defined pecs his shirt merely hinted at.

I couldn't seem to get enough air. Swimming in that sexy magic was slowly turning to drowning, only I didn't want a life raft. Something about him called to me. Something smooth and silky. Decadent. Like a rich, complex chocolate made with the finest ingredients. I wanted to taste. To experience.

To let him take me home, strip off my clothes, and show me how powerful he really was.

"Until next time, Alexis." He bent, slowly, and suddenly I worried he'd try to kiss me.

I worried I'd let him.

He turned, and all too soon, though not soon enough, he was slipping by me and striding to the door.

"Arrogant prick," the grizzled old man said as he reached for his drink.

"Yeah." I put out a hand and braced myself against the bar. "He was, right? You don't say those things to people you barely know. Even if you have the kind of magic that makes them want to hear those things…"

"He's dangerous. You ought to steer clear," said a wispy-haired man on the other side of my recently vacated chair, nothing in front of him. "Nothing good can come from tangoing with a man like that. I should know; I was like him once. Young and strong, with the whole world in front of me..."

"Oh, for crying out loud," the grizzled man said, and turned back to face the bar.

"Women wanted me and men wanted to be me. I was in my element. Nothing could tear me down..."

"And yet here you are," I said, grabbing my chair. "Clearly you took a wrong turn somewhere."

The grizzled man snickered, and Liam stared at me from the other end of the bar.

I pressed my lips closed and hefted my chair, walking it back to its rightful place.

"Good for you," Liam said as I set down my chair. Once I switched it for the wobbly one, I scooted in and sat down with a sigh.

"Good for you," Liam said again. "Don't let that bastard try to intimidate you."

"Don't show that he does intimidate me, at any rate, huh?" I took a big sip of the Guinness that had been waiting for me.

Mick growled something and reached for his beer. A moment later, he said, "Get me a whiskey, will ya, Liam?"

Liam ignored Mick. "All those powerful magical types do is throw their weight around," he said. "They don't care that this isn't their territory. They come in here and bark commands like they own the place. Well, they don't."

"No, they do not. I'll drink to that." I raised my drink in the air before lifting it to my lips, trying not to gulp the whole thing down. I only half succeeded.

"And next time you see him, you just keep putting him in his place, Alexis," Liam went on, quite chatty this evening. "You have the law on your side. If he tries to do anything you don't like, you just go ahead and find the nearest cop. They'll sort him out."

"That's...great, thanks," I mumbled. I doubted any underpaid dual-society cop would want to mess with a guy like that.

"Because once those types get a whiff of something they want, they keep going until they get it. I've seen it before," Liam said. "They leave young girls like you in a wake a mile long."

"Feck sakes, what did someone do, pull your string?" Mick grumbled.

"But not with you, Alexis." Liam nodded knowingly. "He's met his match with you. You just keep on sticking up for yourself. You'll give *his royal highness* a run for his money, you will."

The sarcasm rang out loud and clear. There was ob-

K . F .   B R E E N E

viously a reason Liam worked in a place like this, where he never had to meet influential or powerful people. Usually.

"It doesn't matter." I waved the whole thing away, hoping Liam would get the hint and bugger off. "I won't be seeing him again. His curiosity has been satisfied. He had some misperceptions about me. This should be the end of it."

I did a terrible job of selling that lie, not least of all because I still had to get that blanket back to the confusingly sexy yet clearly unhinged stranger, lest he think I'd changed my mind on which blankets would be keeping me warm...

Chapter 14

KIERAN

KIERAN TURNED THE corner outside of the bar and stopped in the shadows, his whole body tense and his fingers curled into fists. He sucked in deep breaths and tried to clear his head.

He had completely lost control.

Completely.

And without any warning.

His mother's selkie magic throbbed within him. The ocean, only a mile away, sang to him softly. Sweetly. But, pulsing within that compulsion, he could also feel the power of the tides, the might of the currents.

His parents' magic came from the same place, the ocean, but it manifested in entirely different forms. He'd only used his mother's magic once.

Once had been plenty.

For a selkie, the ability to inspire lust and passion was more of a suggestion. A lure. The weak might succumb, but the strong rarely did, unless by choice.

That was, unless the wielder was also a Demigod.

Then, the selkie magic was amplified. Boosted. No longer just a lure, it became a command. A drug.

He'd tried using it exactly one time, when he hadn't understood the difference. His lover at the time had become a robot. Nothing more than a plaything, eager to do his bidding without control of herself or independent thought. She couldn't have said no if she'd wanted to.

The very idea disgusted him. It had turned a strong woman into mush. Continuing to use the magic would've turned him into a monster.

He'd never done so again.

Until now.

He leaned his head back against the wall, fighting the lingering feeling of Alexis's magic. Trying to cut out the throbbing ache.

What the hell had happened?

Needing movement, he pushed away from the wall and walked to the edge of the darkened parking lot to retrieve his car.

He hadn't meant to call up the selkie magic. He hadn't even consciously realized it was happening. One moment he'd been watching the erotic sway of Alexis's hips, and the next he was lost in a tide of lust and need, his cock so hard he couldn't think straight. He wanted her with a ferocity he'd never experienced. Wanted to unlock her mind and get all her secrets in between bouts of worshiping her perfect body.

Why was she affecting him like this? Her magic was provocative and enticing, but it wasn't anything like the sexual compulsion he'd just thrown at her. And even if it had been, he was a Demigod. Her magic shouldn't affect him like this, especially since the assessment had judged her power level to be fairly weak.

"Bullshit," he said softly.

He shook his head as he opened his car door, still uncomfortably hard.

There was no way he was wrong in his assessment of her magic's potency. No way. She'd somehow withstood his boosted version of selkie magic, for fuck's sake. She'd drunk it in, coasted with it for a moment, and then rejected it with a smile.

He wasn't wrong. And there was no way someone with her magical potency and ability could've simply slipped through the cracks. She was hiding something. She had to be. And he intended to find out what.

Chapter 15

ALEXIS

I TOWELED OFF my hair as I sauntered into my bedroom to check the time. Three in the afternoon. I needed to get my stuff in the car and go pick out my spot. Tonight, I'd be taking to the streets and selling my wares. Time to prove the moneymaker my magic was *not*.

Dressed in my best blouse and my only pair of slacks that actually made the journey all the way to my ankles, I grabbed the oversized sack I used as a purse for these ventures and stuffed in a tie-dyed square of fabric, a few dingy crystals, and my tarot deck. The cracked crystal ball without a base weighed down the very bottom.

Rolling my eyes at myself, I slung the strap over my shoulder and grabbed my jacket from its hook.

In the living room, Mordecai was leaning over Daisy, looking at the laptop on her lap. Both kids had scrunched-up expressions.

"What's up?" I asked, stepping into the kitchen and

grabbing my filled water bottle.

"Gandalf is trying to remember algebra," Daisy said, glancing up from the couch. "He should stick to fire beasts."

"Do you want help or not?" Mordecai demanded. I smiled at the strength in his voice and the turquoise blanket draped loosely over his shoulders. I suspected he didn't actually need it; he just wanted the comfort. That was a good sign, and pretty amazing, since his close call had been only a little more than twenty-four hours ago.

Daisy whistled at me. "Look at you. I didn't know you had it in you. Makeup and everything. Though the blue eyeshadow is...off-putting." She slapped the cheap Black-Friday-special laptop shut and set it on the coffee table.

Mordecai looked over, and the knot between his eyebrows cleared. He smiled. "I think it looks good. The black eyeliner makes her eyes look really big."

"That'll do." I pushed a loose curl over my shoulder. "I figure I should try to look a little more approachable at these things."

Mordecai nodded, straightening without any stiffness. That medicine was a miracle. "I think it'll work."

A part of me hoped it wouldn't. That wasn't the part that realized we needed money, though.

I draped my jacket over my arm. "All right, you

guys, keep the door locked and—"

"Wait, wait. I'm almost ready. Just have to grab my…" Daisy's voice trailed away as she disappeared into her and Mordecai's bedroom. As she bustled out with a new handbag that I hadn't seen before, and a cute little hat with a pompom that only she could get away with, Mordecai slipped past me and headed for the front door.

"What's going on?" I asked, putting my hand out to stop Mordecai. "And where did you get that handbag, Daisy?"

Daisy lifted her arm to look at the handbag. "Oh, Denny gave me this. And hey, his dad still wants me to work for the family business. I mean, I'll say I can't for a couple weeks because…you know. But after that…I might just do it. I'm positive Denny has kept his word—"

"Wait, wait…" I pinched the bridge of my nose. "Why is Denny buying you handbags? And I thought you said he didn't have any money?"

She looked at me with those almond-shaped eyes in her thin, doll-like face. I would kill to swap my ordinary brown peepers for her beautiful blue ones. Then again, she always lamented that I had thick, long eyelashes, and she needed falsies. We always wanted what we didn't have.

"He helped serve food and clean up at some luncheon his mom threw for a charity. She gave him forty bucks for it. He bought me a purse because he's into me. Anything else, inspector?"

"Right. Yes." I shook my head in disbelief as I adjusted the purse strap on my shoulder. "But you just blackmailed him with gay porn so you could rob his dad. Isn't he horror-struck that you are a bad person?"

She huffed. "Obviously I told him why I did it. He's totally fine with it. And I'm a serious catch."

"He's too dumb to know that she is bad news," Mordecai said as he leaned against the wall. "He's thinking with his…eyes, not his head."

Daisy flicked her hair over her shoulder. "I'm not bad news. I'm just trying to survive. If he wants to buy me things so I'll stick around, who am I to say no?"

"To the parents of a little rich kid, that's bad news," Mordecai responded.

"I have to agree with Mordecai on that one," I said. "Plus, you recently committed a crime that Denny helped you cover up. He's an accomplice. It's probably best for you to steer clear in case he wants to confess his sins."

"Using people to buy you things is wrong," Mordecai said patiently.

I paused at the front door. "Right. Yes. That's what I meant. You shouldn't hang around him because you obviously don't respect him, and using people for new handbags is wrong." I didn't remind him of how I'd come by my phone. "And *also*, you don't want him tattling on you. The second he feels like a scorned lover, he'll sing like a canary."

"I should just take over as the guardian," Mordecai mumbled.

"That's probably true." I turned the handle. "Okay—why are you two following me?"

"You're certainly a helluva lot quicker to notice the obvious," Daisy said to Mordecai.

"We're going with you." Mordecai adjusted his blanket.

I studied their faces to see if they were kidding. They weren't, which meant they were just dense. "I don't need a peanut gallery."

"Um, hello?" Daisy put a hand to her hip. "A large and crazy lunatic is stalking you, or were you too drunk last night to remember telling us about your altercation at the bar?"

"I was not too drunk"—I was a little too drunk, because I only now remembered filling them in—"and it wasn't an altercation. It was a calm conversation between an arrogant jerk—"

"Who thought he could use his magic to influence you," Mordecai interrupted.

I put out my finger. "Whose magic can't coerce me."

"No. You don't remember the conversation from

last night," Daisy said, looking skyward.

I blinked, trying to dig through my extremely foggy memory. Looked like she was mostly right, after all—I'd done a great job drowning my sorrows.

"He practically knew your life story," Daisy said, adjusting her shirt in preparation for people seeing her. Which they wouldn't. "He clearly has the wrong idea about you and is trying to push the envelope. He's dangerous. You're not safe out there on your own."

"Oh really?" I asked. "And what are you guys going to do? Throw your blanket at him, Mordecai? How about you, Daisy? Are you going to threaten to raid his porn collection in search of blackmail? Honestly, you guys, you're teenagers. Stay here, learn stuff, and figure out how to dig yourself out of this hole I've dragged you into."

"I like this hole, thank you very much," Daisy said primly, "and now it's time I return the favor. My scream is extreme. People can hear it for miles—"

"We really need to work on your understanding of distance," Mordecai said.

"With three of us, not even a deliciously large, unbelievably attractive, and dangerously charismatic stranger—those were your words, were they not, Alexis?—who knows too much will try to kidnap you," Daisy said before stepping forward.

I grimaced. "I didn't actually say all that, did I?"

Daisy gave me a flat look that told me all I needed to know.

I hated that it was true.

"We may not be good at protection," Mordecai said, "but we can help with customer service."

I shook my head, but he wasn't done.

"That stranger now knows you aren't easy to manipulate. Not one on one, anyway. He also knows you have a soft spot for me. I don't want to be kidnapped to bring you to heel. It would be safer for you to take us with you."

I paused with my mouth forming the word "no." I wasn't sure the stranger knew the extent of my soft spot for my wards, but...he'd have some idea. Only a fool wouldn't be able to put two and two together, and this stranger was by no means a fool. Still, kidnapping was a little extreme. A guy like the stranger, with looks, money, power, and sexy magic, wouldn't stoop so low as to basically blackmail a woman into bed. Talk about a blow to his ego. The odds of that were nearly nonexistent.

Except...he did blast me with the sexy magic, so...

"Just don't teach him how to easily manipulate me." I blew out a breath. "But—" They stepped to either side of me, pushed my hand off the knob, and opened the door while knocking me to the side. "Hey. Freaking hell. Don't mind me, I'm just standing here."

"Come on," Daisy shouted over her shoulder.

"Where are you guys going?" Frank stood in the center of my lawn, watching the kids head to the car parked at the curb. If only I'd had a garage to hide the thing.

"How many times do I have to tell you, Frank? Get off my lawn!" Shaking my head, I stomped down the pathway to the sidewalk and my waiting car. "You can come," I told the kids, telling them something they already knew, "but you are to stick to the rear and keep your mouths closed, is that clear?"

"Where else am I going to go?" Frank asked as I brushed past him. "No one at home will talk to me."

"You know where else you can go, Frank. And there'll be plenty of people to talk to when you get there." I walked around the hood of the car as I unlocked it.

"I'm not ready," he called.

"That is so creepy." Daisy shivered as she slid into the back seat.

"He doesn't mean any harm." I raised my voice so Frank would hear. "He's just incredibly annoying and prone to constant trespassing."

"Heartless," I heard as I got into my seat.

"Daisy, I've picked up a very bad habit from you." I put the keys in the ignition.

"It isn't stealing, because you've tried that in the

past and failed miserably at it," she responded.

"I'm a good person, that's why." I showed her a sour face in the rearview mirror.

"That's not nice," Mordecai admonished.

"Well, since you mutinied and took over the leadership role on this ship, I'm allowed to be a brat. We'll see how much you like taking the high road." I turned the key as Frank drifted closer to the car.

He bent down to look in. "I'll just stay here and wait for you to get back."

I shook my head and stepped on the gas. "I might need to force Frank to leave. This is starting to get ridiculous."

"Starting?" Daisy huffed.

"I picked up the eye rolling from you," I told her, heading to the area of San Francisco with the heaviest foot traffic for all things magical. Strangely, it wasn't in the magical district. Or even in the dual zone where we lived. It was in the non-magical tourist area, visited by solely non-magical folk who wanted to check out magical freaks and their crafts. Magical people had to get a permit to set up shop there, and we needed to re-register each year.

"Ah, crap. I should've told you guys you couldn't come because you aren't included in my permit." I tapped the steering wheel in annoyance. "Missed opportunity."

"Not really. The fact that you're not turning around right now is indicative of how that argument would've gone." Mordecai entwined his fingers in his lap.

I shot him a narrow-eyed glare. "Okay, Mr. Word-a-Day, tone it down with the adult shtick. Not even my mother sounded that educated."

"That's because she wasn't," Daisy said.

"I should drop you two off right here and make you walk back."

"Then you'd be responsible for killing me," Mordecai said. I noticed he hadn't rushed to correct Daisy about my mother's education.

I ground my teeth. "Oh, the regret I now have about bringing you lug nuts. Oh, the regret."

He was right, of course, and we all knew it. The rule was one "stall" per permit, each stall being no more than a number on the pavement. As far as the officials were concerned, you could shove as many freaks as you wanted into the designated empty space.

I hated putting myself on display, another freak to amuse the masses, but I needed money.

It was time to take my magic into the public again.

Chapter 16

ALEXIS

"**H**E BARELY EYED your permit," Daisy said in a hush as I rolled into the mostly empty parking lot, which would later be filled to the brim. It was the closest lot to the choice stalls. All the big players generally parked in this area.

All the big players, and me, who got to join them by virtue of not needing the cover of darkness for my craft and having absolutely nothing in the world better to do than show up before most of the patrons.

"I'm here every time I'm between jobs." I drove to the first row and steered to the corner closet to the walkway. "They've seen me every few months, for about a month at a time, for the last...eight hundred million years. It's only an issue when a new person comes on. Then it takes *forever*."

The "reserved" paint on the first five spaces in each row had long since worn away. The city hadn't bothered to repaint. They probably didn't bother to give out reserved parking permits anymore, either.

It didn't matter. Everyone knew those spots were taken by the *biggest* players, most of whom were non-magical assholes and their chained-up magical beasts. How else would the kiddies get to marvel at badly treated oddities?

I hated those bastards. And while I couldn't help the magical beasts, I could sure as hell piss on their "owners'" parade. Because by the time they got here, the lot would be full, security would be on scene, and their formerly "reserved" spot would be taken. They'd have to head to one of the other lots, and anyone who had a mind for vengeance would be able to tell from the previous scratches on my car that keying it wouldn't bother me at all.

I took turns taking each of their spots. It gave them something in common to bitch about.

The second space was empty, so I took that, next to a shiny black van with a graphic of a wand and a few stars in a circle. Spaces three through five were empty, and a handful of vans and trucks in decent condition had parked beyond them. The owners had most likely come in early and dropped off their vehicles, and their gear, so they'd get top placement.

"Did you two remember to grab a couple of chairs?" I asked as I took the rugs out of the back of the car. I knew they hadn't.

Both of them stopped with their hands on the

doors, staring at me.

I laughed. "Serves you right."

"It's fine. When you don't have old bones, sitting on the ground is fine." Daisy shrugged and swung her door shut.

"And I suppose that when you don't have *old bones*, sitting on ground that was recently defecated on isn't a big deal, either."

They both paused again, and this time they exchanged a look. Then eyed the car.

"Can't sit in the car. You might be kidnapped, remember?" I grinned.

With both kids reluctantly helping, I only had to make one trip to my favorite spot. I set my chair on the faded number fifteen.

"Why are we basically the only ones here?" Daisy looked down the strip of tarmac beside the wide, stain-spotted sidewalk. A few crews of people struggled with tents and other items, but it was still largely deserted. As I'd expected it would be this early. Cars crawled past on the street beyond, fighting the constant traffic on the way to the busy tourist area. Only a few pieces of litter fluttered in the salty breeze coming from the bay behind us.

I glanced up at the white-blue sky, the fog trying to steal the show before the sun set. Then I turned toward the bay and looked out at the sparkling waters splashing against the man-made barriers intended to keep the boats safe in their slips. A massive naval ship jutted out in the distance, docked so tourists could check it out. A ways out, Alcatraz haunted the waters, visited by tourists who occasionally brought a spectral trespasser back to the mainland.

"Two reasons," I said, setting up three TV trays that would act as a barrier for the clients. A normal vendor would have a table, and while I could've afforded a cheap one, I didn't want people leaning on it and getting closer. Where they sat was close enough. "One is because the tourists like a bit of a scare, so they don't typically come out until about dusk. And two, a lot of the magical people who set up shop here think the darkness brings out the ghosts and ghouls."

"And it doesn't?" Mordecai asked.

"No. They're out all the time."

"So why would they think it does?" Daisy asked, strangely giving me her undivided attention.

And then it dawned on me—the real reason they wanted to come with me.

"You two want to know how my magic works, don't you?" I smiled to myself and shook my head. "You had me at 'kidnap.' Very clever."

"Well, I mean, you do need us along." Daisy straightened up in self-importance. "There's that crazy-handsome stranger who gets the ol' heart thumping and that you wouldn't mind taking for a spin—"

I had definitely forgotten a few things from our sum-up chat after the bar last night.

"—who will be less likely to kidnap you or us if we all stick together. And then there is the reason you are not making money at this. Because Pippin the Hobbit looked it up, and for a Ghost Whisperer, we think you're in the top tier. Those people make a lot of money. Like the ones who get jobs solving crimes for cops. The good ones make bank."

"The good ones don't have priors."

"Told you that was why she didn't get a job like that," Mordecai mumbled, elbowing her.

She elbowed him back. "Okay, but you could rid places of paranormal activity." She lifted her eyebrows at me. "Or hunt down loved ones and help them with the transition."

"Only the best make money at those things," I said, checking the arrangement of my furniture. I snatched up the roll of yellow tape and drew a line around the client chair. Then got to work taping down the scarves sectioning off my chair. Everything I put out was the bare minimum. I'd learned the hard way what was necessary.

"But *you* are the best," Daisy said with absolute conviction.

"Only the best, and those with enough money and

connections to get a business going. I don't have either of those things. Most businesses take a loss for the first few years. *Years.* As the sole breadwinner, I don't have that kind of time to work my butt off for no pay. I also don't have any money to advertise with, or people skills to bamboozle patrons into hiring me. Or the desire to do this line of work in the first place."

"I'm sensing a severe defeatist attitude," Daisy mumbled out of the side of her mouth to Mordecai.

He nodded solemnly. "That's the first thing we have to fix."

"How?" she asked. "Hypnosis?"

"Do you think that'd be strong enough to override her personality?"

I sighed and grabbed the tarot deck before flinging it onto the middle rug-covered TV tray. Ignoring their muttering, I dropped the cracked crystal ball next it. It rolled a little before thankfully stopping. I didn't feel like chasing it down the sidewalk like last time.

"I should have brought my clipboard." Daisy clucked her tongue while looking over my setup. "I'll need to take a gaggle of notes to figure out how to fix this situation, I can already tell. I mean, no part of this says 'professional.' Not one part."

"A gaggle?" I chuckled. "And there is one part." I pointed at my hair. "Very trendy." I ran my hands over the rugs on the TV trays to make sure my magic was still firing. "There is no need to revamp. I'm not going to be doing this long enough to make a thing out of it. This will do for a couple weeks, hopefully less." I did the same thing to the other two rugs I'd brought before throwing them at the kids. "Here. Sit on those. The clients can stew in their own…problems."

I adjusted my chair so it was facing sideways, away from the kids, and finally took my seat. I stretched my legs and clasped my fingers behind my head before looking out over the water.

"What are you doing now?" Daisy asked.

"Waiting for my first patron. It'll probably take a while. You might want to settle in."

"Are you sure?" Mordecai asked softly. "Is…that guy…"

"That was fast," Daisy said.

"What?" I asked, noticing a couple of people ambling along the sidewalk, none of them looking my way for too long. They either didn't want to be seen at the freak show in broad daylight, or were legitimately trying to get somewhere and didn't want me to think they were paying customers. Some of the stall owners yelled and jeered at passersby, trying to get business. It wasn't a pretty sight.

"You the witch that sees dead people?" someone asked in an East Coast accent. A rough-looking man in his forties entered my peripheral vision before stopping in front of my TV trays, ignoring the chair two feet behind him. He put his hand on the middle TV tray, intending to lean over the divider and into my space, except my subtle defense system wobbled dangerously. He straightened up slowly, not happy his aggressive approach had been thwarted.

He was the pushy, bossy type who thought everyone was put on this earth to wait on him or steal from him. Or both...at the same time. That about summed up all of my bosses.

Three people waited at his back, an important-looking dude with a buzzcut and a stern face, and two slim guys in their thirties who looked like they needed a good meal.

I redirected my gaze out over the bay. "I'm not a witch."

"Right, yeah. Whatever. You that broad?" The man shifted impatiently. "I was told to look for...this type of setup."

"She's that broad," Daisy said. "The best there is. At your service—"

"Maybe," I said.

"Sign me up," he said. The client chair squeaked as the man sat.

I took a last glimpse at the calming water before turning my head in his direction. "Don't you want to know the particulars? Like the services I perform and the amount I charge?"

"I know all that. A buddy used you a while back. I been wanderin' around this spot looking for you, but you ain't been on scene."

He said it like an accusation. Him and me—we weren't going to end up the best of friends.

I grumpily got up and moved my chair to face him. A couple more people were wandering along the sidewalk now, looking in my direction. They were interested in what I did.

Daisy clearly noticed it. "She needs a sign," she whispered to Mordecai. "Or, like...a scarf on her head or something."

"I don't need a sign," I said. "That just encourages people."

"I don't think she'd do well if she went into business for herself," Mordecai whispered to Daisy.

"Understatement," Daisy replied.

I clasped my hands in my lap so I didn't bitch-slap someone, then calmly looked at the man in front of me. His shiny black hair was slicked back over his head and all the stubble had been cleared from his jaw. A crisp suit covered his stocky frame, bulging up over his belt, where I knew a gun probably lurked. His shiny gold watch screamed expensive, as did his gaudy cufflinks.

All of the glitz and shine didn't detract from the overall feeling of *roughness* he exuded. If I had to guess, his profession was less than reputable. The harsh set of his jaw, his permanently clenched fists, and the way he perched on the chair like he would shake my services out of me—they all told me he was someone I didn't want hanging around for long. I'd end up like those poor sods shadowing him.

"What is it you want me to do?" I asked, though you didn't have to be a genius to figure it out.

He braced his forearms on his knees, trying to cut down the distance between us. "My buddy said you are discreet."

"Yeah. Though if a police officer asks me the right questions, I will answer."

His gaze intensified. "What are the right questions?"

"The ones I can't truthfully evade without going to jail."

He leaned back now, his constant micro-movements indicating the restlessness of a guilty conscience. "How often you got cops asking around?"

"Never. But that doesn't mean it won't happen."

He squinted just a bit before glancing around my setup. He relaxed.

Apparently, he figured the police wouldn't believe a person like me even if they questioned me. That, or his lawyer could easily discredit me.

Both were spot-on assessments.

"I need to get some weight off my back, if you know

what I'm sayin'," he said, then a glimmer of uncertainty crossed his features. "My buddy said you'd know what that meant."

"Are you referring to the three ghosts standing behind you, or does this relate to a haunting of a specific location? Because I don't travel."

"Oh my God," Daisy breathed, and then shivered.

The man in front of me tensed. He just barely kept from looking behind him, I could tell.

"It's… I got…" He swallowed, and his eyes flicked to the kids at my left. "I feel this…weight…all the time," he said, clearly uncomfortable. "But it ain't guilt, because…you know…"

"That weight is the ghosts, and no, I don't know how *not* to feel guilty when I kill someone." I waited a beat and earned a flicker of annoyance. He'd definitely killed them, and definitely didn't feel remorse. He was not a man to trifle with. "But you want them gone, yes? That's why you're here?"

A spark of anger lit up his eyes. "Sayin' that sort of stuff can get you in trouble."

"Clearly." I gestured at the three people pushing up close to his back, eyeing me like a starving man would a steak. "The answer is yes, I *can* get rid of them. For a price."

His shoulders tensed again, and no wonder. His personal poltergeists were practically sitting on them.

The rugs I'd given to the kids would've bought him some distance from them. But if anyone deserved to be haunted, this guy did.

"How much?" he asked.

He had money, he had done a terrible deed a few times over, and he was clearly desperate.

He could also break my jaw if I pissed him off. As he'd said a moment ago, he didn't suffer from a guilty conscience.

"Three hundred, one for each issue." I stared at him, no facial expression, and no blinking.

His eyes narrowed. "Two hundred."

"Look, buck-o, I'm not the one being tailed by my indiscretions. Pay the price, or live with it, because I assume you had someone else try to sever that attachment, and it didn't work, right? How else would you know what's going on? But, I mean, look at 'em. They're on you good and tight. That's gotta be draining the energy out of you."

He shifted to the other side, and the folding chair groaned mournfully. His jaw tightened.

Oh yeah, he'd tried to get help. But those poltergeists were clearly not having it. They had a story to tell, and they weren't leaving until someone heard them out.

I slumped. Guess who'd have to be the big ears of this operation?

"Three hundred, and you're lucky I'm slightly afraid

of what you'll do if I ask for more." I crossed my arms over my chest.

He leaned forward again, and his personal hell leaned with him. I could almost feel the weight of their horror. Of their memories. Of their extreme anger that justice hadn't been served.

I only wished I could do something more for them than send them on. Someday this guy would certainly go to jail for what he'd done. These types of guys always did, one way or another. Visiting Alcatraz would tell you that much. But I knew, to them, it wouldn't be soon enough.

"Fine. Three hundred." He didn't make a move toward his pocket.

I didn't bother getting started.

His eyes narrowed again. That was clearly his reaction *du jour*. "You tryin' to scam me, wanting the money up front? I ain't payin' if this don't work."

"Oh yes, you fucking will pay if this doesn't work," I said in a sudden flare of anger. I had zero patience and a wicked temper. They were the main reasons why I was absolutely wretched at this type of work. "This is going to truly suck. They are just about to open their big traps and spill all. I'm not going to want to hear it, because you seem like a real piece of work. I'll probably have nightmares because of this. So if I'm going to subject myself to this horror, you're going to pay for it. Don't like those terms, get the fuck out. I have better things to do than getting jerked around by a lowlife piece of trash like you."

I'd gone too far, but luckily, I knew exactly how to get myself out of the self-created jam.

I stood in a rush and eyed each and every one of his followers. "I can see you. I can hear you." I held up a hand. "I didn't say I *wanted* to, just that I could. I can't help you in the way you want. I'm not a cop, or someone the cops listen to. But you're weighing on him. You're having an effect. Go ahead and siphon his energy, and then press yourself into him. Do you know how to do that?"

The important-looking dude in the white button-up shirt nodded, his expression determined, and I'd bet on my life that he'd been a cop or agent of some kind. The two slight characters looked to the stern-faced dude, but instead of moving closer and following his lead, they cowered where they stood. They were afraid of him.

So a cop or something similar, and probably a couple of lesser criminals. Basically, I really only needed to feel bad for one of the three. Those were better odds for my overall happiness when I left tonight.

I grabbed my chair by the back, turned it sideways again, and sat. The bay still sparkled pleasantly as the waves rolled by.

"Fine. Fine, okay," the man said, and though his

voice was hard, I could hear the traces of unease lining each word.

Magical and non-magical people alike were discomfited by the thought of the dead walking amongst the living. Hell, even the dead weren't happy about it, especially when they didn't know they'd expired and weren't sure what "crossing over" meant. I was given the side-eye in both societies and from both sides of the "veil"—the line between the living and dead—as though I could help what kind of useless magic I'd been dealt.

If you weren't unlucky, you'd have no luck at all, Alexis, my mother used to say.

She'd been absolutely right. I wasn't sure what power the stranger thought he'd felt, but when it came right down to it, my magic greatly limited my options in life.

Chapter 17

ALEXIS

T HE CLIENT (I didn't plan to get his name) stood and pulled out a money clip stuffed with green. The guy was loaded, and he was squabbling over three hundred bucks?

He slapped it onto the TV tray in front of him.

"Put the crystal ball on it," I instructed.

He hesitated with his hand over the cracked orb. "Won't that...mess with your...thing?"

"No. It's just a prop to make me look legit." I motioned at nothing in particular. "Daisy, count that money."

"This is all...very strangely done," Daisy muttered as her clothes rustled. "Hello, good sir. Thank you for stopping by. I'll just..." Money crinkled, then paper slid against paper. "Yup." The bills crinkled again, and I knew she was slipping them into her pocket.

The folding chair creaked, and the sound of water lapping against the pillars of the pier filled the following silence.

"Do I have to do something else?" the man asked, impatience ringing in his voice.

"Nope," I said, not moving. "I was just giving your friends there a chance to get in one last shot at you."

"It's like she doesn't want repeat business," Daisy said softly.

"I don't." Truth was, I had to gear myself up for the worst part of these gigs. A quick glance at the client's followers told me they were all alert and eager to be heard. My heart sank. "Go ahead. I'm all ears." I brought up the timer on my phone. "You each have five minutes."

"Who…me?" the client said as the important dude behind him opened his mouth.

"Of course not you. When you talk, you have a whole host of people who have no choice but to hear you. Those people behind you only have me. And whatever other poor schmucks like me they happen across. I'm about to shove them across the Line whether they want to go or not. The least I can do is hear them out before they go."

The man licked his lips nervously. Oh yeah, he was a real piece of work. He probably had a whole lot of secrets I shouldn't hear.

I hoped I wouldn't.

I reset the timer. "Go." I gestured to the important-looking guy.

"I headed up the department's investigation of Mr. Romano for some three months on suspicion of drug trafficking," the dude began, cementing my earlier assessment. "We got a tip regarding a shipment…"

I let his voice ebb and flow around me. His words mixed together and became nothing but sound, rising and falling. I didn't want to know the gory details of how he'd been kicked out of the land of the living, because they were probably grisly. I had a good imagination—I didn't need help putting disturbing images into my mind's eye.

"Did you hear me?" the important-looking dude asked, and it was clear that even in death, he thought he was the bee's knees.

"Yep." Technically, my answer was true. He hadn't asked if I was listening. I glanced at the timer. "You've got one more minute. Anything else?"

"Roger McLaughlin. He works in the Central Park precinct in New York City. Tell him that Jim Miller told you to tell him eight-seven-seven in terminal three. He'll know what that means. Can you remember that?"

I kept every muscle in my body loose and my face perfectly devoid of expression. If Mr. Criminal knew I'd just gotten that information, whatever it was, I had a feeling ol' Jim and I would have something in common.

"Can you remember that?" Jim repeated.

"Look, guy, I told you, I don't deliver messages," I

said with the right shade of annoyance. Mr. Criminal (I still hoped to forget his name after this) leaned forward, his eyes gleaming dangerously. "I'm sure your mother knows you love her."

Mr. Criminal's eyes remained alert, but his shoulders relaxed slightly. I'd been down this road a time or two. I was excellent at surviving.

"Will you deliver it?" the Jim asked. "Touch your hair if yes."

Smart guy, this important dude. He could read people well.

Not well enough, of course, since Mr. Criminal had gotten one over on him.

"All right, that's time." I brushed the hair out of my face, because what could I do, *not* pass his message on? Roger McLaughlin would think I was just some nutter, so it wouldn't matter, but I wasn't in the habit of ignoring last requests. It was another reason I tried to avoid using my magic. Each and every spirit seemed to have a last request, and I didn't have the time or resources to comply with all of them. "Nope, that's time," I said into the silence, shaking my head. "I don't care. You're done."

The dead usually only stopped talking once they got their point across. I doubted Mr. Criminal knew that, but I didn't want to barter with my life.

"Next?" I called.

Time couldn't go quickly enough for the grueling stories of violence the other two spouted off. They'd each been tortured for information, and they'd been killed after spilling their guts. I couldn't seem to shut their voices out. They were too hysterical and graphic.

I should've asked for more money.

"Stop. I got it all. Please stop." I pinched the bridge of my nose as Small-Time Criminal Number Two begged me to look after Muffy. "I'm sure your dog is in good hands. I really do. People like dogs. I'm sure Muffy is liked more than you, despite that stupid name."

"Oh shit…" The words rode a slow exhale from Mr. Criminal. "You really can hear them. You're not just yanking my chain."

"Sadly, no." I didn't want to know how he knew the dog's name. "Now shut it. I need to send them across." I closed my eyes and bowed my head, focusing.

I'd heard other people needed to chime a bell, or light a candle, or say a chant to send spirits across the Line (what some people called the *beyond*). Some had to do all of the above. I just thought really hard about pushing them across. Had it required any real work on my part, I wouldn't have been there. These jobs were unpleasant enough without putting in an effort.

"Eight-seven-seven," Jim said, his voice strangely echoing. I opened my eyes, but I wasn't in the trance a human needed to be in to see the Line or the spiritual plane. I could only see him cross into it. His body somewhat dissolved, turning translucent. "Terminal three," he said again, before fading away.

"Johnny Sanderson. He's the runner. He sold me out." Small-Time Criminal Number One followed Jim's lead. "He needs to pay."

"Muffy was a really good dog. She likes a cuddle in the evenings." Small-Time Criminal Number Two turned to a wisp and then blinked out.

"See ya." I gave a last shove before yanking down the divide. I glanced at Mr. Criminal. "You should feel lighter now."

Mr. Criminal rolled his shoulders. Then his neck.

"No, no." I waved my finger at him. "Don't do that here. You paid, they're gone, now get out."

His eyes took on a lethal edge. "I'm not in the habit of allowing people to speak to me like that."

I rubbed my temples. "I can bring them back, if you'd prefer?"

"Don't mind her," Daisy piped up. "She's terrible at customer service. She's always this cranky. Have a blessed day!"

I was still rubbing my temples with my eyes closed when the client chair squeaked then groaned. Clothes rustled.

"See that you keep this to yourself," Mr. Criminal said. "I'll be watching."

I barely kept from huffing out a laugh as he shuffled off. He didn't know my name, hadn't known when I'd show up here, and didn't know where to find me otherwise. But suddenly he'd be keeping an eye on me?

Get in line.

"Blessed day?" Mordecai asked Daisy.

"I don't know, he was scary. I figured he'd be less likely to kill religious people. So…" She let the word linger, and I knew they'd both shifted their attention to me.

"So…" I heard shifting on the rug. "You…listen to ghosts and then push them out of this world?" Mordecai asked. "That's it?"

"I'd thought there was more to it, for some reason," Daisy whispered.

"It's plenty, trust me." I stared out over the water again as the daylight continued to wane.

"Where do they go?" Daisy asked, and I could hear the shiver of unease in her voice.

While the kids did know my magical type, we'd never really discussed it, and they'd certainly never seen me do it. Part of that was because ghosts creeped Daisy out and she shushed me soon after I started talking about them, and another part was that the freak show was no place for a self-respecting teenager, magical or otherwise. It was hard to get a good understanding of my work without actually seeing it.

"Some say it's a place that is infinitely better. Some rant and rave about how annoying it is. But what exactly that place is, I'm not sure. I've never been there. The furthest I've gone is to the Line—the gate to the spiritual plane, basically."

"Could you..." Daisy's swallow was so loud, I could hear it from a few feet away. "Could you go there if you tried?"

I furrowed my brow in thought, watching that relaxing movement of the water. "I honestly don't know. Sometimes, when I send a particularly strong and stubborn spirit across, I have to put so much effort into it that I hear a subtle calling from beyond the veil. And when I bring someone back, it's the same way. My spirit kinda...jumps at it. But I don't know if I could go over, or what would happen to me if I did. Would I get trapped? Would my body die without my soul? Would my body go *with* my soul?" I shook my head slowly, curiosity and fear mingling at the great unknown. "When I'm old and senile and wetting the bed, I'll probably try it. Couldn't hurt at that point, know what I mean?"

One of the kids let out a breath. No comment came for a few moments.

"But...these spirits aren't still people, right?" Daisy asked. "I mean, if they were, we'd all see them... They're...almost a figment of your imagination?"

She sure hoped they were, at any rate.

"They were people, and now they're...wandering souls?" I shook my head, not used to explaining this. "You guys, I honestly don't know. They look like living, breathing people to me. They look as real as you two, except I can see past them if I need to. Like Superman's x-ray vision."

"Then how do you know they're ghosts?" Mordecai asked.

"I just...know. When I'm tired, I overlook it half the time, but normally..." I shrugged. "I just know, that's all."

"I feel like you should get a firmer handle on your magic. I mean...you just made three hundred dollars!" I could hear the excitement in Daisy's voice, despite the way I'd made that dirty money. "If you had a better idea of all your...abilities, maybe you could make even more. Because that man definitely seemed happy with your service. The personality behind the service could use some work, but the actual service seemed to leave him satisfied. That says to me that he felt he received value for his money."

"Well put," Mordecai said. "That junior CEO class taught you something. I should've taken it."

"You guys, I know this one seemed great and all, but I don't usually make that much money. Besides, it isn't fun. The stories I was told—"

"Stocking shelves isn't fun," Daisy said. "Cleaning up dog poop isn't fun. Do you know what the difference is? Those pay badly."

"Just tune them out like you always tune us out," Mordecai said.

"I don't tune you out—I ignore you. Which is easy because you yammer about nothing. People who have been tortured to death are a lot harder to block out. And *this* usually pays badly." I rubbed my face. "That guy was an exception. And obviously dangerous. You're forgetting that I was told sensitive information that could get me in big trouble."

"By ghosts," Daisy said. "That doesn't count in a house of law." I frowned at the odd term, momentarily derailed. "That guy is proof that word of mouth works. Am I right, Gandalf?" I could hear Daisy rubbing her hands together. "I would kill for my clipboard right now."

"Just be patient," I said, resuming my stare out over the water. "You'll see what this job is really all about. And then you'll understand why I only reserve my party tricks for desperate times."

Chapter 18

KIERAN

"A ND YOU SAID this chick can also reach into your chest?" Jack asked Kieran as they sat inside the flowing tent they'd set up. The billboard outside advertised a mystical soap that wasn't on display.

The second he'd gotten word that Alexis was on the move, Kieran had had Jack follow her and relay info back to him. He hadn't been thrilled she'd turned up here, in a place ten times worse than the disgusting half-world in which she lived. She was subjecting herself to ridicule and humiliation by small-minded fools. This market, for lack of a better word, was degrading for magical people as a whole, and it had to be damaging to a person's self-worth to participate in it.

In an effort to keep an eye on her, he'd had his guys set up this tent down the way from hers. This way he could monitor her, unmolested by those who might recognize him. His guys had also set up a couple of cameras, for when the larger crowds inevitably came, wanting entertainment from those deemed less than human.

He planned to move closer once the crowds would properly mask him, but for the moment, he had a clear view from a few angles, and enough audio from the closest camera to make out what was going on. Neither Alexis nor any of her crew—her teen wards, he surmised—had noticed them setting it up. They were completely oblivious to the goings-on around them and therefore defenseless to hostile forces. Kieran included.

"Yes, in so many words." Kieran leaned forward on his wooden chair, resting his elbows against his knees, looking out the small window in the side of the tent. They'd cut it shortly after his arrival. "It doesn't look like that's the power she's using here."

"It looks like she's doing Ghost Whisperer stuff, so the file must've been right. At least in part," said Jack, leaning against the pole in the corner, looking out his self-made window. Donovan stood at the mouth of the tent, keeping everyone moving by making their tent seem as boring and unimpressive as it was. Three tablets sat on a small table at the back of the tent, displaying the camera views. A Bluetooth speaker softly played the audio feed from the cameras. "But a class two shouldn't be able to actually see spirits. Especially not in broad daylight."

"I know," Kieran said dryly. He was well versed in what a Ghost Whisperer could and could not do. As his guys well knew. "I've devoted more time to the report on Alexis than I care to admit, and I can't find any trace of how it might've been altered. The usual signs are absent, and it's obvious she doesn't have any magical connections who'd make the changes for her. She's estranged from the magical society. Has been her whole life."

"So how…" Donovan moved to the right of Kieran and withdrew a large serrated knife. The blade punched another hole in the tent, making an additional viewing window.

"How did she alter that report? I don't know." Kieran leaned back and folded his arms across his chest, watching Alexis. She faced his direction, and not the makeshift desk in front of her, so she could look out over the water.

"After meeting her last night, you're sure about her magical level?" Donovan asked.

"Class five, without question." Kieran scratched his cheek. "Absolutely no question."

"You can see that her power is strong." Jack stepped back and pointed out his window. "She impressed that Chester criminal. We've been around long enough to know it would take an awful lot to get that reaction out of someone like him. She clearly removed whatever spirits were hanging around his back. You could see it in his body language. She saw them, heard them, and sent them away, just like she said. All in the space of…" Jack checked his watch.

"Could you see her facial expressions, sir?" Donovan asked, looking down at Kieran.

Kieran had all the traits a Big Three Demigod should, including superhuman eyesight. The guys knew his range, and had set up the tent on the far boundary of it.

"Yes. If I'm not mistaken, she heard something of interest toward the end of the first five-minute interval. I caught a flash of fear, then tightness around her eyes. I've seen that look a time or two. Then, with the other two intervals, horror. Blind horror. She did a piss-poor job of controlling it. Thankfully, she was facing this way and not toward her…client." Kieran leaned forward again, trying to ease the hunger eating through his guts. "She can hear the dead. See them. It explains what she said in the bar."

"What's that?" Jack asked.

"She wouldn't sit on a barstool because she said it was taken. But it was empty."

"Okay…but—" Donovan jerked before striding quickly to the front of the tent. "We're still waiting for supplies," he told someone who'd stopped to ask after the soap. "We've got nothing."

"But isn't that—"

Kieran didn't bother glancing over, and Donovan

didn't need to tell the person to move along. His expression and posture clearly telegraphed vicious intent.

"But we've been to how many class-five Ghost Whisperers?" Donovan asked, returning. "Five, six?"

"Six," Jack said. "And they all needed the cover of darkness, candles, and various symbols to call in your mother's spirit, sir. None of them so much as claimed to see her, or hear more than echoes of her voice."

"Exactly." Donovan angled himself so he could look down on Kieran. "Could this be an elaborate setup by your father? Maybe he found out what you are trying to do. This kind of premeditation isn't beyond him. Planting someone you desperately need in your path, then using that person to glean information from you, would be right up his alley."

Kieran stood and stalked to the monitors. "I've thought of that. Her magical power and talent suggests that she is in the back pocket of my father. Because not only is a class-five Ghost Whisperer unable to actually see and hear spirits as if they were people, but they also don't have the ability to magically slice into a person's midsection, or to banish a soul with nothing more than a little bit of focus for a few seconds. And they certainly can't withstand my magic, not even for a second. But everything else—literally *everything* else, from her clothes to the free drinks she gets off her ex-boyfriend— suggests her files are accurate." Kieran clenched his fists. "She is not what she seems, but I haven't a clue what she actually is."

Jack blew out a breath.

"Conundrum," Donovan mumbled.

"What about a class-five Necromancer?" Jack asked. "They deal in souls. Raising the bodies of the dead and stuffing souls in them, summoning souls from behind the Line…"

"It could be." Kieran paused for a moment, watching Alexis zone out as she gazed at the water. It calmed her, he could tell. Gave her peace. He felt a kinship with her in that—it had always done the same for him.

He turned away as unexpected warmth rose through him.

"Can Necromancers see and hear people, though, or just summon and manipulate souls?" Donovan asked.

"We need Boman," Jack said, referencing another member of the Six. "He's the magical encyclopedia."

"We need to test her properly," Kieran said, frustration rising through him. "First with a practical application, and then with the machines. I want to know what I'm dealing with. I want to know, for certain, what she can do, what she is, and that she has no affiliation with my father."

He couldn't stop a final thought from curling through his mind.

Then, after that's confirmed, I want her.

Chapter 19

ALEXIS

I LEANED FORWARD as a middle-aged woman trudged by with a bowing spine. She stuck her tongue out to lick a huge puff of cotton candy as if it were an ice cream cone.

"You're eating that wrong," I called before I could help myself.

"She definitely is," Daisy agreed, nodding. "Who doesn't know how to eat cotton candy?"

I hadn't gotten a bite for over an hour. All the spiffy vendors had arrived with their immaculate tents, bleating animals, and high-dollar props. My ramshackle setup had turned into more of a deterrent than an attraction.

I'd only reeled in another three patrons after the first guy had buggered off, and each of those three had only stopped in for a good time because of limited options elsewhere. They'd all thought twenty dollars was a lot for seeing spirits, and two had only paid ten. Because of that, I'd only relayed half of the message.

You got what you paid for.

Mordecai and Daisy now thoroughly understood what I had been telling them.

"We need another mobster," Mordecai said as he watched the passing crowd. His and Daisy's backs both slumped in boredom. "Or maybe I should pretend to be a paying customer. They'll see she is actually open for business and realize this is not a homeless camp begging for money."

"It's worse when you say things like that, Mordie, because you're so genuine," Daisy said, taking the words right out of my mouth. "You should leave me to say those things. She doesn't care about my opinion."

"I do," I said out of duty. "At least...five percent of the time."

"See? Oh...wait a minute. What's this?" Daisy elbowed Mordecai. "Look good. We've got one. Lexi, don't blow this."

I glanced at the crowd, having turned my chair toward the wards so I could talk to them as well as watch the water.

A middle-aged woman walked up with determined strides and a set expression. She stopped beside the visitor chair and nudged the leg with the toe of her Kate Spade flat. "This is broken."

"It's fine. Can I help you?" I asked her, almost pleasantly. I might not have liked putting my abilities on display, but I liked boredom even less.

She gingerly sat down before looking over my setup. Disgust crossed her face.

I waited her out. Daisy didn't.

"Can she help you?" she asked.

"Are these your children?" the woman said with a curled lip, her gaze going back and forth between us.

"Yup," I answered without hesitation. "I started at ten. Why wait, you know?"

Disbelief replaced disgust, and it wasn't because she didn't trust my words—it was because she did. She was probably trying to work out how it was physically possible for someone to have children before puberty.

"You're a witch-medium, aren't you?" She analyzed my crystal ball. "Shouldn't that be on a stand?"

"Depends on what you use it for." I stood and turned my chair. I loved playing with clients like this one. "I'm a witch-medium, yes. In the flesh. How can I help you?"

"But she's not—"

"*Shh.*" I barely saw Mordecai elbow Daisy to shut her up. She was far too gullible.

The woman eyed the kids for a moment before looking back to me. "I need you to call my late husband. I have a question for him."

"Uh-huh. How long has your husband been deceased?" I reached forward and grabbed the tarot cards.

She watched my movements. "Two years."

"I see." I shuffled the cards without looking at them. "And what sort of question are you hoping to receive an answer for?"

She pursed her lips. "That's between me and him."

"But that doesn't make sense, since she has to—"

Daisy was elbowed again.

"Yes, of course. Of course it is." I nodded seriously. "Here you go." I passed the tarot deck across the TV tray divider. She hesitated in taking it. "I need to get your impression of him."

Nodding as though that was A) a real thing, and B) made any kind of sense, she took the deck and lifted her chin a little higher. Soon she'd be looking at the sky.

I stifled a laugh. This woman seemed to perfectly encapsulate the term Chester. She hated magic, hated anything related to magic, and she especially hated people who were magical.

Yet here she was, in her own version of hell, wanting help from a witch-medium. My, what tangled webs...

"Go ahead and cut the deck," I said, because everyone knew you were supposed to cut the deck. "Now put the deck on the table in front of you and pull off the top card. Place it face-up." The image of three cartoon mermaids swimming around with cups in their hands stared at the world. I'd mixed and matched tarot decks to get the most outrageous images I could find. They aggravated the Chesters. "Do you think that image identifies with your husband?"

Her eyebrows lowered and red infused her cheeks. She leaned back and crossed her arms over her chest.

I held back my surprise. It did! I'd never had some-one identify on the first flip. Usually they had to go two or three cards to get something significant to them.

Without warning, a man strolled through the thick-ening crowd. His hair receded from his high forehead and his nose took up entirely too much of his face. He wasn't handsome, but self-importance radiated from him.

No one noticed him as he weaved in and out, his back straight and shoulders squared.

"We need to discuss payment," I said, folding my hands in my lap. "Then I will consult the oracle and ask your question."

"The oracle? Don't you speak directly to the de-ceased?" she asked in confusion.

The man saw my client and a few expressions rolled across his face. The last was guilt. He stopped in his tracks before trying to back-pedal.

"Focus on that card," I said, pointing. "He feels guilty over something. He doesn't want to stay."

She snorted. "Yeah, right." She looked to the side.

Clearly she didn't believe me.

I didn't dare speculate. The card suggested infidelity, but if I was wrong, she'd call me a fake and storm off, taking all my fun with her.

"Please focus on the card," I said, but I needn't have bothered. He was close enough for me to reel in, something I only did in this situation. I didn't much like the wiggly thing it did to my stomach. It filled me with nervousness and anxiety and a bit of nausea. Plus, the feeling of the Line throbbed on the edge of my consciousness.

I put out my hands and swayed side to side, hamming it up a little for effect. Chesters hated that as much as they required it to satisfy their preconceived notions of what we did and how we did it. "I'm getting something. A man. Light brown hair streaked with gray. Five ten or so, with a medium build and a slight stomach. A small amount of hair peeks out of his V-neck."

Her eyebrows stayed lowered. She was not impressed, which meant this guy was either the wrong one, or he'd adopted a different image than the one he'd died with. Each was equally possible.

"Right. Fine." I pointed at the man, still being reeled in by my efforts. This had just turned into a grudge match. I needed to prove to this Chester that I wasn't a fake, and forever upset her equilibrium. Just doing my part.

I also wanted to know why he felt guilty. When violence wasn't on the table, curiosity sometimes got the better of me.

"You." I continued to point at him.

My customer scowled.

The man's eyes widened and his mouth dropped open. "Y-you can see me?"

"Yes. What's your name?"

"Puh-Paul."

"Do you always stutter, Paul, or just when you're shocked?"

The woman started and looked over her shoulder, wide-eyed.

Gotcha!

"It's j-just that, no one hears me. N-no one sees me. I can't get anyone's attention," Paul said, hunger lighting his eyes.

Oh no. *That* look. This one was desperate for human connection.

"Do you know that you're dead, Paul?" I asked, ignoring the woman sitting in front of me, staring at me like I'd just sprouted another head.

"I...I'm... Wh-what?" Supreme confusion made his face go slack, and he gripped his shirt. His image flickered, and a slightly older man, with a large stomach and completely gray hair, replaced it. One was what he probably saw in the mirror, and the other was what other people had seen toward the end of his life. You could tell a lot about a person when they were in spirit form.

One thing was clear: he'd have no problem crossing over.

"Right." I turned my attention back to my stunned-mute client. "So. We need to discuss payment, and then I can ask Paul here a question. It was Paul you were wanting, right?"

"You're..." Her face closed down in fear. "You're a..."

"Witch-medium. Filthy magical worker. Awful soul stealer. Look, lady, you sought me out. I have no idea how this could possibly surprise you."

"It's like I'm watching a train wreck in progress," Daisy said in hushed tones, "and I can't look away."

"I don't want to look away. We should've brought popcorn," Mordecai whispered.

"It's just...when they said you were a..." She swallowed. "I thought all this magic stuff was a hoax."

"The Demigod who runs half the city plays with the weather on a regular basis, the news programs love to run footage of shifters changing shape, and you undoubtedly saw all the magical beasts on your way here. How can you still think magic is a load of crap?" I put up my hands. "Congratulations. You win the Most Willfully Ignorant award. You've come a long way, baby."

"No, she didn't," Daisy whispered before giggling.

I did. I totally did. Non-magical people like this were in a strange bubble that had never made much sense to me. Sometimes a good jolt was all they needed.

"Did Janice tell you I was coming?" Suspicion crossed the lady's face.

Sometimes more than a jolt. By someone with more patience than I possessed.

"I don't know Janice. Just as I hope not to know you. The price is forty bucks. But you'd better hurry. Paul is staring at his hands like a baby who's just learned those appendages are attached."

"*Forty...?*" The woman shook her head and pulled her brown leather purse into her lap. Her cut and styled hair, blitzed with hairspray, barely moved in the breeze. "Highway robbery."

"You're the one with the question." I motioned for Daisy to capture the two twenties. "And my children need to eat. You see how big they're getting."

Lips curled in disdain, the woman held on to her bag with a white-knuckled grip. "Ask him—that is, if you really do see him..." My annoyance flared. "If it's his kid. If *she* was pregnant when he got into that car crash."

"Oh shit..." Daisy bit her lip.

I kept my face devoid of emotion and looked at Paul expectantly. He dropped his hands and shoulders. The guilty look returned.

"Well?" the woman asked, her bearing defiant now. She was embarrassed.

"He heard," I said softly, "and it wasn't your fault, what he did. It had nothing to do with you. He was the scum, not you."

I watched her face change. Watched the emotion bleed through. Her lip started to tremble, and unshed tears shone in her eyes before she flicked her head and squared her shoulders.

She was hurting but trying to stay strong. Her embarrassment here was probably echoed in her social group. Man, that sucked.

"It's mine," Paul said, remorse dripping through each soggy word. "I thought we were careful. I always used protection. I never meant to hurt—"

"Can it, Paul, you lying, cheating, shithead bastard." I held up my hand to him.

Knowing crossed the woman's eyes. Her shoulders slumped. I nodded slowly.

Pain creased the lines on her forehead and between her brows. Her back threatened to bow from the heaviness on her shoulders. Her bearing, once purposeful and arrogant, crumpled into something frail.

"He was slime," I said without thinking. "He was. And he knows it. He knew it when he stalked through the crowd to you. But listen to me…" Her eyes inched up to find mine, the strength in them gone. She was an asshole to magical people, but I still didn't want her to go through life feeling worthless. I couldn't, in good conscience, let someone suffer without trying to help. "When you thought of him, he came. When you called, he was pulled to you. He is attached to you. So whatever he was doing with that—likely small—dick of his"— Paul flinched, the no-good, rotten…—"his heart still belonged to you, for what it's worth. He didn't deserve you, but in his mind, you were his and he was yours."

Her eyes held mine like a lifeline. She drank in every word.

"You have two choices," I continued. "You can go home and call him again and then burn some of his stuff so he can see he's definitely dead, or I can send him out of the world of the living. He's ready to go, I can see it. Either way, he won't be here much longer."

"I need…" A stray tear broke free and rolled down her flushed cheek. "I need to burn his stuff?"

"No. You can just show him his death certificate or something, if you want. I just figured you'd want to burn something of his. I mean…I would. I'd create a bonfire out of that shit."

"Just…" She shook her head and stood slowly. "Just send him away."

"Sure. Any last words for him—" I held up my hand for Paul again. "Not you, dickface. You speak when you're spoken to. You forfeited your right to niceties."

She stared at me for a long time, and I thought she'd ask why he'd done it. Living or dead, it didn't matter. Everyone always wanted to know *why* when they were cheated on. But she just shook her head.

"Since the car accident two years ago, all I've thought about is what I would say, what I would do, if I saw him again." She shrugged. "He's gone. We can't work on it. We can't fix this. He's gone." A tear wobbled at the edge of her eye. "I have to move on."

Without another word, she walked away through the crowd, almost a phantom herself. It would take her a long time to recover, but at least now she could heal. That was the main thing. Hopefully someday she'd meet someone who was worth it. And hopefully this experience would make her stop being such a Chester asshole.

Paul watched her go, fading by the moment.

"I'd burn your shit all day long," I said to him, crossing my arms. "All day long."

"Totally," Daisy agreed.

Chapter 20

ALEXIS

B Y THE TIME full night had fallen, the freak show was buzzing. Crowds of people milled around the various tents or stalls, all splendidly arrayed with decorations and hanging canopies. Colorful signs advertised the best *seer* on the West Coast (quite a few people boasted that unproven accolade) or the best cup of coffee in the world. Non-cracked crystal balls held prominent spots on some of the tables, while other tables had a cleared space for smoking cauldrons.

Some patrons smiled and laughed as they toured what to them were various attractions. Others stalked the grounds with grim determination, on a quest or desiring something specific.

"Clearly we need a sign," Mordecai said to Daisy.

The two had been watching the other vendors with acute focus, trying to learn business tricks that would help me rake in more money. And while it was cute, they didn't understand that doing better at this job meant I would actually have to do the job more, and I was already at my peak level of annoyance.

More people than ever before had sought me out tonight. Usually I'd get one or two when I came out here, but in the last few hours I'd had a nearly constant stream of clients. And none of them were tight-fisted! I'd quote a price, sometimes purposely on the high side to make them go away, and they'd cough it up. If hearing what their ghosts had to say wasn't so taxing on my anxiety, I'd be over the moon about the money.

"A sign, and a real table. Like…what is with the TV trays, you know?" Daisy said to Mordecai, watching a woman with an elaborate setup next to us wave her arms over her bandana-clad head as she danced to silent music. She was apparently trying to call the spirits. Spoiler alert: it wasn't working.

"Alexis could do with a bit more theatrics, too," Mordecai responded. "That woman constantly has people at her booth."

"That woman is a bit cheap, though. Fifteen dollars?" Daisy tapped her chin. "If you didn't have a steady stream of people at that rate, would you even make enough to justify your time?"

"You would if you're a hack. Like that woman," I muttered. "She probably doesn't have nightmares, though. Bully for her."

"I think we have to treat Alexis like she's a niche market." Mordecai scratched his head through his beanie, clearly ignoring me. "Even if she put on an act, she wouldn't be able to pull off good customer service."

"Good point," Daisy said. "We need people who are willing to pay more for quality, and also look past a truly atrocious bedside manner."

"Which they will, if their questions are answered." Mordecai sucked his teeth. "So far, it seems like people have received quality."

"Oh yeah. Like that younger girl wanting to ask her pop-pop where he hid his will so the family would stop fighting? Oh my God, that nearly broke my heart." Daisy leaned her elbow on her knee and rested her chin on her fist. "We should've charged her, though. Cute and sad or not cute and sad, everyone's got to pay."

Mordecai shook his head. "A few charity cases are good for public approval."

I rolled my eyes and looked out at the darkened bay, barely able to see the movement of the water in the fog-shrouded moonlight.

"Here comes someone," Daisy whispered. "And he's hot. Lexi, fix your face. You can get a date while you're at it."

Fear and butterflies coursed through my middle as I spun around, terrified I'd see the familiar face that had been haunting me for the last couple days. Instead, a guy in his thirties with unruly brown hair and a pleasing smile sauntered up like he was having a wonderful time at the circus.

My breath left my mouth in a steady stream, but a tiny thread of disappointment had me stilling in unease. That was the wrong feeling to have when it came to the arrogant stranger who'd looked so thoroughly into my life. I liked to flirt with dangerous guys, but he was in a league of his own. Power, brawn, money, and information at his fingertips...he was not someone to be trifled with.

So why did I have absolutely no interest in the attractive man now sitting in front of me?

"Hey," he said, and a cocky smile drifted up his face.

"Hi. What can I do for you?" I clasped my fingers in my lap as a strange sensation niggled at my back between my shoulder blades.

"I heard you can see dead people." He laughed like that was hilarious.

"Oh, here we go," Daisy mumbled. "One of these turds."

Now you're catching on, Daisy.

"Yes. What do you need?" I swiveled my seat to face him, but when I sat down, I glanced right as the strange feeling increased, spreading across my right shoulder and then down my arm. Awareness bit into my skin like stinging nettles.

"Something is...out there," Mordecai said, and his voice cracked with puberty.

"Oh yeah?" The man in front of me followed our gazes with a crooked smile. The crowd drifted past like usual, no one so much as glancing my way. The client scooted his chair up a little, trying to get closer to me. "What was it?" His smile showered me with appreciation and his eyes sparkled in invitation.

"Handsome turd," Daisy muttered. "Ow. I'm going to have a bruise where you keep elbowing me, Sauron."

"Probably just a ghost. They're all over this place." I widened my eyes in an attempt to add some mystery to the lie.

The man laughed.

Yes, I probably could do a little work on the stage act part of it all.

"Anyway, my buddy says that his friend's aunt saw you once, and you, like, told her exactly what her dead cousin looked and sounded like." He bent forward and rested his elbows on his knees, his face now almost as low as the TV trays. "He didn't mention how hot you are, though."

The itching between my shoulder blades intensified and warning shivers spread across my skin. Mordecai pushed himself up onto his knees, looking across me off to the right.

"That shifter part of you is starting to shine through, huh?" I asked him, trying to focus on the guy in front of me and having a helluva time. There were some bad people at the freak show and I'd had more than normal interest in my "booth" today. If someone or something was targeting me, I needed to think about an exit strategy. "Does that mean you can run fast?"

"I sense…something." Mordecai shook his head. "I've never felt this sensation before. I don't know what it means. But I feel aggressive and wary at the same time, and something is telling me the source is over there."

"Don't point!" I slapped his hand out of the air. "If someone's checking us out, pointing will only piss them off."

"Sweet, are you illegal?" the guy said, and I wanted to club him.

Best just to make him go away.

"Who are you wanting to talk to?" I asked.

"What's up with that group?" Daisy whispered. Five big guys formed a loose horde beyond the midnight-blue tent just in front of my setup, their shirt sleeves stretched tight over their large arms and their mustaches curled at the ends.

"I don't know, but they keep looking over here," Mordecai responded. "That's not where I sense the danger from, though."

"Did you see that? That dark-skinned man holding that snake just pointed at us." Daisy moved off her rug and started rolling it up. "Can you run fast, Mordie?

You never answered her. Because I can run very fast."

"I…was hoping to rid myself of a presence." The guy was looking at the kids in confusion.

I absently reached for the tarot deck. "Sure." The snap of cards competed with shrieks of laughter from the midnight-blue tent. The big guys were staring at us pretty openly.

"Beast handlers," I whispered, ripping my gaze forward. If they were interested in me, that meant they'd somehow found out I'd taken one of their parking spots. But they had more to lose by starting something here, so if I pretended not to notice them, all should be well.

I increased the wattage of my smile to epic proportions and leaned forward, leading with my breasts. The buttons prevented cleavage, but often guys could be swayed by the mere idea of cleavage. "Here." I held out the cards. "Cut."

"This is how you see spirits?"

"Nope. That's how *you* call them. I don't see anyone right now—"

"They're coming this way," Daisy said through clenched teeth.

"I don't see anyone," I repeated, recapturing the guy's attention. "So either no one is actually bothering you, or the spirit that's attached to you just isn't present at the moment."

"Ah," he said. "So…how often do you do this stuff?" He gestured at the setup.

Furious tingles scraped along my skin again. I couldn't help but glance to the side. The crowd moved and shifted, but nothing stood out. If there was danger in that direction, it was lying in wait, hiding within the crowd.

In contrast, the group of beast handlers was now coming at me nearly dead center. They needed only to veer around one booth to reach me. My heart sank at the sight of the approaching wall of muscle.

"Every few months," I said, forcing a smile at the client. "Daisy, Mordecai, get out of the way." I breathed evenly, taking the deck back and trying to ignore my jumping heart. The tingle between my shoulder blades was going crazy and my flight reflex was active. "They can't do anything to me," I whispered out of the side of my mouth. "Not in a public place, and not when I'm with someone. That would reflect badly on the whole outfit."

"Do they care?" Daisy said in a tight voice.

I sure hoped so.

"Okay, so I'm going to flip a card. I'll keep going until—" The first of the big guys, six five and stacked with muscle, reached my area. His hair was slicked back into a ponytail and a stupid mustache with the curled edges balanced above thin lips.

"Show's over," the guy said gruffly, and cold trickled down my spine.

I batted my eyelashes, not standing. "Is there a problem? I'm with a client."

One of the other muscle-bound animal guys stopped by said client and grabbed the back of his chair. His tree-trunk arm contracted, and my client tipped forward out of his seat. He reached out to catch himself, grabbing my TV trays and yanking them down with him.

I jumped up. "What's going on?" I shouted, drawing eyes and, hopefully, the notice of security.

The first guy kicked the downed TV stands out of the way and stepped to my side. "Do you own a puke-brown shitty little Honda?"

I brought my hands to my chest as though ready to clutch my nonexistent pearls. I'd be able to strike out faster if my hands were already up. "Puke-brown shitty Honda. Quite the wordsmith. Hmm. Let me think… Yes. Why?"

A couple of the guys crowded in, yanked the TV trays up from around the scrambling client, and flung them to the sides. They clattered across the cement and nearly smacked into the setup of the medium next to me. She and her client startled and half stood.

Mordecai bent to grab one of the TV trays, his blanket coming free from his shoulders and blowing to the ground.

"No!" I held out a hand. Daisy froze in the act of rushing to help him. "Leave it. Stand down."

"Do what she says if you know what's good for you," the lead muscle said.

"Calm down, Mustache. Don't trouble yourself with trying to threaten multiple defenseless persons. You look like you could use a break."

"My boss wants me to deliver a message." Mustache leaned down in my face.

I grimaced and blew out a breath. "Holy smokes. Does your diet consist solely of raw garlic, or what?"

"Stay out of his parking spot," he seethed.

One of his friends threw one of my rugs toward the water. It thunked down far away. He ripped the remaining TV stand from the ground before beating the cheap metal frame against the cement walkway. Another guy looked around at the chairs.

"I found all that on the street, lug nuts. You think this is my first rodeo?" I waited patiently, easily hiding the adrenaline and fear running rampant through my body. Because no, it wasn't my first rodeo, and I knew how to present myself to bullies, no matter how stupid their facial hair.

"Do it again, and you'll be the one smashed on the ground," Mustache said, blowing his hot breath stench into my face.

"Except...no, I won't." I picked at a button on my shirt to keep my hands up, unfortunately not able to hide my shaking.

This was when it would seriously be nice to have some useful magic. Because even if I was queen of the Ghost Whisperers, and had an army of spirits following me around, there wasn't a damn thing they could do to help me besides drain a little energy from my attacker.

I looked over the enormous muscle layering the gigantic frame.

Nope, not a damn thing they could do to help. Not against the five very real guys huddled around my area, waiting to do me harm.

The best I could do was try to keep a cool head.

"Despite my magical blood," I said, "I am protected in this establishment by the Articles of Coexistence, section thirty-two point eight. I have all the necessary, up-to-date paperwork. I am at least four feet from any other stall, and even if I wasn't, I was here first. I parked in a space that was not clearly marked *reserved*. Said space had no signs or paint informing me that I might not be able to park there. Therefore, there is no official claim on that space, and it is governed by the first come, first served policy. I was there first. It is mine. You are welcome to take me to court. Or to petition with the governing body of this fair. Both have been attempted. Both have failed. But still, with your impressive powers of oration, you might stand a chance." I stared at him with watering, unblinking eyes (the breath was intense), letting that sink in. "Oh. And by the by, you wrangle magical beasts, do you not? Did you know that's illegal? It's a punishable offense if you can't prove their origin and come up with a sales document verifiable by the magical governing body. Do you have…such a document?"

I resumed my stare, letting that enormous bluff work its way through his thick skull. They likely did have a fake sales document, and no one would press them to go to the magical governing body. Still, it never hurt to remind these guys that they weren't the top of the food chain. Not when dabbling with magical people. Not even close.

Mustache huffed, and I nearly passed out from the fumes. "Big words for a little girl."

"Actually, I kept the words as small as possible so you could understand. Should I try again?"

His bushy eyebrows lowered over his beady eyes. Muscles popped out over his frame and his fists clenched. He straightened up slowly. It was a bad sign.

"It's easier to beg for forgiveness than it is to ask for permission," he said as he moved in closer.

That was a threat, and it was a damn good one.

I opened my mouth to scream at the kids to run, but a blur of movement made me flinch back. Mustache's fist lifted, and suddenly another large body was right beside me. A strong arm struck the air in front of me, then pushed back, moving me behind his warm, sturdy body. A body that felt exactly as I'd imagined it would from being wrapped in the aching power of its energy field.

Chapter 21

ALEXIS

I T WAS THE stalking stranger!

His fingers lazily wrapped around Mustache's forearm, and though his arm wasn't as big and he wasn't as tall, his strength and power easily topped the other man's. The stranger shoved, and half of Mustache's body jerked backward, forcing him to stagger sideways into one of his cronies.

The guy hadn't brought any friends. He stood alone against a group of five. If it bothered him even a smidgen, I sure as hell couldn't tell.

"This woman is not to be touched. Not by anyone. Do you understand?" The stranger's voice whipped out through the night, making Mustache jerk back and half the crowd startle. They looked in our direction with wide eyes. A moment later, a dozen people pointed.

The stranger's head swiveled, and I knew he was raking his gaze across the five beefed-up bullies. A look of fear rolled across Mustache's face. They visibly shrank before the stranger, and I couldn't hide my shock.

"I apologize, sir," Mustache said, taking a step back. "I wasn't aware she was with you." He put up his hands. "I'll let the boss know. Sorry, sir. Sorry."

"You do that," the stalking stranger said, his demeanor supremely confident. "Right after you tell him that he'll soon be out of business. I'll be looking into his...collection. Personally."

Mustache's eyes widened, but he didn't say another word.

Stunned, I watched as the wall of muscle limped back into the crowd like whipped dogs.

Who the hell was this dude?

Hands still shaking, I stared mutely at my stuff strewn all over the ground. My legs started shaking too. "And this is why I can't have nice things."

The stranger turned to me slowly, the feel of him washing over me and soaking into my blood. My skin tingled with rich, unadulterated desire. My core ached for satisfaction.

"Quick to turn on the charm, eh?" I forced out, trying to level my voice against the onslaught of heady, potent magic that curled around my body in all the right ways.

The stranger minutely bent, his face now inches from mine. His warm breath dusted my face, smelling of chocolate and salty sea foam.

"Just when I think I have a handle on all your oddities, you show up in a place like this and hold court."

"Holy shi—" Daisy muttered. "Her descriptions didn't do him justice. I thought she was exaggerating, but she was under-exaggerating."

"He's the danger I felt," Mordecai whispered. "I still feel it. We need to get away from him."

"We can all hear you," I said. The kid needed to put down the book on trees and pick up one on stealth.

The stranger's eyes roamed my face for one more moment before his head lifted and turned, taking in my wards.

"They don't get out much," I said, hurrying to put myself between him and them. "I don't even think they know how to turn their mouths off. It's a problem. We're working on it." I took a deep breath, trying to still the tremors running through my body. "Get ready to go, kids," I said out of the side of my mouth.

"I can still hear you." The stranger righted one of the chairs before prodding my non-magical would-be client in the ribs with his black, shiny boot. The guy had curled up into a ball, frozen in fear. He wasn't great at survival, clearly. "Feck off."

Like a kid hearing an ice cream truck jingle from afar, I tilted my head to the side. His accent had sounded Irish just now. Like Thick Mick's, almost.

"I wish to purchase a...consultation," he said, his

accent back to what could best be described as generic American. He put the chair in its tape circle and sat. The non-magical guy stumbled to his feet before taking off running.

I stared at the stranger with a buzzing brain. I simply could not make sense of what was happening. An elbow jabbed me in the ribs, jarring me out of my daze.

"Yes, sir," Daisy said loudly, before elbowing me again. "Come on," she whispered urgently. "If he wanted us dead, he would've let those circus clowns with the mustaches do it. Let him buy a…thing. Look at his clothes. He can afford it."

A crowd had gathered around, staring at the stranger with awe or shock. Phones came out and fingers tapped away.

They clearly knew who this guy was. I still did not. Of all the horrible times not to have done my homework.

"Right…" A tangled mess still littered the ground around me, two TV stands twisted and bent, another on its side. "Uh…"

"Get going," Daisy said through clenched teeth.

"I'll give you a moment to fix your station." The stranger swept his fingers toward what remained of my belongings.

"Oh well, that's magnanimous of you," I said sarcastically.

"He just saved your ass. And ours, I might add." Daisy shoved me toward the rug that had been flung. "The least you can do is give him a...thing."

"That guy wasn't going to kill me. Not here," I murmured. "I would've handled it." Part of me even believed that.

Mordecai joined us, his blanket dirty and looped over his arm. He was barely shivering, and luckily, we had plenty of medicine to ensure another cold wouldn't take root.

"I vote we politely decline and get out of here," he said, his voice almost too low to hear. "I sense danger from him, Alexis. I don't know how, and I've never felt this before, but it's a gut instinct, and I think we should trust it."

"Of course he's dangerous. Those clowns all but pissed themselves trying to get away." Daisy picked up the rug and handed it to me. "Predators love a chase. He is clearly a predator, and he has clearly been hunting her. Give him the reading, Lexi. Make him happy—by lying if you have to—and *then* we'll get out of here."

"She's better at survival than you," I said to Mordecai, feeling the gravity of the situation in my gut. "I don't know what he's after, but I doubt he'll leave until he gets it."

"He's toying with you." Mordecai's voice was still just above a whisper, but it had taken on a vicious tone

I'd never heard from him before.

Daisy frowned at him, then patted his arm. "The ring is taking hold of you, huh?" She turned to me. "Hurry. I don't like this any more than you guys do, but what choice is there?"

"I don't know," I said honestly. "I don't know why he keeps turning up. But I might as well talk to him. Maybe he'll realize I'm largely an untalented hack and finally leave me be."

"Don't hit-and-run yourself," Daisy chided. "That lady next to us, with all the arm waving and moaning— she's the untalented hack. You can actually do the magic stuff; you're just an ass about it." She picked up a smashed TV tray. "This one is trash. Do you need it right now?"

"Be nice to that guy," Mordecai said, nearly aggressive in his unease. "Don't give him any reason to take offense."

"Mordie is starting to make me nervous," Daisy said under her breath.

"That's the shifter coming out in him. We'll probably need to talk that through, but first..." I hoisted up the only TV tray that had mostly made it through the Great Mustache Collision. "Just have a seat. We'll leave after this."

I placed the TV tray and rug in front of the guy's chair, then stared down at the tarot cards strewn across the ground. The crystal ball was nowhere to be found, and most likely it had rolled to freedom. If only I could have glanced through it and predicted that turn of events.

Heaving a tired sigh, I collected the cards and placed them on the TV tray, then sat on my chair, the only thing that had survived the animal handlers' tirade.

"Right. Okay." I clasped my fingers in my lap and finally met the stormy eyes of the most devilishly handsome man I'd ever seen. The wind worried his midnight hair, sending strands across his smooth forehead. His sharp cheekbones and straight nose threw shadows in such a way that he looked both noble and incredibly severe. Stubble adorned his strong features, and his high, arching eyebrows might have pushed his striking looks toward harsh instead of beautiful if not for those lush, shapely lips. Those babies pulled the whole look together, bending his ruggedness into something angels would weep over. He had been made by a divine hand.

He waited patiently for me, his gaze intense, his focus absolute.

I looked away, embarrassed and not sure why.

"Start by saying thank you for saving your face," Daisy coached, still playing the unasked-for role of my business manager.

Though she did have a point.

"Thank you." I inched my eyes up, finding his again. They pulled at me, sucking me into a place that lacked gravity. I hovered there, lost in those eyes. In his intensity.

"And now ask what he wants," Daisy said slowly, as though talking to a child.

And she might as well have been.

"Right. Sorry." I tore my gaze away. "I've had a lot of visitors tonight. I'm a bit out of it. Um…" The throng of onlookers continued to watch our unimpressive show. "This is when stage presence would really come in handy."

"Yes, it would. Just work with what you got," Daisy said.

A tiny smile played on the stranger's full lips, but he continued to wait patiently.

"What's your nam—"

"No," Mordecai said, his eyes rooted to the stranger just as surely as the stranger's eyes were rooted to me. "Do it the same way you usually go about this."

Daisy rolled her eyes.

Far be it from me not to trust the guy just because he was developing shifter tendencies.

"Sure. Fine. Just back off, you two. Sorry," I said to the stranger, wanting his name. Wanting to be on more intimate terms with him.

Except he was a stalker, obviously dangerous, and it

was annoying that a couple of kids had way better sense than I did.

"Okay. Let's get to it." I snapped and half considered borrowing a chime from whoever kept ringing the thing a few stalls down. I needed to jog myself out of this daze. "What is it you're after?"

"What is it you offer?" he countered.

"I thought you knew all that. I can see spirits. Or…maybe just ghosts, if spirits and ghosts are different."

"She *definitely* needs to learn more about her craft before we make a thing of this," Daisy whispered.

"Agreed," Mordecai responded.

With effort, I unclenched my jaw. "That's it. So if you have a ghost plaguing you, or if you want to try and contact a ghost, I'm your girl. The exception is if the ghost is on the other side of the Line, and is content to stay there. Then you're out of luck, because it's not right to disrupt a soul because of your selfish desires."

He didn't comment.

"Sorry." I shrugged. "That's all I got."

His stare beat into my head, and I tried desperately to tear my eyes away. His acute focus had unearthed all of my old insecurities. No one had ever noticed me this much, or for such an extended period of time. It was like he had shrugged off the rest of the world, could only hear and see me, and was enraptured by what he was witnessing.

"We won't speak of my desires at the moment, Alexis," he said, making shivers coat my body. "What we will speak of is how you have been grossly mislabeled. Mislabeled and mishandled. Regardless, take me through your skills. Guide me."

What was he saying? I'd been me for twenty-five years. Whatever power he thought I had, my magic didn't do a lot more than the gamut I'd taken it through tonight, and the only people willing to fork over real money for my abilities were career criminals. Besides, I'd been magically assessed like everyone else. Yes, I might have fudged my power level, but magic type was magic type. That couldn't be changed.

I frowned at him, knocked out of the moment. "Well..."

"Show him the cards," Daisy prompted.

"It's like a never-ending car wreck," I muttered, grabbing the tarot because my brain had completely stopped working. "The thing is, I don't guide people unless I can see people lurking around them."

"People, meaning spirits?" he asked.

"Ghosts...?" I lifted the end of the drawn-out word, making it a question. He was making me question everything now.

"They are the same thing." His lips tweaked upward, as though he were trying to ward off a smile.

"Laugh it up, chuckles," I muttered. "Fine. Whatever. But you don't have spirits lurking around you. So unless you have a question for someone specific and can call them here, I'm not much good to you."

His gaze *finally* flicked away, hitting the kids. A moment later, it bounced back, tensing me up again. "I am confident you will be, in time." His words dripped with innuendo, and a flurry of butterflies exploded through my stomach. "As for now, how do you handle someone who's in my position asking for your services?"

"I haven't had many clearly important stalkers blow through, but tarot is a good place to start." The cards snapped as I shuffled. A glance revealed people were still gathered around us, taking it in. "What is it you do aside from following innocent, unassuming women around and making your demands known?"

He didn't shift, flinch, move, or answer me, all things a normal person might've done if that question was randomly lobbed at them. The only change was a subtle gleam lighting his eyes.

"All right, then." I reached the deck forward.

He looked at the offering, but didn't bend forward in the chair to collect it.

"Really?" I lifted my eyebrows. He still didn't bend for it. "Do you want them on a silver platter?" I stood and reached the cards across the TV tray, getting them closer to him.

Finally, he extended his hand and took them.

"Happy days," I mumbled, sitting back down. If he'd been someone else, I definitely would've told him to get bent and find someone else to wait on him. "Go ahead and cut those."

His eyes dipped before he turned the deck over and fanned out the cards, looking at the pictures. A small crease formed between his brows, but he didn't comment. The cards slid against each other as he shuffled, not nearly as practiced as me.

"Sure. Shuffle, if you want," I muttered. "Have you done this before?"

"What do you mean by *this*? Visit a horror show intent on displaying the worst of our magical society and beasts that could not choose their fate?" He paused for a beat. "Yes. I've torn a great many of these things down. This one, however, wasn't on my radar. It isn't very large compared to some I have seen. It didn't seem of pressing importance. I'd had no idea that magical slaves and imprisoned beasts were the preferred fare, however. Thank you for bringing it to my attention."

"Me?" I flinched back so hard that my chair went up on two legs. That was all I needed—the people in this fair thinking I was the tattletale who'd fucked them out of a job. "Whatever enlightenment you've found has nothing to do with me."

"He followed you here." Mordecai spoke in a level voice, but I could hear the wariness coating each word. "He came because of you."

"Oftentimes, the answer to a question can be gleaned by seeking out more information," the stranger said. "Only, in your case, the puzzle keeps getting more intricate."

"I have no idea who he is talking about right now, because Alexis is, literally, the most boring adult I've ever met," Daisy said to Mordecai. "Except for her weekly jaunts to the bar, she has, quite literally, no life."

"You've reached your quota on using the word 'literally,'" I said dryly. "And we can *still* hear you."

I didn't think I needed to remind her of the kind of adults she'd known prior to meeting me. It was what had landed her with me in the first place.

"Or did you mean," the stranger said, ignoring our family squabbles, "have I paid for the services of a Ghost Whisperer before in order to speak to those beyond?" He paused again. "No, I have not. Because they wouldn't take my money for services rendered."

"No offense, sir, but we'll be taking your money," Daisy said. "Ow! Keep it up, Mordie, or you'll end up like Boromir."

"Or do you mean—"

"I didn't realize there were so many layers to such a simple question," I said.

"—have I ever sat in a fold-out chair struggling to take my weight, in front of a rickety TV tray covered in a stained rug, across from a beautifully entrancing woman who is attempting to be a Ghost Whisperer, while two teenagers organize and practically run the business, with a crowd of onlookers at my back?"

"He called her beautifully entrancing," Daisy whispered. "I think I just fell in love a little."

"He's been stalking her, without invitation, for days, and he won't disclose his employment or any personal information," Mordecai replied. "He's someone we should call the police on."

They both had a point, as usual.

"No, I have not," the stranger said, still (somehow) ignoring the pubescent peanut gallery a few feet away.

"Okay. So you have seen someone who talks to spirits," I said. Best to get the show on the road.

"Yes, I have," he answered. "They were not able to answer my question."

"Ah. There we go. You have a question." I crossed an ankle over a knee. "Great. That's a good place to focus. Do you want to tell me who the question is for?"

"No."

"Super. Do you want to tell me what the question is?"

"No."

"Great. We're off to a fairly normal start. So go

ahead and shuffle until you're content, then put the cards on the rickety old TV tray that I found on the street—in case you were wondering—and we'll get started."

"One might look at the conditions in which you live your life and assume you have no pride in yourself, your magic, or your profession," he said matter-of-factly.

"Many assume that, actually." I rose, picked up my chair, and turned it sideways. I couldn't see much of the water, but I enjoyed feeling the salty air softly muss my hair. I'd rather ignore his handsome face and look out at mostly nothing than attempt to relax within his hard-core focus.

"That doesn't bother you."

"Not at all. It's liberating, actually. I know what box they've put me in, and I generally know how they'll act toward me, too."

"You are creating a predictable environment in an unpredictable life situation."

I turned down my lips in thought, then shrugged. "That sounds about right, yes."

"I assume this is the…young man for whom you bought the turquoise blanket?"

"Was it the turquoise blanket wrapped around his shoulders that gave it away?"

"Yes."

I couldn't help but laugh. "You've nailed it. Amazing that I'm such a puzzle to you, what with your fantastic powers of observation."

"What ails him?"

I closed my eyes against the breeze, letting calm roll over me. "That's not my information to disclose."

"I apologize. I wanted to give you the chance to tell me yourself. The nature of his...condition is in his file."

"Which you looked up," I said softly.

"Naturally. A young person in his situation, living in poverty and without the resources of his pack, would rarely live past the beginning of puberty. He is nearly cresting, if I'm judging the surges of his power correctly. How have you kept him alive?"

"Hope and a prayer." I clasped my hands. "And a few ugly blankets."

"She sacrifices for us," Mordecai said with a note of pride in his voice. Also sadness. "She sits here, with her rickety setup, and lets the masses belittle her. For us. She takes odd jobs that are way below her intelligence level. She begs, takes handouts, and doesn't have any use for pride, all because she wants to give us the chance at a future. So while you sit there on your high horse, inspecting her choices like she's some colorful yet insignificant bug, she's busting her ass to give us a chance. She's forfeiting her own life so that we get to have one. You won't ever find a truer, bigger-hearted person in the world. So you should pack up your enormous ego and go find someone else to mildly threaten with your presence and your interest. We have enough problems around here."

Heat prickled my eyes at his speech, overcome a moment later by fear. I didn't know what the stranger's situation was, but he had clout if he could keep the non-magical people in this freak show away from me. I also knew there were limits to the amount of abuse the guy would take. Being a woman who perplexed him, I'd gotten a momentary pass while he toyed with me a while longer.

Mordecai wouldn't get the same lenience. And I didn't know how to protect him.

Chapter 22

ALEXIS

"**D**ON'T MIND HIM." I tried to keep the worry from my voice, still looking out over the bay. "He's—"

"Exactly right," the stranger finished softly. "Thank you, Mordecai. You have fit a piece of the puzzle into place."

"Good job, Mordie." Daisy sniffed.

"Do you get that medicine at a discount?" the stranger asked.

"I thought you had extensive records on magical people?" I couldn't help it. There didn't seem to be any rhyme or reason to what the guy knew and what he didn't.

"Mordecai was left for dead, and the pack has been operating on the belief that nature took its course. Their records are lacking, and as such, so are—" The chair squeaked as the stranger shifted. I glanced over, but his face was a hard mask, giving nothing away. "The girl is not in our records at all."

"I'm a Chester," Daisy said. "Also left for dead."

"*Shh.*"

"I swear to God, Mordie, if you elbow me one more time—"

"She's not a Chester." I cradled my head in my hand, suddenly exhausted. "She's not nearly that ignorant. Or arrogant. But she is non-magical, and her situation, if she were to go back to the non-magical foster system, would be a nightmare. And no, we do not get the medicine at a discount."

"Does a five-finger discount count?" I could hear the laughter in Daisy's voice.

"Elbow her, Mordecai," I said.

"I see." The cards slid against each other in the stranger's hands.

"Do you?" I wasn't sure what prompted me to ask, but there it was, out in the world.

Silence dropped around us, then stretched. The heaviness of it competed with the shrieks and roars of the fair around us. Finally, when I was about ready to turn my head and look at him again, if only to see what danger clouds lurked on his expression, he said, "No. I've never known poverty. I've never watched a loved one suffer because I couldn't afford the treatment she— or he—needed."

That had been a slip, and now I did turn my head.

A shadow sliced across the stranger's face, partially

covering the simmering fury in his expression. One eye, catching the light of the fair, shone bright with viciousness.

But under it all existed pain. A hollowness he couldn't seem to fill.

His magic rose around me, but this time it was different. Instead of the sexiness and passion I'd felt at the bar, which had nearly driven me to questionable life decisions, I felt a vast emptiness. The salty breeze took on a life of its own, its caress turning into a longing for the rise and fall of the waves. The song of the ocean drifted to me from the bay, mournful yet beautiful, blanketing my heart.

A tear slipped from my eye as I tucked into this feeling like I had the sexy-type magic. Its beauty captivated me. Its vitality invigorated me. But that sadness weaving within it broke my heart.

The presence came slowly, from a place I never would've thought to look.

Turning my head toward the bay, I saw it despite the darkness: arms swinging up and down, stroking a path through the water. The body attached to them rode a wave up, then sank into the swell. The person disappeared as he or she neared the edge of the large dock, only to float up again. This time she ascended the dock, revealing a long, white flowing dress and bare feet pointed elegantly like a ballerina's.

The wind whipped her raven hair around her beautiful face, the breeze she was experiencing different than that of reality, her chosen place of un-rest wild and blustery. She hadn't, or maybe wouldn't, acclimate to her new surroundings. This wasn't her home.

Her bare feet, still wet, touched down onto the dirty ground beside the dock, and spirit or not, I couldn't help but grimace with the grime they'd be touching. Her movements were elegant as she drifted toward and then past me.

Slightly in awe, because I'd never seen anything like that—and I thought I'd seen it all—I rose and turned my chair to again face the stranger. The woman stopped beside him, staring down at him with adoration.

"You were expecting a woman, I take it," I said, clasping my hands in my lap. I didn't notice the stranger's reaction because I couldn't take my eyes off her, she was so beautiful. "In life, was it like an ethereal glow radiated out from her? Like she was lit up from within?"

"Yes," he said in a release of breath, and though I could tell he was trying to keep his voice flat, a slight tremor jiggled his words.

"She's young. My age." High, arching eyebrows sat above large blue eyes and a thin, dainty nose. Sharp cheekbones and a strong jaw defined her face, the look completed by lush, shapely lips. She was a soft, feminine version of the stranger. "Is she a sister, or is this her chosen age and not the age she was at death?"

"You see her?" His throat was tight, and I finally switched my focus.

He'd leaned forward, staring at me, not in the intent way from earlier, but hard, like he was willing words to come out of my mouth. Earnestness and longing clouded his expression, and the muscles on his sizable frame flexed.

"She's here, yes. Beside you. Looking down on you. She loved you very much, and it transferred into death." I scratched my chin. "So your mother, then, because I don't think a sister would be that gushy about the situation."

"Your age, you said?" he asked. "Twenty-five?"

"Around there, yes. I'm not a master at telling ages."

"Before she met my father." His jaw clenched.

"Hey, look." I leaned forward as well, dropping my hands to my knees. "That doesn't mean she loved you any less. It just means that she was happiest with her appearance at that age. When my mother died, she assumed the age of twenty-two. She told me I'd ruined her body beyond repair and she was happy to go back to a time when she didn't grimace every time she looked in the mirror. So that's probably all this is."

"Can you speak to her?"

It didn't seem like he'd heard anything I'd just said.

"Yes. What would you like me to say?"

"Just…speak to her. See if she can hear you."

I frowned, because that was weird. Of course she could hear me. She could hear everyone in the living world, trapped here as she was.

"Her name?" I asked.

He shook his head.

"Look, I'm trying my best to be respectful of the situation, but you're making things awfully difficult." When he didn't offer any more information, I sighed and went about things the way I normally did. "Hey, lady in the white dress…"

"She can be professional, it's just that she usually doesn't want to be," Daisy said, always thinking about business. That would be good someday. If only she'd put it off until then.

The woman's head turned slowly toward me.

"Yes, you. I can see you," I said, suddenly showered in a kind of regal regard that made me want to sit up straight and comb my hair. The woman's eyes drifted over my body and then back to my face before glancing back at the stranger.

"He can't see or hear you. Only I can. Try me out. See how it goes."

She adjusted her stance until she was facing me, her eyes soft and kind, but expectant. She was a woman who'd had support staff, but she hadn't been a dick to them. That was at least nice.

"You can just…say anything you want. Anything at all. Maybe your name? We can start there." She stared at me. To the stranger, I said, "She obviously passed that stare down along with the looks. My God, the two of you probably made people quail when you were in the same room."

"What is this place?" she finally asked in a voice like a bell.

"Holy crap, this woman was a heartbreaker," I murmured. "We're in San Francisco. In America."

"San Francisco…" A flash of soft anger pinched her expression. I'd never known anger could be soft, but she did it well. "My son is trying to free me. Even still."

"Are you trying to free her?" I asked the stranger. His eyes hardened and his fists flexed.

"To admit it would be death," she said in a harsh voice, and I felt like a whipped dog. "His father would never permit it."

"How dumb of me," I said quickly. "Stupid me. She said *be* her. Dress in skirts, that sort of thing."

"Oh boy," Daisy said.

"Forget it." I waved the issue away. I was terrible at improv. "Why haven't you crossed over?" I asked her.

"A selkie is trapped by the land without her skin," the woman said. "And in death, trapped in the world of the living."

I pushed back against my chair, sadness washing over me. That issue rang a bell in my memory.

If some asshole land-dweller stole a selkie's seal skin, the selkie would be trapped on land until the skin was returned. In that time, the selkie, a very sexual, loving, and clearly forgiving creature, would marry said asshole and have kids with him or her.

Rumor had it that selkies never stopped looking for their skins. It was like a shifter who couldn't heed the moon's urging to change. Like Mordecai. Given what I saw him go through every month, with or without that medicine, denying the magic created a horrible itch inside him, impossible to completely ignore.

And now I saw that even death would give a selkie no comfort. She was here until she reclaimed her skin.

"So…does the skin…die with you, or is it just…hanging out wherever the dickhead thief stashed it, or…?" I asked.

"It is in this strange plane with me. Somewhere."

"Hmm. Mmhm. So you just need to pull it to you and slip it back on then?"

Her head tilted and she took a step toward me. "Pull it to me?"

"Yeah. Just…think about it really hard, and feel it with everything you have, and long for it, and it really should come sailing back to you. I mean, that's what your son did, and here you are, all the way from…?"

A crease formed between her brows, matching the one on her son's face. She minutely shook her head, and I just barely registered the stranger's intensity beating into me, his gaze now determined as well as vicious.

"Right. So that's another hush-hush topic. Got it."

The stranger wanted to find her skin for her so she could be at peace. That was what she'd meant by setting her free.

"How'd you know she needed her skin?" I asked.

"As I said," he replied, "I've seen a few of...your kind before."

The hitch in his speech made it seem like he didn't think they were my kind at all. But then, if he had a habit of visiting fairs like this, he'd probably gotten the losers of the trade.

"They were useless," his mother said, her tone dripping with arrogance. Somehow, she still seemed lovely despite it. A true gift. "The strongest of them did not look at me, as you are doing. They did not hear me. They felt me, sure enough, and got a few of my words correct, but they all mangled the message before sending him on his way."

"Right. Well, in fairness, most people who have my magic set up shop as mediums because they don't have enough juice for the big-paying jobs, like with the cops or on TV or whatever."

"What did she say?" the stranger asked.

I told him quickly.

"One of the women was employed by the Demigod of London," the stranger said with derision. "She was heralded as the top of her trade. Useless."

"You two have spent a lot of time together, I can see." I mock-grimaced at them before moving on. "So you've tried to pull...*it* to you, and nothing happened?"

"I felt the need for it when I first entered this strange plane," she said wistfully. "The longing. But though it continues to call to me, I cannot find it. I have searched every place I know, including my husband's many estates..."

Her voice had turned harsh by the end, still lovely and lilting, but more like the sea surging over jagged, ship-smashing rocks.

"Huh." I bit my lip, racking my brain for an answer to this riddle. "And you know you're dead, I take it?" Her look was enough to wither flowers. "Right. Of course."

I rested my forearms on my knees, thinking.

"She's smart and talented. You should enlist her aid," I heard the woman say.

"Thankfully, he can't hear you," I replied.

"What?" the stranger asked.

I ignored him. I'd already been sucked into helping one dangerous criminal; I didn't need to get sucked into helping a man who was probably ten times as dangerous, especially since that man was an extremely powerful magical person who didn't understand personal boundaries.

"Have you enlisted the help of a medium specializing in calling the dead from the other side?" I asked.

"Isn't that what you do?" the woman countered.

"Well...yes. But your skin isn't dead, and I've had no experience with this. I just meant a person with all the bells and whistles who can put a lot more *oomph* behind the calling."

"If we don't push through our fear, we will never learn what it means to achieve true success," she said.

I lifted my eyebrows. "I'm not afraid. I just don't know how I'd even go about something like this."

"Then you must try." She trailed the back of her hand down her cheek, a dainty gesture indicating she was tired. "I must go. I have no stamina in this plane. Please hurry. My son has suffered for far too long. He must release me so he can finally live his life in peace. Help him."

With that, her form flickered, then blinked out.

"It wasn't lack of energy; she just wasn't comfortable so far away from her un-resting place," I mumbled, mostly to myself.

I blew out a breath, thinking it all over. Somehow, without actually asking, she'd roped me into helping her.

No. Not roped me in, *tried* to rope me in. I felt for her situation, I really did. But I had absolutely no experience in these matters and wouldn't know the first thing about calling someone's shifter skin. Like…was that even possible?

I leaned back in my chair, utterly spent, belatedly realizing the crowd that had gathered around my space was now at a distance. As in, someone had pushed them back and kept them there.

That was when I saw the crew of guys, all in suits, standing guard at the edge of the crowd. The stranger had a team of men, it seemed, and clearly he didn't want anyone hearing his business. I had no idea how long they'd been there.

"So that's what all this has been about, huh?" I asked, making a circle in the air with my finger. "The stalking, the checking up on me—you're trying to get someone to help…that certain person…find the thing so you can go about your business?"

"Has she gone?" Sadness crossed his features before they snapped back to stony. His body tensed. "Did she ask you for your help?"

I let my eyebrows crawl up my forehead and lied like a thief. "Nope. No. She didn't. Because I don't have any experience in this stuff and couldn't possibly help. So." I stood so fast that the blood didn't have time to get to my head, and I staggered a bit. "Come on, kids. Let's pack up."

He stood like a snake uncoiling, smooth and grace-ful. His hand dipped into his pocket, but before I could tell him not to pay, he nodded and turned. He stalked off through the crowd without a word. His men peeled off after him, a well-oiled machine.

"What the…" Daisy hopped up. "Did he just take off without paying?" She scoffed and stamped her foot. "What a cheap… After you did all that?" She shook her head. "Bitch better give us our money. I'll knock on his damn door if I have to."

"Leave it," I said softly, ignoring the people pushing toward me. Clearly the stranger was an attraction all his own, and now they'd want in on it. No, thank you. "Let him go."

I rolled up my rug, a very bad feeling lodging in the pit of my stomach.

"Unfortunately," I muttered, "I have a feeling he'll be back."

Chapter 23

KIERAN

KIERAN COULD HARDLY speak. He'd given powerful Ghost Whisperers ten times as much information as he'd just given Alexis. Uttering one word would've been more than he'd just given her. And yet she'd read the situation perfectly.

The others had tried to send his mother beyond the Line. They'd chimed their bells and fanned their candles, but in the end, he'd received only their condolences. They couldn't force a spirit that did not want to go.

Alexis hadn't even tried. She'd listened to the problem, directly from the source, and immediately tried to problem-solve. His stomach exploded in fireworks.

"She's legit," Zorn said, voicing Kieran's thought. Zorn caught up to Kieran and kept pace. They walked along the sidewalk to a distant parking lot. People stopped to gawk, recognizing Kieran's face. "I had my suspicions, but…"

"I've had people testing her all night. She has left

them in complete awe." Kieran shook his head and threw out his hand. Fog blasted down from the sky before swirling through the street, creating a thick white wall.

Drivers slammed on their brakes, squealing to a stop. He was already walking, crossing in front of them before waving his hand again and dissipating the weather effect.

"*I'm* in complete awe." He stepped up onto the far curb. "Make sure she gets home okay."

"Donovan is on it."

"Tear down that fair. Make sure those beasts are placed in the magical reserves, and ensure the slaves have enough resources to start an independent life. Let the mayor know that I can be reasonable with regards to a magical fair, but it must be run correctly. What he allowed is appalling."

"Of course, sir." Zorn climbed the stairs of the parking garage behind him. "The standard letter, then?"

"Yes." Kieran reached his car and paused, his mind and body both buzzing. "She didn't slice down my chest once tonight."

"Progress."

"Was it? Or are there different magics at work?" He pulled his wallet from his pocket so he wouldn't be sitting on it, then opened the car door. "Bring her in to be tested. I need to see what's under the hood."

"And the boy?"

Kieran stopped, having descended halfway into his car. He eyed Zorn in confusion. "What about him?"

"He has incredible potential, and he is one of the two things she cares about most in the world."

Kieran had been so blinded by her incredible beauty, and the rich feel of her delicious magic, that he hadn't noticed much else. She was becoming a weakness. A distraction. Something he craved when having spent too long without her quick wit and sparkling eyes.

Something he should cut out of his life immediately so as not to be consumed by her. But he needed her. He needed her magic.

He stilled for a moment, letting the rush of feeling course through him. Heavens, he wanted her. Like he'd never wanted any other woman. She was exciting and mysterious. The things she did for those kids would inspire saints, and she'd stood up to those beast handlers with unbelievable courage. She was strong and fierce, but soft-hearted. Utterly unique. If he wasn't careful, she would become an obsession.

He gritted his teeth, forcing his thoughts away from her and focusing on the boy. The power within him was raw and mighty, throbbing with the need to break free. He was probably a class four now, but he'd see a huge power boost as he continued to go through puberty. He'd be a class five, easily, like his father before him.

"He should be dead," Kieran said. "How has she kept him alive?"

"I think that is a mutual achievement. She and the girl ward fight to keep him alive as much as he fights through the pain out of his fear of hurting them, even in death."

Guilt, sharp and hot, rose through him, riding the coattails of more memories of those sick kids in the hospital in Galway. Of their struggle to keep going, even though their bodies were riddled with cancer. Of the way he'd watched them, day after day, and done nothing. Not until the end, when half of them had been lost.

"Get him tested. See if he can be cured," Kieran said, getting into his car.

Zorn nodded and turned away.

Kieran shut his door but didn't turn on the car just yet. Guilt still tore at him.

Because he knew he wasn't just doing this for the kid's sake.

If he helped the boy, he'd reel in the woman. When it came to manipulating a situation, Demigods were in a league of their own, and he was better than most.

Of course, Alexis didn't seem like a woman to let a stranger dictate her future.

A smile, unbidden, curled his lips. He looked forward to the fireworks.

Chapter 24

ALEXIS

"**M**AIL," DAISY CALLED from the front of the house.

I heard paper slap against wood and knew she'd thrown it down on the kitchen table.

I straightened up from the laptop and worked my knuckles into the knots in my back. I'd been bent over the thing all day, researching the situation regarding a selkie unable to obtain his or her skin in death. I hated not knowing things, and a part of me did feel bad for the stranger's mom. Being stuck in the world of the living had to feel like purgatory. It was a crappy existence.

There wasn't a whole lot of information, though. Apparently, it was widely known that if the holder of the selkie's skin had any sort of respect for the selkie at all, he or she would return said skin to the selkie on their deathbed so that he or she might slip into the eternal waters upon their demise. In fact, in many places, it was regulated by law.

That failing, the holder of the skin would burn it so that the selkie could easily find the skin on the other side. *That* failing—because let's face it, only an asshole would imprison another creature for their own benefit, and assholes didn't give two shits about what was moral, in death or otherwise—it was widely believed the selkie could call the skin as a spirit, thus making it disappear.

Well, the stranger's mom had clearly been calling the skin, and nothing was happening.

So what the fuck?

"Did you—"

I jumped at the sudden sound as Daisy poked her head into my room.

"Wow. Jumpy much?" She grinned. "Did you hear me? Mail."

"Yes. Thank you for that pressing news. I haven't been able to sit still out of anticipation. Now I can rest. Finally."

"Ew." She turned her eyes to the ceiling and disappeared. "One's official looking, though."

"Is it a bill?" I called.

"The house isn't that big, you guys," Mordecai said from his bedroom next door. "You don't have to shout."

"Go back to your trees, Treebeard," Daisy shouted. "And I don't know if it's a bill. It's from a magical committee of something-such."

Frowning, I shut the laptop and pushed up from the bed. I stopped in Mordecai's room and handed off the computer. "I'm finished."

He looked up from his book before reaching for it. "Find out anything?"

"Nothing useful."

"Did you hear from that guy?"

I leaned against his doorframe, thinking back two nights. After the stranger disappeared into the crowd, the kids and I had cleaned up as best we could and lugged all our stuff to the car, continually telling the onlookers that we were closed for business. One of the men who'd been on crowd control stood by the car, strong and stoic, his glare making everyone give the car a wide berth.

He'd gotten there a bit late, though, since a new key scratch adorned the right side. It had a few friends.

"No," I said, "but it's only been a couple days."

"Yesterday was the only day he hasn't stalked you since you two met," Mordecai said, his eyes somber. He had not been taking this situation well. I couldn't tell if it was his shifter traits coming through more strongly now, or just plain ol' sense. "Something is up."

I shrugged. "I told him I couldn't help, while letting him see my life in all its poor splendor. He probably recognized a bad bet when he saw one."

Mordecai studied me for a moment before bending

back to his book. "I can see you don't believe that."

He was right. I didn't. But there wasn't a whole lot I could do about the situation.

"What'd you get up to today, Daisy?" I asked as I walked into the living room.

She had just grabbed a badly used textbook from the coffee table before sitting down. "Had an interview with Denny's dad, let Denny take me out to lunch, and read with him in the park. All in all, a pretty nice little day."

I paused on my way to the kitchen, because it was time to be a parent, no matter how much I didn't want to. "I thought we talked about you spending time with Denny, and about you getting a job for his dad."

"We did." She flipped open the hardcover. "But we also discussed what that mobster's ghost said. I knew we shouldn't send that kind of letter from here, so I grabbed an envelope from Denny's dad's office on the sly. I told him the job wasn't for me. It's fine."

I stared at her with a gaping mouth.

She licked her thumb and turned the pages, hunting for a specific section.

"I was just going to call it in," I said.

"There's no way they would have let you leave an anonymous message." She flicked a page. "At best, they would have only taken your name. Then, if the lead checked out, they would have come searching for the source of the information. Hello? Don't you read detective stories?"

"No, I don't. And also, I've called in loads of anonymous messages. It's always been fine."

"Have any of those tips been incriminating to a mobster who may or may not have people on the inside?"

"We don't even know if that guy was a mobster."

"Don't we?" She lifted her brows before flicking another page.

I sighed, giving up. "Stay away from that family," I said as I turned. "I mean it, Daisy."

"I will, I will. But Denny is pretty good company."

"Stay away!"

"*Fine.*" She huffed.

At the kitchen table, I separated the mail into a large pile (the trash) and a tiny pile (stuff that mattered). I pushed aside a water bill that I could blessedly pay because I'd helped a criminal and probably upset my karma, and picked up the letter Daisy had alluded to.

"SF's Magical Governing Committee," I read, slipping my finger into the end as apprehension wiggled my gut.

The SFMGC, comprised of officials chosen by the Demigod's office, didn't have anything to do with the freak show, so it couldn't be a notice that my permit had been revoked. With the large haul I'd taken in a couple nights ago, and the trouble I'd caused, I'd decided to take the rest of the week off. But I hadn't been looking very hard for a job. I'd need to go back to the fair on Monday, after the hubbub died down, and see if I could stay under the radar a little better. I'd even leave the choice parking spaces to the big dogs.

Why else would they have written to me? I'd only ever received letters from these guys when they'd wanted to test me...

My thought trailed away as my ire rose.

I ripped the rest of the way into the letter and scanned the contents.

"That filthy bastard," I said too loudly.

"What?" The couch protested in a series of squeals before Daisy jogged in. "What happened? Is it the insanely hot guy with the unbelievably banging bod that we all hate? What did he do?"

"He wants me to be retested for magic, which is fine. I don't know why this is necessary, since he clearly thinks he knows everything, but whatever. It's an annoying afternoon followed by too much Guinness. But he also wants Mordecai tested again, which..." I crunched the letter in my fist. "Which is not going to happen."

"Why? Aren't you curious?"

"No. Do you know why?"

"*Obviously.*"

"Because when Mordecai was tested last, he was

young, in bad shape, and everyone thought he didn't have much longer to live. Well, he's still alive, he is definitely going to be a powerhouse, and he's almost at the age where the alpha of his old pack can challenge and kill him." Hot tears blurred my eyes. "I have busted my *ass* to keep Mordecai under the radar. People thought he was dead, which meant he was safe. And now this asshole thinks he can waltz into my life and endanger my kids?"

I slammed the paper down on the table.

"Over my dead fucking body." I swatted hair out of my face and wondered if I could call the stranger's mother. I mean, I *could*. Once I'd met a spirit, I could almost always summon them. I could get that woman in here so fast she'd wonder who'd ripped the water out from under her. And I'd give her a good talking to on how she'd raised her entitled, arrogant, life-endangering son.

But what would that do? He couldn't see her or hear her. I'd be badgering a dead woman. Though she kind of deserved it, considering the monstrosity of a man she'd cultivated.

No. No, I was better than that. Slightly.

But I wasn't better than tracking that bastard down and giving him a piece of my mind.

"I'm going to the pub." I stalked to the counter and snatched up my handbag. "I'm going to summon up a little liquid courage while I take to Google, and this time, I'm actually going to find him. No more letting a bunch of celebrity gossip crap deter me. I'll do it, and then I'm going to bring the fight to him."

I wasn't awesome at stalking people, online or otherwise, which had proved a huge stumbling block in my attempt to unmask the handsome stranger. With my burning curiosity about his mom weighing on me, I'd given up before I'd found anything.

"Oh my God. Wait." Daisy stood in the entryway of the kitchen with her hands out.

"You're not going."

"Of course I'm not going! It's a bar and he's dangerous. But…you need…something."

She dashed out of the kitchen.

"I need an army of large men, and probably an Uzi. That's what I need. But I have my mouth, and I can stoop to foul play. I know stuff about Mommy dearest, after all. And you know what? Since he decided to fight dirty, I will make him rue the day he challenged me in a battle of 'who will punch below the belt the hardest.'"

Daisy's feet thundered back down the hall and she appeared in the kitchen holding an ankle brace fitted with a dagger. "Use this."

"Oh." I'd forgotten I had it. She'd clearly been rooting around in my stuff again.

That discussion could wait until later.

"Great, thanks." I strapped it on and practiced pulling it out. "For reachability's sake, it would be better on my thigh."

"Your thigh is too fat."

"It's muscle, you twit." Ish.

I draped my purse across my body and took a deep breath. I was about to go out in search of a fight with a giant, super-fast, super-strong, super-magical, super-rich, super-handsome dude.

What was I thinking?

"I'm thinking that Mordecai will not be pushed around, that's what I'm thinking." I balled my fists in determination.

"Okay." Daisy nodded at me and braced like she was about to lift something. "Good thinking. You are strong. You are powerful. You can. You can."

"What?"

"That's a mantra. I am strong. I am powerful. I can. I can!"

I could get my butt beaten up. The other two were just wishful thinking.

"I am good in a pinch," I corrected, making up my own mantra. "I am good at surprise-hitting powerful people in vulnerable places. I will. I fucking will!"

"Yes. Okay. Go with that!" Daisy followed closely behind me to the front door. "Call the house if anything happens. I've driven before. I can run a bitch over, no sweat."

"That's good to know."

I opened the door to Frank standing outside, wringing his hands.

"Not now, Frank," I said without stopping.

"Ew. Just send that poltergeist to the other side," Daisy said, her bravado fading quickly.

"It's not nice when they don't want to go," I called, power-walking to the sidewalk. "Besides, Ms. Merlin is a real jerk and could use some haunting."

"Where are you going?" Frank caught up with me quickly, and because I needed something to keep my mind off what I was doing, I didn't chase him away.

"I am going to protect my homestead, Frank, in a brash and possibly crazy way."

"Oh. So how was your day?"

"It was lovely, Frank. A real nice time."

"Oh. That's good." And Frank, taking one of his few opportunities to talk to someone who could hear him, launched into a series of annoying and mostly boring stories about how he was nearly positive he had a ghost in his house.

He'd died with Alzheimer's, and half the time, he forgot he *was* the ghost.

"Okay, Frank," I said once we reached the bar on the outskirts of the neighborhood. I was somewhat winded. It had been a fast walk that had seemed significantly faster with Frank's chatter. "Time for business."

"Okay." Frank looked around. "Do you know how to get home?"

"Yes." I pulled open the door, greeted by the low light and stale aroma of sick and alcohol. A roar of laughter rolled out of the back by the pool table, from a crowd of people keeping to themselves. I marched up behind the row of patrons sitting at the bar, my eyes on Cindy the bartender. If felt like the heavens had opened up and sung.

I'd forgotten all about her! She was a huge gossip. If anyone knew anything about that handsome stranger, it would be her.

As I rounded the soft corner at the other side of the bar, aiming for my seat, a large back greeted me. A jet-black head of wind-swept hair turned a fraction. The owner had clearly seen me walk in and now monitored my progress.

The stranger, and he'd been expecting me.

A wave of adrenaline dumped into my middle. I stutter-stopped—or maybe jumped and staggered, I couldn't be sure—before stalking forward again and stopping behind my chair. And it *was* my chair, too. He hadn't stolen it. He'd stolen the one next to it, on the non-Mick side.

"Good. I'm glad you're here. I have a bone to pick with you," I said to the stranger in a thick, hopefully scary voice.

Chapter 25

ALEXIS

"**I** FIGURED. SIT." The stalking stranger gestured at my chair as though he owned it.

Best to establish independence in this situation, or he might think he'd gained the dominant position.

"I'd planned on it." I pulled out my seat so I could slide in without brushing my front against his large, powerful arm. "What's up, Mick?" I said to the ever-present moody regular.

Mick grunted. "Not a lot has happened since you left. I'm just keepin' on top of it," he said dryly, his thick Irish accent made thicker with heavy drinking.

Half a beer and a mostly gone tumbler of whiskey sat in front of him. He was on his way toward getting sloppy, sleeping-at-the-bar drunk. Once he started the whiskey, he wouldn't stop until he'd thrown a barstool and been kicked out, or landed on his face somewhere.

I scooted in as Cindy bustled down the bar, a smile on her face and lipstick on her teeth. Her dyed red hair didn't dare let the gray creep into her part. "Hiya, love, what can I get ye?"

"Guinness, please."

"I got that," the stranger said, lifting his finger.

"No." I held out my hand, hoping he understood the next phrase. "I'm on my own." I didn't want him to buy me a drink for obvious reasons, but also because bar etiquette said I would then owe him a beer in return. Doubly bad news.

"You'd piss away your hard-earned money at the bar?" the stranger asked disapprovingly. "Let me buy you a drink."

"Give me a break, Mr. I Know Everything but a Bunch of Important Details. I'm sure you're entirely aware that the owner of this place pays for my drinks. Everyone knows it."

"Does he, fuck!" Mick jerked and looked over at the same time. That had been his way of asking a question.

Apparently, everyone but Mick.

"I would ask if that bothered you, given the owner is your ex, but…" The stranger let the sentence hang.

"But you've already ascertained that my pride isn't affected?"

He didn't respond, and I didn't really care what he had to say for himself anyway.

"Listen," I said, putting my hand on the bar between us. "What the fuck?"

"Yes!" Mick clenched his fist and shook it in the air.

He loved random acts of swearing and violence.

The stranger's eyes glittered. "I'll need more details," he said, but I knew he was full of crap. He knew exactly what I was talking about.

I played along anyway. "First, what is your damn name? You know all about me, and all I know is that you are a meddling, stalking, aggravating asshole."

Mick slammed the bar top. "Big, slopey-shouldered bastard," he barked out.

"That you haven't already heard my name is telling," the stranger said cryptically.

"Yes, it is clear you are very important," I said. "Well done. Speaking of, where is your entourage tonight?"

"I do not require their assistance just now."

"Uh-huh. Formal answer." I adjusted my seat, more for appearances than an actual need to get comfortable. Mick continued to mutter away to himself in the background. "Your name?"

"Why are you here, Alexis?"

The stranger wrongly assumed that his name would be enough information to clue me in. Little did he know that I didn't know anything about the magical hierarchy because I tried to avoid the whole governing body like the plague. Something that would be increasingly difficult if he kept sticking his big nose in and forcing me to visit the headquarters.

"Right. Fine," I said, letting it go. "Listen, you saw Mordecai the other night, right? That sick kid for whom you bought the blanket?"

"I still haven't gotten that blanket back. Does that mean you're intent on keeping it?"

"Really? *Now* you're worried about getting the blanket back?" I couldn't help but smile. "Cold at night, huh?"

Fire lit his eyes. "Yes. I've denied anyone else the pleasure of my bed. I'm waiting for you."

I nodded in a businesslike fashion. "I'll make sure to get you that blanket as soon as possible. You'll need it while waiting for hell to freeze over."

A smile played on his lips.

"Anyway," I went on. "Earlier this week, he was coughing blood. He was barely hanging on. We got lucky and found him some medicine, but it was a close call."

His smile melted away and the glimmer in his eyes turned somber. Thankfully, he was at least taking this seriously.

"As you've noticed"—putting the stranger's name there would've really helped with a personal touch—"we don't have a lot of money. Nearly none, actually. He usually suffers a week out of a month. Suffers like you couldn't possibly imagine." My eyes stung, and I cursed my constant fear/sorrow/heartache for my inability to cure Mordecai. Talking about his struggles always jacked my emotions. "He can barely move around the house sometimes. Right now we're riding high on medicine, so he's in decent condition. Last night, you saw him at his best." I paused so my words would resonate. "That was his best. Ponder that for a moment. He had a cheap, thin turquoise blanket wrapped around him in public, a beanie covering a head to hide the patches of hair that have fallen out, he's thin as a rake… I mean, need I go on? That was him at his *best*."

I paused again as my Guinness arrived. Cindy beamed at the stranger and leaned against the counter. "Now. How's it goin'? Are ye well?"

Mick leaned more heavily against the bar, his expression deadpan. "Wonderful. Great. Time of our lives."

Cindy wasn't fazed. "Have you heard about Shamus hanging around with that younger girl?" Her eyes widened. "He's nearly double her age."

"I'd say he's got a good supply of Viagra," Mick said, then burped. "He's got the whole town nervous."

Chuckles bubbled up through my middle, laughter never far away when Mick was in one of these moods. But this wasn't the time. I needed Cindy to find something else to do so I could finish my business with the stranger.

I elbowed Mick.

"Would ye fuck off?" he roared.

Cindy startled, having no idea he was actually talking to me, before pursing her lips and heading to the other end of the bar to tend to the only other live patron. If only the dead actually drank, she'd have plenty to do.

"Effective," the stranger murmured.

"You shouldn't try it," I said. "He'll throw a punch if a guy messes with him. He'll likely miss and fall out of his chair, but he'll still throw it." I batted at the hair clinging to my face. The smell of detergent, sweetness, and salty sea wafted toward me. The stranger had clearly inherited a little something from his mother.

I remembered the wave of sexy magic he'd hit me with earlier in the week.

Maybe a whole lotta something.

"I saw your ward. What is your point, Alexis?" the stranger asked.

"My point is, if you demand that he go in and get tested, his pack will know he's still alive. They'll be intimidated by the threat he could be if he were healthy. The alpha will want to kill him, and in a couple years, when Mordecai is of age, the alpha will legally be able to challenge him, regardless of which zone he lives in."

"It seems you didn't read the summons very closely."

I hesitated in reaching for my drink, my eyebrows

nearly at my hairline. The scant few words I'd read tumbled through my memory. I distinctly remembered reading that I was being called in for testing, and farther down the page, I'd definitely seen Mordecai's name. I said as much.

"Yes. He is being called in for a diagnosis," he said.

"We already know his diagnosis. It only gets worse with age. The only possible cure is a risky procedure. End of story."

"The field of magical medicine has come a long way in the last few years. The procedure to cure Mordecai's situation is now commonplace. No riskier than, say, heart bypass surgery. And just as easy to schedule. The cure would be within reach for a great many people."

"Fine. But I'm not one of those people. Which means his condition isn't going to change."

The stranger took a drink of his Guinness, sucking down a good helping in one gulp. Mick's muttering invaded the silence.

"You are shortsighted if you think the alpha of the Green Hills pack won't circle back at some point when Mordecai is of age to make sure the potential threat is wiped out. Will is thorough and ruthless."

Fear froze me. "But they think he's dead."

"Every alpha signs off on a death certificate for the shifters in his or her pack. It's protocol to identify the cause of death. Mordecai is technically in the Green

Hills pack. Will has noticed the death certificate hasn't passed his desk, trust me. I don't know the man well, but he sits on a very fragile throne. He isn't well liked. He'll make sure all viable threats are squashed, no matter how sickly."

"Then why don't they kick his ass out?"

"Because, like I said, he is thorough and ruthless. Not to mention cunning and he doesn't fight fair. Do you know how he killed Mordecai's parents?"

"Happened upon them late one evening, I heard."

"Yes. Ambushed them. Came upon them when they were out on a date night. The two were heavily intoxicated and walking home. They were at a severe disadvantage. The official report is that Will challenged a sober Ray. Moesha, Ray's wife and beta, Mordecai's mom, apparently jumped in to help, so Will killed her, too. There was no mention of the bar, the late hour, or the couple's disadvantage… But Will and his closest followers handled the forms related to the takeover. Backdating is an easy way to get around sticky situations like murder, especially when you're in a shifter pack and killing isn't all that uncommon."

I couldn't do much but stare at him in shock. "I'd never heard that."

"It wasn't advertised. The governing body tends to let the alphas handle their own affairs as long as all the i's are dotted and t's are crossed. The autopsy reports acknowledged some inconsistencies, but the matter was dropped." His jaw clenched. "This outlook is viewed by…many as a weakness in the current magical governing body."

"Yeah. I'll say. So what happens to the weaker members of the pack? How do they get help if they need it?"

"They can leave, if they want. They can appeal for a transfer. There are options. Many more options than back before magic was out in the open."

I shook my head. "I'm thankful I'm not a shifter. A self-serving asshole trying to boss me around would not sit well."

"No." A smile tugged at his lips and his eyes intensified as he looked down on me. "I don't suppose it would. Your fire and determination wouldn't allow it. You would be a wise and just leader, but a mouthy, troublemaking subordinate."

"I don't know about one of those things—half the time the kids act like the parents and I'm schooled on how to properly behave. But the subordinate thing is true enough."

"You lead when you must, and you allow others their free will. It's the sign of a good leader. And many of the packs have good leaders. I never met Ray and Moesha, but the reports say they were well liked and respected. They led their people to prosperity. A prosperity that has dwindled."

"So how will a renewed diagnosis help? Why bring him in to reestablish what is already in the files?"

"His condition, if left untreated for too long, will have permanent effects. It may damage his body to the point that he can no longer be healed. He'll then have to be on medication until he dies."

"O-kay, but still, how will knowing that help? You may be right, but even if the alpha comes after him, it won't be for another few years. Besides, the guy could very well have forgotten. You can't say for sure. But if you bring Mordecai in and check him out, and we can kiss even that small chance goodbye."

"It's worth the risk."

"For who?"

"Don't you want to know if he can ever be cured?"

I traced the sweat down the side of my glass. "I'm dreaming small at the moment. Right now I'm job hunting and working on increasing my stockpile of money. I did well at the freak show the other night, even though you stiffed me. If I keep getting that kind of business, I can hit the fair for a month or so and then—"

"No," he said.

"What?"

"You won't be going back to that fair. You're above that."

"Thanks, Mom. That's nice of you to say. But I *will*

be going back, because I need the money—"

"Alexis, no." His commanding look jabbed through me, followed by a jolt of his magic. I felt it in every inch of my body, filling me in a way I would be hard pressed to explain. My chest tightened and my blood heated, the magic's presence inside of me...*delicious.*

I grabbed on to the bar and closed my eyes. This magic was different than the sexy magic from earlier in the week, but no less pleasurable. I'd never felt anything like it, unique and potent, exciting yet homey. It spiked my energy while covering me in a blanket of safety.

Aggressively protective. Primal. Sensual. Butterflies filled my stomach as the feeling of his magic settled low, tightening my core and making my sex ache with need. I craved fulfillment. I wanted to feel the stranger's exquisite body as it pressed me into a soft mattress. To run my palms over his back as the muscles flexed and relaxed, moving to the rhythm of his powerful thrusts. The man was so damn sexy that it defied logic. Almost made me want to forget the way he'd tampered with my life so I could go to bed with him.

"I'm not sure what your magic is meant to do," I said, slowly coming up to the surface. "But you're not the boss of me. You have no control over the freak show. It's a non-magical affair, and they've granted me access. That's the end of it."

His intense look held utter bewilderment, but not

anger. He wasn't pissed off that I'd thwarted a direct order, just confused. Possibly no one had ever said no to him before, and he needed a little time to adjust.

"Anyway, to answer your question, no, I don't want to know if I've damaged Mordecai beyond repair. Because if I have, I will never forgive myself. And if I haven't, I'll be terrified I will. When a miracle falls in my lap, and I can get him that procedure, *then* I'll want someone to look at him."

"I am your miracle," he said, his voice husky and his eyes hungry. "Because if you work for me, I'll make sure you and your wards have magical medical. The ability to cure him will be within your grasp."

Chapter 26

ALEXIS

FIREWORKS WENT OFF in my middle—joy and fury both. I'd known he would try to get me to work for him. I'd felt it the other night. I'd also known he would piece together the one-sided part of my conversation with his mother and realize I'd lied.

I just hadn't known he would use emotional blackmail to get me in the door.

"What do you have in mind?" I asked, staring at my drink.

"I want you to help me put my mother to rest."

I closed my eyes and minutely shook my head. "I don't know how. I've researched the matter a bit further, and her inability to call her seal skin doesn't make sense. She should be able to summon it."

"I think you're the only person capable of figuring out why that is."

I put out my hands and half turned to him. "Who am I gonna ask? A bunch of derelicts at a forgotten pub in the dual-society zone? That's the extent of my social circle. And I can't even ask them if they know anyone I can talk to, because they're all dead."

A few of the guys looked up, one clearly angry. He'd get lippy if I didn't head him off. It had happened more times than I could count, and it wasn't cool to look crazy while arguing with what others thought was an empty seat.

I stared at him. "Don't pretend what I said is a surprise. Only a sad sack doesn't want to cross over because he'd rather sit in the bar all day, which is the thing that killed him in the first place." I refocused on the stranger, who had paused patiently. "You're the one with the connections. Why don't you consult a few selkies about how this type of problem might manifest?"

"I have. They don't know. Largely because no one has heard of this situation. If it has happened before, and someone figured it out, they didn't or couldn't pass the information on."

"Right. Correct. And they are gone now. I can't randomly call out across the Line and hope someone turns up to help me. I need an actual person or thing to focus on. Without specifics, I'm no good. And any spirits on this side of the Line are unlikely to have any answers. Either way, I can't help."

"My mother seemed to think otherwise."

"How do you know?"

His head tilted a little, a silent gesture telling me not

to insult his intelligence. It had been worth a shot.

"Fine. But your mother was only focusing on my ability to see and hear her. Like I just told you, that isn't enough. You might need someone with different magic. Or someone who's good at detective work."

"You just mentioned that you researched the matter. Someone who wasn't at least curious, who could tolerate unanswered questions, wouldn't have bothered. You want to know for your own benefit. I can see the frustration in your eyes—"

"That frustration is from trying to explain logic to a blockhead."

"You want to help. You want to solve this riddle. And I want peace for my mother. Not to mention the fact that you have no job, I pay well, and I can help cure your ward. There is no reason for you not to take this job."

"Oh my God," I said, exasperated. "No one is this arrogant." I finished my Guinness and raised my hand to Cindy at the other end of the bar. "There are plenty of reasons not to take this job. The main one is that I don't trust you. You won't even tell me your name, so I'm not sure what other actually important details you might hold out on me. You nearly ran me over, and have been stalking me ever since. News flash: that's not normal, balanced behavior. You're dangerous, you're unhinged, and I want nothing to do with you."

"You're lying," he said, and just like that, he turned on a dime. His sexy magic slid across my skin, warming me instantly. Inviting me into his embrace.

"I stand corrected. I want to soak in your magic. But I'd want to do that if it was attached to Mick. So let that sink in for a moment."

His stupid eyes glittered again. He pushed his seat back and slid off his barstool. "I have you cornered, Alexis," he said in that rich, deep tone. "I have everything you need. *Everything*. All it'll take is for you to give in."

I sniffed. "Even if I wanted to, I can't. I run a democracy at my house, and I'd need to run something like this by the kids. They'll say no, Mordecai especially. Without question, they will say no, and then they'll tell me to hurry up and get that blanket back to you so you have nothing on me."

"I have plenty on you, and tomorrow, after you are forced to reveal the magic you're hiding in that sexy little body of yours, I'll have everything I need to escalate this to the next level. I am your only option, Alexis. I'm the miracle you've been waiting for."

He swaggered out of the bar, supremely confident in his control over the situation. Over me.

"That smug bastard," I said, only then noticing that Mick had his forehead on his arms, sleeping on the bar. How the guy didn't roll off was beyond me. It was talent. Or just a lot of practice.

Cindy brought a fresh Guinness and a wide, excited smile. "Can. You. *Believe* it?"

"No. I can't believe it, no." I ran my fingers through my hair, dread pinching my gut.

Would it really be so bad working for him? He'd stalked me, but he hadn't hurt me in any way. Actually, he'd helped and protected me. Surely that couldn't be all bad.

"What made him wander in here, I wonder?" Cindy widened her eyes at me again, turning a little so she could gaze across the bar at the door. "And chatting with you like you were on his level? I'd heard he was stiff and closed off, but he was as chatty as you please. A real gentleman."

"You know that guy?" I asked, suddenly all ears. I'd known I could count on Cindy.

"Do I know that guy?" She looked at me like I was too dense to function.

"Yes. The big one who just left."

She spread out her hands, leaned forward, and opened her mouth wide. The dramatics were strong with this one. "Yes, I know that guy! That's Kieran! When I told Miles he was here the other day, he absolutely *flipped*. He keeps missing him, though. He's in a meeting with a vendor. He'll be *livid* he missed Kieran again."

"Kieran?" The name held no relevance. "What does he do in the magical community?"

"The rock you're hiding under is enormous, Alexis." Cindy rolled her head. Not her eyes, her entire head. "Demigod Kieran. He's Demigod Valens's son, sure." She paused while my world bled of color. "He's been in town for a couple months. And he came *here*! Can you believe it? I wanted to ask for his autograph, but I didn't want to anger a god, you know what I mean?"

Cold dread trickled down my spine. A sensation like biting fire ants spread across my skin. Fear that I had never known threatened to stop my heart.

"Did..." I swallowed through a suddenly parched throat. "Did you just say he's the...Demigod's son? Valens's son?"

She laughed, my reaction tickling her. "Yes! Kieran. The uncrowned Demigod of Ireland. He wasn't in power there, you know. His mom was sick, so he mostly took care of her. He deferred to their governing body. She passed not long before he came here. I heard..." She moved a little closer and lowered her voice. "I heard he was here to learn from Valens so he can go back and claim his mantle. I mean, Kieran is from Poseidon's lineage, and Poseidon is one of the top three gods of power. It would be a shame for him *not* to take charge of a territory. All that power would go to waste."

Bladder weakening with each word and legs shaking

so badly I didn't know if I could stand on them, I rolled through my memories. Each of my dealings with Kieran rose to the surface like a dead body—things I'd said, threats I'd made, my extreme attitude. This new information cast each horrible deed in a whole new light.

"Just so I'm clear…" I held up my hand. This could not possibly be true. "That man, the handsome one who just walked out, is *the* Demigod who lives in the castle in Ireland? The guy who was just right here." I pointed at the empty chair next to me. "He is a Demigod. *He* is a *Demigod*." I wanted to be absolutely clear about my incredible, unbelievable stupidity.

"Cindy," the guy at the other end of the bar called.

Cindy's jowls wiggled when she nodded at me in delight. "Exciting, right? To be this close to greatness?"

She winked and moved away.

No. No, it was not exciting. It was freaking terrifying.

Valens probably would've killed me on the spot if I'd walked out in front of his car. He would've killed my whole family if I'd tried to mace him.

Denying him? Calling him names?

A cold sweat broke over me.

No wonder Kieran had followed me that first time. He'd probably been completely blindsided by my attitude. He'd had to catch up with me and set matters to rights. After that, he'd probably only played nice to get the skinny on my magic so I would help his mom.

I'll have everything I need to escalate this to the next level.

For once, my magic had saved me. For now.

It was safe to say that Valens, the Demigod of San Francisco, was above the law. Hell, he *created* the law. By rights, the man was a god wandering through the lives of mortals. Not all Demigods could live forever, but Valens, I knew, would live, and had lived, for a very long time.

His son thought he'd cornered me. That he'd force me to get my whole life on the books, and then strong-arm me into doing his bidding.

Could he force me into his bed, too?

I wasn't sure. He could certainly coerce me with magic. Valens had been rumored to do that as often as he pleased, though it wasn't like women ever said no to him. His son probably wasn't any different. He'd merely been playing with me like a cat plays with a mouse.

I blew out a breath as tremors ran through me. Working for the Demigod would be suicide. When I couldn't figure out how to help his mother, he'd likely decide I knew too much about his problems. He could dispose of me and say it was an accident. Or wild dogs run amok.

Hell, he could just say he accidentally killed me in bed with his awesome powers. *Oops*, he'd say, then flash that perfect smile.

"Oh God," I said, hardly able to breathe.

If you didn't have bad luck, Alexis, you'd have no luck at all.

Chapter 27

ALEXIS

"HE CAN FORCE us to register our magic," Mordecai said the following day as we drove toward the magical governing body building, "but he cannot force you to work for him and he can't force you to live in one of the magical zones. I looked it up. It's against the law. He *certainly* can't force you sexually. That's a federal law, and it applies to *everyone*, in all zones and territories and holes and whatever."

As expected, I'd told the kids everything, and they'd given me an absolute *no*. They didn't want me to work for that man for any price, even a possible cure for Mordecai. An all-powerful Demigod could crush my life in his large, strong hands. Mordecai had pulled up stats—Valens kept everything in check and running smoothly, but he ruled with an iron fist, and if you displeased him or broke the rules, you were dealt with viciously.

I remembered the deadly glint that was often in the stranger's—Kieran's—eyes. Sure, he looked a lot like his mom, but he had the power and ruthlessness of his dad. I could see it.

"It doesn't surprise me that Valens would withhold a selkie's skin," I said, my opinion of him lower than I had thought was possible. "He probably found a way to withhold it from her even in death, just to cement his dominance over her. To prove he was better than the call of the sea..." A connection tried to ignite like a couple sticks rubbed together to make fire. "You know, his lineage is the god of the sea. He holds most of his power there. One would reason that he could withhold a sea creature's power by virtue of supernatural might alone."

"Except death is not his realm. That's Hades'," Mordecai said.

The spark fizzled out. "True."

"And he'd have to focus on it all the time. Maybe not while she was alive, trapped in reality, but it seems like death doesn't have the same restrictions. Spirits move about pretty easily."

"Yes and no. They move around familiar places easily, often returning to wherever they felt most comfortable, or knew the best, or died in, but they get lost in unfamiliar places. Confused. They fizzle out and find their way back to their comfort zone."

"Why is one of Frank's comfortable places in our front yard?"

"I have no idea. Honestly, I'm scared to ask."

"Why?"

"Because he's about my mother's age, and like I just said, ghosts often hang around a place of comfort."

"Ew."

"Yeah. And you don't even know what he looks like." I grimaced. I did not like thinking of my mother's love life.

"You're not taking that job." Mordecai glanced down at my phone where the GPS map was displayed. "A right up here."

"Right. True. I am curious, though. I want to know if I can call magical objects like I can people."

"Then try."

"I can't without a solid foundation. Something special of hers would probably do the trick, if a trick could be done."

Mordecai nodded and pointed so I would turn. We approached the guarded gate in the six-foot-high brick wall encircling the magical zone, the height almost daring non-magical people to come in illegally and attempt to create mischief. And foolish kids did. All the time.

Most of them paid the price. Some of them were never heard from again.

"Have your ID out," I said, and slipped my ID from my wallet. "If I could figure out the riddle, though, and get his mother back that skin…"

"Don't even say it," Mordecai warned.

I slowed behind the line of cars seeking admittance into the magical area. In the clear lane beside me, intended for higher-powered personnel, a large Mercedes SUV glided by, barely slowing before the guard in that lane touched his first two fingers to his forehead, letting him pass without showing identification.

I couldn't not say it. I couldn't not say it, or not think it, or not dwell on it constantly. "You'd be cured, Mordecai. You would get complete access to your heritage."

"And then what?" he asked, his voice hushed. "Right now, I don't have any strength. I don't know how to fight. The alpha might not bother with me because I'm nothing. One look at me would tell him I'm no threat. His people would see a strong alpha picking on a sickly boy. He'd get nothing out of it. My weakness is my greatest protection. In fact, he'd get points from the pack for acting merciful. But if I was healthy, he'd have no reason not to challenge me."

"That would make really good sense to leaders like your parents probably were. And clearly like you would be. That's why they were loved. But I told you what the Demigod said. The current alpha doesn't fight fair, and he isn't loved."

"The Demigod might've been telling you what you

needed to hear. Demigods are also cunning, and they also don't fight fair."

I paused with my mouth open. I was too freaking gullible by half. "Dang it. You're too smart."

"No, I just have a lot of practice talking you out of very bad ideas. If only I was half as good at talking Daisy out of them."

"The difference is, she somehow pulls off her terrible ideas, and I always get caught."

As we approached the head of the line, I rolled down the window, squinting into the frigid air. A little bit farther and the temperate weather of the magical zone would welcome us in.

"Good afternoon, kind sir," I said, handing my license to the stern-faced guard in a black uniform with two green stripes down the arms and legs. "Lovely day for a kite, isn't it?"

His jaw set firmly, he brought up a blacklight reader to catch the watermarks in the license.

"Rest assured, there is no way I'd try to sneak in." I smiled up at him.

He turned and slid the card through a reader, waited a beat, then handed the ID back. He looked at the car behind me.

"Lovely chatting with you. I feel refreshed." I waved at him and continued on through the wall.

"That's the way to get them to remember you,"

Mordecai said.

"Not hardly. They only remember important people who are full of themselves. He'll disregard a poor girl desperate for a little back-and-forth." I turned left on the cleanly swept, pristine road. Full trees waved in the strong breeze, some flowering out of season. Brick buildings and cute little houses lined the streets. All of the neighborhoods were as expensive, well maintained, and cozy as this one. Tufts of fog floated ahead, thinning dramatically the farther in we got. The Demigod had the weather looking fine.

I wound through the blocks until I hit a larger thoroughfare and followed Mordecai's directions to a bluff overlooking the Golden Gate Bridge.

"Nice view," Mordecai said as I parked as close to it as I could. I only wished I could live in a place with this view. Of course, the houses that looked out on the bridge were astronomically expensive in any of the zones, magical or otherwise.

"I bet Kieran has a great view," I murmured wistfully. "That might be worth trading a night for."

"Did you fall off the logic truck and hit your head on stupid?" Mordecai asked as he opened his door.

"I wouldn't really do it," I grumbled, though I half wished I was a person who would. He probably had a sweet house, and a giant, fluffy, comfy bed.

He certainly had that body. And those eyes…

Mordecai shook his head, looking around the half-filled parking lot. Unlike government buildings in the non-magical areas, the buildings here rarely had lengthy lines, long wait times, and heavy foot traffic. Valens wanted everything in his city to run smoothly and efficiently, something other magical leaders worked on emulating.

"Okay. Just keep your head down, get in, and get out," I said, grabbing Mordecai's lean bicep and directing him to an artful stone path leading toward the high, arching marble front entrance. Valens also liked grandness.

"Are you giving yourself that advice, or me?" he asked. It had probably been meant as a joke, but it came out sounding nervous.

"It's going to be fine. All they want to do is check you out."

The columns along the sides of the building reminded me of those in Ancient Greece or Rome, but the shimmering decal of thousands of inlaid tiles cast a modern appearance that made a person think of the moving ocean.

"Say what you want about Valens, he has a real eye for beauty," I said in hushed tones, marveling as we descended a set of stone steps that matched the walkway.

"Just ask his wife," Mordecai replied.

His body tensed as we entered the door and turned left for the information desk. A chipper woman with blueish skin and bright blue hair beamed at us as we approached. I had no idea what kind of a magical person she was, or if she had any idea a forlorn-looking granny stood behind her, staring down at her. I imagined that only the severely closed-off wouldn't notice the tingle of constantly being watched, even if the watcher was no longer in a visible body.

"Good afternoon—" She cut off the greeting when I shoved the crinkled letter across the high desk. "Ah." She looked up with a smile. "And you are Alexis?"

"Me." I tapped my chest, not intending to be quite so caveman-like. What could I say—official places made me nervous. I was usually only in them when I was in trouble.

Her smile lifted her cheeks. "Fantastic. You are right on time. You'll just head down the corridor on the left here, to the very end, and knock on room one-oh-seven."

"Super."

"Annnd… Mordecai." Her unnaturally green eyes flicked toward Mordecai. "Yes?"

He nodded.

"Fantastic. You'll just head upstairs and to the right. Room two-oh-one. They'll look after you there. Let me just check you in." She tapped a keyboard off to the side with long purple nails. The *click-click-click* made me grind my teeth. "And it looks like transportation has been arranged for your return home, Mordecai. So they'll—"

"No." I leaned across the desk to get a look at the computer screen. "I'll be taking him home. He doesn't need your transportation."

Her disarming smile didn't do anything for the tightness in my chest. "It's standard procedure, Miss Price. Sometimes the various tests can take a lot out of patients. We like to make sure they get home safe."

"Yeah? Well if he goes missing, what happens then?"

Her smile faltered. "I assure you, he will be quite safe."

"I know he will. Because I'll be taking him home." I gestured toward the computer. "Type that in. He declines the transportation service."

Now her smile said she was ready to talk down a hysterical woman. "Supplying transportation is—"

"Type it in, cupcake. That's the end of it." Cripes. I was starting to sound like my mother.

"We don't—"

I gestured at the computer again before turning Mordecai away from the desk. "Let's get you where you're supposed to go. At any time, if you feel you need to, and can, run like hell. There's no shame in taking flight. There're no heroes among patients."

Mordecai nodded stiffly.

Up the wide marble staircase and to the right, we walked into room two-oh-one. Two people sitting sat on the plush cushions of the wooden chairs pushed against the artfully decorated wall. A leafy green plant adorned the corner beside the check-in window.

"A doctor's office in a government building. What could possibly go wrong?" I asked quietly, my hand still on Mordecai's arm. I didn't want him to take off running prematurely.

The man at the desk, as plain as they came, with brown hair and an average face, glanced up when we stopped in front of him. Before greeting us, he checked his computer screen. "Mordecai?" he said.

"Yes," I answered, leaning against the desk.

"Fantastic. Just have a seat and we'll be with you shortly."

I nodded and ushered Mordecai over to the line of chairs, perching on the seat next to his. "You're going to be fine. Everything is going to be cool. They're going to poke you, and take blood, and hook you up to computers. I'll be here to pick you up when they're done. Okay?"

"What about you?"

"I have to go to that room downstairs somewhere."

"I mean…" He swallowed. "What are they going to

do to you?"

It occurred to me that his nervousness hadn't been for himself. It had been for me.

I smiled and put my hand on his shoulder. "They're going to hook me up to a machine and attempt to read my power level. When that goes wonky, they'll try another. Then one more. They'll draw blood, curse the machines, and probably scratch their heads. I've done this a time or two. It's nothing."

"The more powerful Demigods can sense the power in magical people. If Kieran is calling you in again, he won't let you bamboozle them this time."

My stomach rolled. I wasn't a huge fan of unpredictable authority figures. I shrugged it away. "Whatever comes, I'll deal with it. I've been hustling for a long time. I can handle whatever they throw at me."

Chapter 28

ALEXIS

"AH. ALEXIS PRICE, correct?" an elderly woman with thick glasses and curled white hair said as she looked up from an appointment book. A younger woman roamed in the back of the square office attached to the sterile waiting room, sticking papers into a row of boxes.

No plants, flowers, or racks of magazines adorned the beige walls of the waiting room. No rugs jazzed up the cream linoleum floor. Simple wooden chairs with no cushions dotted the left wall, ample space between them.

"You guys really went above and beyond for this department, huh? A real eye for decorating, this." I gave her a thumbs-up. "Very welcoming. Nailed it."

"I'll be with you in a moment," the younger woman with smooth bronzed skin said as she worked through her stack.

"You're here for an assessment, is that correct?" the older woman asked, looking through those thick glasses at me.

"It's got to be damn annoying that no one ever answers you, huh?" I asked, cocking a hip and leaning it against the lip of the desk.

Her cloudy gray eyes took in my face for a long moment as the pretty younger woman turned with a furrowed brow.

"I don't appreciate that tone, young woman," the older woman said. She made a note in her appointment book.

"What happens when the other employee needs that chair?" I asked.

The younger woman distributed her last paper and bustled toward me, her skirt-suit formfitting and her manner professional. She wasn't doing a bang-up job of hiding her wariness and confusion, however. She probably thought I was one of those magical nutcases who couldn't handle her powers, had said goodbye to reality, and opted to live in her own world with imaginary people.

She was only half right.

"Can I help you?" she asked, pulling out the chair.

The older woman looked up with a frustrated scowl before her form flickered and vanished.

"I'm being passively forced to get tested," I responded. "Alexis Price. An appointment was made for me. Tell me, should I have brought my own straitjacket, or will those be provided?" I laughed a little. "I mean, I feel like I've showed up to a black-tie affair in jeans, know what I'm saying? My ensemble does not fit in with the surroundings."

Her eyes flicked past me before turning to her computer, a smile revealing a small dimple in her cheek. "We get all manner of magical people through these doors, and it's thought that keeping a blank canvas will allow their imaginations to roam."

"Uh-huh. And people actually buy that line?"

Her smile widened. "No one usually asks about it, actually. This department sees magical beings with the highest power levels."

"So they are more interested in themselves than in their surroundings?"

She fought the smile this time and pressed her lips together. In other words, *exactly*.

The printer whirred to life and she squinted at the screen, her expression slipping. "Oh." Wariness crossed her features and she darted a look behind her. When her eyes hit mine again, they held fear and a question.

She'd just read what my magic entailed and pieced together what she'd witnessed earlier—how I'd appeared to talk to someone who wasn't there.

It always tickled me that magical people, who rolled with so many oddities in life, like people changing into animals, causing things to spontaneously combust, or controlling others through mind manipulation, took pause at the fact that the dead walked among them.

"Just…go ahead and fill out this paperwork." The woman attached the printouts to a clipboard and handed them through the window. "Someone will be with you shortly."

Ten minutes and a bunch of annoying questions about my mental stability regarding my magic later, the door off to the side of the waiting room opened, emitting a bald man with bushy eyebrows. His dark eyes roamed my body in an analytical way before coming to rest on my paperwork.

"Miss Price." He took a stiff step into the room. His eyes dipped and his eyebrows rose, telling me this wasn't a guy who was in the habit of making eye contact. He probably had a big brain and a lot of social awkwardness. "May I call you Alexis?"

"Call me whatever you please. It won't make this situation any more or less unpleasant." I stood and tucked my clipboard to my side. They wouldn't ask for it until I was in the room.

"Of course. Alexis, my name is Mountebank Iams, and I'll be assisting you today." A mountebank was the magical equivalent of doctor, a title derived from an old-timey word used to denote a charlatan who sold fake medicine. When the magical community had forced their way out into the open a century ago, they'd had a sense of humor about the way they organized things. "If you will follow me…" Eyes still downcast and brows still raised, he lifted his hand toward the door.

Ignoring my flip-flopping stomach, I lifted my chin and held my shoulders straight as I entered the small sterile hallway.

"You guys don't employ shock treatment, right? That hasn't been brought in as a special measure?" I asked as I peeled off to the side so he could regain the lead.

"You have nothing to worry about, Alexis. We are experienced and skilled in determining the power level of someone your age. It will take no time at all."

Did it count as lying if the person didn't know they were lying?

"Here we are." He stopped in front of an open door with a large wooden B nailed to its surface.

Pretending like I was eager to cooperate, I stepped into the room and glanced around. Three empty chairs waited, each one pushed up against a differently colored wall that didn't house the door. My wall color options were green, red, and yellow. I felt as though I'd been reintroduced to preschool and was about to be asked whether I could fit the differently shaped blocks into the right holes. The chair I chose would be their first clue into something related to my personality or brain that I wasn't educated enough to understand.

Each corner hosted one of the evaluation machines, the tubes and wires arranged in such a way that it looked almost organized. The knobs and dials were not labeled, and the screens were all black.

"Pick any chair you like," Mountebank Iams said, gesturing at the chairs.

I'd already been rolling through *eeny, meeny*, and then counted five more times so they didn't know what I was doing. It was as random as I could make it. I sat in the red chair, looking on the yellow wall, a color that I wasn't fond of.

"Perfect. If you'll excuse me for a moment, the nurse will be in for some preliminary checks, and I'll continue from there." Mountebank Iams left the room and closed the door behind him, that wall white. He'd now go write down my selection and the time it took to make it.

A moment later, a red-faced nurse with a can-do expression and a tight bun strolled in.

"Good afternoon, Miss Price," she said, her smile absent but her tone kind. She clicked a button on the machine next to me, and it whirred to life. I didn't bother telling her it wouldn't work. They'd just assume I was an idiot. "Let's see what we have here."

She put out her hand, and I relinquished the clipboard.

"You've been tested three times before, is that correct?" she asked.

"Yes."

"And each result was different?"

"Yes. Though the third was in the ballpark of the first."

"Right, yes." She traced her finger down the page on the clipboard before folding the sheet in half lengthwise. She traced her finger down the next page. "You can see those who haven't made the transition to the afterlife?"

"Yes. There was one in the office area of the sterile check-in room."

To her credit, she didn't even pause.

"Have you experienced any fluctuations of power?"

"Nope." Just like I'd answered on the questionnaire.

"Any reason to suspect your power has grown or changed in any way?"

"Nope." Also like I'd answered on the question-naire.

"Can you call people back from the Line?"

"Anyone close to a spirit can call them back from the Line. Are you actually asking if I can call them back from beyond the Line?"

Her eyes flicked up. "Can you call people back from *beyond* the Line?" Her emphasis had been slight, but it was there.

The marathon of annoyance had begun. It would start with her and spread to the other staff.

"Yes, I can," I answered.

"Can you then send them back within the same session?"

"Yes. God, I hope people don't call spirits if they don't have the power to send them home again when they're done. What turds."

Her stern brown eyes held a warning about giving my opinion or talking out of turn. A warning I intended to ignore. They weren't in control here. Nor were they in charge. They needed my cooperation to get what they were after, and I did not plan on giving it. I might as well amuse myself while I was trapped in the chair, waiting for them to exhaust their efforts.

"What percentage of the day are you able to see spirits?" she asked, back on target.

"It is a wonder I bothered filling out that questionnaire at all. A hundred percent of the waking hours."

Her eyes drifted up from the paper, but I couldn't read the look in them. Her assessment lasted only a moment, and I suddenly wondered if she thought I was lying.

Why the hell would a person lie about something like that? It wasn't something to brag about. The opposite, in fact.

"And sleeping?"

"Your mind controls your dreams. Spirits don't have access to your mind." When she didn't immediately continue her line of questioning, I simplified my answer: "None."

"You don't dream about spirits?"

"I dream about people who may have died, as I do about the living, but the dreams are controlled by me. They are puppets on the strings of my subconscious, or my conscious mind if I gain control of my dream."

Her eyes were on me again, still unreadable. "You can control your own dreamscape?"

"Not like a Dream Walker. Anyone, magical or otherwise, can do what I'm saying. It's called a lucid dream. You control your dream, but you aren't physically in it. You're...wakeful dreaming." I crossed an ankle over a knee. "I feel like you should know what I'm talking about. They have schools for what you do, right?"

Her eyes hardened, and a little tingle at the base of my spine said not to mess with her.

I had rarely listened to my gut feelings in the past— why would I now?

"The spirits you see, how transitionary are they?" she asked.

"I'm not sure what that means, like I said on the questionnaire. Do you mean how close to the Line are they?"

"How solid is the form of the spirit?"

"Oh. Completely solid. Like looking at you."

Her eyes were like Chuck Norris's fists. "Every spirit

you see is as solid as a living person?"

"Yes."

"How are you able to differentiate between the two?"

"In short, I just can. I can feel it, I guess. Sometimes there is a soft inner glow, sometimes a soft outer glow, but mostly...I just know. I've never really thought about how. No one taught me to do this stuff, I just...do it."

Her look said she wasn't impressed. In her head, she was certainly saying "I see" in a disbelieving sort of way.

"Do they talk to you, these spirits?" she asked.

And on she went, sometimes asking for a painful degree of explanation to a question I'd already answered. Finally, when her efforts were exhausted and her patience had worn thin, she gave me a crusty look and told me the mountebank would be in shortly.

A half-hour wasn't shortly. By the time he strolled in, clearly without any sort of urgency, I was tapping my foot and wondering how Mordecai was getting on. I hoped he wouldn't be done before me. They might just send him home without waiting. Which would've been fine, had I been positive he'd end up at home.

"Hello again, Alexis," the mountebank said, his attempt at being chummy ruined by his lack of a cheery voice and eye contact. "Now, we'll just connect you up and get a reading, and you'll be all set."

I was tempted to let them get what they wanted

without hassle. Tempted, but not willing. Kieran was trying to put me in a box to use at his leisure. Besides which, the governing body kept more records on powerful magical people—and they also encouraged them to move into the magical zone. Even if I could afford it, I didn't need a bunch of busybodies sneering at my weird magical traits.

So I settled in, squishing my magic into a little ball and shoving it way down deep, where even the strongest machines couldn't read it. Tubes and bands and whirligigs in place, on went the machine.

It took three minutes for the mountebank's face to droop into a grimace. Another minute for his brow to bunch. One more to peer down at the machine, then over at me.

Yup. That's how it's going to go. Your expectations, no matter how hard you try, will not be met. Good day, sir.

And he did try. He moved me from one machine to the other. Then back to the first. The tubes sucking strangely at my skin were checked. The headpiece altered. My vein slapped before another sample was taken.

All the while, he kept getting different results. If I were better at this, I could target one result and keep hitting that. That'd satisfy him. But alas, I was only human.

"Now, Alexis," the mountebank said twenty minutes later with sweat standing on his brow and frustration in every line on his face. The no-nonsense nurse stood by the machine on the red wall, accusation clear in her stance. "Something is not adding up." His smile was condescending. He pointed at the long sheet of perforated white paper in his left hand. "We've taken these readings three times. All are different, but *all* of them suggest a lower-powered magic." His eyes flicked up, then back down. That was as close as he usually got to checking my expression. "And yet the type of magic you've described is indicative of someone with a substantial power level."

"Huh." I tapped my chin. "Conundrum. Maybe there's a plate in my head that I'm unaware of? You know"—I snapped—"everyone always says my personality is electric. Maybe that is messing up the machine."

The nurse's lips tightened further. The mountebank shook his head, reading the printout again. He glanced at the machine. "I need to make a call. Nurse Jessub, come with me, please."

She glared at me all the way out the door. We wouldn't end up friends, she and I.

Fifteen minutes later, I was unsurprised to see the mountebank bring in a lanky man with a buzzcut, keen eyes, and a smile that said people did what he wanted if they wanted to keep their appendages. The nurse filed in after him with an expression that said, *This is for your own good.*

"Hello, Miss Price," the new guy said, his hands behind his back and his smile oily. "I'm Rob Stevens."

"Hi, Rob," I said.

"I am an Authenticator. Do you know what that is?"

My heart sank and a bead of sweat ran down my back.

His smile spread. "I can see that you do. Yes, I can read the shades of truth within lies, and vice versa."

I hadn't reacted because of what he could do. He could figure out the problem all day long, but that didn't mean they could get any closer to discerning the level of my magic. Not unless shock treatment had returned to medical practice (they never had given me an answer on that).

No, my problem was that magic like his was rare and prized. He could demand a good price for his work. The fact that they'd brought him in with me, paying him an arm and a leg for his services, meant Kieran was not messing around. He wanted proof of what I could do, and I was scared by the lengths he was willing to go to get it.

"I've heard Mountebank Iams is having some problems matching up your account of your magic with the readings of the machine."

"I've been hearing the same thing," I replied.

"Her connections are all correct, and when we—"

"It's okay, Mountebank Iams, I'll take it from here." Rob glanced around the room, choosing the chair in front of the yellow wall. Once seated, he leaned back and crossed an ankle over a knee before entwining his fingers, getting comfortable. "I'll call you when I'm ready."

The mountebank stiffened and his jaw clenched. He'd just been chucked out of his own assessment room, and it galled. Despite the situation, it tickled me.

"Now," Rob said when he were alone. "Let's start from the beginning."

I started with my impression of the bland waiting room, the spirit I'd seen in the office, and why and how I'd chosen my seat in this very room. Throughout our preliminary chat, I peppered in some white lies about arbitrary things, like the number I'd added onto *eeny, meeny* and how much I liked the nurse's attitude. Talking about my magic came next, and there I didn't lie at all. My mother always said that choosing to keep information to myself was okay, but outright lying would just land me in the stink.

By then, his smile had vanished and his body had tensed somewhat. He looked over at the machine in confusion. "Did they try another machine besides this one?"

"They tried all three."

"Of course," he said, blinking slowly. "Do you want to know my assessment?"

"No."

He shook his head, looking confused. I'd been confusing a lot of people lately.

"Which means," he said, as if the words had been drawn from him with a string, "you know vaguely what it is."

It wasn't a question, so I didn't give him an answer.

"You think that machine works just fine, don't you, Miss Price?"

"Yes. I love your tone when you call me Miss Price, by the way. It's soothing."

The silence between us lingered. I could really get used to having a guy like him around. I sounded as sweet as can be, but we both knew I was being sarcastic.

Because I did not like his tone at all. It made me want to throttle him.

"Why can't the machines get accurate readings, Alexis?" he asked.

"Why, indeed? Tell me, what's the status with shock treatment? Or torture?"

His crossed ankle swung to the ground. I was getting under his skin.

"That's the thing about your magic," I said, fighting for the upper hand. "It's only useful when you have information to pore over."

I would not let them get control over me. The power to choose my own fate was the only power I had. The one thing I couldn't bear to give up. The day I let someone else rule me was the day I lost my will to keep fighting. It was the day my mother would not know the daughter she had raised.

"I don't frighten you, do I?" he asked.

"Why would you frighten me?" It dawned on me. "Ah. Because liars are frightened of people discovering the truth. And those are the type of people you usually deal with."

"You're a clever girl."

"I have my moments."

"Though I knew that earlier, from the way you inserted silly lies to point at the utter truth of everything you said regarding your magic." He stood. "You are not what you seem, Miss—Alexis. You think you know what you are. I believe that. But in this situation, it's not just your power level that isn't adding up. You are as ignorant as the mountebanks at this office have been."

"Oh…kay…"

He paused with his hand on the door. "I've done all I can here, since no, I am not permitted, nor do I care to, torture you. Someone else can handle that."

"Oh, goodie. You know, I've really enjoyed our time together. This place is great."

"You're laying it on a little thick, Miss Price," he

said, before shutting the door between us.

I sighed. Two down, how many more to go?

Later I would learn that it was only one. One more. The worst one of all.

Chapter 29

KIERAN

"THE ENCOURAGER IS up next, sir," Zorn said, standing by Kieran's side in the large medical monitoring room.

The staff in this room sat at their computer terminals in their white coats and analyzed stats on various subjects from a multitude of departments. Only two staffers were working on Kieran's case, in addition to the personnel who actually went into the assessment room, but it still felt like too many. He wanted the least amount of people to know his business as possible. But he also needed to be thorough. He wanted this done properly. There was no more hiding for Alexis Price, not from him.

"He's a class five, like you requested," Zorn went on.

An Encourager could influence another person's thoughts and actions. A class five was on par with mind control.

Without warning, rage flared up from deep inside of Kieran, hot and possessive. His body tightened up of its own accord, ready to fight. Something about the idea of another man entering Alexis's mind, able to access her most intimate information, turned his stomach. The thought of that man being able to control her fanned his rage higher until red tinted his vision. If she would give control up to anyone, it would be Kieran, and it would be done willingly.

"No," he said, leaning over the desk, watching the monitors. Four in all, capturing every angle of the room. Alexis sat with a loose posture in her chair, her fingers entwined in her lap and her confidence supreme. She thought she'd come out on top of this situation, hiding her magic like a thief, just as she had in the past.

One thing was certain: Alexis Price would not go down without a fight, no matter what he threw at her.

"I doubt an Enforcer could crack her," he said quietly, not wanting anyone else in the large medical monitoring room to hear. It wasn't just a good excuse not to use the Enforcer; it was the truth. A truth that would raise eyebrows—even more so than she already had. "Turn off the recording. I'll handle it."

The door at the far end of the room swung open and Rob entered, his brow furrowed and his expression contemplative. He made a beeline for Kieran.

"She's unique," he said without preamble, clearly forgetting his position. "She's hiding something. She knows I know it—she knows *you* know it—but she isn't anxious about it. She's downright confident. And she should be. She handled me more than I handled her. Only the best-trained industry professionals sit through an interrogation with that much detachment. No..." He put a finger to his lips and looked down. "Detachment isn't the right word. With that amount of...insouciance. She artfully tucked lies within the truth like it was a game, and she was assured of winning." His look held suspicion, but he wasn't acting disrespectful, which was the only reason Kieran didn't call him down. "Are you testing me, sir? Have there been any complaints regarding my abilities?"

Kieran barely checked his surprise. He'd expected something unusual—Alexis always kept him guessing—but he hadn't thought she'd be able to twist the Authenticator into so many knots that he was doubting his own ability. Rob thought she'd been highly trained. That she was assessing him, and not the other way around.

"We'll be in touch," Kieran said, forcing a flat expression. It was not the right time to smile at the absurdity of the situation. "Zorn..."

Zorn stepped forward, his arms out to herd the suddenly imbalanced Authenticator. A half-hour ago, Rob had thought he was at the top of his trade. Now he wondered if he'd be sacked. What a strange twist of events.

Jack drifted to his side from behind one of the staff monitoring Alexis's vitals. "If you hope to keep her under wraps, you should probably cut this short. Get the assessment and get out, know what I'm saying?"

Kieran barely nodded, already stepping forward. Scientist types spent their life explaining the unknown—they'd want to dig into the weird that was Alexis and her undocumented talents. Unless Kieran ushered her out of here as quickly as possible.

He let himself out of the monitoring room and walked down the hall, briefly thinking about how he wanted to approach this situation. She already mistrusted him, and for good reason. He'd been shadowing her for days. Even the completely untrained would have a problem with that, and the trained would be thinking of ways to kill him, Demigod or no. Forcing her to cooperate with the testing would only make matters worse. He needed to drive her to the brink...and then pull back and let her make her own decision.

If that decision was to continue messing with his testers and their machines, he wasn't sure what he'd do.

He stopped at the assessment room door with his hand on the handle and took a deep breath. He had no idea why he still wanted to smile, and even less of an idea why he felt nervous. Kieran never felt nervous.

"Hello, Alexis," he said as he opened the door.

A look of blind fear washed over her face and she

licked her lips before glancing at the green wall, then the machine.

She would've picked the green wall if she'd made a personal choice instead of trying to mess with the mountebanks, and she knew he could force her to give up the goods and let that machine properly assess her.

When had she become so easy to read?

"How are we?" he asked, pausing in the doorway, wondering if a fleeting hope of escape would cross her face.

As if she'd slipped into a coat, a new wave of confidence washed over her. She didn't so much as glance out of the room. If he hadn't seen her handle those beast handlers at the magical fair, he would've bought it all. But she'd been terrified then, and she was terrified now.

He would soon find out why—what she was hiding.

"We?" she said, her voice strong and even. She did excellently under pressure. "Well, you seem to be fabulous, and I am rather humdrum. Thanks for asking."

He smiled and stepped into the room before closing the door behind him. He eyed the wall colors. "I think I'll choose green."

"Great to know. Should I jot that down?"

"You don't have any paper. Make a mental note. I like when my women know every minute detail about me. It makes my life easier."

Her lips tightened, and he barely kept from laughing. The mountebanks found her deflective, dry humor exasperating. He had no idea why. He found it refreshing that someone didn't agree with his every word. It kept things interesting.

"My name is Kieran. Demigod Kieran, Valens Drusus's son." Her eyes narrowed instead of widening. "Or did you finally figure out who I was?"

"Your people have the gift of gab. Cindy at the bar filled me in."

"My people?"

"Yeah. Irish. Awful gossips."

He did smile this time before leaning back in his chair, getting comfortable. "Cindy, yes. She pours a good pint." He let his gaze roam her face, snagging on that inviting, heart-shaped mouth. "Do you know why I'm here?"

"In this room, or in this city?"

"The room. You know...in part, why I'm in this city."

She glanced around at the walls. "These rooms are usually bugged, right? Do you want the whole world hearing what I know? Because I have no problem with snitching."

"These rooms are usually monitored, yes. But not right now." He hoped Zorn knew to plug in some earphones if he wanted to keep listening. "I hoped you'd consent to a proper assessment test."

"I have. They've tested me three times."

"With varying results."

"The machines are clearly buggy."

"Just so we're clear, the room was monitored before I came in."

Her jaw set stubbornly, but she didn't say anything.

"I have the ability to bend an individual's mind to my will, Alexis." He kept his tone light, but fear flashed within her eyes. No, she did not want to be controlled. She'd given up much in her life—she did not want to give up her power over her mind. He respected that. Only a weak person would. "I'd rather not do that to you."

"I would rather you not do that, too. Look at us—something in common."

"But I need that assessment, Alexis."

"Conundrum." So, she was digging in her heels. He'd expected no less.

"That's how it's going to be, then?"

"Do your worst," she said, using a different voice. He wondered if it was a reference from a movie he wasn't getting. Regardless, he grinned and gave in to her command.

Chapter 30

ALEXIS

I WONDERED WHAT Kieran would do. How far he would go. He was a Demigod, and with the magnitude of his power, he could make me grovel at his feet like a starving, begging child.

Please don't make me grovel.

He half rose and scooted his chair closer, stopping in the center of the room.

"I'd stay out of kicking distance, if I were you," I warned.

That sexy grin twisted his lips again. "Noted. So…" He entwined his fingers, as calm as they came.

"So," I said, trying to mimic it. I did a horrible job. It came out like I wanted to put a spike through his heart.

"It seems you are somehow preventing the machine from getting accurate readings. Because this facility has not had experience with that before…" They had, because my mother had been the master at it. She'd always hit her target within a few points, a talent I couldn't seem to duplicate. These guys just hadn't caught anyone doing it before. "...they don't know how to get what we need."

"So they called in the big guns."

He bent his head, and that damn grin stretched a little wider. He thought all this was hilarious, the dog.

"I'll give you one more chance to—"

"No," I said. I could withstand his magic in the bar; I might as well try to withstand it here. Maybe he couldn't—

The thought cut off as a wave of unadulterated bliss swept over me, promising unbearably sweet rewards. My core tightened to pounding, desperate for fulfillment. My nipples budded in anticipation of being suckled by his luscious lips.

I moaned—I couldn't help it—before dropping my head forward and riding the wave of pleasure, revving up to orgasm right here in the assessment room.

I hoped he really had switched off the monitoring equipment, because I was about to make a fool of myself.

Then again...Kieran wanted me sexually. He'd said as much, and proven it in the bar. If I showed how much pleasure his magic caused me, it would drive him crazy because he couldn't touch me.

Or, at least, I hoped so. This tactic would be ruined if he decided to ignore the law.

Heat pounded through my middle. I raked my teeth across my bottom lip before spreading my legs and leaning back. "Yes," I sighed, not having to pretend. Pleasure coursed through me, throbbing and aching. I arched my back, soaking into it. Feeling the build. Right on the edge.

"Cut off the cameras," Kieran said with what sounded like a clenched jaw, his voice hard and tight. Hard like his cock, I was certain.

But I didn't have time to reach that big O, or be embarrassed about who else might've seen my little display. Hot spikes of agony ripped across my skin before digging in hard. I was dunked, headfirst, into more pain than I'd experienced in a very long time.

"Dick move..." I ground out, taking it. This was a battle of wills, and I would not give in. I only wished I had better magic so I could fight back. "Not letting me orgasm."

"You'll orgasm with me, or not at all," came the reply, his voice still tight.

I laughed despite the pain. "My big pink vibrator begs to differ. You can suck it."

"I will suck it. And lick it. And make you writhe in pleasure before screaming my name."

It felt like daggers had been punched through my eyes. Fire burned across my scalp. I opened myself up to the pain, letting it consume me. Letting it drag me where it would.

"There you go," I said, trying to stay loose and absorb the sensations. It made the magic bearable, somehow. Tolerable. I could handle this. "You've just proven yourself a liar, unless you'll be jacking off while you eat me out?"

The magic switched on a dime, and I knew in a flash he was alternating between his mother's and father's magic. Sweet and sensual, then vicious and dominating, both utterly consuming. I wondered if he was even in control, or if his magic was instinctively reacting to my verbal pokes and prods.

Passion flared, erasing the sharp bite of pain from the moment before.

"You're so fucking sexy, Alexis, you drive me to distraction," he said in a low growl. I peeled my eyes open, hot and aching and needing his cock buried deeply inside of me.

The same heat burned in his eyes, as though he was using the magic on himself. As though I had the same effect on him as he was having on me.

Suddenly, I wondered how much of this was actually his magic, and how much was my reaction to him. I was scared of the answer.

"But this is too important," he muttered. His jaw clenched, and for a moment—a split second—I thought I saw regret.

Then the pain rolled through me again, tearing down all the heat and sensuality from my sex-addled brain. God, he was good at keeping someone on edge. I had to hand it to him.

"You can end this whenever you want, Alexis," he whispered, and I heard it that time, faintly. Regret.

"Where's...the fun...in that?" I clenched my teeth, then tried a new tactic. Instead of sinking into his magic like I usually did, I floated through it—and I reached out a mental hand and tugged him in with me.

He grunted, as if I'd struck him. A moment later, without warning, a huge wave of his vicious magic crashed over me, blistering me as it tore me apart. Black spots danced before my eyes before enlarging, cutting out my vision. Fear choked me and pain blotted out my awareness. My equilibrium went next before something hard and immovable hit my side.

"No more."

That rough, sexy voice was much too familiar. The spine-crushing pain dried up, evaporating like raindrops on hot cement.

One minute I was in mental hell, and the next I was panting, lying on the floor, flat on my back, looking at white, puffy clouds painted on the light blue ceiling. Apparently, I wasn't the first person who'd ended up flat on her back in this room. I was glad I didn't know that coming in. Nothing had hit me—I'd hit the floor.

Kieran knelt by my side, his face pale.

"Are you okay?" he asked, and the sentiment was genuine.

"That's an odd question, given that you just smashed me with godly magic."

His gaze raked down my body, but it wasn't sexual. He was checking me over. "I apologize. It was a defensive reaction to your magic. I didn't mean to strike that hard."

My brain tried to process what he'd said, but it felt like he'd peeled back my scalp and stuffed my cranium with cotton candy. I couldn't focus just yet.

Kieran's arms came out, and I knew one moment of panic before they snaked under my body and he lifted me, holding me tightly to his chest.

"Please don't crush me. I've had a bad day."

"I'm not going to crush you," he said before depositing me back into my chair.

He pulled his seat closer, right in front of mine, definitely within striking range of my legs. He settled slowly onto it.

"I don't want to control you, Alexis," he said, his voice intimate, just for me. "I don't want to force your secrets out of you. I want to coax them out, one by one, in long, sweaty sessions that last all night." Passion dripped from each syllable, and the effect was like vibrating panties. I barely kept from moaning. "But you've put me in a tough situation. You've become a talking point out there. They are scratching their heads and looking up your various magical traits. And while the magic tied to seeing spirits is a known quantity, your ability to suppress your magic, and run circles around experienced interrogators, doesn't fit the profile. Your power is clearly off the charts, but what you do with it is strange. Or, I should say, what you choose not to do with it on a daily basis is strange. You are an anomaly, Alexis. A sexy, gorgeous anomaly that I can't let off the hook until I know what's lurking under the surface. I have more power than you can withstand. Please, don't make me prove that."

I wheezed out a laugh, slouching. "You just picked me up off the floor. I'm pretty sure you just proved it."

"I'm prepared to compromise. It's rare that I would. If your results are something my father might desire for his…team, you have my word that I'll protect you from his influence. There are few in the world who could make such a claim. I have that power. In your case, I will exert it."

I blinked in confusion, my thoughts still moving as slow as molasses. "What in the hell could I have that Valens would ever want?" I shook my head. "Look, to end this ridiculousness, fine. Test me. Just promise me that if I have enough power for the government to care, you won't make me move to the magical zone. Daisy can't live there, and Mordecai would be in constant danger. Just…please, promise me that."

"Is that all it would've taken?" He cocked his head, mystified. "All this, just so you don't have to move to the magical zone?"

"It would put my wards in danger. Where would Daisy go?"

He stared at me for a moment. "I should have seen that. How shortsighted of me."

"Well, now that you mention it…"

He nodded. "That is an easy promise to make. And once you are categorized properly, the mountebanks' burning curiosity will be put to rest. I've seen it before. They hate unanswered questions, especially when the subject is the one in control of the answers. But soon after they answer this riddle for me, I've seen to it they'll get someone new to marvel at. Someone my father will be desperate to control." A vicious smile crossed his face. "That subject belongs to someone else. He wandered away in search of mortal pleasures, and I swooped in to pick him up at the right moment. I'll fabricate where and how I found him, feign ignorance to his magic and who has a claim on him. Given that he responds to authority about as well as you do, he'll give you the perfect way to slip out from under the radar, providing me with enough cover to alter your records."

That seemed like an awful lot of effort for one assessment, but I wasn't about to say no. It solved both of our problems—my desire to be ignored, and his need for something constructive to do.

"Yeah. Sounds good. I'm in. Whatever."

He stood and slid the chair across the room, the graceful movement contrasted by metal screeching on linoleum. "Don't give them a hard time," he said as he made his way to the door.

"Yes, but they make it impossible," I yelled after his retreating, muscular backside. He was doing great things for those slacks.

"Get your head back in the game," I muttered to myself furiously. The man was unsettling on so many levels. It was starting to mess with my head.

Biting my lip, I kept all snarky comments at bay when Mountebank Iams and his stern-faced nurse trudged back in. "Cooperating the first time would've saved everyone a lot of time and effort," he said.

"Just think about all the things we would've missed out on had I done so. Our chemistry. Our witty banter." I grinned at him. "Tell me true. You loved it."

His face could've cracked glass.

I held out my arm so they could wrap the band around it. All the hookups from the last machine had been yanked off when I'd tumbled to the ground.

"It really is strange that you have three machines in here with the sole purpose of knowing a person's favorite color," I said. "Just do a color test."

"Some magic lends better to multiple people working in sync. For those types of magical people, we need multiple machines running synchronistically."

"Ah."

"Now, please relax *so we can get an accurate reading.*"

I was grateful to do as he said. After Kieran, I was exhausted. I just hoped this test would finally satisfy Kieran's curiosity, and he'd be done with me once and for all.

Chapter 31

ALEXIS

IT ONLY TOOK ten minutes, but it seemed like a lot longer in the company of the stuffy mountebank and his disapproving nurse. At the end, they looked at me with wide eyes, stunned by whatever the machine was telling them, and then escorted me out of the room as though the past two hours hadn't happened. I wished I could be excited, or feel any other emotion but unease.

As promised, I was free to go. At least that was a good sign.

No one was in the waiting room where I'd dropped off Mordecai. I lugged myself to the check-in desk and waited for a small-statured woman to glance up from her computer screen. Her brow furrowed just a bit before she plastered on her chipper customer service smile.

"Hello. Can I help you?" she asked.

"Yes. I'm just checking on Mordecai Wolfram."

"Oh, yes. Mordecai. What a lovely young man. Let me check his progress." She turned back to the computer screen. "Let's see... Ah. All the tests are done, and we're waiting for the stat sheet to make sure we have everything we need. Sometimes the numbers are skewed and an additional test is needed. It looks like Mordecai is... Yes, he's in a massage currently. He should be out within the hour."

"In a *massage*?" I asked.

"Yes. Given the wait times, and the nature of our patients' illnesses, we offer a variety of services to help them relax. It looks like"—she moved the mouse—"Mordecai opted for all three." She turned back to me with a sad smile. "That's fairly standard for patients who suffer chronic pain."

"A massage, and what else did he get?"

"A facial and a mud bath."

"Right." He needed it, deserved it, and I was glad he had access to it, but man, after being poked, prodded, and mentally messed with all day, it took a second to like him. "So an hour?"

"Yes. And you are Alexis Price?"

"Yes. I'm finished...with my thing. Downstairs."

"Yes, of course. He mentioned that you'd be taking him home. If you give me your number, you can feel free to use our resources and I'll text you when he's ready. Or, if you'd prefer, we can arrange—"

"Texting me would be great," I cut in, not about to argue again about someone else driving him home.

"What resources?"

"We have a state-of-the-art fitness center. Clothes and shoes can be provided if necessary. We also have a library with over thirty thousand volumes…"

I rubbed my eyes, noticing she hadn't mentioned a cafeteria, though I was pretty sure the place must've had one. Was she trying to tell me something?

"Where's the library?"

A couple of wrong turns later, I finally found the hall that housed both the library and the fitness center. But when I reached the large archway that led into a cozy place with overstuffed chairs, huge wall-to-ceiling bookshelves, and people quietly reading, I couldn't bring myself to go any farther. The second my butt hit one of those comfortable-looking reading nooks, I'd pass out. The best bet was to keep moving.

Continuing on, I heard the metallic clanks and rhythmic pounding of people working out. The opened double doors showed off a myriad of machines and free-weight areas, half of which were currently being used. A check-in desk sat off to the side, and I very nearly wandered over to see about getting some clothes.

Instead, I drifted in, working myself up for any sort of physical activity. To the right, legs jutted into the air before slowly lowering again. Upon closer inspection, it was a yoga class of clearly advanced students, because they went right back into a handstand.

That wasn't for me.

A group of five men and women followed a bulky lady out through a back door, each with a weight in one hand and a jump rope in the other. That was probably a class of some sort, like boot camp or CrossFit or something. To the left, way in the back behind a setup of medicine balls, more weights, and padded mats, another set of double doors stood open. Soft light fell through, illuminating the person who stood just in front of them.

A shock of butterflies ripped through my stomach as I noticed the large, well-built man in loose sweats and an unzipped sweatshirt. His torso was nude. My tongue nearly stuck to the roof of my mouth as I feasted my eyes on that impeccable slice of pec and six-pack heaven.

Kieran was just as defined as he was built. The man was a legend.

No, Alexis, he's a god.

He turned his head, glancing around, like he was doing something mischievous, before he reached the doors. He grabbed first one side, then the other, exiting the gym and closing the doors behind him.

Instead of drifting to a stop and turning around, like I definitely should've, my stride lengthened and my speed increased. Something in me wanted to see how he liked being stalked. How he liked thinking he was alone, doing his own thing, when someone was watching him from the shadows.

Besides, I had a burning need to see what someone like Kieran got up to when he thought no one was looking. Was he like a normal person, or did Demigods lead more extravagant lives?

He knew all there was to know about me. Time to turn the tables in this little power play and get what I wanted for once.

I got to the double doors and did as Kieran had done, inspecting my surroundings to see what was what. The desk was out of sight from his area, and only two people were taking a break from their machines, patting their face dry or slugging water out of a bottle. Neither one glanced my way.

Some of the fatigue lifted as stealthy excitement coursed through me. I cranked the handle, surprised it wasn't locked, then pulled the door open a crack so I could peer inside. Light filtered down through a glass dome high overhead. A walkway led right, flanked by a banister with nothing but air on the other side.

Confused, I slinked in and closed the door behind me, staying near the wall. A shout echoed up from below, followed by a spattering of laughter. A splash of water drowned them out before another burst of shouts and laughter took over.

The walkway to the right curved around the banister to a small landing. From there, the walker could either continue on to the other side, a walkway similar to this hugging the wall across an open chasm, or go down a wide stairway to the floor below.

Speaking of the floor below…

I took a couple steps forward and peered over, listening for any sounds of possible pursuit. I didn't want to be caught unawares, which might lead to someone trying to teach me to fly by throwing me over the banister.

My eyes widened at the layout below me. It was a course of some kind, with ropes and scaffolding suspended over water, each item an obstacle, dumping the athlete into a safe water landing should they mess up.

"Go!" someone shouted.

A horn blared and a large electric timer hanging at the end of the course started rolling numbers.

A guy with lean muscle and the flowing elegance of the truly athletic practically danced across a series of raised round steps, all spaced at odd distances, each of the surfaces at a different angle. The man made it through quickly, his hands barely raised at his sides to keep his balance.

He scampered up one of the carpeted scaffolding platforms, jumped across empty space, and grabbed a rope hanging in the air. He swung to another platform before climbing onto a log balanced lengthwise on a metal rail about ten feet above the ground.

My mouth dropped open as I watched him roll through the air toward a floating island hovering at the end of the rail. It was like watching a real-life Mario Bros. character run, jump, and parkour his way to the finish flag.

When he reached his destination, a cluster of guys clapped off to the side, keeping pace along a walkway that would eventually pass right under me. I spied Kieran at the center of the crowd, his height matching the others' but his physique setting him apart. His focus was entirely on the man struggling to stand dizzily and move on to the next obstacle.

Somewhat fascinated and also let down that he wasn't doing something more exciting, I pushed back from the banister and hurried toward the stairs. Once there, I edged out enough to see that they were now staring at the athlete as he climbed up a rock wall, made of real rock. The obstacle partially blocked their view of the stairwell, so I skulked toward the hidden side and hurried down, hoping their entrancement with the athlete would keep them from noticing me.

Once at the bottom, it was easy to scamper to the opposite side of the obstacle course, ducking from one large structure to the next. A splash made me pause, my heart in my throat. There was no way the athlete would get out on my side, was there?

As the onlookers clapped and shouted encouragement, I caught a glimpse of their bodies moving back toward the beginning. It was time for someone else to go.

Between two large pillars, I saw the fallen competitor climb out of the water with a delicious display of back muscle. Once up, he shook his head with a smile.

"Let's see you take that wall, Thane," he shouted, running his hand through his hair while laughing. "They made it ten times as hard."

"For *you*."

I hated how intimate I was with that rough, sexy voice.

"I got this," Kieran said.

"Hit it," someone shouted.

"Hold on, let me reset the timer," someone else said.

I snuck forward until I noticed some steps leading up to a viewing platform. I hesitated, knowing I should stick with the lower walkway, where it was easier to hide behind the large obstacles. At the same time, I wanted to see what he could do. An obstacle course seemed so mundane. It didn't seem like something a Demigod would waste his time on. Unless impressing his minions and pumping his already massive ego was what got Kieran's rocks off. Probably.

Without another thought, I climbed the steps and hurried to the bench by the wall. I was now about halfway between the lowest floor and the upper walk-way connected to the gym. The course opened up in front of me, and I had a perfect view of Kieran stripping his gray sweatshirt off before tossing it aside.

The V of his upper body reduced into his sweats-clad, trim hips. He swung his arms, and his large biceps grabbed my attention like a hypnotist at a magic show.

The newly wet guy draped a white towel across his shoulders and joined the others waiting for Kieran, some with sweatshirts and some with bare torsos. All the guys moved and stood with a lethal, toned grace.

"You ready?" one of them shouted.

Kieran nodded, and the horn blared.

He started forward, faster than a mere human, run-ning across the round pedestals like they were even and flat. At the platform in no time, he climbed the rope hand over hand, his ease of movement staggering. Up on the log next, he wrapped those long arms and legs around it before rolling, holding on while spinning through the air like it was a normal mode of transporta-tion.

The side of another obstacle blocked my sight, but the whooping of his buddies as they moved along the walkway made it clear he'd landed on the floating island. I edged out to the side so I could watch him run along an uneven surface, scale a bending wall, and then launch himself at the rock wall that had beaten the other athlete.

Glorious muscles popped out along his frame as he reached and strained for hand- and footholds, making his way up the sheer face. Moisture glistened along his perfect back.

My body was aching so badly that I almost didn't notice the movement from the other side of the room.

Shock and fear coursed through me. It was Mountebank Iams, his brow furrowed. He held a file folder, and nervous butterflies fluttered my stomach. Did he have my results?

I pushed back a bit, losing sight of Kieran as he made it to the top of the wall, turned with one hand gripping the tiny ledge, and swung himself out of sight.

"No way!" yelled the guy who'd fallen into the water earlier. "I thought for sure that one would knock him down."

"Pay up." Another one put out his hand before they noticed the newcomer.

A shiver collectively went through the group, their postures and expressions changing at the same time. Whereas before they'd been relaxed and loose, now they were wary and on guard. They turned to the mountebank as a group, their backs to Kieran, who'd moved on to another part of the course.

"No one is allowed through here when Demigod Kieran is working out. You know this," one of the guys said, the tallest of the group, with bronzed skin and huge arms.

I grimaced and pushed back toward the shadows.

"He asked that I bring...certain results"—the mountebank's pause was smug—"as soon as they were in. And believe me, he's going to want to see these." He held the file folder close, clearly not intending to offer it up to the peons.

The mountebank had better check his attitude, or he'd end up facedown in any one of the many pools of water around here.

The guy who'd just gone for a swim, whose wet blond hair now stood every which way, glanced back to check on Kieran's progress. "He's almost done."

I expected them to get moving to keep pace. Kieran was flying through the obstacles, clearly having as much trouble here as he would on a stroll through the park. But instead the men had shuffled together to form a wall, blocking the newcomer from going any deeper into the man den. Their bodies remained poised and alert, clearly ready to react aggressively at a moment's notice.

I got the distinct impression it was a well-known fact that no one should be in here except for the Demigod and his chosen few. A sign wouldn't have gone amiss...

Like it would've mattered.

A few moments later, a horn sounded, making the mountebank jump. He looked mostly calm and collected, but he'd been reading the postures of the guys around him. No doubt he could feel the tension in the air.

Two beats later, and a blur of movement ripped along the walkway. Kieran stopped behind the guys. He rolled his shoulders, and the muscles along his robust chest flared dramatically.

I swallowed audibly.

"Well?" Kieran asked without preamble.

His men parted like the sea before Moses.

"Yes. Um…" Mountebank Iams held out the files, the sturdy paper trembling in his grasp. "It's as you expected. Her power level is a class five."

Freezing cold dripped down my middle. That was impossible! A class five was the highest level of magic a non-godly type could have. Class fives could do fantastic things, like play with the elements, create illusions, or fly. There was no way I had that much power. There was clearly some mistake.

Kieran opened the folder as silence trickled through the room. I could hear my heart pounding through my eardrums. He turned a page and kept reading. No one so much as shifted.

I leaned forward, nowhere near that patient. Everything in my person wanted to yell, *Welllll?* while simultaneously telling him to throw those results away, forget this whole thing, and let me get on with my mundane life in the crack of societies. Or, if he really wanted to help me, he could put in a good word at my local ice cream establishment, where I was hoping to rise in the ranks to executive scooper if I played my cards right. I wasn't cut out for class-five magic. It wasn't in my nature, and certainly wasn't in my bloodline.

Not to mention, my magic didn't have too many exciting manifestations. Unless you liked dead people.

Even if I *was* a class five, it didn't change anything. Not one thing. Kieran had to see that.

"Has anyone else seen this?" Kieran asked, his voice even and flat and not giving anything away. I picked at my nail in unease.

"No, sir, just as you requested."

"And her mother? Could she have passed this down?"

"Well, sir, it's hard to know without further analysis. Genetics can manifest in unique ways."

"So we're blind to how this happened. With her mother deceased, and no recorded father, we're at a standstill." Kieran turned another piece of paper. I was dying to know what he found so interesting. "Is there any reason to suspect she knew any of this?"

The mountebank's mouth turned downward. "Given my briefing with the Authenticator, it seems unlikely. From her file, it seems as though she's been struggling for most of her life, without access to training or guidance. She displays the characteristics of a mutt, and has reached for and honed that which would help her the most. I doubt she even has a name for what she was able to do in the assessment room today. As such, it would be interesting to study further. She could provide valuable insight to those of my craft…"

Kieran snapped the file folder shut and held it to the side and slightly behind his body. The blond guy with wet hair took it without comment.

"I have all I need from you," Kieran said, his tone harsh.

"Yes, sir." The mountebank cowered and took a step back. "I understand, sir. I just want to press the point, sir, how extraordinary the events were in that assessment room today. I very much think further assessment—"

"Get out," Kieran barked.

The mountebank flinched and took two more quick steps backward. He bowed submissively. "Yes, sir. Sorry, sir." He turned without another word and scurried from the room.

After the door shut behind him, silence rained down. Nobody moved or shifted. I could hear myself breathing.

"I want her watched," Kieran barked finally, his eyes distant. "Day and night. Find out her schedule, what she does in her alone time, and who she communicates with. I want to know her better than she knows herself. Watch her wards, too. Run interference if someone tries to contact her. We'll need to set up a training schedule, but first I need more information about her magic. Arrange for blood work. I want to know who her father is. Find out if he knows she exists."

Anger at his continued stalking shifted to furious tingles running down my back.

My father? What did he have to do with anything? He was a one-night stand my mother had claimed not to remember. I'd figured she was lying, but hadn't felt the need to press her. She'd always acted in my best interests. She'd also had a soft spot for assholes. If she'd thought I shouldn't know him, or vice versa, I was good with that. I didn't need more struggle.

But hearing that Kieran would try to find him set me on edge. It felt like my entire life was being cracked open, changed, and I was powerless to stop it.

What the hell is in that file?

Anger rose like fire in my blood.

It didn't matter. My life wouldn't change. Not because of more power, or some secret magic I apparently didn't know about and certainly didn't know how to use, and not because of some stranger showing up out of the blue and calling himself my pappy. I had two kids to take care of. My only important job was making sure they reached adulthood with enough of a head start to have a chance at life. Nothing else mattered.

As for Kieran's cronies following me around, watching everything I did?

I barely kept from chuckling.

My magic might not be able to grow things or fight people off, but I could arrange for an entire neighborhood of invisible busybodies to bombard these bastards. My spies were bored as hell and anxious to tattle. Kieran's guys wouldn't be able to fart without one of my people knowing about it, and their hiding places would be given away instantly and constantly.

"Get Jim reassigned and get people on him," Kieran went on. "I don't want him trying to take this further. If he does, or even breathes a word of it to anyone, get rid of him for good."

My mouth dropped open.

"The records?" an intense guy asked, standing beside Kieran now.

"Amend them with old data but a slightly improved magical score and post them. Don't dally. I don't want to give anyone a reason to look more closely. Make sure the distraction is up and running by the time you post the info. Put the originals on my private network. No one is to see those, do I make myself clear?"

"Yes, sir," the man said, and a growing unease gnawed at my gut.

I wanted to pull the ejection cord. I wanted to pack all this in, go home, and crawl under a rock. I didn't know what was going on, but the implications had turned my blood cold.

"Get it set up," Kieran said, starting back toward where the mountebank had exited. "Keep me informed of when she goes to that pub. I want to know the moment she sets out."

"Yes, sir."

I watched him go, followed by his groupies, thinking through the names I'd contact in the neighborhood. Hopefully most of them hadn't yet allowed their boredom whisk them away across the Line. I only tended to check in when I needed something, and that was a rarity reserved for desperate matters only.

I wondered if a few of them would like to stalk the stalkers, heading back to their homes and haunting them. No one enjoyed being haunted.

Bing.

The breath caught in my throat and everything in me froze solid.

It was a text message. I hadn't turned off my ringer.

Kieran stopped abruptly, followed by his groupies. As one, they turned in my direction, too slowly. Predators ready to prowl.

Bing.

This couldn't be happening!

I couldn't see eyes from this distance, just faces tuned in to the sound's location.

I knew the very instant Kieran recognized me.

It was the same moment a wide smile flashed across his striking face.

Chapter 32

ALEXIS

"**G**ET OUT," HE ordered his guys in a low, growling voice. An excited voice. The predator had spotted his prey.

"Shit turds." Heart suddenly rampaging, I burst forward and down the steps. He was across a sea of obstacles in a single moment. If I ran like hell, I had a chance to get to the door.

Then what?

I had no idea.

"Where does she think she's going?" I heard.

"Get out!" Kieran demanded.

No witnesses.

"Batshit and tiaras." I took the steps two at a time, catching one wrong near the end and pitching forward. I turned it into a roll, going a little sideways but stopping before I slammed into an obstacle beam.

I was up and running in a flash, not superhuman, but fast enough. I dodged behind an obstacle and quickly scanned for another way out. Nothing but wall.

Metal tinkled, and from the corner of my eye I saw a rope swing out from behind scaffolding. Nobody came into view.

Bing.

"Shut up, you bastard." I saw more steps leading up to another platform, this one higher, but no outlet that I could see. I couldn't chance going all the way up there to find a door. Besides, that wall probably signified the end of the gym. I'd have to cut across at some point.

Maybe I could lure him over to this side while I cut across the other?

He can move at superhuman speeds, you dumb shit. That won't work.

My inner dialogue was not very kind when faced with stupid ideas.

Feet pounded on a hard surface before the sound abruptly ceased. I looked around wildly.

The course looked clear. Nothing moved in my line of sight.

A hard thump sounded, followed by two more.

I paused where I was, breath coming quickly and heart pounding in my ears. That sound had been in front of me, in the middle of the two paths. But where?

I stalked to the side, near a large obstacle, my feet edging toward the side of the walkway. I scanned all I could from my position leaning over the sparkling water. Nothing. No large bodies and no sound. He was waiting for me to go by.

So maybe I had to go across instead.

This is stupid.

Yes, it is, inner asshole. But I have no other choice.

Each obstacle looked harder to navigate than the one before it, but finally I found something that looked like some sort of balance exercise. A collection of round balls dotted an expanse of water. Going lengthwise would be a true challenge. Going across would only require courage and surefootedness.

Amendment: this is really stupid.

I annoyed even myself at times.

Gritting my teeth, I prepared to tempt fate and cut across. But suddenly an idea clicked on the light bulb above my head.

I turned back the way I'd come. There had to be a door at the end. Why else would there be a viewing platform on this side?

Much better idea.

I took a moment to turn off the ringer on my phone before I jogged as slowly as I could while remaining silent. A light squeak behind me sounded like shoes on a slippery surface. Then pounding, like someone trying to get out of an obstacle.

Oh shit!

I put on a burst of speed, no longer trying for quiet, just trying to get out of there before he could clear the obstacle. I passed the stairs to the viewing area I'd been on, not even sparing them a glance. All my focus was on getting to that theoretical door at the end.

A shape swung from God knew where and dropped twenty feet directly in front of me. Kieran bent with the impact, and straightened slowly, his eyes shimmering with lust and malice.

"Fuck. Fuck, fuck. Oh fuck." I pivoted on a dime and was jumping before I'd thought it through.

I grabbed a blue rope midair, my momentum swinging me over the water. But there was nothing on the other side to grab. I swung back, chancing a jaw-clenching glance behind me.

He stalked up the walkway slowly, that devilish smile lingering on his handsome face.

"Crap, crap, fuck, crap," I muttered, looking around wildly. The rope was losing its swing. Soon I'd be hanging over the water. I needed to jump. But to what?

"There aren't many people who can sneak up on me, Alexis," he said, his voice thick with eager anticipation. "Those who get caught trying…are punished. How should I punish you? It is in my power to do so. You're on magical soil now. You're in my house, and you must play by my rules."

"Fuckety crap." I tried for more swing, but my hands were losing their grip and the rope wasn't complying. I strained to the side, reaching for one of the pegs in a sideboard with a bunch of holes, barely wrapping my fingers around it. The wood came out of the hole, and I swung the other way. "What the…"

"I'm almost disappointed I caught you. You were angry, weren't you, hearing my plans? A girl like you would rebel against something like that. I wonder what you would've done to retaliate. I can't say I don't deserve it, but I can't say I'm sorry, either."

I braced myself to launch off the rope.

"No!" he shouted, his teasing tone gone in an instant. "You'll hurt—"

One of my hands gave out before I had the momentum right. I hardly flew forward at all, but my body somersaulted. I smacked the water with the side of my face, my mouth open to scream, and my hands and legs spread out like a frog.

Bone-chilling water assaulted my mouth and pushed up into my nose. Cold rushed up over my head and body. My buoyancy slowed me and I paddled wildly up to the surface, already shaking from the plunge in temperature.

A hand grabbed my arm, and I struck out, catching Kieran's stomach with my foot. He only tightened his grip. It wasn't the reaction I'd been going for.

I crested the surface and gulped for air. Water sloshed into my mouth, antagonizing a cough already in progress. I sputtered hoarsely. The primal fear of drowning clawed at me, and I struggled to get away from him. To swim and keep from going under.

"I have you." He yanked me, turning me as he did so.

He trapped my back to his chest before two sure strokes moved us to the side of the pool. I might as well have been a baby for how easily he pulled me from the water, laid me out along the side, and knelt over me.

I heaved, coughing up water and gasping for air. I couldn't have run if I'd wanted to, not that it would've done any good. Horrible cold shook every inch of my body. My teeth chattered uncontrollably.

"Why...so c-cold," I stammered before taking another moment to cough up a lung. I hugged my arms around my middle. "F-feels...like...i-ice."

"C'mon. Let's warm you up." For the second time that day, he scooped me up and hugged me to his chest. Before I knew it, he was running with me, so fast that everything beside us blurred. "I keep it that cold as a punishment to the guys for falling in. They have extra...protection against...certain elements, so it needs to be cold enough to ice over. My magic keeps it from actually icing over." I could tell he was choosing his words carefully, probably so as not to give away secrets. He apparently thought I gave two rats or knew anyone with friends they could tell. "I had other things on my mind when you were dangling above the surface.

Without…protection, the temperature of the water will give most mammals hypothermia."

"Probably…n-not. W-wasn't in…for long."

He lowered me onto a blue exercise mat still within the private obstacle course area, next to a bundle of sweatshirt. Without ceremony, he hooked two thumbs in the waistband of his sweats and slid them down his legs. Black boxer briefs hugged his powerful thighs and put a very large bulge on display.

I probably should've asked what he thought he was doing, or done more than slap at his hands as he went to lift my shirt over my head, but for one solid moment, I could do nothing but stare at the size of that bulge.

It wasn't one of my finest moments. I blamed the deathly cold cocooning my thoughts.

"S-stop." I slapped his hands from the bottom of my soaked shirt, hanging limply off me like a pliable ice cube. He'd already removed my cross-body purse and lowered it to the ground. There went any receipts I needed. "Wh-what are…you do-doing?"

"You need to get out of these wet clothes, Alexis. You can keep your underwear if you want, but the pants and shirt have to go." He captured both of my wrists in one of his large hands before lifting them over my head and grabbing my shirt with the other hand.

I probably would've struggled if I weren't so damn cold.

The sopping, freezing fabric on my face made me feel like I was being dunked again. It hadn't warmed up in the least. Definitely magically treated.

It fell to the side in a wet *glop*.

My lacy bra with more holes than lace and very little support gave him an absolute eyeful, but if he noticed for more than a moment, he didn't show it.

"Here." He snatched his sweatshirt up off the ground and pulled it around my shoulders. "Tuck in."

I didn't need to be told twice. I pushed my hands through the armholes and wrapped all that material around my torso. His smell permeated my senses. Clean cotton, masculine spice, and crisp ocean. I closed my eyes and breathed it in while swimming in the sweatshirt's warmth.

Which was why I was late to the party when he unbuttoned my jeans and slid them down my wet thighs.

"Are those...poop emojis on your underwear? Is that a warning?" he asked.

"Oh my..." I bent in mortification and pulled down the sweatshirt, covering what I could. "They were free, okay? I wouldn't have worn them if I'd thought they'd be seen."

He chuckled darkly. "And to think, if I hadn't chased you into the water, I never would've seen what you wear on a day-to-day basis. Step out."

Still bending with the sweatshirt pulled to cover

what I could, I braced a hand on his hard shoulder and jerkily lifted my legs out of the jeans.

"Here." He ran to the wall, a blur of movement, and extracted sweats from a basket beside a rack of weights. Back in a moment, he bent and opened up the leg holes for me to step into them. "You'll probably have to hold them up. They're made to fit me."

"I sure as h-hell hope I have to ho-hold them up." I pulled the sweatshirt a little tighter as he brought up the sweats.

"I wouldn't have hurt you," he said softly as he bunched the sweats around my middle. His mostly nude body stood nearly pressed against mine, and his warm breath dusted my face. "Not in a way you didn't like."

Tingles raced the shivers across my skin. I fought from leaning in, craving the warmth I knew his body would provide.

"Don't fear me, Alexis. Don't ever fear me. I may hurt a lot of people before this is through, but never you. Do you understand?"

"Before what is through?" I asked, struggling to keep my teeth from chattering. "Helping your mother?"

He looked down at me for a moment, but didn't answer. Instead, I felt one of his hands tighten into a fist, pulling the sweats around me that much tighter. His other hand slid upward until the heat of his touch burned across my lower back.

"Did you hear what I said? About your magic level?" he asked, stepping just a bit closer. His arms tightened around me, pulling my body flush with his. "About my plans for you?"

I could hardly breathe. His proximity vibrated through my body, his power drilling into me until it soaked deep down into my middle. His hand drifted a little lower on my back, and his grip on the pants loosened, his fingers dipping down into the waistband.

My whole world stilled in that moment. I let my eyes drift shut, feeling the glorious heat from his magic and body. I wanted his touch much, much lower. I wanted those shapely lips to skim my fevered skin as I moaned out his name.

I wanted to feel the rush of his size as it thrust into me.

"Please…" I meant to say "stop," but the word wouldn't come out. He was, quite possibly, the epitome of a bad idea, but I just wanted to throw caution to the wind and take him for a ride.

"You're mine, Alexis," he whispered next to my ear. His hand dipped lower, his fingertips brushing the top of my panty line.

And that was part of the reason he was the epitome of a bad idea.

I tried to reel away. To back up. But my body

wouldn't obey.

In a quick movement, he pulled his hand from my back and nudged my chin up.

His lips settled against mine, soft and full. He increased the pressure of his kiss as his first two fingers slid along my jaw, the touch light and teasing, making my insides dance. He sucked softly on my bottom lip before his tongue flitted in, teasing.

I fell into that kiss. That sinfully decadent kiss.

Fireworks went off in my middle and color exploded behind my closed eyes. Lightness filled my body until it felt like I was floating up off the ground. My skin felt alive, brimming with electricity. My core burned for his touch.

"Your magic feels...unbelievable." His kiss deepened as his hand roamed down my chest.

My own hands betrayed me, loosening their grip on the sweatshirt to allow his hand to slip in and cup a breast.

I moaned, reaching out now and running my palms across his cut body. I'd been with a couple of lookers in my day, but no one who could even remotely compare to the perfection that was Kieran.

He pinched a nipple softly, and I gasped at the shock of pleasure that speared through my center and boiled in my core.

"I want to fuck you, Alexis," he said against my lips,

his hand moving faster now. It slid over my belly and down to my panties. His fingers traced along the edges before slipping in. I moaned. "I want to fuck you right now."

Chapter 33

ALEXIS

MY BRAIN BUZZED with desire, blocking out all thought. All of the many reasons why this was a terrible idea.

Kieran's tricky fingers slid along my wetness before dipping in, nearly buckling my legs and sending me to the floor. His thumb massaged my clit while his fingers plunged into me, starting up a rhythm, the perfect speed.

His other hand rubbed a nipple, the pleasure from all the stimulation pulsing within me.

I yanked on his neck with one hand, the kiss bruising now, while running my other palm along the hardness in those boxer briefs. His rigid length filled his underwear and then some, straining to get out. His fingers worked me higher, his skill with his digits just a glimpse of what was sure to come.

A soft buzzing wormed through my desperation to have him inside of me. A phone ringing somewhere.

A phone ringing!

Mine had been in my pocket when I'd fallen in the water. It was surely dead, which meant Mordecai wouldn't be able to get a hold of me!

Panic blared, cutting through my passion-dizzied mind.

I yanked my hands up, leaned back, and then shoved with my palms, hitting Kieran square in the chest.

"No," I said, taking a big step back before remembering the state of my borrowed sweats.

My feet caught on the fabric, but my weight continued to move backward. I staggered and then tipped, stupidly expecting to be saved and instead landing right on my tailbone.

The last traces of desire fled, and I blinked in the chill of the air, getting my bearings. The sweats were around my ankles and the sweatshirt lay wide open, exposing my mess of a bra and my nipples, still budded, sticking out through it.

"That's embarrassing." I yanked the sweatshirt closed and quickly zipped it up. I struggled to my feet, this time stupidly thinking I'd get a hand. Still a nope.

Kieran stood stock-still, looking confused, surprised, and wary, his large hard-on raging against the confines of his briefs.

"That's probably also embarrassing, given the change in our situation." I brushed my wet hair out of my face before bending for my clothes. A pat and a few squeezes revealed empty pockets. No phone, dead or otherwise.

I glanced down at my sopping purse, but knew it had been in my pocket. I spun, looking back toward the pool, before hurrying that way.

"Alexis, wait…" Kieran's voice was wispy, completely unlike him. He clearly wasn't used to girls saying no when he'd gotten them that far.

"I shouldn't have let him get me that far," I quietly berated myself, stopping at the edge of the pool and looking down. The sweats slipped down to my thighs before I could grab them and haul them back up.

Water shimmered on the surface, distorting my view, but even still, a certain sleek black object that I'd worked very hard for could be seen at the very bottom.

My heart sank. It had been in there for a while now. I should've had Kieran fish it out before I'd shoved him away and shouted no in his face.

"Okay. Surely there has to be a net around here somewhere…"

"I've got it." Kieran sauntered up like he owned the world, his hard-on still going strong. No embarrassment about that fact bled into his poise, gait, or expression. He didn't even seem annoyed. It was business as usual for him, like the moment before hadn't happened.

In a smooth motion, he dove into the freezing water, straight down to my phone. He grabbed it without hunting, turned, and kicked back to the surface, utterly at home in the water. Of course, he was a descendant of the god of the sea and the son of one of the sea's creatures. He belonged in the water.

He grabbed the lip of the pool and pulled himself out. Without a word, he handed my phone over.

"Shit," I breathed, taking it in hand, not even bothered when the sweats slipped down around my ankles again. "What if Mordecai was trying to get a hold of me?" I looked up at him. "Do you think my phone is dead forever?"

He studied me for a quiet moment before glancing at my phone. Without a word, he turned and strutted away.

A twinge of guilt pinched my gut. "I should probably apologize for how I handled that other thing," I mumbled, watching his muscular backside as he moved away. "Then again..." I tore my gaze away and turned my phone over in my hands. "He's the reason my phone is possibly dead, and that I might've missed a call from the medical office, and that my life has been turned upside down." I lowered my eyebrows. "He deserved that harsh no. And maybe a kick to go along with it. Hopefully he takes the hint—"

"I have superhuman hearing, Alexis," he called from

the beginning of the obstacle course, interrupting my private conversation with myself. Rude. "You're mine, and you just proved you feel it. I protect what's mine." I saw him bend for something, but couldn't see what. Probably his phone. "We'll talk soon about my job offer."

I caught a glimpse of him stalking away before he turned a corner. The soft click of a door said he'd gone.

All I could do was stare in disbelief for a moment.

Between showing up to the appointment and this moment, I'd made my situation infinitely worse.

"Crap," I said quietly, letting the silence soak into me. "Crap."

After a few deep breaths, I worked my way back to my clothes, only to stop in confusion when all I saw was a wet stain. Confused, I glanced around the floor. Nothing beyond a few mats and a scrap of paper that had been discarded.

"He took my fucking clothes?" I put out my hands, opened my mouth, and dramatically turned in a circle. "What the…"

The guy was a lunatic. There was no other explanation. Power had gone to his head, cracked something vital, let sense and reality seep out, and left behind only a great face with a breathtaking body.

And now that great face and breathtaking body had my good jeans and non-stained shirt.

"What a royal dickface fucker. I hope I get the chance to kick him right in that huge dong of his."

Muttering to myself, in between cursing the giant sweats that didn't want to stay up, I made my way to the closest exit that everyone else had used. Double doors housed a sign warning people away from Demigod Kieran's private fitness quarters.

"There's more than one door, you bunch of nit-wits," I groused, shoving the doors open and leaving them that way.

Three steps out, a presence niggled at my awareness. Already annoyed, I stopped abruptly and spun around. A half-naked man crouched behind a fake plant, watching me with a straight face.

It was the blond guy with still-damp hair. And now that he was closer, I saw that he was the same guy who'd been standing guard over my car after the freak show.

"Hello, Magoo," he said nonchalantly, his smile large and beautiful and about to get a foot in it.

"Fantastic." I didn't know what else to say about that nickname.

I clutched the large sweats a little tighter, holding my wet purse out a little farther from my body, as I turned away. "You didn't even bother to put on a shirt before starting your detail, huh?"

I started walking. He was big, toned, and moved like he was lethal. If he intended to follow me around, there wasn't a lot I could do about it besides get home as soon as possible.

I needed to come up with a plan.

"I worked hard on this body. Why not show it off?" he said, drifting behind me.

Obviously that wasn't the reason why he wasn't wearing a shirt, but I didn't bother commenting.

At the stairs to the second floor, I glanced back as I walked around the banister and onto the stairs. With a start, I realized he was gone. Somewhere along the way, he'd drifted out of sight again without my knowing.

I didn't know if that was good or bad.

The waiting room was empty but for the guy at the check-in desk with a phone to his ear. Something told me he'd dialed my number and was hoping I would pick up.

"Hey," I said, hurrying up to him. "Sorry I'm late. I dropped my phone in the pool."

"Ah." He beamed at me and lowered the phone to its cradle. "We were starting to lose hope. I'll just bring him up for you."

A few moments later, the door in the corner of the room opened and a desperately drained Mordecai trudged out, leaning heavily on an orderly.

"Oh my God, what did they do to you?" I asked as I rushed forward, my heart in my throat.

"It's fine…" Mordecai blinked at my outfit. "Where

are your clothes?"

"Do you want help, ma'am?" the orderly asked.

"No. I got it." I ducked into Mordecai's outstretched arm and slung my arm around his middle without thinking.

I'd let go of my sweats.

"Crap." I grabbed at them with my other hand, slapping the wet purse against my leg. "Shoot."

"Ma'am—"

"What is going on?" Mordecai asked, a smirk fighting the concern in his eyes.

"Ma'am, do you need—"

"I'm fine," I yelled at the orderly, because I needed to take out my humiliation turned aggression on someone, and it couldn't be a sick teenager. "Just…give me a minute."

"Would a stapler do?" Mr. Smart Guy at the front desk asked, returning.

"Maybe," I muttered.

A few helpful staff, a lot of staples, and a host of safety pins later, I was ready for the road.

"So…" Mordecai leaned against me, his shoulders bowing heavily. "Where are your clothes, again?"

Trying to tamp down my fear for him, I swallowed my rage and frustration over the situation with Kieran. Mordecai didn't need to bear the burden of my shitty problems.

"Never mind. It's nothing."

"Your underwear is leaking...hopefully water through huge gray sweats, your hair is dripping, and your bag has been dunked. It's nothing?"

He was so nice that he didn't even mention my failure to answer the office's texts and phone calls.

"Let's save it for when we get home. I don't want to repeat myself for Daisy."

I helped him out of the room and turned toward the stairs. A moment later, though, he stiffened and slowed. He glanced behind him, his fingers digging into my back.

"What?" I asked, stopping to turn around.

"Keep going," he whispered.

"What?" I repeated, whispering now, at the head of the stairs.

"Someone is...back there. They seem...dangerous."

"Wow, look at you. Your shifter senses are blossoming. Can you see anyone?"

"No. Come on—what are you waiting for?"

I searched the hall, not letting him turn me around. A girl of about Mordecai's age waited next to a small alcove, her fingers picking at the big plastic buttons on her shirt and her face lowered, as if she didn't want people to see her. Shy, probably. On her right hung an oil painting of the running of the bulls in Spain with a man flying through the air, propelled by a horn gouging his butt. A metal-looking tree climbed the wall beside it, its branches hanging down to give the girl's nook some cover.

"Hey," I called, not worrying about my volume. This was a magical place. Hopefully I wasn't the weirdest person around.

The girl started and her head snapped up. Her gaze zeroed in on Mordecai and me before sweeping the hall in front of us, looking for the person I was addressing. When she didn't see anyone, I thought her gaze would return to us.

Instead, it drifted upward, toward the branches of the tree crawling across the ceiling.

"No…way." I followed her gaze and found widened eyes in a partially strained face. "You're an odd-looking banana, sir."

Chapter 34

ALEXIS

THE GUY WITH the huge arms from Kieran's posse clung to the branches of the metallic tree, which did *not* look strong enough to hold him. Those incredible arms probably comprised most of his weight, but his legs were active, too, holding his lower half.

Seeing that his cover was blown, he swung his legs down before he gracefully dropped, slightly bending with the impact. He rose, huge, at probably six four or five, with large hands and a solid frame. His severe expression matched his cheekbones, and his eyes were hard and dark.

"Come on." I finally turned, yanking Mordecai with me.

"Who is he?" Mordecai asked, looking behind us. "Why is he following us?"

"He's the Demigod's version of a joke." I veered to the side, dragging with Mordecai's weight. "Grab that banister."

His arm shook as he gripped the wood, and his other fingers clutched my shoulder. He tipped, and I staggered to catch his weight, half falling down two stairs.

A strong hand landed on my bicep and the large man stepped in front of us, his other hand coming up to brace against Mordecai's chest.

We both froze.

"This is why they like to take the patients home," the man said before pulling my arm, moving me away from Mordecai's side. "It is also why we have wheelchairs. And elevators." He slid into my place, easily taking Mordecai's weight, and started slowly down the stairs.

My heart squished as I hurried down in front of them. The man didn't have to do this. He was under no orders to carry my ward around. That he would help, without being asked, told me he was at least a decent guy.

Unfortunately, it would make it harder not to like him.

Lines creased Mordecai's face by the time he reached the bottom, some from uncertainty, and some from fatigue.

I bit my tongue, wanting to ask if the mountebanks had told him anything.

"I think I can manage," Mordecai said. Even his words sounded strained.

"You're being helped out by one of Demigod Kieran's Six," the man said. "Take the style points. They're free."

"Well… They aren't exactly *free*, are they, since you're on spy duty?" I asked, not as accusatory as I'd meant it to be.

Mordecai looked at me, troubled, but he didn't ask for more details. That would come later, when the stranger was gone.

"Touché," the man said, not at all perturbed or arrogant. It was slightly infuriating that he seemed like a cool guy.

"You've got a good frame," the man said to Mordecai as we moved toward the door, slow and steady. His accent was distinctive but difficult to pinpoint—whenever he spoke, his tongue rolled and vowels rounded. "If you have enough fuel, you'll fill out like a powerhouse."

"Someone else would need to supply the meat for that fuel. Alexis is a vegan," Mordecai said.

"A vegan?" The man gave me a sour face. "Why would you do that to yourself?"

"It's good for you. And saves the environment. And…" I squinted, reaching for another reason. Being poor and not having any hookups in the meat and dairy department were the only real reasons I could think of.

"I'm just kidding," Mordecai said with a smile, and I

wondered why he was suddenly so comfortable. Did he somehow fail to understand what accepting this man's help meant?

"You let me know, and I'll make you a roast that will knock your socks off," the guy said. "You'll feel like a million bucks."

I bit back a snarky comment when I noticed the teenage girl from upstairs standing near the empty front desk. Her eyes were just as large, her body just as hunched, but this time she watched me with a hungry intensity.

I turned my gaze away, but it whipped right back when she stuck out her finger and pointed behind the empty desk.

Ah. This was where the blond guy must've gotten off to.

I sighed before elevating my voice. "You might as well come out from behind the desk. I know you're there."

"How could you possibly know that?" the guy carrying Mordecai asked.

"I cheat, that's how. Why do you think no one wanted to play hide-and-seek with me as a kid?"

The blond guy, his hair nearly dry but still sticking out all over the place, stood slowly from behind the desk. His gaze lingered on the large man for a moment, something passing between them, before he stalked forward.

"Well, aren't we a merry bunch," I mumbled, nearly to the door now.

"Can you hear me?" the girl asked softly.

I sighed again, fatigue dragging at me. I really wanted to ignore her. I wasn't in the mood for a last will and testament. But she'd helped me twice, now. I owed her.

"Hold up," I told the others.

"What is it?" Mordecai asked, but I'd already turned.

"Yeah," I said to the girl. "Do you need to get something off your chest? Or would you like me to send you across the Line? I can't bring your killer to justice or contact anyone, but I'll listen for five minutes if you want."

"I can't go beyond the Line." She disappeared before reappearing right beside me.

I jolted and back-pedaled, a wall of my *fuck off* magic dropping down between us to keep her at bay. I stopped and clutched my heart, my eyes widened. "Did you learn to teleport after death, or what, because it is surprising. That's why people don't like ghosts, I'll tell you that much."

"Apporter," she said, and the plant by the desk disappeared, only to reappear on the other side. The guys behind me all sucked in a surprised breath.

Surprising, indeed.

In life, she'd been able to teleport not just herself, but other people and objects. That was a rare and neat kind of magic. A spirit who could move objects in the living world must have been extremely powerful when alive.

"Okay, well…" I took a deep breath, letting my heart slow down. "Don't do that to me again, okay? Walk like normal."

A man in a brown suit slowed his pace as he walked across the lobby. He glanced behind him, confused, wondering if I was talking to him.

"Not you," I told him, waving my arm to get him to go by.

"They killed me," the girl said in a small voice. "They won't let me leave."

"They killed you to keep you from leaving?"

The man slowed further, his eyes searching for my conversational partner. He clutched his briefcase a little tighter.

The girl shook her head. "They killed me, and now they won't let me leave."

A wave of goosebumps washed over me.

I stalked to the glass wall before dropping my head, letting my surroundings disappear and inducing a light trance. Almost immediately, a strange feeling of electricity shocked into my hand, a repellent force I'd never felt before. It tried to push through my body, digging into my squishy middle where I was pretty sure my soul was housed. The place Kieran could reach into and poke with his most delving stares.

I shivered, hating to admit that, even to myself.

"How in the bloody hell?" I whispered, putting my other palm to the glass. Electricity spread through my body.

Ghosts could usually go wherever they wanted, but this girl literally couldn't leave the building.

The girl drifted toward me. "They're punishing me for moving a trainer outside of the window."

"Wait…they killed you for moving a trainer outside of… Oh." It dawned on me. "What floor were you on?"

"The fourth floor."

"Right. So…yeah, if you kill someone, the powers that be typically serve you a piping-hot death sentence. That's kind of how things work here."

"I couldn't help it! They were shocking me with a cattle prod to get me to behave. I was mad. I didn't have complete control." She balled her fists. "It wasn't my fault."

Who'd treated her like that?

This girl had been quick to identify Kieran's minions. I blinked rapidly, then glanced over at the two guards waiting with Mordecai.

No, I couldn't believe that. Kieran was a lot of things, but he'd never been cruel. Besides, her clothing suggested she'd been haunting this area for a few years, at least, given the stale style of her sweater and jeans. Daisy couldn't afford the current teen fashions, but that didn't mean she stopped pining for them. I vaguely knew what kids this age wore.

"Were you being groomed to be in the Demigod's squad?" I whispered.

The girl drifted closer. "They called it his Elite. As in, I would be an Elite. But I didn't want to be! They took me from my house. They didn't even ask. It wasn't fair!"

"How long ago?"

She picked at her button, suddenly unsure.

I'd asked an unfair question. Spirits had a hard time monitoring the passing of time. Time simply failed to register.

"And you're talking about Valens?"

"Yes." Spite and hatred rang through that word.

A picture was starting to form. My heart sank for Kieran's mom. "Do you know how he is keeping you in the building? I don't recognize this magic."

"A man with white eyes and really long white hair. It moves around like it's alive, his hair. Sometimes a stick appears in his hand. It sounds like rattlesnake tails when he shakes it. He can't see me, like you can, but he feels me. Then he turns toward me with those white eyes. He tries to capture me. So I teleport away."

"He comes often?" She nodded, fear crossing her face. "How long between visits?"

"I…" She shook her head, looking helpless.

"Right, right…" I scratched my temple. "Sorry, I keep forgetting about the time thing. Okay." I exhaled. "Have you tried to move beyond the Line?"

"Yes. I see it. It's flashing. Like a beacon. But when I move toward it, I hit a wall. I can't get through."

"Let's see about that. Any last words?"

"Make sure my parents are okay. That they know what happened."

"O-kay…" I was sure her parents already knew. An Apporter killing a dude and getting sentenced to death would have circulated through the news—and if she'd been stolen from her bed, no doubt her parents had been looking for her. This was all assuming the magical government hadn't followed protocol and sent them an official statement, of course. Bottom line: I wouldn't have to do anything for this one.

"Ready?" I asked. She nodded and fell back into the light trance. A soft breeze rolled over me as the plane shifted. The Line materialized, just off to the side, always in a different place, but ever-present. Blues and purples spread out from a long black center, their colors like a nasty bruise, but the feeling of its call—soft, urgent, and comforting—tugged on my soul. Around me, real-life colors bled into ultraviolets and neon shades, throbbing within the power of the spiritual plane. I was standing in the spirit crossover point, while also standing in the lobby of the magical government building. For some reason I'd never bothered to think more thoroughly about, this didn't confuse or bother me. It just *was*.

That was when I saw it. A wall cut through the gloom, made up of shifting colors of reds, pinks, and yellows, stationed directly in front of the Line.

"That's...weird," I said, furrowing my brow. I grabbed hold of her spirit and shoved her toward the Line, ready to let go as she neared it. Since she was willing and ready, it should grab her and reel her in. It wouldn't take as much energy that way.

When she was almost there, my grip on her loosened, I ran smack into that unnatural, color-shifting wall, and a strong electrical current surged, flinging me back. The effect flash-burned my body and fried my insides. I gasped and clutched at my chest, staggering backward. Tremors shook my legs and arms and my teeth chattered.

The blond guy flung a strong arm around my shoulders, preventing me from falling, as Mordecai asked, "What happened?"

I shrugged the blond guy off, needing to stand on my own.

"Someone is messing with my shit, that's what happened," I said, facing the Line physically, even though it wasn't a physical realm. Anger rose through me, chasing away the uncomfortable residual buzzing from shock.

What in the holy fuck? Life was hard enough, but when a spirit finally wanted to be at peace, who would purposefully prevent that? You'd have to be the biggest turd alive.

And I would not stand for it.

I shoved the girl's flickering form to the side. She didn't need to be a part of this. I'd help her out once I burst through that manufactured wall of bullshit. Because while it was powerful, I'd only been pushed back because I'd allowed the shock get to me. I could rip it down. I knew I could.

Then something occurred to me.

I was in Valens's house. And he was a territorial motherfucker. He'd clearly hired that white-haired guy to put up this strange spirit block. If I messed with it, the old guy would find out when he came around to maintain the spell, which I assumed he regularly did, based on what the girl had said. Valens would retaliate, hard and viciously.

Maybe this was what Kieran had been talking about. Freeing his mother would mean defying his father, and his father would strike out. Since I was needed to free his mother, he wanted to hide me from the fallout.

Aw, whadda guy.

I rolled my eyes.

But one thing was clear: if I tore down this wall right now, I'd paint a huge target on my back. My file said Ghost Whisperer. Plenty of people had seen me in the building. It wouldn't take them two seconds to figure out who'd tampered with their spectral prison.

"I can't do this right now," I said, backing away.

"What?" the large guy asked. "What's the matter?"

I turned to the girl. "Valens has locked you in. I don't know if I can do anything about it. I have two kids to look after. If I jeopardize myself, I'll be jeopardizing them. But you have my word on this—before I die, I'll send you across that Line, okay? And hell, maybe I'll just follow you over. Hopefully it kills my body and doesn't leave Valens with anything to punish. Win-win."

"We gotta go," the blond guy said urgently, grabbing my arm and tugging.

I didn't resist, but I got one last look at the girl's baleful eyes before being pulled through the door. There wasn't anything more I could do for her right now, anyway. She'd just have to wait.

"What's the problem?" I asked as I was being marshaled to the car.

"You know what the problem is," the blond guy said, hustling me up the stairs in front of Mordecai and the big guy, "and it isn't something you need to discuss out loud in a magical zone. Demigod Valens has eyes and ears everywhere. He can't know about you. Not your power, not what you can do, not any role you may play in helping Kieran's mother—nothing. You gotta keep a low profile."

"I *was* keeping a low profile. A very low profile. I had absolutely no problems from magical people at all, especially not powerful ones. That is, until your boss crashed into my life and started lighting bonfires."

"I realize that, but here we are. So tone it down, okay?"

I gritted my teeth but bit back a response as the big guy helped Mordecai into the car.

I had every intention of "toning it down," but my mind started whirling.

Demigod Valens had someone on staff who could trap spirits in the land of the living. He used it as punishment. For the girl, he'd trapped her spirit directly, but for Kieran's mom, he'd trapped the spirit of the skin. I'd never heard of any of this before, but it was clearly possible. Step one was analyzing that wall and figuring out how it had been done. The magical user might not have the same power profile as I did, but he was setting up shop in my house, so I ought to be able to figure out the setup. Step two...

No—what was I thinking? I couldn't go to step two.

I didn't want to get tied to Kieran, and I certainly didn't want to go up against Valens. History told us that people didn't live through that. Hell, he kept people confined after he killed them.

I shook my head and got into the car, ignoring Mordecai's questioning gaze.

The best thing to do would be to forget all of this. To walk away.

I just needed to return to the way things had always been. Easy.

Chapter 35

KIERAN

KIERAN LOOKED UP from the biggest shock he'd had all day and picked up his vibrating phone. "Yeah?"

"She can figure it out," Donovan said. "She can figure out what is trapping your mother."

Kieran sat forward and leaned on the desk, his elbows pressing into Alexis's open file. Fatigue drained away instantly. He waited for more.

"It seems Valens is trapping spirits in the government building, and who knows where else," Donovan continued. "He put up a wall of some sort. She tried to get a spirit through, but it physically knocked her back. Damn near put her on her butt."

"How is that possible?"

"She doesn't seem to know, but you should've seen her face. It pissed her off good and proper. She didn't like someone cutting her off from the spirit world. She might not like that facet of her magic, but she's righteous about it. She's protective of it."

Hope surged within Kieran as a smile worked his lips. His Alexis didn't like to be told no, she didn't like to be ruled, and yet she wanted him as much as he wanted her. He knew all of those things as well as he knew how to breathe.

"She started talking about forcing down that wall and sending the spirit through," Donovan said, his voice dropping. "I had to get her out of there in case someone heard her. She's wild, sir."

"I like wild."

She was also highly intelligent and extremely magical. She wasn't using even a tenth of her ability.

The problem was, how could he get training for her without alerting everyone to what she'd been hiding all this time? Her father could be one of three people. One of those three would kill her outright if she were his. He wouldn't care about creating a lineage—as an immortal, he had no need for heirs. He'd be more concerned that she might rise up to tear her parent down. Like Kieran was about to do. History was filled with such cases. Less so now that the magical world was out in the open and organized, but immortals had long memories.

The other two... Kieran wasn't sure. They were both mortal and had a defined line of succession already in place. Alexis would put a wrench in their plans, but would she be a wrench worth dealing with?

One thing was for sure—she could help his mother.

Help him. Donovan had just cemented that fact. She had everything it would take, including determination, courage, and cunning. She was the whole package.

The luckiest day of his life had been when he'd nearly run her down.

"Keep watch on her. Keep her safe. Call me with updates."

"Yes, sir. And sir?" Donovan paused for a moment. "They don't have any money, and that kid looks grim. He needs food. He's a shifter, and she's got him eating vegetables 'n' shit—" Donovan's voice hitched with the slip in decorum. This was business, and that talk was out of line.

Kieran let it go. "And?"

"And if everything goes as planned, he's going to need some real sustenance. Shifters need meat. If he doesn't get it in human form, the second he can turn into his animal, he'll take down the first red-blooded thing he can find."

"See to it. Don't let her know it's coming from me, and don't take no for an answer."

"Yes, sir."

Kieran dropped the phone. For once, he wasn't showing goodwill to get something out of it. This time, he was helping a sick kid, like he had with that blanket. No strings attached.

He heaved a sigh and thought of his mother. She'd

be proud of him. Maybe there was hope for him yet.

His thoughts hardened a moment later. What he'd have to do to tear his father off the throne.

Or maybe not.

Chapter 36

ALEXIS

"I DON'T LIKE the interest you are taking in the Demigod's situation," Mordecai said as we pulled up in front of the house. The minions hadn't followed us out of the parking lot, and I got the sneaking suspicion that someone else was on car-tailing duty. It would have to be a pretty ratty-looking car not to stand out around here. They were probably hunting the used-car dealerships.

I hurried to his side so I could help him out. "I'm not taking an interest in his situation. Honest. It's just that the girl's situation is similar to that of Kieran's mom, and I don't know what the heck that magical wall is. I've never seen anything like it before. It's not right, putting that up. It's a shit thing to do. They killed that girl because she possessed a type of magic that scared them. Sound like a familiar story?"

"And if you stick your nose in, they might kill you, too."

I blew out a breath, forcing out the image of the

girl's desperate face. "I know."

"So you need to steer clear."

"I know."

"You don't sound like you mean it. When you stumble on something that doesn't make sense to you, you pick at the thread until the entire sweater unravels."

He was right. It was a personality flaw that usually didn't result in huge consequences. Now, though, crushed between two Demigods who had a fragile relationship, it could have consequences of epic, astronomic proportions.

Frank stood in the center of my lawn, his face lighting up when he saw us.

"Frank, seriously, why do you have to stand on my lawn?" I asked in annoyance. He looked down at his feet. "Anyway, there are some people who are trying to spy on me. Can you keep an eye out for anyone hanging around here who shouldn't be?"

"Sure, yeah. What do they look like?" he asked, walking toward the door.

"Just look for trespassers, okay?"

"Okay. Should I call the cops?"

I stopped at the door and just stared at him for a moment. This was clearly one of those times he'd forgotten he was dead. "No, Frank. That's okay. Just let me know, all right?"

"Of course. I'd be happy to."

"And hey, can you ask around and see if anyone wants to watch the neighborhood as a whole? I want to keep tabs on these guys."

"Well, the president of the neighborhood watch fell off his ladder last week. From what I've heard, he landed on his back, right up near his neck. He's in the hospital…"

No, he wasn't, he was in the cemetery on the other side of town.

"Then it would be a good idea to organize everyone in case the thieves hear what happened and try to take advantage of the situation." I unlocked the door.

"Yeah…" Frank nodded slowly. "That's a good point. Okay." He straightened his shoulders. "I'll take care of it."

"Thanks, Frank."

"Oh my God, Mordie, you look terrible." Daisy rushed to the door and put her shoulder under Mordecai's other arm. "Are you okay? What did they say?"

I held my breath as we got him to the couch. When I returned to shut the door, Frank was standing on my walkway, facing the street with his hands on his hips.

"They verified my illness," Mordecai said, burying himself in blankets.

"All that, and all they did was tell you what you already know?" Daisy's voice burned with anger. "You could've stayed home for that."

I ducked into my bedroom really quickly and grabbed the blanket Kieran had bought. Returning it wouldn't do a damn thing to get him off my case. We might as well use it.

"They did tests on how much it's progressed, but I have to wait for the results. Not that it will do any good. I told them it wouldn't matter—" He frowned when I stretched out the blanket. "What are you doing?"

"Wait…" Daisy scanned my clothing, lingering on the office-supply seamstress job and then my hair. "What the hell happened to you, and where are your clothes?"

"I don't want this." Mordecai tried to ward off the blanket. "Take that back to him, Alexis. Just because—"

I held up my hand to stop them both, before launching into what had happened to me at the magical government building.

"So you see?" I finished. "This blanket has nothing to do with anything. I doubt he'd even let me return it, let alone back off if I did. He's got that file to hang over my head now."

Daisy's eyes narrowed. She took the blanket and threw it on top of Mordecai. "He stripped you down?"

"I was freezing and my clothes were wet. I had to get out of that shirt." I turned quickly for the kitchen.

"Yes…" Footsteps thudded against the floor. "But *he* stripped off your shirt?"

"It happened so fast that—"

"What about your pants?"

My face burned as I filled a glass with water. I didn't answer.

"Alexis, what did you do?" She stopped at the entrance to the kitchen. "He's the enemy, remember? A crush is one thing, because the man is seriously hot, but—"

It was definitely role-reversal day. First Mordecai, and now this.

"I kissed him. That was *it*." I gulped down my water. "It's not like I meant to. It just happened."

"Was that really it?" Daisy asked with a cocked hip, suspicion and anger clear on her face.

"Yes," I lied. Even if I wanted to spill all, they were too young for the nitty-gritty. And I certainly didn't want to spill all. "Then I shoved him away because I remembered about my phone and Mordecai."

"*Then* you remembered about Mordecai?" Daisy accused. "After making out with the enemy?"

"If that water hadn't been magically treated, it would've had ice on it. That's how cold it was. I couldn't get my thoughts straight."

"So you're a class five," Mordecai said softly, thankfully not wanting to dwell on my terrible decision-making. "Do you think that's why he's interested in you?"

A wave of heat washed over me.

This would probably be the new normal. Every time I thought of that whack-job Demigod, I'd remember his searing touch, paired with the light, teasing kiss that boiled my blood. Even now, my breath sped up and my heart rate increased.

"Or is it the mutt thing?" Mordecai asked.

A knock sounded at the door.

I pointed at him. "That was a real knock?" Sometimes I had to ask to be sure. When Frank had enough energy, he used it to affect the physical world.

After Mordecai nodded, I motioned for Daisy to get into the kitchen and padded softly to the door.

"What about the bat?" Daisy whispered.

I ignored her as I wrapped my fingers around the knob. How many people could it be? Only three possibilities came to mind: my stalker, his minions, or a salesman who wouldn't last ten minutes trying to sell me something. Much like Mountebank Iams and his Nurse Ratched, salesmen tended not to find my witty personality in any way charming.

I swung the door open, revealing the large man with the huge arms and sharp cheekbones that would break a fist.

Two canvas grocery bags hung from his right hand, one with something leafy sticking out.

"I'm Jack," he said. "I'm here to make that roast."

"Holy Moses," Daisy said from behind me, peeking around at Jack. "He's a big guy. Seriously, should I get the bat?"

Jack flashed straight white teeth, the smile making his dark eyes glitter. "You'd need more than a bat to take me on."

"Well, it's a start," Daisy said.

He hefted the bags. "Can I come in? Mordecai needs some fuel."

"Fuel, as in food?" Daisy shouldered me out of the way and pushed the door wider. "Because I'm starving." This was an incredible change of pace, even for her. But then, food had a way of changing minds. "You're one of the Demigod's guys, right? You look vaguely familiar from the other night."

Jack ducked in and had a glance around. If he was unimpressed, he didn't show it. It was nice of him.

"I'm one of his Six, yes. I'll be hanging around the yard for a while. Keeping the beasties away." He motioned toward the kitchen, and I nodded to his silent request to enter.

"Oh, good. So if that mobster comes here to try and shut Lexi up, we've got some backup." Daisy nodded at me as Jack set up shop on the counter. She glanced at his muscular back before fanning her face and dropping her voice to a whisper. "He seems nice and he's super hot. Ditch the Demigod for him."

"What mobster is this?" Jack asked, glancing back. A good-natured smile adorned his bronzed face. Daisy was right—he was handsome. All of the guys I'd seen around Kieran were. They had nothing on him, though. Except when it came to manners and personal boundaries.

"Nothing," I said, walking to his side. "Just some criminal from the freak show the other night. One of the ghosts asked for a parting favor. I need to make an anonymous call, is all."

"You should really just do the letter," Daisy muttered.

I looked over the ingredients as he was unpacking. Organic, fresh produce, two packages of butter, heavy cream, a hunk of meat… "I should say no and turn you away. I want nothing to do with Kieran."

"Say no and turn me away after you eat. After what you went through in the assessment today, you deserve it." He pushed over some carrots. "I hear you know how to work with vegetables."

He was so easygoing and relaxed that it was hard to remain uptight and standoffish. I huffed out a laugh as Daisy sat at the table.

"We all do, yeah. But we're not used to the carrots being this firm." I delegated the carrots to Daisy along with a peeler. "I'd offer you some wine, but—"

"Here." He bent down to the canvas bag and extracted a bottle. "I got you."

I definitely wouldn't be saying no now...

"This isn't going to change my mind about working for your boss, just so you know." I took the wine and found my out-of-use wine opener.

"I'm just trying to get a couple kids a good meal. But since you brought it up, he's a good boss. A fair boss. He pays well, and he looks out for his own. He pulled me out of a rough spot. He's a man that a guy—or gal—can respect."

"I bet he didn't stalk you, though," Daisy muttered. "And force you to get an assessment out of the blue. And steal your clothes..."

Jack's brow furrowed and he glanced at my getup, reminding me I hadn't changed yet. "I did have to take an assessment—we all did; Kieran likes to know exactly what he's working with—but yes, I got to keep my clothes. Then again, I didn't go for a swim."

"That's because you didn't get chased across an obstacle course like a gazelle running from a lion," I replied.

"Touché," he said, chuckling.

"He's probably going to make a shrine out of the clothes." Daisy jerked the peeler over the first carrot, taking more of the skin than was absolutely necessary. "After he gets whatever he wants, he'll kill her off. He's already collecting mementos. Whack job."

"Daisy," I chided.

Jack laughed harder as he unpacked the meat. "You don't have to worry about Demigod Kieran. He's trying to shelter you from what may come. He may not reveal all his cards at the get-go, but if you put your trust in him, he'll see you through any storms. I know from experience."

I shook my head as I washed the potatoes. If Kieran planned to go up against Valens, he might not be able to see himself through, never mind me. Working for him might be a suicide mission.

I needed to find another source of income, and quick.

Chapter 37

ALEXIS

"**A**LEXIS!"

I jolted straight up in bed, ready for an emergency. Light blanketed my curtains, telling me it was already full day. I'd had a late night on Sunday, poring over all the listings on several job boards, sending resumés until the crack of dawn. Frustratingly, lower-level positions hiring magical people were as sparse as ever, and half of the companies listed I'd already worked for (and been fired by). The scant few left paid next to nothing.

It looked like I'd be at the freak show for a while longer.

"Alexis," Daisy shouted again.

"Coming." I ripped the covers away and swung my legs over the side of the mattress. "Coming!"

Fear pumped through me, all the things that could've unexpectedly befallen Mordecai running through my head. I pulled open the door and staggered out, never entirely alert after coming out of a deep sleep.

"Here she comes," Daisy said as I thundered down the hall.

A strange tent of scarfs, old blankets, and weird mystical pictures greeted me at the edge of the living room near the front door. A weathered wooden chair sat in front of the setup, and my trusty fold-up chair was tucked inside the makeshift fort.

Mordecai and Daisy stood off to the side, surveying the mystical monstrosity.

"What's...going on?" I rubbed my eyes, swaying as adrenaline, fear, fatigue, and the beginning stages of annoyance created a heady cocktail.

"It's afternoon. We need to get some training in before heading to the fair." Daisy held a clipboard and a pen, with an architect's pencil tucked behind her ear. "Let's go over the setup first, shall we?"

Annoyance took over. "You woke me up to walk me through how to properly sit in a festival of awful?" I noticed Mordecai's "beloved" turquoise blanket mixed in with the other pieces of the "tent."

He slumped under the force of my accusatory stare.

"Daisy said that it adds brightness to the overall ensemble," he explained. "And I have that gravity blanket now, which is warmer than all three of my other blankets put together. I don't need as many."

"Oh, sure, pick a domineering Demigod's gift over mine. Great." I pulled my hair out of my face as I turned for the kitchen and a giant cup of coffee. Mordecai's explanation had stung me. I knew almost everyone could provide for this family better than I could, but the fact that it was *him* doing it...

"We've got another one," came Frank's muffled voice through the door.

I groaned, finishing the trek to the kitchen counter and reaching for the empty coffee pot. Frank had kept checking in all day yesterday, cataloging the many movements of strangers around my house. Jack and the smiley blond guy, who'd introduced himself as Donovan when he'd forced his way in to make pot pie yesterday evening, had been spotted numerous times, but a couple of others had been hanging around too, taking shifts and going so far as to peek in the windows.

That wasn't all they were doing, though.

They were trying to make their lives easier by setting up surveillance around my property. So far, Frank had spied them putting up four cameras, covering both exit points (the front door and a never-used back door) and the sides of the house. I'd left them to it. I wanted my watchers to rest easy, comfortable in the knowledge they could monitor me from afar. Then, when I needed to get out undetected, I'd rip down their electronic eyes and set them to scrambling.

"He's hiding in his favorite bush. I've got my eye on him, don't worry," Frank yelled. "I got Genevieve out back. She has eyes like a hawk."

Frank was working on a network of nosey spirit neighbors, but so far, the two other spirits he'd brought around were more than pulling their weight.

Class-five magical worker, look at me. Invisible network at my service. If only they could, I don't know, throw a punch or push someone off a cliff. Then I'd be cooking with gas.

Beggars can't be choosers.

"Hurry up, Alexis," Daisy said with obvious annoyance.

"She thinks she's created a genius business plan," Mordecai said.

"I *have* created a genius business plan, you troll," Daisy shot back. "This setup will bring all the freaks to the yard."

"She is the freak. We want the norms."

"Whatever. Ew. Stop raining on my parade."

I was getting it from all sides. I didn't think I was up for it. Not before caffeine, anyway.

"I'll be right there," I said tiredly, scooping grounds into the filter. My plastic scoop scraped the bottom of the metal tin, and buying more wasn't in my budget until I got a new job.

All sides.

"He's big, but I can take him, don't you worry, Alexis," Frank called through the door. "The bigger they are, the slower they are. I move like the wind."

"He must register that strangers can't hear him," I said, clicking the on button and wandering back to the living room, "or why would he be screaming at me through the door?" Daisy's eyes widened, and she looked warily at the door. She was trying to help me with my trade in spite of being constantly creeped out by it. It showed her commitment to the cause. "But then, he is talking about tumbling with a large magical person hiding in the bushes. It makes no sense."

"It's easy to picture yourself taking down enemies when you know it's only a fantasy," Mordecai said softly.

Daisy shook herself out of her creeped-out daze and put her hand on his shoulder. "We've got this, Frodo. We can't help you carry the ring up Mount Mordor, but we can help carry you."

"Wow." I braced my hands on my hips. "You need to stop watching that movie."

"I see you," Frank called. "I see you looking."

I shook my head and tried to ignore the aggressive spirit turned poltergeist outside. "Okay. What of this"— I gestured at the makeshift setup—"will you let me burn?"

"Um, none?" Daisy scoffed before stalking to the visitor chair. "We need to paint this, obviously. I found it a block away next to a dumpster. It looks like it was sitting there awhile." That was an understatement. With the weathered, badly stained wood frame, and wet, rotted-looking cushion, it appeared to have been sitting there for decades. "Ms. Nicolas, next door, has some extra paint from the latest art…thing she's making. It's sitting by her back door. I'm pretty sure she's just waiting to illegally dump it like last time, so I'll grab one of those when she goes on her walk."

"Stop peeping in Ms. Nicolas's backyard," I muttered out of parental duty. Ms. Nicolas created horrendous paintings and sculptures that were impossible to ignore. How they sold, I did not know, but it was a train wreck Daisy hated to miss.

"Okay." She waved the comment away. "But it's really sturdy. Check it out."

I was a little afraid to touch it.

"Instead of your TV trays—"

"He's moving," Frank yelled. "He's on the move. Where are you going, you—"

Frank's voice drifted away.

"—we have a lovely little breakfast bar." Daisy lifted the edge of one of my rugs, revealing a length of badly pockmarked wood with a stretch of empty spider web spanning the top. I shrank away. "It needs a bath and a paint, and it will look just fab. Check out those legs. Strong and sturdy. That'll give our clients confidence."

"Our?" I asked, pushing the pad of my finger

against my temple and rubbing.

"We're all going into business together," Mordecai said, and he wasn't being sarcastic.

"No"—Daisy pointed at my face—"don't do that. I can see you about to pull hero and try to go it alone like some cowboy out of the Wild West."

"Cowboys in the Wild West were actually farmers in most cases," Mordecai said. "Hence the term *cowboys*. The fabricated idea of gun-slinging cowboys was made famous by Hollywood, and nowhere near depicts real events—"

"We don't care," Daisy interrupted.

"I care," I said. "I did not know that—"

"Okay, then, we'll table that for circle time." Daisy used her pen to point at the top of the tent, which was two peaks at different heights held up by leaning broomsticks. "Everyone else has a tent, so we need to join that parade. It makes us look legit. Once we have more working capital, we can replace these blankets with more scarfs, but for now—"

"I'm impressed with the lingo," I said, smelling the coffee and heading back to the kitchen.

"This has actually been a good independent study for us," Mordecai said, drifting after me. "It's empowering, creating a business."

"Uh-huh." Empowering meant it would take longer for them to give it up. How annoying.

"Your chair is still the same," Daisy continued, and I wondered if she'd even noticed me leaving the room. "You need it light. I like the idea of you moving your chair around. It creates a sense of urgency in the client. They'll want to impress the Great Seeing Eye in order to get her help."

I paused in pouring the coffee. "The *what*?"

"It's a working title," Mordecai assured me.

"Keep working." I eyed the messy stack of mail in the middle of the counter. Daisy had been so busy with this new venture she wanted to force on me that she hadn't insistently alerted me that she'd gotten the mail.

"We still need a sign. I need to get some poster board and pens, but I figured we should work on a budget first," Daisy went on, scribbling on her clipboard.

"Uh-huh. What's the pencil behind your ear for if you're using the pen?" I asked before taking a sip of my coffee. I wandered to the table and pulled the stack of relevant pieces of mail closer. Daisy had sorted the junk out already.

"Because that's what builders use," she said.

"Right." I frowned as I noticed an envelope from the city's Parks and Rec Department. Daisy's voice drifted to the back of my awareness as I set my coffee down. Unease flowed through me—a sense that I was waiting for the shoe to drop. A moment later, the air dried up in my lungs and a feeling of helplessness washed over me.

"It isn't fair." I pulled out a chair and plopped down, my eyes stinging in frustration. "It isn't fair!" I yelled.

The kids were next to me a moment later. "What happened?" Mordecai asked.

"What's not fair?" Daisy peered over my shoulder.

I set the letter on the table and dropped my face into my hands. "The freak show has been shut down."

"*What?*" She snatched up the letter. "'Dear Patron,'" she read, then mumbled, "Off to an intimate start... 'Dear Patron. Due to circumstances beyond our control, the Magical Showcase, held at Pier Thirty-three'...yadda yadda...'has been permanently cancelled. All permits have been suspended, and access into the area has been closed to all persons of a magical nature.'" Her voice drifted away and her eyes roamed from side to side, reading on down. "Oh look! Here we go. 'Plans have commenced to *move*'"—she gave Mordecai and me poignant looks—"'the Magical Showcase to a neutral location wherein magical and non-magical people alike will be welcome to showcase their talents. Permits will be granted to those applicable. For more information, please contact your specific governing body.'" She beamed at me. "So you see? This is *good* news. They're moving it to the dual-society zone and opening it up to everyone. It'll be bigger! We'll get more people actually interested in magic instead of just looking for entertainment." She nodded and tapped the letter. "This is a stroke of luck. This will be great for our brand."

"First, we have to actually create a brand," Mordecai said dryly.

Daisy glared at him. "Rome wasn't built in a day, Mordie. Instead of pointing out the flaws, why don't you help solve the problems?"

"Permits will be handed out from our specific governing body," I said, my head still resting on my palms.

Mordecai exhaled loudly. "Oh," he said.

"Why is that bad?" Daisy asked.

"Because a certain stalking Demigod wants me cornered," I said, "and now he has the power to deny me the ability to make money he isn't supplying. The ball is in his court."

Chapter 38

ALEXIS

"Like hell the ball is in his court." Daisy slapped down the letter. "He's not in charge of this city. His dad is. And his dad doesn't give two rats about us. We'll apply, and if he sticks his big nose in, we'll appeal. Worst case, we'll fire up the computer and create a fake profile. We can get around him."

A knock sounded at the door. I glanced around at the others. "Did you guys hear that?"

"Yes. It was a real knock," Mordecai said.

I lugged myself up, suddenly too exhausted for any of this. I was tired of being kicked in the jugular. Tired of Kieran getting his way so easily.

Tired of this life.

"The other one left, and this one took his place," Frank said, standing behind one of Kieran's minions, this one with wavy brown hair, piercing gray eyes, and a sun-kissed face that beamed raw hostility. "Don't let the suit jacket fool you—he's just like the others in their black jumpsuits."

"Thanks, Frank," I said, eyeing the pristine, tailored suit of this minion and noticing a thick manila envelope in the hand resting at his side.

"Alexis Price," the minion said in a thick, scratchy voice.

"Stalking creep," I answered.

On a normal day, his animalistic stare promising pain if I sassed him might make me zip the lip. Right now, he could suck it.

Without another word, he held up the manila envelope. After I took it, glaring all the while, he turned and made his way to a Beemer double-parked in front of my house. He revved the engine before speeding away.

"I probably don't want to know what this is," I said, dropping it to my side. "Kieran seems to have a flare for timing. It's like he knows exactly when to kick me when I'm down." I remembered the cameras, stepped out a little farther onto the porch, and flipped the bird.

"Well now, that's not ladylike," Frank said in distaste.

"Go ahead and keep talking, Frank. Find out what happens…"

His lips thinned, then whitened. Clearly the effort to hold back was intense.

"They've been roaming around all day," he finally said before walking to my side and turning, staring out at the street with me. He braced his hands on his hips.

"One was peeking in the front window when I got here this morning. There was a crack in the curtains. Well, I gave him a good kick."

"Oh yeah?" I said, trying not to move my lips. I didn't want neighbors to glance out their windows and catch me talking "to myself." "What did he do?"

"He jumped and looked around." Frank preened. "I didn't know I still had it in me."

The lurker had probably felt a sudden icy stab that had set his hair on end. Knowing what I was, he'd probably guessed exactly what had happened. That would freak a great many people out.

I smirked. "Keep up the good work."

"Yes, ma'am." Frank saluted me in a way that made it clear he'd never served in the armed forces.

Back in the house, I debated throwing the envelope in the trash. I even opened the lid and held it over the bin, staring down at it. But I caved, the silence ringing loudly in the kitchen. The kids clearly knew who had sent it, and what it possibly held.

The first sheet of paper held a simple message and directions, followed by a small picture of a map.

Meet me to discuss. —Kieran

Butterflies swam through my belly.

I separated two packets, each with its own cover letter. The first was from the office of Kieran Dursus.

"The details of his job offer," I said quietly, skimming the cover letter before turning the page and reading through the description of the services he'd requested. The simple job of helping his mother cross over was described with a great many unnecessary details from someone who thought they understood my job and clearly did not.

Mandatory séance? Spirit communication devices?

"Why the hell would I use a tape recorder?" I muttered. "Those things catch one word in ten. Spirit box? Oh now, they're just taking the piss altogether."

I kept flipping through.

My breath caught.

My hand started to shake.

Without another word, I passed that page on to the kids.

"What is it?" Daisy asked Mordecai, taking the page and quickly huddling with him. "Holy shit."

"Language," I said in a wispy voice.

"A hundred thousand base salary, with perks." Her eyes rounded and she looked at Mordecai. "What do you think the perks are?"

"Breakfast, maybe. Some companies do donuts in the morning." He took the paper, skimming the contents. His eyes stopped moving and a wistful expression crossed his face.

He'd seen the benefit section, which covered all of

my family, including undocumented wards (their names were listed). 401k, dental…and full medical, both magical and non-magical. Mordecai's medicine would be covered, he'd have access to routine checkups, and if he was a candidate for the cure, he'd have access to it.

He tossed the packet on the table angrily. "He's trying to buy her."

"Obviously. But wow." Daisy blew out a breath. "He thinks she's worth *a lot*."

"That's because she is." Mordecai turned away toward the fridge.

"Yes, Mordie, *we* know she is worth more than a basket of gold and chocolate. But usually we're the only ones." She moved closer to the table. "Then again, she's a bona fide class-five magical worker." She reached across the table for her clipboard. "We need to find out what someone like her is worth in the job market. He could be shortchanging us. That bitch already owes us money for the freak show thing. I haven't forgotten. I'll be damned if he's going to get one over on us again."

"That one's mine, right?" Mordecai asked softly, glancing at the shaking packet in my hands.

I didn't look up from the cover page. I didn't want him to see my fear.

This packet would tell me if my inability to keep him stocked up on medicine had damaged him for life. That, or it would tell me there was still hope, but only if

I willingly put myself into the hands of an egotistical, possessive Demigod who was about to be in a fight with his homicidal father.

"I'll do the honors," Daisy said softly, putting down her clipboard. She'd clearly noticed my expression and read the situation. She gingerly took the packet.

Mordecai turned to stare out the window, not seeing the curtain in the way.

She took a deep breath, pulled the cover page up, and then tucked it behind the rest of the packet.

"Read it out loud," Mordecai said. "It doesn't matter regardless. There's no sense in beating around the bush."

"Forty-four percent corrosive cells," she read, her brow furrowing. "Seven-two percent responsiveness…" She shook her head and turned another page. Then another. "Ah. Here. A summary." A relieved smile crossed her face. "Damage rate is borderline critical, *but*"—her smile widened—"likelihood of… I can't pronounce this, but the procedure for people like him is ninety-two percent likely to prove effective!" She looked between me and Mordecai excitedly, then went back to the summary. "If he does not get the procedure, likelihood of his condition improving with continued medication…is dim, okay, fine, *but*…" She traced a line with her finger. "The likelihood of his condition staying stable with continued medication is a strong possibility." She dropped the page, joy radiating from her whole body. "He's okay! He could be better, sure, but as long as he gets his meds, he'll be okay."

Pain soaked through my middle and tears welled in my eyes. I turned away toward the coffee pot so they didn't see. "Except I don't have a job, Daisy. And now I don't have the freak show. I have no way to earn money. What happens when the meds run out again?"

"You don't need the freak show. We can take your act to the streets." Daisy snatched up her clipboard. "There has to be a dark alley where your caliber of magic would really sing."

Her enthusiasm was admirable, but it didn't stop the tears from rolling down my face. Utter helplessness dragged at me. Fear for the future. Sorrow at what Mordecai was going through. I could end this. I could fix it.

What was a Demigod's gilded cage if it saved a loved one from a life of pain?

"We still have that other medicine to sell," Daisy said, her voice ringing with determination and confidence. "You can ask around at that bar you go to. From your stories, it sounds like those people would know how to unload it, or they may be in the market themselves." I heard her pen scratching on paper. "I can still take a job with Denny's dad. I won't give myself away. I know I won't. So that'll hold us over for a while..."

"You're not taking that job, Alexis," Mordecai said softly, cutting through Daisy's planning.

"No way." Daisy's pen smacked the paper. "Like, really? He's going to try to blackball you, then deliver this, and expect you to just cower at his feet? No." She was writing again. "I say we egg his car. Didn't you say he had a really nice car? Well, eggs would ruin the paint. The punishment would fit the crime."

"I would be down for that," Mordecai said.

I blew out a long breath, letting my emotions run their course. Letting all this wash over me.

"We can make it," Daisy said. "We can. I know we can."

"I agree." Mordecai turned away from the sink. "Next year, I'll be sixteen, then I can get a work permit. I can get medical myself, or just help with the bills. We'll have enough. We just have to get through one more year."

"Easy," Daisy said. "We just need to figure out this dark alley idea until we can get into the new freak show. I know, what about—"

I laughed silently through my tears. They were resilient, these kids. True survivors.

"Okay," I said, marshaling my resolve. "Okay. We'll do this as a family. But…" I wiped my face really quickly and turned toward them with my finger held out. "If we run out of medicine again, I'm taking that job."

"We won't." Daisy gave Mordecai a comforting look. "We won't run out. We'll keep you steady until we can get you that procedure. We'll do it."

I nodded as determination rose through me. Followed by anger.

That meddling Demigod asshole thought he could strong-arm me into getting what he wanted. He thought he could play Mordecai's condition against me.

But he didn't realize that, in my moments of weakness, I had two awesome kids to band together and raise me up.

"Keep that egging idea on the back burner," I said, my natural fire and aggression coming to the surface. When life gave you lemons, find someone to chuck them at.

Even if that someone was a Demigod.

"What are you going to do?" Daisy asked.

"I'm going to tell a Demigod where to shove it."

I grabbed a sweatshirt from my room and marched toward the door.

"Keep your clothes on this time," Daisy yelled after me.

Chapter 39

ALEXIS

"ANY OF THEM in the yard?" I asked Frank as I slung my purse, now misshapen as well as discolored, across my body.

"Yes, ma'am, there is. Right over there." Frank pointed at the overgrown shrubs hugging the corner of my house.

They weren't thick or extremely high, but if it hadn't been for Frank, I never would've guessed some big guy lurked within them.

I stalked that way, Frank at my side. "Should I check in with the eyes at the rear?" he asked, clearly digging this bit of spy speak.

"No need."

Donovan, with his perpetually tousled hair that worked so well for him, looked up with haunted eyes, his smile long gone. He wasn't nearly as excited about his job as Frank was about leading my surveillance team. Then again, he had been kicked in the keister by a ghost.

He stood slowly, knowing the jig was up. He didn't bother asking how I knew he was there.

"Tell your boss I'm on my way to meet him," I said without preamble. "I assume the location in that envelope is good?"

Donovan looked down at his arms before shivering. His hairs were probably standing on end. He felt Frank's presence. "Yes. He's already there."

"Is he, now? So sure I'd accept his offer?"

"Do you have any choice?" Donovan shrugged. "It benefits everyone. Why wouldn't you take it?"

"Oh, I don't know, because he's manipulating me? Because he's trying to trap me into giving him what he wants?"

"If you want to beat the player, you have to learn how to play the game," Donovan said with a smirk.

I narrowed my eyes at him. "Kick him again, Frank."

"With pleasure." Frank rubbed his hands together.

I spun and stalked across the grass to my car.

The meet-up wasn't far, on the cliffs overlooking the ocean. I parked as close as I could, next to his shiny Ferrari that sorely needed a key scrape down the side and a few eggs, before hiking up the hill toward the brick wall enclosing the magical zone. The paved path ended and a dirt trail took over, turning sandy as I wound around a couple of trees and along the steep cliff.

A mostly broken wood and wire fence leaned badly, warning people and dogs alike from going too near the cliff's edge. Huge sections were missing, and others dangled down, falling as the cliff eroded away.

Not far in the distance, the non-magical fence sparkled silver in the late afternoon sun. Coiled barbed wire looped on top and little white signs hung at chest level, their words lost to the distance, but I knew they warned of a life-threatening shock should anyone touch the fence.

I checked the map Kieran had sent, then followed the curve of the cliff through another outcropping of wind-whipped trees. My shoes sank into the sand and the cold ocean breeze bit my cheeks. At the edge of the tree line the world stretched out before me, blue water reaching from one side to the other. Cold gray sky sank until it met the ocean in the distance.

A small green bench sat in the middle of a flat area overlooking the magnificent view. Ten feet beyond, the land dropped abruptly, and no fence stood in the way of that expanse of land and sky.

Kieran sat on that weathered bench, his large back bowed as though the weight on his shoulders was too heavy for him to sit up straight. And it was. His mother stood beside him, her hand resting on his shoulder in comfort, staring out at the sea with him. The memories of the lost were plaguing his mind.

The fire, and the frustration, the intense anger—it all dried up within me. My heart swelled...then sank.

He was a little boy in grief. A man traumatized by loss. A son pinned between the actions of a father and the suffering of a mother.

I remembered losing my own mother. Remembered getting that call from the hospital, and feeling the world come crashing down around me. I had been able to assist her through the transition to the other side, but Kieran felt helpless to do anything for his mother. I could see it in the droop of his large shoulders, and I'd bet there were grief lines on his face.

I was witnessing his personal Vietnam, just as he'd witnessed mine when watching me try to buy that blanket.

He was asking for a way out, in exchange for offering me a way out.

The scene before me swam in tears as his mother slowly turned toward me. Her sorrow-infused eyes pleaded with me more than any words could. "Help him," she said, her voice like a bell, her tone aching. "Please. Help my son. He doesn't deserve this."

I turned to the side and blinked away tears.

This was why I hated getting involved. Because in these situations, saying no just wasn't in me. I couldn't, in good conscience, let someone drown in grief when I could help. I just couldn't.

"Hey," I said softly.

The effort it took Kieran to straighten up was obvious.

"Take your hand off him," I told his mother. "You need to know when it's helping, and when it's hindering. Right now, it is hindering. He needs to be able to snap out of it so he can function."

He spun around then, his eyes haunted and his face lined in grief, exactly how I'd predicted.

"Help him," she said again, walking toward the cliff. With a last look behind her, she stepped off the edge and fell.

"Good...God." I clenched my teeth. "Seeing that is hard. I mean, I know she's already..." I cleared my throat. No need to remind the poor guy.

I gingerly sat at the very edge of the bench, trying to put as much room between us as I could. Even still, a delicious (though worrying) hum settled within me, responding to the electricity passing between us.

"Alexis." His gaze roamed my face. He turned back to the ocean. "I knew you'd come. Angry, sad, desperate—I wasn't sure which mood I'd get, but I knew you'd come."

"Congratulations. You've manipulated me into getting what you want."

Surprisingly, he shook his head and leaned back like

his whole body ached. "I got the opposite of what I want."

I lifted my eyebrows. "So...you didn't want me to come?"

"I wanted you to come. I want your help. I want you spread and panting beneath me."

Out of nowhere, heat roared through my body. I clutched the edge of the bench, fighting the impulse to run a hand up that defined arm.

"But I don't want to coerce you," he went on. "Not like this." He blew out a breath. "My father trapped my mother. He met her one day, walking along the beach, and her beauty and her strength—both the strength of her magic, and her as a person—entranced him. Like you do me." He paused for a moment, looking over at me. Fire lit his eyes and matched that of my body. "He wanted her for his own. To keep her. At first, she was more than willing. She forgot about her skin for a time, losing herself to the exotic pleasures of dry land. But to a selkie, the call of the ocean is impossible to ignore. One day, he woke up, and she was gone."

"Which is how things usually go with a selkie, right?" I said quietly.

"Exactly." He turned back to the ocean. "But my father is not a rational man in many things. Nor a forgiving man. I'm sure you know that."

Everyone knew that, yes.

"As a Demigod of Poseidon, lord of the sea, my father had the rare ability to have her tracked down. To have her brought back to land. He couldn't accept that the ocean had more power than he does. He rules the ocean, after all."

"But…as his son, so do you, right? He's not actually all powerful in that respect."

A brief smile pulled at Kieran's lips. "Yes. As I said, my father is not rational in some things. He has a fragile ego."

"Well…I mean…he is a man, after all."

"Once she was back, he took her skin. Hid it. Which, at first, I think she treated like a game. She loved him, after all. She fell into a life of luxury and power, pampered and treated like royalty. But, as before, the ocean called."

"And he wouldn't let her go to it."

"She was pregnant at the time, but even if she hadn't been…" Kieran's fist clenched. "His love is of power. Of complete dominance. When she begged to leave again, even promising she would return, his regard for her turned. She became a prisoner. A prisoner he no longer sexually desired. He banished her, kept her at arm's reach. Kept her landlocked."

"And you?"

He ran his fingers through his hair. "One in ten children created from the union of a Demigod and a non-Demigod develop a Demigod's power. My mother was a class five. That surely helped. My father has had twelve children, but only one Demigod materialized. I am the heir. Together, we can control more territory."

"But…you lived with your mother, right?"

"Ah. I see what you're getting at. I forget, you don't think like the people around me." His look said that was a good thing. "I was banished with her, yes, but just for safekeeping. He kept tabs on me my whole life, first to see if my powers would materialize, and then because they did and he wanted to groom me."

"To sculpt you into a clone of himself."

"Essentially, yes."

His tone raised my small hairs. I swallowed a sudden dose of fear.

"He made sure I had excellent tutors," Kieran continued, "who taught me about ruling and warfare. He invited me here after my mother died so I could expand the family business."

"And you came to free your mother?"

His penetrating stare reached down into me, baring my soul to him as he was baring his to me. Silence descended between us and heat built, fueled by the passion and electricity burning between us.

He leaned my way slightly, and expectation washed over me. I licked my bottom lip, remembering the feel of his kiss. Of his hands on me, and the gloriousness of his body.

His gaze dipped, lingering on my tongue. His pupils dilated and he bent, cutting the distance between our lips in half. My body pounded and I couldn't get enough air.

"Among other things," he said softly.

Chapter 40

ALEXIS

S HIVERS COATED MY body, and suddenly I wasn't sure what he would do, and what I would do in reaction.

I needn't have worried.

A wrinkle wormed between his brows, and with a surge of strength, he rose from the bench. He jammed his hands into his pockets, and my gaze snagged on the bulge between them.

"I may not have kidnapped you, but I forced you into this position," he said, his voice pained. "I want you, that's no secret. I want to fuck you so hard you forget your name."

A small moan escaped my lips. When I was near him like this, feeling the electric chemistry between us, I wanted the same thing. I wanted to let go and give in to his awesome strength and power.

"And I need you," he went on. "I need you to free my mother. Fate brought you to me. What were the odds that I'd meet someone with your rare ability in the place it would do the most good?"

I could barely feel confusion through the pounding in my body. Rare ability? Weren't there plenty of Ghost Whisperers in magical San Francisco alone?

"I found your weakness, and I exploited it." He glanced back at me. "Just like my father would've done."

I unstuck my tongue from the top of my mouth and wiped my sweaty palms on my jeans. "I came here to refuse your job offer."

His head jerked my way before he turned slowly back toward the water. His brow furrow didn't match his gorgeous smile.

"Did you?" he said.

"I did. Don't get me wrong—you didn't underestimate me at all. I would've caved in a heartbeat. But the kids don't want your money. They're convinced we can do this on our own."

His stormy eyes assessed me, glimmering. His smile grew. "Strangely, I'm relieved to hear it."

"But I will be taking the job." A mental gut punch took all the breath out of me. I struggled to get it back, sheer panic trying to steal the moment.

He cocked his head, and his smile dripped away.

"Yeah." I cleared my throat and beat on my chest a little. "I really don't want to. If you can't tell."

He shifted, his back nearly to the ocean. "Then why are you?"

"Because of your mother. She pleaded with me to

help you. And because I've lost a mother too. I can't imagine how helpless I would feel in your situation. Actually..." I held up my hand, still struggling for air. "I can imagine it. It's how I feel about Mordecai."

He nodded slowly. "It is the same, yes. Exactly the same. Which I realized when I was sitting here, waiting for you. That's why I called and made an appointment for Mordecai before you got here. The details will be delivered to you tomorrow. I've prepaid for the procedure, but everything's in his name. I meant it as an apology, of sorts, for having forced your hand. But now..." His smile drifted back. "Let's call it a nod of respect, for misjudging you...while still getting my way."

An unexpected laugh shook me. I looked away, trying to get my bearings. This version of Kieran was the man his minions saw, I had no doubt. A real guy with a surprising sense of humor. If I was around this guy too much, I was liable to forget about his possessive, domineering side. And that was dangerous.

"You bought the blanket for Mordecai before you knew what I was," I said, back to reality (except for the deep ache that would not *go away*). "Why? Or could you feel what I was even then?"

"Without assessing you, I never could've known the entirety of what you are."

I shifted on the seat. This was the second time he'd

alluded to my being more than someone who could see and work with/boss around spirits. But before I could ask about it, he'd already plunged on.

"My mother died a slow death," he said. "The sickness of a selkie kept from her skin is like cancer. I watched her erode from the inside out." He clenched his jaw, and rage burned brightly in his eyes. "Toward the end, we couldn't rely on in-home care. We needed machines. Equipment. It was in those trips that I learned, firsthand, what it was to be poor and sick. What it was to see suffering people who couldn't get help. At first, I shrugged off most of it. I ignored it. But one day, a child with a scarf on her head walked by, so weak she could barely keep upright. She was dying, but her parents couldn't afford treatment to ease her pain. It…" He turned away. "It woke me up, to say the least. It struck me deeply. So when I saw you studying those blankets, trying to figure out a way to afford the one that would comfort him most…" He shook his head. "It was the least I could do. A tiny gesture."

"It wasn't a tiny gesture for him." I shrugged and smiled. "Well, it wouldn't have been if the situation hadn't involved stalking and unresponsive mace."

"We've already discussed my struggle to avoid being like my father."

"Right, yes. Yes, we did. Anyway…" I clasped my hands and leaned forward, not really sure where to go from here. My perception of him was changing. Had changed.

I wasn't sure if that was a good thing, since now we'd be working together, or a really, *really* bad thing.

"Anyway," he said, mimicking me, back to facing the ocean. "I'll let you get your affairs in order and look over the contract. After Mordecai is seen to—if you haven't changed your mind—then let one of my guys know. We can handle the paperwork and get started."

Hearing the finality in his voice, I stood from the bench. "No one gave me their phone number. Besides, my phone is dead, remember? It's sitting in a bowl of rice, but won't turn back on."

"Just walk outside and let them know. They won't be far."

I froze in my turn. "Wait. They're going to keep hanging around my house?" He didn't answer, which I took for a yes. "But what about my free will? And this job being my choice?"

"Working for me is your choice. Sharing my bed is your choice. Setting up protection for you is *my* choice."

"Protection? From who, random bored spirits who want to chat? The only person I need protection from is you."

He turned and hit me with a hard stare. "You will never need protection from me. I hope I just proved that. But the magical world is not a kind place. You've drawn my interest. That will be noticed, despite my attempts to safeguard the knowledge. Your magic will draw more interest still, if someone pokes around. I'm being cautious. I told you, I protect what is mine."

I put my hands out, my mouth hanging open, completely incredulous. All the soft warmth that had been building over our conversation flew out the window. "We literally just talked about this. You said you didn't want to corner me into doing your bidding."

"I'm not cornering you. I'm safeguarding you."

"Yeah, until you browbeat me into submitting to you."

Passion sparked in his eyes. A smile curled his lips. "I very much want you to submit to me, but I don't need to browbeat you to do it. I must merely wait until you're ready. You want me, Alexis. I can see it, even now. Even in your anger. You crave me, as I do you. One day you'll give in. I was raised among the Irish. I know what it is to be stubborn. To dig in one's heels and never say die. You don't have it in you. Not in this. You'll come around, and when you do, I'll show you delights you've only dreamed of."

Tight bands of desire squeezed my chest. My legs trembled. I didn't dare speak because I wasn't sure what I'd say.

"You haven't asked what was in your file, Alexis. Are you not curious about your results?"

I opened and closed my mouth like a fish, fighting through the hunger boiling my blood.

"I'd planned to keep them from you, but…" He walked toward me slowly. I stood frozen, unable to back away. Not allowing myself to go forward. "You're more powerful when you control your fate. One day you'll be my equal in all but power, and I have every reason to suspect you'll find a way around that. Or else your wards will."

He smiled again, stopping mere inches in front of me. He looked down into my eyes.

"I'm scared to know those results," I blurted, betraying myself. "I'm scared it will change my life, and endanger the kids."

"It will change your life. I'll make sure it doesn't endanger those kids." His warm hands cupped my shoulders before sliding down my arms. "You have the blood of Hades in you. It's potent. You are not a Demigod—but as a class five, his gifts have manifested in you in intriguing ways. You are a Spirit Walker, Alexis. You are the rarest and highest form of necromancer. But more, your gifts have been amplified by the boost of divine blood. That is why you can see spirits as though they were people. That is why you can easily call them, send them over the Line, bring them back—all of it. You are one in a million."

I stared mutely, horror-struck. "I'm a soul stealer? I

joked about that the other day to some Chester. With-out knowing it, I was actually being truthful."

His hand came up and he traced a thumb across my chin. "You have that ability, yes. To rip a person's soul out of their body." He stepped back and drew a line down his chest. He fisted his hands near his middle and then spread them, as though pulling open a trench coat to flash me. "I felt it the first time I met you. I feel it right now. It's a helpless feeling. Terrifying, if I'm being honest. More so because you don't know you're doing it. You don't know how to control it."

I clasped my hands together. "I'm not doing any-thing."

"Yes. Exactly." He stepped closer again, and this time ran his thumb over my bottom lip.

I barely felt it.

Shock riddled my body. Fear. Disgust.

Soul Stealers were the most ruthless villains in any magical society. Everyone knew that. They could walk through a battle and rip the very life out of a person. Then they could shove that life right back in, creating a sea of walking corpses. Lifeless bodies lay in their wake, or mindless drones followed behind them. It was like being an extremely powerful Necromancer and an Encourager rolled into one, and the very idea made me shiver.

"I'm not one of those," I spat. "Your test is wrong."

He studied me for a moment. "In the hands of my father, you would become everything you fear, but I will not let that happen to you, Alexis. I swear it. I will protect you, from him and from myself. You already have a just and moral heart. You help others. You protect the realm of the dead, whether you realize it or not. *That* is the job of the Spirit Walker. A soul stealer is what happens when the corrupt prey on the less power-ful. When good people are mind-raped and used for ill." His grip was hard on my arms. His eyes held ruthless determination. "Trust in me, Alexis. I am not always a good person, I don't always have the best of intentions, but I *will not* allow that to happen to you. I will protect you with my dying breath. I vow it."

I blinked back tears, fear and hope swirling into a cocktail in my stomach. I didn't want to believe the results. Couldn't. But I wanted to believe he'd protect me. If the results were true, I wanted him on my side, even though he was...him.

"I have to think about all this," I said.

His eyes roamed my face. He nodded slowly.

"I want proof."

He nodded again.

"That's why you thought you could find out who my father is. He's a Demigod." My heart tightened with the words that came out of my mouth. I could scarcely believe it. And if it were true, I knew my mother had known. She must have. And given her love of ass-holes…

"It's Magnus, isn't it? The Demigod who kills his children. She'd want to keep me away from him at all costs. Including moving out of the magical zone and into the forgotten crack of the societies. That's why she made sure I hid my power and, apparently, most of my magic in the assessments."

She'd claimed to prefer the crack because she didn't like the roughness, or iron-clad rules, of the magical society. Besides which, the people she wanted to help were the ones who didn't belong anywhere.

But this news painted a different picture. Maybe my mother and Kieran's mother had had something in common.

"Yikes." I backed up until I could sit down hard on the bench. "One moment I'm a normal Joe with a useless kind of magic, and the next…"

Sorrow crossed Kieran's face for a fraction of a second. "I don't know who your father is," he whispered, sitting next to me. "Regardless, it's a safe bet whoever it is doesn't know about you. We'll keep it that way. I just need to know what I'm working with so I can get the right training for you. Not all of Hades' gifts manifest in his heirs. I want to know which gifts are possibly lurking in you. Testing only gives us a general idea. Now we need to push you and lure it out."

I blew out a breath and leaned without thinking, resting against him. "I need to take a second and hate you with my whole body for dragging me into all this. For exposing me."

He lifted his arm and put it around me. "Hate sex can be fun," he murmured, rubbing my back. "I'd be happy to let you experiment on me."

"Hate sex is the stupidest thing I've ever heard in my life. Only men would think that was a thing, filthy bastards." I shook my head, giving myself over to the moment. I needed to let it wash over me, before I could push it aside and get on with my life. Because I *would* get on with my life. I had to. I had two kids relying on me. I'd figure this out like I figured everything else out.

"Okay." I straightened back up. I needed to get Mordecai his cure first. Then I'd confront this thing head-on. I didn't know if my mom had purposefully hidden me, but if she had, she'd done so for good reason. She'd want me to take care of myself, even if that mean taking cover. No shame in the hideout game. "Okay."

Kieran chuckled, standing with me. "Just like that, huh? Your world is flipped upside down, and you're ready to go?"

"Sometimes that's all we can do." I flicked my hair out of my face. "I'll look forward to getting the appointment information for Mordecai. And I won't be paying for any training. You started this, so you have to foot the bill."

His smile weakened my knees. "No sweat."

"And get your people out of my yard. No one knows about me. No one bothered me until you came around. I don't need them."

"Nice try."

I affixed him with a glare before I brushed it off and turned for the trees.

"Oh, and Alexis?"

I stopped at the tree line.

"I know that you know about those cameras," he said, his good humor now in full force. He thought my annoyance with his "protection" was hilarious. "I also know that your neighborhood doesn't have a home-owners' association, nor do they have any rules about drones. Take down my cameras, and I'll have two drones over your house twenty-four/seven. I don't fight fair, as you may have already noticed."

"Mark my words: you and your minions are going to rue the day you tangoed with me." It was a good, strong bluff.

His laughter was not the response I'd been hoping for. "I can't wait."

Head held high, I marched off through the trees. One thing was for certain: this guy was never going to get in my pants. I'd work with him, I'd help his mom, and I'd satiate my curiosity for how Demigod Valens was trapping spirits, but lusting after Kieran was as far as I was ever going to go. He could bark up that tree till he was blue in the face, but he wasn't getting anywhere.

A thought curled out of the back of my mind before I could help myself.

With a kiss like his, his prowess in bed would surely blow my mind. He'd be like rich, decadent chocolate. One taste, and he'd ruin me for anything lesser.

Gritting my teeth, I knifed those thoughts and buried them in the proverbial backyard.

But egotistical jackass or no, I did have to own that Kieran had granted me a miracle. He'd helped materialize one of my Big Dreams.

He was giving a future to a very sick kid.

Regardless of the torture he'd likely put me through in the months to come, he was trying to save Mordecai. I would allow a soft spot in my heart for this selfless action.

Now we just had to get through the procedure itself. Mordecai wasn't out of the woods yet.

KIERAN WATCHED ALEXIS disappear through the trees as supreme confusion stole over him.

He'd just vowed to protect her. With his life, if need be. It was like a stranger had said those words. He hadn't even made that promise to his Six. To *anyone*.

But even now, when the energy of her presence and her entrancing quality drifted away, allowing cold logic to resume, he didn't want to take it back. Couldn't.

The warm heaviness within him wasn't lust. It wasn't the result of their electricity or the delicious burn of her magic rising through him.

It was deeper than that. Not attraction, but affection. Somewhere along the way, she'd gotten under his skin. In trying to learn about her magic, he'd learned about her as a person. About her life.

He liked what he'd discovered.

He blew out a breath and turned, surveying the ocean. He had a long, dangerous road ahead of him. First, he'd free his mother, something he was confident he could do now that he had Alexis on board. Then he'd take on his father. And though Alexis, if trained, could help him with the latter, freeing his mother would be the end of it. She was too good of a person to be tangled up with him for the long haul. He would only bring her down, not to mention possibly get her killed.

No. No matter how much he needed her, or wanted her, he'd only employ her for the first leg of the journey.

Chapter 41

ALEXIS

TWO WEEKS LATER, I checked the clock on my nightstand and shoved down the rampant anxiety coursing through my body. Three-oh-one. An hour until checkout. Time to go.

True to his word, Kieran had gotten Mordecai an appointment for the procedure that would quell his body's response to the shifter genes. Being the son of Demigod Valens, not to mention a Demigod himself and extremely influential in any circle, Kieran had ensured Mordecai got sent to the front of the line. Considering the waitlist was six months long, that was pretty incredible.

I wasn't under any illusions that this was strictly a kindness on Kieran's part—the quicker Mordecai improved, the quicker I could start working for him.

"Daisy, are you ready?" I called, grabbing a light coat and my keys off my dresser.

"Yeah," she said tiredly as she passed my door toward the living room.

We'd been at the hospital all day yesterday while Mordecai was in surgery, then half the night while he was unconscious and hooked up to various machines that would finish the job. According to his last checkup, the procedure had great odds of working for him. But I'd been unlucky all my life. I didn't trust percentages and ratings. Life had plenty of room for error.

So Daisy and I had hung around, wanting to be on hand if anything were to happen.

Thankfully, nothing had.

We'd tucked him into bed at one o'clock last night and wished him goodnight.

We'd woken up this morning to a message left on the machine. "I'm alive. I'm tired and sore, but they say that's part of the recovery process. They said I'm already out of danger." I could hear the smile in his voice. "My body took to the procedure really well, and once the issue was resolved, my body started healing at abnormal rates. Which is apparently good. So I'm just going to sleep. You guys should, too. I'll see you for check out at four. Love ya, bye."

"I looked online," Daisy said as I joined her in the kitchen. She had a glass of water and puffy blue bags under her eyes. "They usually keep patients for a few days after the medical thing Mordecai had done."

I nodded. "We can ask the doctor about it when we get there."

"I mean, even really magical people."

"I know, Daisy. We'll ask the doctor." I grabbed my sleek new phone, an anonymous gift that had been waiting on my porch after the meeting with Kieran two weeks before. The service had been prepaid for a year.

I wasn't so stupid as to have no idea where the phone had come from. Nor was I too proud to keep it. As far as I was concerned, Kieran was responsible for breaking the other one. He could damn well make restitution, thank you very much.

"Same place as usual," Frank said as we exited the house, standing in his favorite spot while surveying the lurkers hiding in my yard. "They even have a mat over there now to get comfortable while spying."

"Good work, Frank. Stay vigilant," I said distractedly. "And get off my lawn."

"I don't understand why you care that the...spirit"—Daisy shivered—"is on the lawn. It's not like he's real. And we barely mow it."

"It's the principle of the thing." I got into the car, catching a glimpse of a bush moving at the side of my yard.

Apparently, the minions weren't actually hiding from me—they'd given that up after a few days of getting constantly called out by me—they were keeping out of the public eye. They didn't want anyone knowing they were there.

Jack had brought by the "official" assessment of my magic and power level, then the one that had actually come out of the machine. Kieran hadn't been lying about anything. My mom had banged a Demigod with a lineage to Hades. I was likely a mistake, and she'd kept it a secret. Kieran still didn't know which Demigod was my father. He was apparently stepping lightly so as not to raise suspicion.

I didn't want to know. Coming to grips with the fact that I possessed one of the most feared types of magic had been hard enough—I didn't need to duke it out with Daddy dearest. One day I'd have to circle back and learn how to use my powers just in case Kieran brought more trouble, but for now...I wanted to pretend my life hadn't changed in a horribly dangerous direction. I wanted to focus on the kids.

"Does this mean we can stop giving Mordecai the medicine?" Daisy asked in a small voice. A dozen questions had been on repeat since Mordecai had checked into the hospital, this being one of them.

"If the procedure worked, then yes, we can stop giving him the medicine."

She nodded, staring out the window. "And we're positive that meddling bastard can't get his hooks into us or Mordie for this?"

"Kieran has no legal way to use this goodwill to his benefit. We can walk away."

"And we will? Walk away?" She side-eyed me.

I hadn't yet told them that I would be taking the job. But Daisy, very astute when someone was trying to get something over on her, had noticed when the contract disappeared from the kitchen table. She'd asked about it, I'd fibbed and claimed I'd filed it, and the questions had come pouring in.

I was pretty sure she was onto me.

"Totally," I said, and it almost sounded believable.

I showed my badge to the guard at the magical gate. "Lovely afternoon, gov'na. Fine weather we're having," I said in a horrible British accent.

He passed my ID under the scanner before readying the light to shine through the back. The machine beeped and his gaze snapped to me. "This is the old ID. Where's the new one?

"What...new one?" I asked, pushing up in my seat to make sure I'd given him the right card.

He zeroed in on the screen. "Newly issued. Check your mail." He handed my ID back. "In the future, use that lane." He pointed at the fast-track lane beside me.

"But..." I glanced over before looking at the grim face pictured on my ID.

"Meddling bastard," Daisy grumbled.

"Keep moving." The guard waved me on.

"Right, yes. Because bumping me up in the world is a great way to keep me on the DL, Kieran," I mumbled, stepping on the gas pedal.

"You need to get rid of him," Daisy said, still looking out the window. "I enjoy all the hot guys hanging around the house, but it's a bit much."

Yes. It was. But try telling that to a possessive Demigod. He'd laugh in your face.

This one had laughed in my face, at least.

At the hospital, I parked near the back and took an extra few minutes meandering in. Instead of taking the lead and urging me to walk faster, Daisy kept pace, silent.

She was just as worried as I was that this was all some trick, and we'd show up to bad news.

Mirroring her deep breath, I made my way through the hospital doors, the anxiety a live thing in my middle.

"Will he need therapy?" Daisy asked quietly as we entered the elevator.

"No. He'll be just like you and me. Healthy. A normal kid."

"But weak."

"As weak as he's always been, yes. He'll need to start running and exercising. But he can get stronger now." *Hopefully.*

"At least those hot minion guys are still cooking. They're making us a lot of protein stuff, I've noticed. They're getting him ready to bulk up."

I nodded as the elevator chimed and the doors

shimmied open. "I should stop their charity, but…"

"He needs it," Daisy said softly.

I didn't comment.

"He won't need any medicine at all?" she asked.

"No. No medicine," I said patiently, taking her hand as we walked slowly down the hallway.

A large figure stood outside Mordecai's door, and for one heart-stopping moment, I worried it might be a shifter, here to wipe out the new threat. But a moment later, I recognized the face and body: Zorn, the minion with wavy brown hair and piercing gray eyes.

"Hey," I said as we approached. I was thankful for his presence. Mordecai wasn't well enough for the alpha to issue a challenge just yet, but an alpha with no morals could kill him in his sleep.

Zorn nodded and stepped to the side, his hands clasped in front of him and his tailored suit wrinkle-free.

I wrapped my fingers around the cold metal door handle. I couldn't seem to will myself to turn it. "How is he?"

"He is healing at an incredible rate, even for a shifter," Zorn said in his heavy, scratchy voice, as though it had been damaged from aggressive screaming over an extended period of time. "His body has been waging a serious war all these years. The doctors are amazed he survived it. A lesser shifter wouldn't have, not with the way his body was fighting his power."

A weight pressed on my chest. Heat prickled my eyes. "But he's okay? He'll...be fixed? He won't hurt anymore?"

Zorn looked at me full-on now, assessing. His expression softened, if a stone could be said to soften. "He'll be better than new. Some shifters become tough because they're subjected to cruelty, but the rough treatment turns them into unbalanced individuals, like the current alpha of the Green Hills Pack. Battling his condition, with you and Daisy at his back, has amped up Mordecai's resilience and endurance. You helped shape a well-rounded boy, who will turn into a power-house of a well-rounded man. He owes his future success to you, Alexis. You did good."

Tears dripped down my face and sobs choked me. I'd never expected to hear something like that. Not in my wildest dreams.

"Thank you," I said, trying to calm my quivering voice. "For saying that. It helps."

He turned his head, looking straight. "I wasn't trying to help. I was speaking the truth."

"He's like a robot half the time," Daisy muttered, but I could hear the emotion in her voice. "Or a zombie."

I took a deep breath and turned the handle. The foot of the bed came into view, and a moment later, I stalled as Kieran turned toward the door. His eyes rested on mine for a long beat, stormy but sparkling, in that face the angels had clearly blessed.

Butterflies swarmed my stomach and my heart gave a worrying lurch.

I hadn't seen him for these last two weeks. Not once. He hadn't stopped by the pub, nor had he hung around the house. He hadn't even called.

I swallowed past the sudden lump in my throat and moved into the room on stiff feet.

Mordecai sat up, his back resting on a pile of white, fluffy pillows. His turquoise blanket sat in a ball at his side, the one thing he'd insisted on bringing. His eyes widened when he noticed me, then Daisy, and a smile stretched across his relaxed face.

Without his tight eyes and the creases in his skin from the constant pain, he looked like a stranger. Like a normal fifteen-year-old kid who had his whole life ahead of him.

The sobs I'd stuffed down upon entering broke free, shaking my body.

"You look good," I said, smiling through my tears and wiping furiously at my face.

"I feel good," he said, beaming now. "I just feel…like I'm sitting here. I don't even have to try at it. I'm just sitting here, enjoying the day."

More sobs took me, my heart aching with happiness

and guilt, knowing what it must've been like all these years. I was so happy he could be in a place of peace. That he didn't hurt anymore.

I looked at Kieran, my eyes leaking like faucets. "Thank you for doing this. You didn't have to."

Kieran shifted and slipped his hands into his pockets, like he was embarrassed. "There wasn't anyone more deserving."

I nodded, because that was absolutely true.

"Thank you," Daisy said tersely, staring at Kieran like she wanted to kill him. It was a defense mechanism. "You saved my brother. And for that, I respect you." She flicked her hair. "It doesn't mean I'm cool with…" She waved her finger in my general direction. "But this was big…and you deserve credit for that."

Kieran nodded slowly, his expression not changing, but the glimmer in his eyes turned up a notch. "Alexis, may I speak with you?" he asked politely, motioning me toward the window in the corner of the room.

Daisy worked around me to get to Mordecai's head. "You look really good, Mordie. Except for your hair. That hasn't come back in. We might need to look into Hair Club for Men, because you can't go around looking like that now that you're well…"

I tuned her out as I drifted toward Kieran, electricity surging through my body and heat warming my blood. I lifted my eyebrows, streams of tears still cutting tracks down my cheeks.

"His rate of recovery is incredible," Kieran said quietly, his gaze roaming my face. "It speaks to his power. All of this has been entered into his files. I can't change that, not now. He's already been assessed at a shifter class five, and this boosted rate of healing, no doubt his body's natural response to his years of sickness, will elevate his overall attractiveness. Given that he has no true pack affiliation, organizations from around the world will be interested." His eyes took on a hard edge. "Some of those organizations will seem powerful and prestigious, but their interests are less than reputable. I know you don't trust me, but—"

"Mordecai can ask advice from whoever he wants. I'm his guardian, not his brain."

Kieran's lips curved upward and his gaze intensified as it delved into mine. "So you do trust me."

"No. I didn't say that. I just said—"

"I heard you." His grin flipped my stomach before seriousness stole his expression. "As I'm sure you know, he'll also get challenges as soon as he's better. Almost all challenges stop at losing consciousness, but some are to the death. He'll need to plan for both."

I nodded, looking over at Mordecai listening to Daisy ramble on about something. "I know."

"He'll need to train. Hard. He's lost time. He has a powerful frame, but he needs—"

"Fuel," I said, rolling my eyes. "Don't play dumb. I know you know about the meals."

He exhaled a laugh and his breath dusted me, sweet, like chocolate.

"Yes." His volume lowered and his tone took on an intimacy I hadn't expected, sucking at my focus and making my body tingle. "Do you need anything? Money? Food?"

I looked into those turbulent, deep blue eyes, and a part of me understood what he was really asking—if I'd allow him to provide for me. If I'd let him take care of me as well as protect me.

Emotion welled up again. I'd been offered plenty of pity in my life, and occasionally some compassion, but no one except my mother had ever wanted to look after me. No man had ever wanted to take on the hunter role in my life.

The part of me that recognized his interest desperately wanted to say yes. Wanted to be saved for once and let someone else shoulder the burden that was my life as the poor, immature matriarch of a cobbled-together family.

But a bigger part of me knew I needed to stand on my own two feet. I may be immature, but I *was* a matriarch. I would not yield or give up my power to a possessive stranger who only *sometimes* did the right thing, something he'd admitted himself. I'd worked too hard to hand over the reins.

Not to mention the kids would *never* go for it.

I smiled and shrugged in a blasé sort of way. "Now that we don't have to pay for medicine, we'll be okay. Thanks for asking."

His eyes lingered on mine for a moment, and I saw his understanding.

He nodded. "Look over that contract. I'll be in touch." He strode past me, but paused and turned back when he reached the door. "It occurs to me that I never paid you for our session at the Magical Showcase. Since I was never quoted a price, I took the suggestion of your…associate." His gaze flicked to Daisy before he nodded at a large white bag in the corner that I hadn't noticed.

It was a testimony to how focused I was on Mordecai that I hadn't noticed a huge bag with *Burberry* written on the side.

"No." I shook my head while excitement bubbled through my body. "Nope."

He watched me for a moment, and a smile ghosted his lips. "I'll leave you to it, then."

"No." I crossed my arms over my chest. "He didn't." I looked at Daisy. "You told him to buy me that as payment?"

"I don't know. Look in it." She squealed and crossed the room before grabbing the bag and bringing it to me.

"How'd you…" I pulled tissue paper out with a shaking hand. "Oh my God," I breathed, then stared with my mouth open, speech leaving me.

It was a buckle medium tote. In pink! The exact bag I'd had to leave behind the day we'd met. He'd returned it to me.

"No way." Tears fogged my eyes.

"This bitch owns a Burberry, what?" Daisy pointed at me before lifting her hands in the sky. "Watch out, fancy ladies, we all up in your business."

"I'm proud of you," Mordecai said as I slid the bag up my arm.

"Why?" I petted the side. "Because I have a ward who knows how to wrangle fashionable presents out of a conniving Demigod? If so, I'm proud of me too. Good work, Daisy. And no, you can't borrow it."

"Too soon. That joke came too soon." Daisy paused. "It is a joke, right?"

"Because you recognized that the Demigod wasn't offering you pity," Mordecai said, "he was offering you a leash, and you didn't accept it."

I felt a frown bud as I thought back to what Kieran had said. "I don't know that it was a *leash*, per se…"

"It was a leash. I heard him." Daisy nodded confidently. "Don't let no dick rule you. You be the boss of you."

"All right, fourteen-year-old. Thanks for the life lesson." I rubbed at my face.

"Are you going to take the job?" Mordecai asked.

I lowered the handbag. It was now or never.

After tucking it back into the bag and gingerly placing it to the side, I crawled in next to him. Daisy squished in on the other side.

"Yes," I said. "For a few reasons. But yes. I am."

"Finally. The truth!" The bed jiggled, and I knew Daisy had made some sort of dramatic gesture.

"You should know that Daisy sent a letter of negotiation to his office," Mordecai said. "Ow!"

"I told you not to tell her!"

"What?" I leaned forward and turned so I could look at both of them.

"You're a terrible liar, so I figured I'd get out in front of you. *Someone* has to protect your brand." Daisy straightened up with a determined expression. "I gave the letter to the robot two days ago. You weren't being undercut, but your experience wasn't being fully taken into account. I figured they could come up a little. Plus, he owed us for that session. I wasn't about to let that go. That's why I recommended the bag. You never would've bought it for yourself."

I looked back and forth between the two of them. "You're not going to bust my chops on this? You're not going to tell me I shouldn't take it?"

Mordecai shrugged. "It's a bad idea, getting mixed

up with a Demigod, but…"

"He's got mommy issues, not to mention big daddy issues, and you have a thing for helping out people with issues. I mean…hello?" Daisy raised her hands. "You're going to do it anyway. We might as well sign up to do damage control so you don't get in over your head."

With a squishy heart, I leaned back and swung my feet up onto the bed. Daisy elbowed Mordecai and yelled something about Samwise Gamgee and tatters before finally settling. We all crowded together.

"I'm sorry you guys don't have normal teenage lives," I said softly.

"At least we *have* lives," Daisy said. "Without you, we'd both be dead. I'm exactly where I want to be. With you fuckers."

"Really Daisy, with the swearing?" I wiped away a tear.

"Daisy got her miracle," Mordecai whispered. "I got my miracle. Now, Alexis, you need yours."

I didn't have a miracle in my future. I had a nightmare. But as long as they were taken care of, I'd just be happy with a pint. Dream small.

THE END

About the Author

K.F. Breene is a *USA Today* Bestselling and Top 10 Kindle All-Star author of paranormal romance, urban fantasy and fantasy novels. With two million books sold, when she's not penning stories about magic and what goes bump in the night, she's sipping wine and planning shenanigans. She lives in Northern California with her husband, two children and out of work treadmill.

Sign up for her newsletter to hear about the latest news and receive free bonus content.

www.kfbreene.com

CPSIA information can be obtained
at www.ICGtesting.com
Printed in the USA
LVHW031130260522
719652LV00001B/1

9 781955 757089